Netherfield Park Revisited

The acclaimed Pride and Prejudice sequel series

The Pemberley Chronicles:
Book 3

Devised and Compiled by
Rebecca Ann Collins

SOURCEBOOKS LANDMARK™
AN IMPRINT OF SOURCEBOOKS, INC.®
NAPERVILLE, ILLINOIS

By the Same Author

The Pemberley Chronicles
The Women of Pemberley
The Ladies of Longbourn
Mr Darcy's Daughter
My Cousin Caroline
Postscript from Pemberley
Recollections of Rosings
A Woman of Influence
The Legacy of Pemberley

Published by Sourcebooks Landmark, an imprint of Sourcebooks, Inc.
P.O. Box 4410, Naperville, Illinois 60567-4410
(630) 961-3900
FAX: (630) 961-2168
www.sourcebooks.com

Originally printed and bound in Australia by SNAP Printing, Sydney, NSW, 1999.
Reprinted in June 2001, March 2002, and June 2004.

Library of Congress Cataloging-in-Publication Data
Collins, Rebecca Ann.
  Netherfield Park revisited / Rebecca Ann Collins.
    p. cm.
  ISBN-13: 978-1-4022-1155-3
  ISBN-10: 1-4022-1155-4

  1. Young men—England—Fiction. 2. England—Social life and customs—19th
century—Fiction. I. Austen, Jane, 1775-1817. Pride and prejudice. II. Title.
PR9619.4.C65N47 2008
823'.92—dc22

                          2008012617

          Printed and bound in the United States of America
                  VP 10 9 8 7 6 5 4 3 2

Dedicated to
Averil, with love, 1999

An Introduction . . .

DEVOTEES OF JANE AUSTEN WILL not need to be reminded that the news of the arrival at Netherfield Park of Mr Charles Bingley, "a single man, possessed of a good fortune," begins the story of _Pride and Prejudice_.

It affects dramatically the lives of the Bennet family at Longbourn—in particular, Jane and Elizabeth.

In the end, after the inevitable heartrending exasperation that plagues every romance, Jane marries her beloved Bingley, while her sister is claimed by his enigmatic friend Mr Darcy. Both young women marry and move away, out of provincial Meryton society, to live, we are assured by Miss Austen in the final chapter, happily ever after.

Having observed their passage through some of the following years in _The Pemberley Chronicles_, the author's first book, I have long been intrigued by the prospect of a return to Netherfield in a new era, by another, younger Mr Bingley.

It was a story that asked to be pursued; hence the new Master of Netherfield, Jonathan Bingley, son of Charles and Jane, returns to his father's former home at a crucial time in his life in this third novel in the Pemberley series: _Netherfield Park Revisited_.

Jonathan Bingley's decision has some interesting and unforeseen consequences for himself and others. Inheriting from his parents not only a sizable fortune but also his engaging nature, Jonathan Bingley could quite easily have walked into or out of one of Miss Austen's own stories. The circumstances in which he finds himself are both probable and believable in the context of mid-Victorian England. A man of passion and integrity, he faces some difficult choices, and a more complex fate than that of his amiable father awaits him.

For the benefit of readers who may need reminding, a list of the main characters in *Netherfield Park Revisited* is provided in the Appendix.

RAC/ June 1999

Prologue

THERE CAN SURELY BE NO more anticlimactic occasion than the day following a wedding in the family, or as was the case at Pemberley in the Spring of 1859, two weddings in the family.

The wedding of Julian Darcy, son of Mr and Mrs Darcy of Pemberley, and Miss Josie Tate, daughter of Mr and Mrs Anthony Tate of Matlock in Derbyshire, had brought together a vast number of family and friends, some of whom had not seen one another since the last wedding in the family. Even more so, since it was held together with the wedding of Louisa Bingley to Dr Matthew Ward.

Jonathan Bingley, the only brother of Louisa Bingley and eldest son of Mr and Mrs Bingley of Ashford Park in Leicestershire, being a dutiful and courteous young man, decided to call on his favourite aunt and uncle before returning to Kent, where he managed the estate and business affairs of Lady Catherine de Bourgh.

His wife, Amelia-Jane, stayed behind at Ashford Park, complaining of tiredness and a headache, while Jonathan set off for Pemberley.

He was not expecting his visit to result in anything more exciting than cakes and tea and a pleasant exchange of views with the Darcys, who were always excellent company.

They greeted him warmly. Their nephew and godson was a special favourite, and since he was not as often in Derbyshire as they would have liked, he was always welcome at Pemberley.

"Jonathan, how very nice it is to see you and how good of you to come especially to see us," said Mrs Darcy, while her husband rose to congratulate him on the news that he had recently been rewarded for his services to the nation with a significant civilian honour.

Jonathan, with his usual modesty, protested that it was, if the truth were told, a reward for services rendered to his party—being a most loyal and active member of the Reformist wing of the Whigs during some twelve years in Parliament. He did add, however, that he was very proud to receive it all the same.

The morning room in which they sat was filled with Spring sunshine while outside, the servants cleared away the debris and dismantled the great marquee which had accommodated the wedding guests.

Turning to his aunt, Jonathan said, "Aunt Lizzie, you know I could never have left for London without seeing you and Mr Darcy again. There was so little opportunity at the wedding to talk of anything but the two singularly handsome couples and the excellent repast provided for your guests. Of course it goes without saying that Pemberley looked splendid, as always."

Elizabeth thanked her nephew for his generous compliments as she took his arm and went out onto the terrace and into the garden, promising to show him her latest roses. Darcy fell in beside them and asked, "Jonathan, am I right in believing that Lady Catherine has asked that you supervise the transfer of some of her treasures from Rosings to her residence in Bath?"

"Yes indeed, Sir, I imagine it will keep me very busy throughout this month and well into the next. Her Ladyship has sent a long list of items—many of her particular favourites," he replied, with a tiny grimace.

Elizabeth smiled. "With detailed instructions as to how they should be packed for transport, no doubt," she said.

"Indeed, how did you know, Aunt Lizzie?" asked Jonathan, unaware that Mrs Darcy had previously experienced Lady Catherine de Bourgh's very particular form of instruction on the correct way of doing everything from packing a trunk to practising the pianoforte!

Mr Darcy remembered and laughed at Jonathan's surprise, recalling an occasion many years ago when his aunt had urged him and his cousin Colonel

Fitzwilliam to procure the services of a particular valet to have their coats pressed and packed before leaving for London.

"She declared that he always packed Sir Lewis de Bourgh's trunk when he travelled and he was a perfectionist, of course," said Darcy.

"Of course," said Jonathan, echoing a sentiment he had heard often enough. They were all laughing as they returned to the house, when Jonathan drew their attention to a carriage that had just driven into the park. It was an unfamiliar vehicle and neither Darcy nor Elizabeth was expecting any visitors.

"I wonder who it could be," said Elizabeth, as they went within.

Soon, however, their callers were announced as they were shown into the saloon: Dr and Mrs Faulkner and Miss Anna Faulkner.

Instantly, Elizabeth rose and went to them, greeting them cordially, for it was her dear friend Charlotte's younger sister Maria, her husband Dr John Faulkner, and their daughter, Anna.

They had been at the wedding, too, and Jonathan, standing a little apart, recalled seeing the handsome young lady at the reception, but he had totally failed to recognise her.

On being introduced, he confessed, "Miss Faulkner, of course—it is Anna. Good heavens, you must forgive me, my recollection of you is of a mischievous little girl in a smock, with your hair in braids. It is completely at odds with your present elegant appearance, Miss Faulkner. This is a most pleasant surprise."

Miss Faulkner, handsome and tastefully dressed in the most modish European style, smiled cheerfully and extended her hand to him.

"I am not surprised, Mr Bingley, I do not think we have met in almost ten years. I have a vague recollection of your wedding, when I was a very little girl, I think," she said, looking to her parents for confirmation, "and later, when I was about fourteen, we attended a session of Parliament at which you spoke quite passionately, although I must confess I have quite forgotten your subject. We were, I recall, in London for a family wedding."

Astonished at her recollection, Jonathan laughed. "That must have been either the Ten Hour Day debate or the Public Health Act; we were pretty passionate about both matters. Those were most exciting times," he said as they moved to sit down.

Elizabeth, who had ordered more tea and cakes, joined them to ask what Anna had been doing with herself over the last few years.

Before Miss Faulkner could reply, her father intervened to tell them that Anna had spent most of the last four years in Europe. "Mostly in Brussels and Paris, to be exact," he said, "with a family named Armande, recommended highly by Mrs Collins. They run an excellent school for young ladies wishing to improve their knowledge of French and study the Fine Arts."

Dr Faulkner was clearly proud of his daughter's achievements and took plenty of time to detail them. Anna, he told them, was "especially interested in Art and Music." She had excelled at playing the pianoforte and the harp and her drawings had been highly praised.

"Indeed," he went on, at the risk of severely embarrassing his daughter, "her watercolours of fruit and flowers are quite remarkable."

Elizabeth, who could neither draw nor paint, was most impressed. Turning to Anna, she said, "You must let us see some of your work, Anna. Do you only paint in Europe or have you been working over here as well?"

"I'm afraid most of my pictures are at the Armandes' studio in Brussels, Mrs Darcy, but I have been doing a few smaller paintings since I've been home. However, there is some prospect of seeing some of them when Monsieur Armande comes to London to conduct a Summer school in French Art. I have hopes that he may include a few of mine in his students' display," she explained, trying modestly to dilute some of her father's fulsome praise.

"You must let us know when it is to be open to the public," said Mr Darcy, whose interest in Art was well known, and Jonathan expressed the hope that he might come up to London to view them, too.

They were all quite disarmed and charmed by the artless manner in which she acknowledged their interest, without presumption or false modesty.

Jonathan, whose interest in the Fine Arts had been rather neglected of late, was quite fascinated by Miss Faulkner's accomplishments.

While her parents and the Darcys became engrossed in family small talk, he struck up an interesting discussion with the young lady.

The Faulkners, who had admired the situation and elegance of Pemberley were delighted to be invited to take a short tour of some parts of the house. Sensing Miss Faulkner's interest at the mention of the gallery, Jonathan offered her his arm and they joined the rest of the party as they toured the music room, the library, and the picture gallery, before going out to view the grounds and walk across the lawn towards the lake.

Dr Faulkner and Maria had gone on ahead with Mr and Mrs Darcy, but Miss Faulkner lingered in the gallery, stopping to admire the remarkable collection of Italian masters.

Jonathan asked if she had been to Italy, and she answered with alacrity, "Indeed, I have, but while I admire their Classical Masters, such as we have seen here, I must confess my present favourites are the new French painters. They seem to have a very special genius, they make it appear so effortless; there is not the painstaking detail, the quality of artifice that marks the work of the old masters, more a simplicity of line and splashes of glorious, glowing colour … it is all quite magical."

Jonathan, who had not heard such articulation of form and colour before, had to confess that he knew very little of the new French painters. Names like Degas, Manet, and Pissarro meant little to him, unknown as they were in England and certainly in Kent, where the decidedly traditional range of the De Bourgh collection had rather dominated his world lately.

Miss Faulkner explained that the new French artists were finding it difficult to gain acceptance even in their own country, but she was most enthusiastic.

"They are too good and too many to be ignored," she declared with a smile. "Monsieur Armande is convinced that they will be the next generation of great European artists, and I am sure he is right."

Her enthusiasm was infectious, and as they moved to join the rest, Jonathan promised himself that on his next visit to Paris, he would attempt to seek out the work of these new painters. Anna had convinced him it was an experience not to be missed.

"It must be one of the greatest of God's gifts," she said, "to capture light and texture with brushes and paint as they do. I would give anything to paint half as well."

While they had been talking, Elizabeth's younger sister Kitty, who was married to the Rector of Pemberley, had come around to meet her dear friend Maria, and more time was spent in greetings and conversation. They were old friends and had much to talk about.

Later, the Faulkners left after Jonathan had promised to call on them at Haye Park when he was next in Hertfordshire, for as he observed, they were but a few miles from Longbourn, where he visited regularly.

Following their departure, he continued to express astonishment at the accomplishments and charm of their daughter Anna.

"I have to say I am at a loss to understand how young ladies of today become so accomplished," he declared. "They can all play and sing as well as draw and paint and speak two or three languages ..."

Elizabeth wondered aloud why Anna Faulkner, clever and lovely as she was, had remained unwed.

"Is it by choice, Kitty?" she asked. "For I cannot believe she has had no suitors."

Kitty waited until the servants had removed the tea things and left the room before she told a story of great sadness that explained why the Faulkners' daughter Anna, now almost twenty-five years old, was still single. Jonathan Bingley, though feeling some degree of embarrassment as an outsider, was too intrigued not to want to listen.

The tale Kitty told was of a romance some six years ago, between Anna Faulkner and a Captain Lockhart in the Royal Navy, who had achieved rank, but had not as yet a ship to command. This was not uncommon, for in the forty years of peace since the Congress of Vienna, it was the British Merchant Navy that had grown prodigiously.

However, while their friendship had flourished and an engagement had been generally expected, the outbreak of the Crimean War in 1854 had precipitated his urgent recall to active duty on board a ship bound for the Black Sea.

There had followed a proposal of marriage, to which an almost immediate answer was required, since he was commanded to sail for the Crimea within the fortnight. Dismayed at the very thought of war, which she abhorred, and revolted by the idea that she would have to endure the sights and sounds of battle, young Anna Faulkner had refused his offer of marriage, to the astonishment of her family and the utter consternation of poor Captain Lockhart.

It was not that she did not love him, she had said repeatedly, but she could not bear the thought of being there to see him die; and die he did, at the horrible carnage that was Sebastopol. He died not, as she might have expected, in the midst of some heroic action, but of the dreaded cholera, well before confronting the enemy, like so many other young men.

As Kitty told it, Anna, being not yet twenty, had been terrified at the prospect of being aboard the ship, witnessing daily scenes of death and destruction in the midst of a war of which she had no understanding whatsoever. Born in the long period of peace and prosperity that had followed the final defeat of Bonaparte, she had never expected to be confronted with such a conflict.

Jonathan, astonished at Kitty's tale, was, nevertheless, understanding of young Miss Faulkner's predicament.

"Surely," he said, "it should not have surprised anyone that such a young woman would have found the prospect of marrying a man and sailing immediately for the Crimea, where we were at war, considerably daunting. I cannot believe that any of my sisters would have found the proposal attractive, nor would my parents have welcomed such a marriage, fraught with danger as it would have been."

Darcy agreed, pointing out that the catalogue of blunders that had followed Britain's ill-prepared and unnecessary entry into the Crimean War would only have served to confirm her fears.

"The consequences for thousands of our troops and their families were absolutely appalling," he declared, supporting Jonathan's contention that, in the circumstances, no criticism could have been fairly levelled at Miss Faulkner for turning down Captain Lockhart's proposal of marriage.

Staying longer than he had at first intended, Jonathan learned that Anna, since the death of young Captain Lockhart, had been unwilling to enter into any new engagement, though it was known she had had other offers.

"She seems apprehensive and disinterested," said Kitty, "and since she has little interest in gossip and flirtation, finds herself left out of most invitations to picnics, parties, and such gatherings, making it even less likely that she would meet an eligible partner."

Jonathan felt and expressed some sympathy for Miss Faulkner, who had struck him as a charming and intelligent young woman.

Although he said nothing more, he could not help contemplating the difference between her and some of the young women he had met in London and among his wife's circle in Kent. Art or Music would have been the very last thing to engage their minds, which were filled with such fluff as to be quite impenetrable.

Some time later, on a visit to Longbourn, he was to learn from Miss Faulkner's aunt, Charlotte Collins, that Anna had suffered deep remorse at the death of her captain, but had not let it blight her life.

"She busied herself with study and hard work, improving her mind and skills, increasing her knowledge of Literature and History," said Mrs Collins, who had soft feelings for her niece, "and on my recommendation, her parents sent her to Europe to the Armandes in Brussels, where she proceeded to excel in Music and Art. Monsieur Armande is full of praise for her work. She seems a good deal happier now."

All this, however, was to be revealed much later.

For the moment, Jonathan returned to Ashford Park, where he was not surprised to find that his wife's headache was much worse and necessitated the postponement of their journey to Kent.

Casually mentioning his meeting with the Faulkners, he received two completely contradictory responses from his mother and his wife.

In the first instance, Mrs Jane Bingley readily agreed with his account of the family, speaking well of the good sense of Dr Faulkner and Maria, and recalling that her daughter Sophie had met Anna Faulkner in Paris and been quite impressed with her.

"I believe she paints, draws, and plays both the harp and the pianoforte," said Jane, "and is a charming young person, as well."

Amelia-Jane's reaction was quite the opposite; she claimed she had never been able to have any kind of conversation with her cousin Anna, and dubbed her "dull and boring, though perhaps not quite as boring as her parents!"

Jane noticed the uncharacteristic sharpness in Jonathan's voice as he retorted, "That a young lady should be called dull and boring merely because she has made the effort to improve her mind and cultivate some artistic skills is more than unfair, it is downright uncharitable!"

Adding her support, Jane spoke gently of the great value she and Mr Bingley had placed on education for their daughters. She would not have it put down, she said.

Amelia-Jane, unaccustomed to being contradicted in any way, decided that she would go upstairs and lie down, in the hope that her headache would go away. It was her way of declaring the subject closed.

❧

Some days later, the Darcys were engaged to dine with the Bingleys, and inevitably, the subject of Miss Anna Faulkner reappeared in the conversation between the two sisters.

Elizabeth, wondering whether Jane had met the Faulkners recently, and hearing that they had indeed been staying in London only last month, within walking distance of each other, remarked that it was most refreshing to meet a young woman who seemed far more interested in pursuing her study of Art and Literature than in pursuing—or, indeed, being pursued by—young men.

"Would you not say that was a pleasing change, Jane?" she quipped.

Jane agreed, "Indeed, Lizzie, remembering the unhappy and often undignified scenes we have seen in times past, with our Lydia and even poor Mama, I would say that Miss Faulkner and her parents appear to be blessed with a good deal more common sense than most."

As her sister smiled, Jane went on, "Lizzie, you will not be surprised to hear that Jonathan, on returning from Pemberley last week, was of the same opinion. He remarked that Miss Faulkner was surely very fortunate to have such sensible parents as well as the means to remain single, if that was her choice. He did, however, hasten to add that he did not mean to imply that Anna was destined to remain unwed, for, he declared, 'Miss Faulkner is young enough and, certainly, handsome enough to marry and may yet do so."

Elizabeth laughed. "Jonathan has certainly mastered the gentle art of composing a compliment to a lady, even if it is in her absence," she said, adding, "But Jane, he is not wrong. As Mr Darcy pointed out after they had left Pemberley, the Faulkners can be proud of their daughter. Anna's accomplishments and undoubted intelligence should make her a most desirable partner for a man of culture and good sense, but, were she never to marry, she would still be one of the most charming and well-informed women one could hope to meet."

Jane agreed, and Elizabeth observed that Jonathan, on hearing Darcy's words, had remarked, "It is surely better that young men and women should have the capacity and the courage to remain unmarried, unless and until their hearts and minds were both equally and deeply engaged."

Elizabeth added, "I was just about to tease him about being so philosophical after the event, when I could not help noticing the grave, almost sad expression on his face as he spoke, and I confess, I remained silent."

Jane said nothing, and Elizabeth continued recalling that Darcy had agreed with Jonathan. "He said he had seen too many unhappy unions in which rash, hasty, or worse, merely mercenary decisions had brought couples together, who would within a year or two discover the misery of incompatibility."

"Oh indeed, Lizzie," said Jane, "there can be nothing worse than a loveless marriage."

Both Elizabeth and Jane, who had been singularly blessed in their marriages, could recall familiar examples of the type Mr Darcy had referred to, but though Jane had on one or two occasions expressed some anxiety about her son's happiness, she had no knowledge of any particular problem in his marriage.

Elizabeth, on the other hand, had long been feeling some disquiet about Amelia-Jane and had sensed that Jonathan and she were no longer as content together as they had been. It was difficult not to notice the growing coolness between them, and she was concerned, lest it be a symptom of a deeper malaise.

However, despite her anxiety, she was reluctant, so soon after two weddings that had been celebrated with great hope of future felicity for their children, to rake up what possibly were the dying embers of Jonathan Bingley's marriage.

NETHERFIELD PARK REVISITED

Part One

1859

I F JONATHAN BINGLEY HAD not previously recognised that there was developing a serious problem that threatened his happiness and the stability of his marriage, he was certainly made aware of it as they returned to Rosings Park.

Throughout the journey, Amelia-Jane remained seated on the opposite side of the carriage to her husband, rather pointedly placing their youngest daughter Cathy, who was nine, and her lady's maid between them. She also insisted that the blinds be drawn down on her side of the vehicle, so as to preserve her, she claimed, from suffering another severe headache on account of the glare.

Their two eldest children, Charles and Anne-Marie, had already returned to their respective educational establishments on the previous day. Jonathan knew that they, like him, were uneasy about their mother's changing moods and uneven temper, for indeed, of late, she had changed greatly from the vivacious, light-hearted girl he had married and the easy-going, compliant mother they had known.

Jonathan was very troubled indeed; troubled and grieved. He had, at first, attributed the change to the loss of their two little boys, Francis and Thomas, born two years apart, both of whom had not survived longer than a year after birth. The terrible trauma of their deaths had affected all of them, but it had affected his wife more deeply and for a longer period because, with her elder children away from home and his own work keeping him busy, she seemed to find no solace at all.

Understanding the weight of the blow she had suffered, Jonathan had tried to reach and console her, but had failed repeatedly. Each time he tried to comfort her, she seemed to retreat even further into her own grief or break into heart-wrenching sobs. She was reluctant to talk of the children to anyone and, if pressed, would take ill and retire to bed.

Jonathan was too loyal a husband to breathe a word of this to his mother, who knew only that Amelia was still deeply distressed following the death of their sons.

The problem, however, continued to plague them and had recently worsened. Though devoted to his wife and family, Jonathan found it increasingly difficult to keep it to himself and finally sought his sister Emma's advice.

The opportunity to do so presented itself quite fortuitously, when some weeks later, his brother-in-law James Wilson, a long-standing and dedicated member of the Reform Group in Parliament, wrote inviting Jonathan to dine with him at his club in London. He had, he wrote, an interesting political proposition to put to him.

Jonathan, who had spent some twelve years in Parliament representing a constituency in the Midlands, had left the House of Commons some seven years ago, tired and bored with the bickering and dissension that had, in his opinion, opened the way for the Tories and set back Parliamentary Reform for a decade.

Thanks to the recommendation of Mr Darcy, he had been appointed by Lady Catherine de Bourgh to take over the management of her vast estate and business affairs—a prestigious position which included a very pleasant house in Rosings Park.

Others may have felt that the task of reporting regularly to Lady Catherine and being on hand whenever she felt the need for congenial company was too high a price to pay for the modest remuneration offered, but Jonathan, being an amiable and easy-going young man, had not been unduly troubled by Her Ladyship's demands upon his time.

The move to Kent had meant that Amelia-Jane, who had felt very isolated in Derbyshire, had found herself drawn into a new social circle, in which she seemed to find some enjoyment. There was also the very great advantage of being settled near Hunsford, the parsonage where her sister Mrs Catherine Harrison lived. Catherine provided invaluable support to Amelia-Jane when she needed help with the children, and, more than her mother or her husband, it was to Catherine that Amelia-Jane had turned for comfort following the loss of her sons.

Practical and mature, Catherine had been better able to cope with her younger sister's demands. Jonathan had seen clearly the advantage of their situation.

More recently though, he had begun to feel restless; irritated by the superficiality of the social round at Rosings Park, he had begun to miss the involvement in politics and the brisk jostling of ideas in the public arena of Parliament. Which was why he had accepted James Wilson's invitation; there had been a promise of something interesting to do.

James, an active member of the Reformists, had insisted that Jonathan should maintain his membership and interest in the party.

"You are far too young to give up on politics, Jonathan," he had said. "We may yet have you back in the Commons, one day." And when

Jonathan had modestly pointed out that it might not be easy to get back in, James had laughed and assured him that "room could always be found for a good man."

Jonathan was eager to discover the reason for the invitation, wondering what his brother-in-law had in mind. James Wilson had married Jonathan's sister Emma after the death of her first husband, David, whose abuse and mistreatment she had borne secretly for years. James, who had given her a new lease of life, was a man of absolute integrity, and Jonathan felt sure he could trust him.

When they met, James was as good as his word. He was hoping to involve Jonathan in the negotiations following the elections, which had given the opposition parties a majority, but ironically, it seemed their disunity would deliver government to Derby, again.

James pointed out that some skilful negotiations were needed if the Conservatives were to be defeated in the house and, by participating in them, Jonathan could perform an invaluable service for his party and the nation.

"Just think, Jonathan, if Russell and Palmerston were back in government, reform would be back on the agenda. Is it not what you have always wanted?" he asked.

"It certainly is," Jonathan replied, "but how could I or any other ordinary party member have much influence on the negotiations? Is it not for the elected members to realise they owe the nation a duty?"

"You are too modest, Jonathan." James' words were almost a reproof. "You do not know your own ability. You above all, with your commitment to reform, your eloquent powers of advocacy, should be involved in lobbying members and winning them to the cause. You would be best placed to persuade recalcitrant Liberals that it is better to have Palmerston in office concentrating his mind on Italy, while Russell brings down a new Reform Bill, than to have Lord Derby back again, kept in power by our disunity alone."

James argued passionately and Jonathan assured his brother-in-law that his commitment to reform had never waned and, together with the excitement of a new government and the prospect of an active role in the party, the offer was very tempting indeed.

He asked for time to consider it, a request that was gladly granted with an attached invitation to Standish Park.

"Emma and I would love to have you to stay. Amelia-Jane and the girls too, of course," said Wilson. "Stephanie and Victoria seem to be very fond of your Teresa. I believe they became good friends at Louisa's wedding."

Jonathan agreed that they had and promised to convey the invitation, pointing out that they would probably appreciate a change of scene.

For his part, he preferred by far the comfortable elegance of the Wilsons' family home to the rather more ostentatious grandeur of Rosings Park.

The two men parted after a most satisfying evening, Jonathan promising to visit Standish Park very soon and have an answer for James. He left for the Bingleys' town house in Grosvenor Street, where he stayed overnight, returning on the morrow to their home at Rosings Park. He was excited and pleased with the news he had to impart to his family. He anticipated a whole new career opening up before him.

But, if he hoped that James Wilson's proposition for him to play a more active role in politics would be welcomed by his wife, Jonathan was due for profound disappointment.

After dinner on Sunday, at which they had exchanged little more than a few morsels of information of the kind that may pass between husband and wife at table, Jonathan accompanied Amelia-Jane upstairs, intending to tell her of Wilson's proposal and his inclination to accept it.

Amelia-Jane had appeared to have recovered somewhat from the headaches and dizzy spells that had assailed her during most of the previous month. Indeed, he had been glad to see that she had taken to driving out in fine weather around the park and sometimes to her sister's at the parsonage at Hunsford.

Jonathan had hoped that with this obvious improvement, she would be more receptive to James Wilson's proposition.

But it was not to be.

In fact, it was the very opposite. Even the mention of a return to politics seemed anathema to her and she cried out as if physically hurt by his words.

"You surely do not mean to go back into the Commons! Oh, Jonathan! I could not bear it, if you did. I certainly have no wish to return to London and attend all those dreary charity fairs and boring garden parties again. It would kill me!" she protested, tears filling her eyes.

Nothing he could say, no amount of reassurance that he was not intending to re-enter the Commons, that he had no offers of a seat, and anyway, the election was over—none of this seemed to penetrate her remorseless opposition.

As for the invitation to Standish Park, she viewed it with great suspicion as part of a conspiracy by the Wilsons to lure him back to Westminster. In vain did he try to point out that his role would not be as arduous nor would it keep him as busy as being an MP. She was unconvinced.

"I do not trust the Wilsons; Emma supports everything James proposes. I cannot believe that they would let you go once they have you back at Westminster. It will be exactly as it was before. I can see it, and do not tell me that you will refuse them, because I know how dedicated you are to the party. You will put the party before us, to be sure," she complained, plaintively.

"Amelia, dearest, that is not fair. I have always put you and the children first; it was the reason I agreed to leave the Midlands and move to Kent. You know that to be true," he protested.

"I know nothing of the sort!" she cried. "I recall very clearly that whenever there were debates and votes in the House, you thought nothing of rushing back after dinner, night after night, or staying overnight at Grosvenor Street, while we returned home."

It was a litany of complaint and it soon became abundantly clear to him that it was of no use to pursue the matter any further. He would have to make his own decision and travel to Standish Park alone, for clearly, Amelia-Jane would not accompany him.

Later that week, their son Charles, who was diligently pursuing his medical studies, came to inform his parents that, having consulted Dr Richard Gardiner, for whom he had great respect and affection, he had applied to enrol at Edinburgh in the new Academic year.

"It does not sound as grand as Paris, I grant you, Father, but Dr Gardiner assures me it is the right thing to do."

Jonathan agreed that Richard was probably right, and told him of his own decision to return to work at Westminster.

To his surprise, he received his son's immediate support. "That has to be the best news I have heard in many months," Charles declared. "I have often wondered how long it would be before the business of managing Rosings would bore you back to politics."

"Then you approve?" asked his father, a little unsure he had heard right.

"Indeed, I do, and I encourage you most assuredly to take up Mr Wilson's offer. He cannot have made it lightly; he takes his involvement in Reform politics very seriously."

Jonathan was so pleased that his countenance reflected his satisfaction. Charles, seeing the relief on his father's face, was moved to add, "And I am sure your work will prove most valuable. There is no more important cause than Parliamentary Reform at this point in England's history. One more term of stagnant government and we would be the laughing stock of Europe. We have a great opportunity and must not throw it away."

With his son's encouragement and his own commitment, he left for Standish Park the following week.

He had not brought the matter up with his wife again, having resolved to accept James Wilson's proposal. He seemed resigned to the fact that Amelia-Jane's opposition was inevitable and unshakable and would have to be borne with as much patience as he could muster.

He set out looking forward to seeing his sister and his charming nieces and nephews in an environment in which he always felt life was lived just as it should be.

❧

Emma Wilson greeted her brother warmly on his arrival at Standish Park, and if she was disappointed that his wife had not felt fit enough to travel the relatively short distance between their homes, in the same county, she concealed it well.

Emma's good taste and sensibility, combined with her excellent education, had seemed to present an insurmountable obstacle to her young sister-in-law, whose lack of serious learning often left her outside of their conversations. Despite Emma's best efforts to nurture a friendship between them, Amelia-Jane had always held back. Recently, she had taken to avoiding their functions.

"I never quite know what to say to James and Emma," she would complain to Jonathan. When they were first married, her exquisite youth and charm had sufficed to dismiss any qualms he may have had. Later, though, her reluctance to make any attempt to cultivate and enjoy the fine taste and genuine values of his sister had begun to embarrass and even occasionally distress him. Neither elegant surroundings nor cultural pursuits involved her mind for very long.

He recalled an occasion when Emma's very talented young daughters, Victoria and Stephanie, had been invited to perform after a family dinner party and as they did so, Amelia had begun to chat to a woman sitting beside her, very softly at first, but gradually reaching a point when her whispering so distracted and irritated those sitting around her that they had finally requested her to stop. Whereupon she had been so mortified that she had left the room in tears and refused to return.

It was but a small incident, and Emma had dismissed it as nothing to be concerned about, but Jonathan had never forgotten it. Neither had Amelia-Jane, who afterwards complained, quite unfairly, that she felt awkward and unwelcome at Standish Park.

On this occasion, however, there was no awkwardness at all as Emma embraced her brother, welcoming him after a long absence.

"Jonathan, it is so good to have you here. It has been too long since you have been with us," she said as they went indoors.

They had always been close, and this time, Jonathan looked forward to the visit especially because he felt impelled to speak to his sister of the increasingly concerning situation in his marriage and, particularly, his ailing, unhappy wife.

On their first evening together, they were only the family at dinner, and it was a happy occasion, with Jonathan producing gifts for everyone. His two nieces, being well-read young ladies, appreciated the volumes of romantic poetry, while his two young nephews, Charles and Colin, were easily captivated by the latest mechanical toy train. Good-humoured and fond of children, Jonathan was a favourite uncle.

James and Emma were overjoyed when he disclosed that he had decided to accept the position at Westminster.

"I cannot tell you how delighted I am, Jonathan," James declared, adding, "I promise, you will not regret this decision. You will be performing a very important service to your party and the nation."

Later, as they repaired to the drawing room to be entertained by Emma and her daughters, Jonathan, sensing the warmth and happiness this family enjoyed together, felt increasingly isolated and alone as he contemplated his own wretched situation.

It was not long before Emma, noticing his subdued mood and solemn countenance, came to sit with him and asked if there was anything wrong.

Jonathan, although aching to pour out his heart, realised that this happy evening was not the time. He promised Emma that they would talk; indeed, he wanted very much to discuss some important matters with her.

Concluding from the seriousness of her brother's demeanour that he meant exactly what he said, Emma assured him she would find the time and the occasion for them to talk privately, very soon.

Later that night, after most of the family had retired to bed, Emma sat with her husband discussing Jonathan's situation.

James Wilson was absolutely certain that he had made the right decision. "It is high time that he returned to doing something more significant than Her Ladyship's books," he quipped, revealing that Jonathan had confessed to being somewhat bored with his current occupation. "It is no job for someone of his calibre. There is much more important work for him to do. Jonathan Bingley is exactly the kind of man we need to produce the ideas, the policies we must introduce if we are to carry this nation forward. He has a truly civilised mind—a sense of idealistic purpose and patriotic duty, combined with tolerance, humanity, and practical common sense," James declared, and Emma wondered why, with such remarkable qualifications for public office, he had ever been permitted to leave Westminster.

"He should have remained in Parliament. Why did the party let him go?"

James could not recall the circumstances, but Colonel Fitzwilliam had suspected that it was due, for the most part, to his wife's unhappiness with the time he spent at Westminster.

"If that was the case, how do you suppose she has agreed to let him return? Is she not far more likely to oppose it now?" Emma asked.

James smiled. "That, my dear Emma, presupposes that Jonathan is still as strongly influenced by his wife's opinions. I may be mistaken, but I think you will find that your brother has discovered the value of emancipation."

Emma laughed, but not with any great degree of mirth; remembering her brother's sombre expression, she could not help feeling that if he had emancipated himself, as James had suggested, it had been achieved at a considerable personal cost. It was something about which she would discover more on the morrow.

As James put his arms around her and suggested that it was probably late enough to go to bed, she smiled and thought only of the great good fortune that had brought them together.

Never had she felt the need to use her position of privilege as his wife to oppose or thwart her husband's chosen path, even when it had meant sacrificing some of their precious time together. While she loved him with a depth of passion she had not believed possible before, she would never use it to manipulate him.

Like her cousins Caroline and Cassy, Emma had found her deepest satisfaction not in passively accepting her role, but in actively working with her husband to advance the ideas and achieve the goals in which they both believed.

Having known both the barren despair of a loveless marriage and the fulfilment of her present life with James, Emma felt deeply sorry for her brother and wished with all her heart that she could help him.

When she told her husband of her fears, he surprised her by admitting that he'd had his concerns too, and he urged her to speak with her brother and, if necessary, stiffen his resolve.

"Emma, if Jonathan is unhappy, you will help him most if you support him so he can fulfil his wish to perform some service of consequence. It may need a great deal of strength and determination, but I know that neither you nor your brother are lacking in either of these qualities. Jonathan probably needs a sympathetic and supportive listener."

Emma smiled. If that were all he needed, her brother would have no further problems, for she could give him all the sympathy and support he could ever ask for. But she had a frightening presentiment that his problems were of a far more complex nature.

On the following Monday, when James had left for London and Mrs Elliot had departed for the library with the girls, Emma sought out her brother.

He had left the house soon after breakfast to take a walk through the grounds, which were particularly beautiful at this time of year.

Standish Park was certainly looking its best, but it was not the fine stands of trees nor the display of late Spring blooms that attracted him there. He was seeking to clear his mind and put his thoughts in order before speaking with his sister.

When she caught up with him, Emma found him in a quiet part of the park overlooking the river, looking rather lost.

Though a little surprised to see her, he welcomed her and smiled as she approached.

"I did not expect you to find me quite so easily. You must know the park very well," he said, and she replied lightly, "I've had years of practice with the children. The boys like me to pretend that it is harder to find them than it really is."

Even as they laughed, she detected a mirthless quality in his voice and, turning to him, came directly to the point.

"Now, Jonathan, would you tell me what on earth has happened to make you so unhappy? No, my dear brother, do not deny it; it is quite plain to anyone who knows you that there is something very wrong. I knew it the instant I saw you, and then last night after dinner, James mentioned it, too. He is very concerned about you. We both love you and want what is right for you, but we need to know why you are so downcast. Why Jonathan, even the children have noticed. Stephanie thought you looked tired, but Vicky, she is more discerning, she said you looked more anxious and sad than tired. What is it, my dear? Will you not let me help?" she asked.

Jonathan, who had stood before her shaking his head with astonishment, was, for a moment, speechless. He had not expected his secret would be so easily discovered.

Emma, sensing his sorrow, had no wish to subject him to any further ordeal by questioning him about his life. Speaking gently and taking his arm as they returned to the path, she said, "Jonathan, let us return to the house, where we will not be disturbed and you can tell me whatever you wish me to know. I promise I shall listen and not give you any unwelcome advice."

"Unwelcome advice? Indeed, Emma, advice is just what I need, for I am truly at a loss to understand what has gone wrong with my life and how on earth I am to put it right again. If you or James have any advice for me, I shall welcome it."

There was such a tone of urgency and hopelessness in his voice that she was moved almost to tears. She had not ever seen him in such a state before. He must be truly miserable, she thought.

"Then, will you tell me what has brought you to this state and let us, together, consider what might be done. If there is any way in which James or I may help, we will do all we can." Her sincerity was never in doubt. Jonathan was silent again, recalling his sister's wretched, unhappy marriage and the death of her first husband, which had ended the pain she had borne for many years before finally finding happiness with James. He knew she was no stranger to suffering.

When they reached the house, they went directly upstairs to her sitting room, where, having ordered tea, Emma asked that they should not be disturbed unless some urgent matter required her attention.

In the hours that followed, Jonathan described to his sister the curious and difficult situation that existed between him and his wife Amelia-Jane.

Though it was clearly painful for him to talk about it, he did so honestly, and as Emma listened, interrupting rarely to ask a question or two, she was struck by the great sadness in his voice and the fact that he attributed no blame to his wife at all.

While Emma could understand that the loss of her two boys could have caused Amelia-Jane's problems at the outset, her rejection of her husband's efforts to comfort her puzzled Emma greatly. She could not understand it. They had seemed such a close and affectionate couple.

The confusion led her to ask honestly and frankly if he had ever given his wife cause to distrust him or doubt his faithfulness, and she had to beg his pardon when he swore he had done neither, because he loved his wife and had never paid undue attention to any other woman.

"Good God, Emma, you cannot imagine I would do such a thing. Nothing I have said or done could be construed as disloyalty or unfaithfulness. Do you not believe me?"

His tone, expression, and attitude reflected his outrage. His sister was immediately anxious to reassure him.

"Of course I believe you, Jonathan. I am concerned, however, that from your account of her behaviour towards you, your wife may not."

"If she does not, it is an irrational caprice, with no basis in fact," he retorted, "for I swear, I have given her no cause."

Emma decided to try another tack and inquired after his work. Was it engrossing him to the extent that she might feel neglected? she asked, only to be told that, in fact, since he had left the House of Commons, he had spent far more time with his family. Indeed, he declared, it was Amelia-Jane who was out more often, visiting her sister at Hunsford or driving to Rosings, where she had made friends with the librarian who was charged with cataloguing Lady Catherine's art treasures.

Confounded, because she could see no likely reason, nor any possible solution for her brother's problems, Emma rose and moved to the window where she stood looking out, when an express was delivered to the door and brought up immediately by the maid.

It was for Jonathan, from his wife's eldest sister Catherine Harrison at the Hunsford parsonage. It brought grave news.

Word had been received at Rosings Park of the death, in Bath, of Lady Catherine de Bourgh. The family, including Amelia-Jane and her youngest daughter Cathy who was Lady Catherine's goddaughter, were leaving immediately for Bath to attend the funeral. Jonathan, it was expected, would follow and meet up with them at the Camden apartments, not far from Lady Catherine's own residence.

Mrs Harrison said messages had been despatched to Mr Darcy at Pemberley, the Bingleys at Ashford Park, and her mother, Mrs Charlotte Collins at Longbourn.

Jonathan stood in the middle of the room, astonished not by the news, for it had been known that Lady Catherine had been seriously ill for many months, but at the calmness with which Catherine Harrison had attended to all the arrangements at Rosings. She was a practical and sensible woman, whom Jonathan had come to admire and respect. He was well aware of the high regard in which she had been held by Lady Catherine herself.

Emma realised that Jonathan would have to leave almost at once to meet the coach to London and there was no real purpose to be served by returning to their earlier discussion. He was, however, eager to assure her that he had every intention of returning after the funeral.

"Emma, I promise to return as soon as I possibly can and I must thank you very much for listening. I cannot tell you how much it has helped to talk with you. I do need and value your advice. Please tell James I shall keep my appointment with him at Westminster next week. Indeed, now that Lady Catherine is no more, it will be easier for me to ask to be released from my duties as her manager—once I have completed all the formalities, of course. The Trust could appoint a new man in the Autumn."

Emma helped him pack and prepare for his solemn journey.

Neither the Bingleys nor the Darcys had spent much time in Bath over the past ten or more years, making only short, occasional visits there.

Elizabeth and Darcy, though they admired its fine city architecture, disliked the "hot house" atmosphere of Bath society, while Bingley had hardly any close friends among its collection of retired, gouty, military men and pretentious but often impoverished county families. Though his two elder sisters, Mrs Louisa Hurst and Miss Caroline Bingley, had settled in Bath, Bingley and Jane were not frequent visitors.

Twice a year, Mr Darcy dutifully called on his aunt and her invalid daughter, who had moved here for, it was claimed, medical reasons, but he rarely stayed more than a few days.

Jonathan Bingley, on the other hand, was a frequent visitor to the city; as Her Ladyship's manager he reported regularly on her estate and business affairs and, being a modest, intelligent, and amiable man, had found considerable favour with Lady Catherine. Furthermore, she had always appreciated his wife's deferential manner towards her and her daughter.

When the families gathered for Her Ladyship's funeral, it fell to Jonathan as her manager to make the necessary arrangements and ensure that all the appropriate formalities were carried out.

He was kept so busy by his various solemn duties, which he took very seriously indeed, that he did not at first realise that Amelia-Jane had arranged to stay not at the Camden apartments with the rest of the family, but with the Bingley sisters.

They had a very fine house in Barton Place, not as close to the Royal Crescent as they would have liked, but close enough to Lady Catherine's prestigious neighbourhood to suffice. On their invitation, Amelia-Jane and her daughter Cathy had joined them, together with a Mrs Arabella Watkins, a widow recently arrived in Bath, who seemed to have become, very quickly, a particular friend of Miss Caroline Bingley.

Later, when Jonathan went to call on his aunts in order to accompany his wife and daughter to church, he was introduced to Mrs Watkins, but being preoccupied with other more sober matters, he had not noticed her with any particularity. So, when Amelia-Jane spoke enthusiastically of her new acquaintance, he was unable to proffer an opinion, one way or another.

Meanwhile, Elizabeth and Jane had settled in at the very comfortable apartments they had taken at Camden Place and were preparing to dress for the funeral, while their husbands had gone to call on Miss de Bourgh, who was, sadly, too unwell to attend the funeral service at the church.

Jane was trying on a shawl she had purchased that morning in Milsom Street, hoping to add a further degree of sobriety to her gown, which unlike her sister's was not wholly black, but had a design of embossed roses on the skirt.

Jane was not entirely happy with her appearance. "Lizzie, do you suppose the family will forgive me if I do not look totally bereft, not donning the deepest mourning? I am sure the other Bingley women will make up for it," she said anxiously.

Elizabeth, despite the solemnity of the occasion, had to smile at her sister. "Dear Jane, with your sweet, serious face, complete with black bonnet and veil, no one will notice that your gown has not also gone into deep mourning," she said, adding, "I had to, for Darcy's sake—he was her favourite nephew and still carries the main responsibility for her family Trust. I daresay I would otherwise have felt quite comfortable in semi-mourning."

Jane shook her head. "No doubt Miss Bingley would have persuaded Amelia-Jane to don a black bonnet and veil too," she said, adding with a little grimace, "Oh, Lizzie, I have to confess I am very uneasy about the friendship between those two. Caroline is too old and sophisticated to be a suitable friend to Amelia-Jane. I wish I knew what Jonathan thinks of it, but he is so loyal, he will say nothing that may reflect badly upon his wife, even if only by reference to her friends."

The sudden return of the gentlemen caused them to suspend their discussion, but Elizabeth understood her sister's qualms. There was little love lost, even after all these years, between herself and Caroline Bingley, whose supercilious, sneering remarks had caused her so much aggravation at the very beginning of their acquaintance. Now she was Jonathan's aunt, and Elizabeth had no doubt that the aunt's influence upon her nephew's wife would not be beneficial.

She had her own concerns, too.

However, it was time to put aside these thoughts, don their black bonnets and veils, and go forth to the church and pay their respects to the redoubtable Lady Catherine for the last time.

After the formalities were over, however, Elizabeth did get her nephew Jonathan alone, as the mourners milled around the tables laden with food, and on asking him how he was, she received such a look of resignation and sadness that she was convinced something was very wrong indeed.

Despite her awareness of the occasion, she felt compelled to inquire, "Jonathan, what is it? I can see you are not happy and I cannot believe it is all on account of Her Ladyship," she said, softly, but he only looked askance and hurried away to attend to some aged lady who needed a drink.

Elizabeth was most unhappy. She had hoped to get more from Jonathan than an uncharacteristic shrug and a crooked smile. She determined to speak to Darcy on the earliest possible opportunity.

Mr Darcy and Jonathan remained in Bath for a few days, to support Miss de Bourgh and attend the reading of the will, but the rest of their party left the city on the day after the funeral.

Travelling as expeditiously as possible, they arrived at Ashford Park, where Elizabeth proposed to stay until her husband returned.

Inevitably, the subject of Jonathan's marriage—never far from their thoughts these days—came up again, as Jane recalled observing the couple at the funeral.

"Was there not a terrible coldness between them, Lizzie?" she asked sadly. "I am very anxious for them. Poor Jonathan looks so unhappy and I do believe Caroline Bingley's influence upon Amelia-Jane is doing no good."

Elizabeth, trying not to add to her sister's distress, suggested it might be only a temporary problem in their marriage, some misunderstanding which might well work itself out, but Jane would not be comforted.

Exacerbating her unhappiness, the returning Mr Darcy brought the news that Amelia-Jane had remained in Bath with Caroline Bingley and her sister Louisa, while Jonathan had travelled with Mr Darcy and the Grantleys as far as Oxford, where they spent the night before Jonathan had continued his journey to London, alone.

"He was clearly upset that his wife was not returning with him, I had no doubt of that. I gathered he had an important appointment on the Monday with James Wilson at Westminster and could not stay on in Bath, as she had asked," said Darcy, who confessed to Elizabeth, when they were alone, that he was concerned that Amelia-Jane seemed determined to thwart her husband's desire to return to Westminster.

"Do you believe he means to return to the Commons?" Elizabeth asked apprehensively, knowing already that Amelia-Jane abhorred the very idea.

"No, not to the Commons—there's no opportunity there, now the elections are over, but I gather he has been offered a chance to work for James Wilson, who is keen to get the Reform agenda running in the new Parliament. He hopes Lord Russell will soon be back in government. Indeed, Jonathan believes that a united opposition will succeed in defeating Derby and get Palmerston and Russell back on the treasury benches."

"And would you consider that to be a sound development?" asked Elizabeth, who, being rather disinterested in matters political, was usually content to be guided by her husband's opinions on this subject.

Darcy had no doubts at all. "Anyone would be an improvement on Derby," he replied, adding almost as an afterthought, "I have little time for Palmerston—the man is more interested in foreign adventures than Parliamentary Reform—but I agree with James Wilson that Russell is a genuine Reformist. Jonathan believes that given the opportunity, Russell would work with men like Gladstone to liberalise the electoral laws and extend the franchise."

"And is that what James wants Jonathan to work on?" his wife inquired.

"Ultimately, yes," he said, and explained, "But before they can achieve any of that, they need to negotiate an agreement with the Liberals, to help them defeat Derby in the Commons. Jonathan believes it can be achieved, and I know he would give anything to be involved."

Darcy spoke with the certainty of someone who had discussed the matter thoroughly, which he had, with Jonathan on the journey from Bath to Oxford.

"And how does Jonathan propose to pursue this goal at Westminster, while continuing to manage Rosings?" asked Elizabeth.

Darcy knew his wife would always ask the pertinent questions.

"Ah, yes. Well, as a matter of fact, he does not. He has spoken to me of this already and will write to the Trust, after all the legal formalities following upon my aunt's death are completed, requesting that he be released from his duties as her manager in the Autumn. Jonathan feels, quite correctly, that he cannot responsibly undertake the duties of both positions and seems to have decided that his political work must take precedence."

Elizabeth was very surprised to hear this account of her nephew's intentions, so clearly proclaimed.

"And has he told Amelia-Jane of this decision?" she inquired.

"I do not believe he has had the opportunity yet," Darcy replied. "I gather he intended to tell her as soon as the funeral was over, but her decision to stay on in Bath has rather ruined his plans. I don't suppose she will welcome the news; he intends that they should move to Grosvenor Street, temporarily, while he looks to take a place in the country."

Suddenly, Elizabeth felt cold and reached for her shawl.

She knew, from everything Jane had said that Jonathan's wife would oppose the entire plan. She had become far too comfortable with her style of life at Rosings to agree to a change.

"Poor Jonathan," she said, as Darcy helped her with her shawl. "No wonder he looked so sad. I certainly do not envy him."

Understanding her melancholy mood, Darcy took her hand in his and held it. They loved their nephew dearly and were most unhappy that his seemingly contented life appeared to be going badly awry, with circumstances tumbling out of his control.

They were almost home; as the carriage negotiated a deep bend in the road and the lights of Pemberley came into view, Elizabeth sighed with relief. It had been a long and difficult week.

❦

Not many days after their return, Elizabeth received an unexpected visit from Jane, who came alone and brought with her a letter from Jonathan, recently written from London, the contents of which had obviously caused her much grief. She was plainly distressed and would take neither tea nor any other refreshment until both Elizabeth and Darcy had read the letter.

When Elizabeth first began to read, she could not quite understand the reason for her sister's anguish, but as she continued reading to the final page, she could better appreciate her feelings.

Jonathan had honestly and unambiguously informed his parents of his decision to return to public life and placed before them his reasons for doing so. He wrote:

Dearest Mama,

I had hoped to inform you of my decision sooner, but I had, perforce, to wait until Amelia-Jane and Cathy had returned from Bath, as I wanted to tell them first.

I intend to resign from my position at Rosings and accept the offer from Mr Wilson to work with the Reform Group in the Parliament. It is the best opportunity I have had in years to perform some significant public service.

I have long felt the need to do more than manage the private estates and business affairs of Lady Catherine de Bourgh—important though it was to Her Ladyship and her tenants, it is nothing to what this position at Westminster offers.

I do not mean in a financial sense, for the remuneration is not very much greater and there is no house, nor are there other privileges included. But it is a great opportunity to make a worthwhile contribution to my country.

Others may find satisfaction in military service or commercial enterprise, but as you know, I am not cut out to be a soldier or a successful businessman. I do believe however, and Mr Wilson believes, that I can contribute to the work of the Reform Group in Parliament, which is so vital for the future of England. It would be a great privilege to be involved, in whatever modest capacity I am asked to serve, in such an historic enterprise.

I might add that my dear sister Emma is wholly in agreement with me on this matter. I hope you will understand, dearest Mama, why I have decided to accept Mr Wilson's proposition. Indeed, he has even offered us the use of his town house in Grosvenor Street, until we find a suitable residence, which is extraordinarily generous of him, do you not agree?

None of this could explain his mother's anxiety, until the final page was reached.

There is, however, one unhappy consequence, which I had not anticipated and which I still hope and pray may be averted.

Amelia-Jane is implacably opposed to the entire scheme and will not agree to move to London. She claims she has no liking for London society and prefers to stay on at the Dower House with Teresa and Cathy, at least until I have found a suitable country residence to which she may move.

I am exceedingly grieved and have tried very hard to persuade her, but she has made up her mind and I must respect her wishes.

She may continue at Rosings conveniently until the new manager is appointed, which will probably happen before Christmas, whereupon she and the children will have to move out of the Dower House.

Dear Mama, if you will write to Amelia-Jane, inviting us to Ashford Park at Christmas, I am sure it will help to mend things, as I do expect to find a suitable property by the New Year.

The generosity of Lady Catherine's bequest to me will make this much easier to achieve. I shall be forever grateful to Her Ladyship for her kindness.

Elizabeth, who already knew of the bequests that Georgiana Grantley's boys, Colonel Fitzwilliam's sons, and their own Julian had received, had expected that Jonathan would be similarly rewarded.

Lady Catherine's nephews had not been forgotten in her will, nor had several of the young women in the family, who had received gifts of jewellery; Amelia-Jane and all three of their daughters had been likewise favoured.

But, it appeared that Jonathan Bingley had been singled out for his loyal services and been well rewarded. Whether or not it had been Her Ladyship's intention, the considerable sum she had left him would undoubtedly help Jonathan purchase his own place in the country and pursue his career in public life, as he clearly desired.

Unfortunately, it appeared, his ambition would be achieved at the cost of alienating his wife and fracturing his family. Was Jonathan fully aware of the risk he was taking? Elizabeth wondered.

Jane clearly did not believe he was. She was distraught. "Lizzie, what is to be done? Mr Darcy, please, can you not speak to him? I cannot believe he intends to sacrifice his marriage and family in this way."

Elizabeth had never seen her sister in such a state before. She looked up at Darcy, who read the letter through again before he spoke.

He was very gentle, but quite firm. "Jane, it is quite plain that Jonathan has made up his mind. I do not believe for a moment that in doing so, he has decided to risk the destruction of his marriage. But, I do believe that Amelia-Jane has done so. She is not without blame in this matter. Is there not something irresponsible and even presumptuous about her total opposition, her absolute refusal to accommodate his chosen career, upon a whim?" he asked.

"Were she to continue at Rosings for a short while, there would be no great harm in it. The distance between them would not be great and it may be argued that it is convenient, because their children and Mrs Harrison's share a governess. But should she continue this obstinate opposition even after he has purchased a suitable place in the country, I would find it difficult to apportion any blame to Jonathan."

As both Jane and Lizzie listened, he continued, "Surely you must agree that, at forty-two, he is entitled to pursue a career that interests him. The Law and Commerce, at which his father excels, hold no attractions for him."

Jane seemed confused. "But is it not his own desire to return to Westminster that is at the root of all this trouble? Is that not rather selfish and irresponsible, too?" she asked. Even as she spoke the words, it was quite clear that it pained her to contemplate such a thing about her beloved Jonathan.

Darcy smiled and shook his head. "My dear Jane, I would gladly wager the entire Pemberley Estate against the possibility of your son ever acting in a selfish and irresponsible manner. It is not in his nature; it would be simply impossible," he declared.

After many hours of discussion and several cups of tea, Jane was finally persuaded to let Darcy speak to Jonathan and discover what he intended to do if his wife remained totally opposed to his plan. Meanwhile, she agreed to write to her daughter-in-law inviting them all to Ashford Park at Christmas.

Jane hoped by this means to bring them together and settle their differences. Elizabeth, however, was unsure that it would help, but had not the heart to discourage her sister's efforts.

~⚭~

Later that year, the two sisters and their families travelled to Woodlands, Lizzie's farm in the south of England, as they did every Summer.

Lying in a fold of the Downs, amidst some of England's loveliest country on the border between Surrey and West Sussex, it was a place Darcy had purchased for his wife on an impulse; a place they had all grown to love.

It was of a size and character that was convenient and comfortable and they shared its delights only with their favourite people.

This year, because their uncle Mr Gardiner was, sadly, not well enough to join them and Mrs Gardiner wished to stay with her husband, Colonel Fitzwilliam and Caroline came instead with their youngest daughter Amy, who was pretty and accomplished and not yet nineteen. Her remarkable resemblance to Caroline at that age was always a talking point among their friends.

Elizabeth had hoped that she could entice Jane away from her unhappy concentration upon the problems of Jonathan and Amelia-Jane, but it was not easy. Jane wanted with all her heart to help solve her son's dilemma, but Elizabeth, being rather more realistic than her sister, doubted that a resolution could be found especially because the two participants were themselves reluctant to seek it.

"How is it possible," she asked Darcy, as they lay awake one night, discussing the matter, "to find such a solution when we know so little of their own wishes? What good would it do?"

Darcy sympathised with her concern, but he had a different opinion. "Lizzie, my dear, Jonathan Bingley is unlikely to rush into anything without giving it a good deal of thought. I have been speaking with Fitzwilliam about this situation at Westminster that he has been offered and he believes it is a most responsible position, requiring a man of utmost integrity, who commands the trust of all parties."

He was keen to emphasise the importance of the work that was being undertaken and explained patiently. "Negotiations are proceeding to achieve a coalition of members that can defeat Lord Derby's Conservatives, and Jonathan is to be involved as an honest broker. It is not reasonable to ask him to turn down such an opportunity simply to satisfy the whim—and I might add a rather petulant whim—of his wife."

Elizabeth was struck by the seriousness of Darcy's tone and the terseness of his words. "A whim? Is that all you think it is?" she asked.

He would not retreat. "Can it be more than that, Lizzie? Surely not, my dear; there is not one good reason why Jonathan should not accept. How will it harm him or his wife and family? Consider this: with Lady Catherine's business affairs being placed in the hands of the Trust, the opportunities for his advancement are few. Much of the work will be legal and commercial in nature, for which Jonathan has little liking. On the other hand, he is offered a real chance of preferment at Westminster."

"But what about his wife's objection, is that of no account?" she asked.

Darcy had an answer for her. "Certainly, if there was some evidence his decision would lead to neglect or if it were just self-indulgence on his part, I would have some sympathy for Amelia-Jane, but as it turns out, I can only conclude that the merit is almost all Jonathan's. His wife's obstinacy, her current childish conduct does her little credit. It reveals a total lack of understanding and judgment."

Seeing that his wife was about to protest at the harshness of his words, Darcy held up his hand and continued, "Please understand, my dear, that if the Reform Group does succeed in their plan, it will be a considerable achievement and all those involved will be credited with it, most particularly Jonathan. And should he, at some future date, attain higher office as a consequence, his wife and children will all benefit greatly.

"No, Lizzie, I must agree with Fitzwilliam. And indeed, Bingley thinks, too, although he feels deeply for Jane in the circumstances, that there is no justification to blame Jonathan at all and no reason to try to dissuade him from his chosen path."

Elizabeth felt helpless. "Then what is to be done? How are they to be reconciled?" she asked.

Darcy was thoughtful. He had a strong aversion, born of bitter experience in his youth, to interfering in the personal lives of his friends and family.

After a while, he spoke rather tentatively, "Catherine Harrison has always struck me as an eminently sensible and practical sort of woman. I know Amelia-Jane is close to her; they are often together. Perhaps an approach through her may succeed where others have failed. I cannot believe that she would support her sister's present attitude. Her advice may help Amelia-Jane see things differently."

Elizabeth, seeing what looked like a glimmer of hope in the gloom, decided she would speak with Jane after breakfast on the morrow.

The following morning, Caroline and Amy decided to drive into the village, leaving Jane and Elizabeth to prune and store the rosemary and lavender that grew in great profusion in the kitchen garden. It was a task the sisters had always enjoyed.

While they were so employed, Elizabeth took the opportunity to broach in a casual manner the subject of Jonathan and Amelia-Jane and suggest an approach to Catherine Harrison, but found Jane quite unwilling to interfere.

"Should Jonathan hear of it, and you may be sure he will, he may be very unhappy. He has told us honestly where his problem lies, but has never asked for our intervention. He may consider it unwarranted interference and I should be most upset if he were to be angry with us. As it is, he knows well that he can call on us for help at any time," she said quite decidedly.

"Have you written to Amelia-Jane inviting them to Ashford Park at Christmas?" Elizabeth asked, and Jane said she had, but had not heard back from her daughter-in-law.

"Perhaps she is reluctant to write until she has settled matters with Jonathan," she said, carefully and deliberately carrying on her task.

Elizabeth broke the silence. "Jane, do you recall a discussion we had after I had returned from Italy, during which you related the news that Emma and Jonathan were both engaged?" she asked. "It was during that cold, bitter Winter following the deaths of Edward and William."

Jane remembered it well. She had always felt that the haste with which both her elder children had rushed into engagements in the months following the terrible accident that had taken the lives of their two young cousins, was due to the shock and sorrow occasioned by those tragic events. Grieving and missing the two boys, both Emma and Jonathan had seemed to grasp at the comfort and hope offered by young love.

They had both become engaged before the Winter was over, Emma to David Wilson, a most eligible man about town, and Jonathan to Amelia-Jane, who was not sixteen at the time, but was so pretty she was admired wherever she went.

When she spoke, Jane's voice and countenance reflected her thoughts. "Yes, I do remember, Lizzie; you were astonished at the speed with which it had come about in those few months when you were in Italy with Emily and Paul. I confess that, while I had my reservations, I was pleased for them. They seemed so happy with each other. Jonathan actually rediscovered the art of smiling—he had been so dejected and melancholy since the boys' accident, I had been very anxious for him. Amelia-Jane changed all that; she was vivacious and pretty and appeared to adore him. It was probably unwise; clearly so in Emma's case, it was disastrous."

"But we were not to know that, Lizzie. Jonathan and Amelia-Jane were perfectly happy until she lost her two little boys, and now it seems he is being punished for it."

Jane sounded and looked so miserable that Elizabeth was sorry she had even raised the subject. She did her best to comfort her, to suggest that it was quite possible that the problem might be solved by the couple themselves, but she knew she was not very convincing. It was only the return of the gentlemen, who had been out shooting, with a good bag of game that brought a change of mood and some light-hearted banter to occupy the hour before lunch.

Afterwards, Jane was clearly tired and depressed, and Bingley insisted that she should rest upstairs. He was less concerned with the stability of Jonathan's marriage than with the state of his wife's health. He knew how she had suffered when their daughter Emma's unhappy marriage had ended in tragedy; it had taken a terrible toll upon her health. Now, it seemed she was taking Jonathan's troubles very much to heart, and Bingley feared Jane might become ill again.

Later that day, with the afternoon sun creating a patchwork of light and shadow in the wooded valleys below them, Elizabeth and Darcy took a walk away from the house, towards the river that cut its way through the chalk hills and green meadows. They had often taken this path, which led to a place they had found on their very first sojourn at Woodlands, when, heartsick and emotionally drained from the accumulated sorrow of three terrible deaths in the short space of two seasons, they had needed time alone to comfort one another and learn to bear each other's pain as well as their own. Woodlands had been their private healing place.

They returned often, and sometimes, it hurt more than at others.

On this occasion, however, it was not their own pain that concerned them. Elizabeth, recalling Jane's words that morning, asked, "Do you suppose that Jonathan and Amelia-Jane have fallen out of love?"

Darcy almost laughed out loud, but seeing her earnest expression he checked himself. "Lizzie, my dear, why should I suppose such a thing? I have no evidence to reach such a conclusion. But, if I were to be scrupulously honest, as I am with you, always, I would have to admit that the thought had occurred to me. Why do you ask?"

She told him of her conversation with Jane, and Darcy agreed that it was possible that Jane was quite right. Since Emma and Jonathan had both been very close to William and Edward, their sudden, tragic deaths must have made them dejected and vulnerable.

"An engagement and marriage may have seemed a way out of the gloom and sorrow that had enveloped us all at the time; people always cheer up for a wedding," he said, adding in a more serious voice, "but now that they are older and circumstances have changed around them, the partners they reached for in their youth may appear in quite a different light. It was certainly true of Emma's marriage, perhaps Jonathan is realising it too … a pretty face, a bright smile, and an amiable temperament can be very appealing in youth."

Elizabeth sighed, "And some years later, things appear rather different?"

Darcy nodded sagely. "Alas, it is not uncommon, Lizzie, for in youth we tend to make judgments that seem perfectly reasonable, but are often indefensible in later years," he said, and his wife groaned.

"As we both know only too well!" she said, recalling their own unhappy errors of understanding, which had resulted in much soul-searching.

"Indeed," he replied, "but we were fortunate enough to discover and amend our mistakes before they destroyed our prospects of happiness; not everyone is as well favoured. To a very few, a second chance is given, as with Emma's second marriage to James Wilson. It is happier and more successful because they share so much, and he is a man of intelligence and sensibility who cares deeply for her. One cannot fail to see their felicity."

Elizabeth acknowledged that he was right, adding with a sigh, "And poor Jonathan, unhappily, seems to have outgrown his early enthusiasm for a quiet life in the country with a pretty little wife, and he seeks a more active political career when she clearly does not share his ambition," she said, and even as he agreed, Darcy smiled.

"You put it well, Lizzie. But, returning to your earlier question, they may have grown apart in other ways, as well. He has certainly become more serious of late and she seems less so. He has a desire to perform some significant public service, while she cares only for her private satisfaction. These things could result in matrimonial misery."

Elizabeth was reminded of her father's words. Based undoubtedly upon his own experience, Mr Bennet had warned his daughter against making "an unequal marriage," pointing out that it could only bring "discredit and misery."

It had held no significance for her, because with Mr Darcy, she had a marriage built upon the strongest foundation of mutual love and esteem, which had only increased with the years. Her greatest satisfaction had been in seeing her father convinced of the rightness of her choice of husband and the happiness they enjoyed together.

But it did seem as if, sadly, young Jonathan Bingley had repeated his grandfather's error and allowed a pretty face and figure to lead him into a marriage in which the promise of perfect bliss had never been fulfilled.

Despite the clarity of her memories, Elizabeth said nothing of this to Darcy, out of loyalty to her father, except to comment on the unfairness of Fate, which allowed Jane and Bingley, who were an exemplary married couple, to suffer so much distress over the marriages of their two eldest children, who were, in every other respect, beyond reproach themselves.

Darcy agreed. He had great affection for both Bingley and Jane and shared their concern for the happiness of their children. Yet, he had to admit that as in the case of Emma, he could see no way out for Jonathan, unless he were to risk destroying his marriage, a union contracted in his youth with feelings and hopes that both partners seemed to have outgrown.

Try as they might, they could not satisfactorily explain Amelia-Jane's behaviour. As she had grown older, she had grown less rather than more committed to her marriage and the husband she had embraced with so much affection at seventeen. Elizabeth was bewildered.

"Why would a young, pretty woman with everything she could wish for— a handsome, faithful, successful husband, a pleasant home and loving family— set her feet upon a path that could lead only to calamity?" she asked plaintively.

Darcy had no immediate answer. He did not wish to distress her further by pointing out that pure petulance and self-indulgence might be a reason. He felt he had already been sufficiently critical of Amelia-Jane, who, of all Charlotte Collins' daughters, seemed to have inherited the least of her mother's excellent understanding and good sense. Even young Josie Tate, Charlotte's granddaughter, now Julian's wife, though not twenty-one, had more practical common sense and discretion, he thought.

Deliberately changing the topic, he reminded Elizabeth of their own daughter Cassandra, whose fifth child was expected in Autumn.

"Now, there is a good marriage," he declared, and to his great relief, Elizabeth, temporarily distracted from her melancholy contemplation of their nephew's problems, smiled, recalling the happiness of their beloved daughter.

"Indeed, yes," she replied. "Richard and Cassy are equally fortunate, and they know it. There will be much to do before the child is born. I have asked Jenny to have a list of things ready for my attention when we return to Pemberley at the end of Summer. She is already training her niece Margaret to help Cassy with the new baby."

Darcy was glad he had succeeded in taking her mind off Jonathan's troubled marriage.

Soon, the shadows would lengthen across the meadows and engulf the valley in darkness. It was time to return to the house.

They rose and walked slowly up the path and through the grove of birch trees. When they reached the house, they were surprised to find a vehicle standing in the drive.

"It's the Grantleys' carriage, I am sure it is," cried Elizabeth, hastening as she made for the front porch. "It must be Georgiana!"

Even before she reached the entrance, her sister-in-law came out to greet them, followed by Jane and Bingley.

Georgiana had seen them approaching as she took tea in the parlour. They greeted one another with great affection.

"Lizzie!"

"Georgiana, what a lovely surprise! You look wonderful. Is Dr Grantley with you?" Elizabeth asked as they embraced.

Georgiana turned to greet her brother, who was standing to one side, and declared that they both looked very well before explaining that she had written a few days ago to say they were to be in Winchester, where Dr Grantley was attending a function at the cathedral, and she hoped to drive down to Woodlands to visit them.

"Dr Grantley is at the Bishops' dinner tonight, and they are going to be busy all day tomorrow," she explained, adding, "I did not know then that Frank was coming, too, but he decided to join us at the very last minute."

"Is Frank here?" asked Darcy, to which a reply came from somewhere behind him as his nephew Frank, who had been enjoying a game of croquet, came towards them, his hand outstretched.

"He is indeed, sir, and very happy to be here," he declared, dropping the croquet mallet.

"So here we are, Lizzie," said his mother, "though it looks as if the post has been remiss and my letter has not reached you in time."

"It has not, but no matter, you are very welcome," said Elizabeth, "and will you stay tonight?"

"We would love to, if you have room for us," Georgiana replied, to which their hosts answered that there was plenty of room and they could all fit in, especially if Frank did not mind taking the room at the top of the house.

Frank Grantley, at twenty-six, was the youngest of the Grantleys' three children, and an easy-going and good-humoured young man. He laughed as he called out that he did not mind where he slept so long as there was a pillow for his head and a blanket for his feet, before returning to the croquet game with Amy, despite the fading light.

As Darcy took his sister for a walk around the garden, Elizabeth went indoors to give orders for dinner and make arrangements for the accommodation of her unexpected but very welcome guests.

The arrival of Georgiana Grantley and Frank considerably lightened the atmosphere at Woodlands that evening.

She was such a pleasant, happy woman that she seemed to add enjoyment to every conversation, and her son, likewise, was determined to keep them all entertained with tall tales and anecdotes aplenty.

Notwithstanding his light-hearted attitude, he was, in truth, a serious student of Theology and Music and hoped to follow in the footsteps of his distinguished father at St Johns College.

He had apparently made friends with young Miss Amy Fitzwilliam, who had spent several weeks with the Grantleys at Oxford, last Christmas. They were obviously pleased to be meeting again unexpectedly, and Amy, an avid reader though not quite nineteen, was clearly very impressed with the well-spoken and exceedingly widely-read Frank Grantley.

"He reads all the time and knows so much about every subject under the sun," Elizabeth heard young Amy declare to her mother, "and he plays the organ as well as the pianoforte!"

After dinner, which was the pleasantest meal, they repaired to the drawing room and, immediately, there were calls from Mr Bingley and Colonel Fitzwilliam for music and song!

Caroline obliged and then Amy, who had brought her flute, was appealed to. Though at first she was shy and hung back, when Frank, who had heard her play last Christmas, agreed to accompany her on the pianoforte, she performed quite beautifully to very appreciative applause.

Georgiana, who was a teacher of music as well as a talented performer, was full of praise and young Amy was clearly pleased to be so noticed. Indeed, it was clear that her parents were very proud of their youngest daughter.

Elizabeth was glad to see everyone enjoying the fine entertainment; even Jane appeared to have forgotten Jonathan's troubles, temporarily at least.

It was a welcome change from the melancholy mood of the past few days.

Georgiana Grantley had no knowledge of Jonathan's marriage problems, being far removed from it all at Oxford. She was, therefore, spared the concerns that had obsessed Elizabeth and Jane for several days.

It meant that all of that evening and most of the following day, their talk was of Oxford and mutual friends, of Art, Music, and the progress of the Grantleys' two older children, Fitzwilliam and Anne. The former had married some years ago and moved permanently to London, where he worked as an architect, while Anne, who had ample talent and could quite easily have studied music professionally, had given it all away to marry a clergyman from Hampshire.

Her mother reported sadly that they saw very little of her, since she had two little ones who kept her very busy and her husband did not like travelling.

"I spent all of yesterday with them, while Frank and Dr Grantley were at the Cathedral, but would you believe that we could hardly speak two sentences together before one or the other of the children would interrupt and demand her attention?" Georgiana complained.

Elizabeth and Jane gathered from her tone that she did not approve. Her own children had always been very well behaved.

The best news of all was that Dr Grantley had been invited to teach next Summer at a university in Italy, and Georgiana would be going with him.

While everyone was envying her the wonderful opportunity, Frank groaned at having to spend Summer alone with both his parents away in Europe.

"Could you not go, too?" asked Jane, but that was apparently not possible.

His mother had already suggested that he take a vacation at Lyme Regis or visit his brother in London, neither of which seemed to attract Frank at all.

The delights of the capital had no attraction for him, he declared, and groaned again at the thought of Lyme Regis, pointing out that he had always hated seaside resorts, ever since his elder brother had buried him under a great pile of sand at Scarborough, from which early grave he had to be rescued by his mother.

Georgiana, laughing even as she attested to the truth of his story, had to agree that he was right. But she urged them not to feel sorry for her son, for he could quite easily occupy himself at Oxford. But Frank protested that nothing he could do at Oxford would rival the excitement his parents would be having in Venice, Florence, and Rome!

"Come now, think of the Palazzo Vecchio or the Chapel of the Medici and tell me, do any of you honestly believe that I, a humble student of Theology, could inform and entertain myself as well in any of the celebrated colleges at Oxford?" he asked, and seeing he had his listeners' sympathy, added, "No, I am resigned to my fate. I shall spend the Summer locked in the vaults beneath the library, perusing ancient texts and deciphering archaic versions of the Nicene Creed, until my eyesight is quite destroyed."

"It will do your soul good, Frank," Fitzwilliam called from across the room.

When they had ceased laughing, Darcy, who had remained silent, said, "If you care for the country, Frank, you could come to us at Pemberley. We cannot match the Palazzo Vecchio or The Bridge of Sighs, but I daresay we could find some things that would entertain you. There's excellent trout fishing and acres of woodland to explore."

Elizabeth added her own voice to assure him that he would be most welcome and she knew he would enjoy the music of their choir and the Matlock Chamber Group, when Fitzwilliam intervened saying, "And if you tire of the pleasures of Pemberley before the Summer is out and would like a taste of the simple life, our farm is but a few miles up the road at Matlock. Caroline, Amy, and I would love to have you, would we not, my dears?" a proposition with which his wife and daughter readily agreed.

"Now there would be a real change from the dreaming spires," quipped Bingley, and before another word was spoken, Frank had accepted all their invitations and was thanking Darcy, Elizabeth, Fitzwilliam, and Caroline for their kindness and promising to look forward to a vacation in Derbyshire, which he was sure would make up for the loss of the glories of Venice and Rome.

Only his mother had some reservations. "Are you sure, Lizzie?" she asked, reluctant to inconvenience them.

"Of course," said Elizabeth. "With Julian and Josie settled in Cambridge, it will be very good to have some company and I am quite sure Frank will find plenty to occupy him in Derbyshire. We shall look forward to your visit, Frank, and do remember to bring your music with you."

The following morning, Elizabeth rose late and, when she came down to breakfast, found only Jane at the table.

"It is such a beautiful morning, Lizzie. They have all gone out," her sister said. The gentlemen are out riding, except Frank, who, I believe, was accompanying Amy and Caroline on a ramble in the woods."

Elizabeth joined her sister and asked for a fresh pot of tea and toast to be brought to the table.

They had not been more than half an hour, speaking mostly of the happy evening they had all spent, when laughter was heard outside and soon Amy, Frank, and Caroline appeared, their arms full of wild flowers from the woods and meadows around the farm.

Young Amy, flushed and rosy from the early morning air and the exercise looked a pretty picture, with a sprig of blossoms tucked into her hair.

"Aunt Lizzie, could we have some vases?" she asked, standing in the doorway like some Grecian wood nymph.

It was so appealing an image; it made Lizzie wish she could paint.

When they had finished putting their flowers in water, they returned to the breakfast room hungry from their exertions and sat down as cook sent in more tea, toast, and honey.

Elizabeth was delighted with her unexpected visitors. They had brought lightness and laughter and a touch of fancy to Woodlands, where before, they had been so disconsolate.

She was genuinely sorry to see them leave and, as the carriage arrived at the front porch and Georgiana moved to the door, there were tears in their eyes as the sisters embraced.

Frank Grantley had kissed all his aunts on the cheek in the French manner, and, though he only kissed young Amy's hand, Elizabeth noticed a somewhat prolonged farewell between them as they parted.

She had heard just a hint of a promise to meet again soon—perhaps at Christmas?

Caroline had said nothing, but Elizabeth assumed that Amy had been invited to spend Christmas with the Grantleys again.

"Now, I wonder," thought Elizabeth, "could there be something beginning there? Frank and Amy?" She recalled Jane's remark after Julian's wedding that

Amy Fitzwilliam would probably be the next bride in the family. Elizabeth wondered, but held her peace.

Many things had happened since then, not least the problems of Jonathan and Amelia-Jane, which had all but overwhelmed their Summer holidays. Amy, she decided, was older and more sensible than Amelia-Jane had been and was unlikely to be carried away by romantic notions of marriage. Even more reassuring was the fact that Amy was Fitzwilliam's daughter and Frank was Georgiana's son! They were cousins and no doubt their families would seek to ensure their future happiness.

It was neither the time nor the place, she decided, to speculate upon another youthful romance.

~❧~

Meanwhile, unbeknownst to most of her family, Amelia-Jane had embarked upon a course of action that would lead her in a totally different direction to that anticipated by her husband.

Irritated by the lack of sympathy and support offered by her sister Catherine Harrison when she had complained of Jonathan's decision to return to Westminster, she had written a long letter to her new confidante, Caroline Bingley, detailing the aggravation and inconvenience of moving to London, as well as the imagined hurt and mistreatment suffered at the hands of her husband.

That Miss Bingley was Jonathan's aunt had served only to increase the bitterness of her complaint. She was also well aware of the general animosity that existed between the families and, cunningly, used it to advantage.

While Amelia-Jane had not had much formal schooling since the untimely death of her father, Reverend Collins, she had read many popular novels and was able to use her knowledge to good effect, creating a sympathetic picture of herself as the unhappy wife, while painting a portrait of her husband as rather unfeeling and selfish.

The romantic writings of women, which filled the circulating libraries, provided her with many dramatic pictures of wives wronged or neglected by heartless men. It was not difficult to adapt the model to suit her present purpose.

"How little did I dream, when we were married and lived so happily, that one day my dear husband would cause me such pain," she wrote, inviting a lachrymose response from the receiver.

> *It seems to me that he is so consumed with ambition that he no longer cares if he hurts or offends me.*
>
> *I am convinced that there is some malign influence upon him, for he has changed. My dear Jonathan would never have treated me with such indifference and coldness …*

… and so on and so on for several pages.

The letter had so moved Miss Caroline Bingley, or so she claimed, and her friend Mrs Arabella Watkins, to whom she had revealed its contents, that the reply came in the form of a visit.

"Mrs Watkins, Arabella, was absolutely determined that we had to come at once, dear Amelia-Jane, for your letter was a cry from the heart. Neither of us could read it without shedding a tear and my sister Louisa agreed. 'You must go to her at once, Sister,' she said on hearing Arabella read it out a second time, 'Amelia-Jane needs you.' So here we are," said Caroline Bingley, a look of alarm and concern upon her face.

Amelia-Jane seemed gratified by their response, but the unexpected arrivals had caused some embarrassment to her eldest daughter Anne-Marie, who was visiting her mother. Having deduced from their conversation the general state of play, she contacted her brother in London to complain.

She wrote, with much feeling, to request his help.

> *I cannot believe that Mother has discussed intimate family matters relating to problems between herself and Papa with Miss Caroline Bingley, and what is much worse, opened up our family's affairs to a total stranger of very dubious repute—a Mrs Arabella Watkins.*
>
> *Who on earth is she? I know nothing of her. What is her status in Miss Bingley's house at Barton Place, Bath? Is she a friend? A lodger? And what allows Miss Bingley to believe that she and Mrs Watkins, whoever she may be, are entitled to advise Mama to leave Father and us in Kent and travel to Bath to stay with them?*

This, I believe, is their advice to her, although one cannot be certain since Mama appears thoroughly confused! She spends most of the day with them, during which time, I have no doubt, they fulminate against Papa, and by nightfall is reduced to such a state of agitation and rage that she is quite pathetic.

I have great fears for her. Charles, I beg you please come down here immediately and help me put a stop to this insane nonsense, before Mama does something really stupid.

Your loving sister Anne-Marie

Anne-Marie Bingley, though a year younger than her brother, often acted as if she were his elder sister. Charles' natural disposition was very like his grandfather's, amiable and easy-going, though not lazy or indolent. Indeed, of late, inspired by the example of Dr Richard Gardiner, he had worked assiduously to prepare himself for a career in the medical profession.

Anne-Marie thoroughly approved of her brother's conversion to serious study. She had herself effected a change in her life not very long ago.

After several years of being treated by her mother as a pretty little doll to dress up in fashionable clothes and expensive jewellery at a very early age, Anne-Marie had rebelled and tossed out all her finery.

In the midst of the worst period of the Crimean War, when she was not much more than sixteen, with daily tales of horror from the front line, Anne-Marie had become mesmerised by the suffering of the soldiers. Later, inspired by the example of Florence Nightingale and her own aunt Louisa Bingley, she had joined a group of women who took extensive training in nursing in preparation for the return of thousands of wounded and dying men at the end of the war.

Despite the protestations of her mother, who tried to dissuade her with dire predictions of contagion and disease, and the light-hearted jibes of her brother, who was unconvinced that his lovely young sister was seriously interested in nursing the sick, Anne-Marie, energetic and determined, had successfully completed an arduous course of training, surprising her friends and family with her skill and dedication.

Soon afterwards, she discarded most of her fine clothes and jewellery, donned a plain gown and took work in a large military hospital outside London, where the reforms initiated by Miss Nightingale were already showing results, as better sanitation and hygienic hospital practices had helped reduce the rate of infection and death.

Her father had been astonished by her determination and capacity for hard work, while her mother bemoaned the fact that dozens of expensive gowns had to be given away because she would not wear them any more.

As for Anne-Marie, she claimed she had never been happier, and indeed, she looked so well that it was difficult to disbelieve her.

While she retained a taste for fun and would occasionally attend a ball or enjoy a dinner party, she dressed with a new simplicity that actually enhanced rather than detracted from her general appeal. Though this had upset her mother, who thought she looked "old and dowdy," it had greatly increased her standing among the rest of her family and friends.

Chief among those friends was young Eliza Courtney, eldest daughter of Emily Gardiner and the Reverend James Courtney, Rector of Kympton on the Pemberley Estate.

Eliza had recently married the son of a distinguished family with a reputation for philanthropic work among the poor. She was, now, Mrs John Harwood of Harwood House, which her husband's family had owned for several generations.

One part of the Harwood property had been opened up for the use of the army as a military hospital for returning soldiers. On discovering, quite by chance, that Anne-Marie was working at the hospital, Eliza had insisted that she leave her modest lodgings in the village and move into a guest room at Harwood House, not more than a mile from the hospital by road and only a short walk across the grounds.

It had marked the beginning of a warm friendship between the two young women. Eliza, who had always been sensible and intelligent, even as a girl, found Anne-Marie's new persona quite compatible with her own.

For Anne-Marie, Eliza Harwood was a godsend. Educated and cultured, with an interest in Literature and Music, she opened up an entire new world for a young woman who had been given little encouragement by her mother to appreciate the Fine Arts. Despite her youth, Eliza Harwood was also practical and could be relied upon in a crisis. She was, indeed, exactly the sort of friend Anne-Marie needed.

When Anne-Marie received no response to her urgent letter from her brother Charles, it was in her friend Eliza she confided.

Her letter to Charles had been written two nights after the arrival at Rosings Park of Miss Bingley and her friend, Mrs Arabella Watkins, whom Anne-Marie had quickly dubbed "The Widow Watkins."

She was horrified by their influence over her mother and was determined to foil their plan to entice her to move to Bath, away from her husband and family.

Eliza Harwood knew very little of the problems presently engrossing the Bingleys. Nevertheless, when she heard Anne-Marie's story, she supported her friend completely.

"I can well understand why you would wish to prevent it," she said. "Why, your mama would know hardly anyone in Bath, and this would make her even more dependent upon Miss Bingley and this other person … Mrs Watkins, whoever she might be!"

"That is exactly my objection, Eliza, but how shall we convince Mama? How is she to be persuaded that it is not in her interest, nor is it in the interest of her family, for her to race off to Bath with Miss Bingley and her friend?"

"Can you not get your brother to speak with her? Most mothers are willing to listen to their sons," suggested Eliza.

So desperate that she was willing to try anything, Anne-Marie agreed to write a note to her brother which Eliza would have sent round to Charles' rooms in London.

As soon as it was done and despatched, Eliza took her friend upstairs and insisted that she take some refreshment and rest before returning to the hospital, where she was due to work the rest of the day. She went with her hopes high that her brother would finally recognise the urgency of her request and come to her aid.

Young Charles Bingley, still busy making arrangements for his journey to Edinburgh, where he was to continue his studies, was distracted and impatient on receiving his sister's note. He wanted to help, but had neither the time nor the inclination to become involved in what he saw as a petty squabble. He had already suffered some embarrassment as a result of his mother's activities and wanted no more. Perhaps even more pressing, he had an appointment with a young lady and took just enough time to write a hurried reply to his sister, which he handed to the man from Harwood House, before leaving in a hansom cab.

When Anne-Marie, returning from her work at the hospital, read her brother's note, she wept. She could not believe that Charles would leave her to struggle on alone, trying to persuade their mother not to destroy her marriage and their family.

Hearing her come in, Eliza had come downstairs expecting to find Anne-Marie having her dinner, which was always set aside for her when she worked late. Instead, she found her weeping quietly, her meal untouched.

Trying to comfort her, Eliza offered to accompany her to Rosings, to see her mother, but Anne-Marie was too distraught and tired to think clearly and after much persuasion partook of a small portion of food and a cup of tea before retiring to bed.

Eliza had promised that they would talk again tomorrow and decide what was best to be done. She hoped that a good night's sleep would help.

In truth, it seemed to have hardened Anne-Marie's resolve.

At breakfast the following morning, she announced that she had decided she would go immediately to Kent to speak with her mother.

"Eliza, I must persuade her to stay, I *must*," she declared in a determined voice.

Eliza's husband had gone North on business, which meant she was free to travel with her friend to Kent.

"I cannot let you go alone, Anne-Marie. I know John would want me to go with you," she said and would not be persuaded otherwise.

On reaching Rosings Park, they went first to Hunsford Parsonage to see Anne-Marie's aunt, Mrs Harrison.

Hearing from her that Miss Bingley and Mrs Watkins had spent most of the previous day at the Dower House with her mother, and that the housekeeper had said Mrs Watkins was helping Mrs Bingley pack a trunk, Anne-Marie was desperate to be gone.

"That insufferable woman! What right has she to interfere?" she cried and, despite the efforts of her aunt and her friend, she would not rest, but determined to go directly to the Dower House and confront them.

Eliza had a great fear of confrontation and prayed they would be spared any unpleasantness.

Whether her prayers had been heard and duly answered, they would never know, but when they reached the house, the birds had flown!

Only the kitchen staff and the manservant remained, since Mrs Bingley's maids had gone with her, and all they knew was that the three ladies had left for London.

They had heard nothing of any plans to go on to Bath. They had understood that the party would be spending some time at the Bingleys' house in Grosvenor Street.

Determined that they would be stopped, if it were at all possible, Anne-Marie sent an express communication to her father, who she knew to be visiting Longbourn, informing him of all that had transpired in the last few days and urging him to return to London.

She then decided to travel the relatively short distance to Standish Park and acquaint her father's sister, Mrs Wilson, with what had taken place.

Eliza Harwood, who was, by now, quite convinced of the seriousness of the situation, even though she did not understand all its complexities, decided to accompany her friend to Standish Park.

Although the drive from Rosings Park to the Wilsons' estate took them through the picturesque Kentish countryside, so tense and distressed were the two young women that they hardly noticed their surroundings. The short journey seemed interminable, so keen were they to reach their destination.

It was almost dark when they arrived at the house, and even Emma Wilson, who was accustomed to late callers for her husband, was surprised to see them at so late an hour.

Fearful they had brought bad news, she cried out, "Has something happened to Jonathan?"

Eliza Harwood hastened to reassure her that Mr Bingley was not the object of their concern, but his wife.

"Why? Has she been taken ill?" she asked, bewildered by this information.

"Indeed she has, very ill; in the head!" said Anne-Marie, before she collapsed into Emma's arms.

In the next few minutes, amidst confusion and panic, Emma Wilson—practical and thoughtful as ever—had her niece carried upstairs, revived, and comfortably tucked into bed. It was clear that Anne-Marie was exhausted.

Emma then sat down with Eliza and tried to discover what had brought about their extraordinary journey and her niece's state of extreme agitation.

Eliza, in whom her friend had confided, had to decide how much to reveal.

At first she was reluctant to speak out without her friend's authority. But soon, realising that if Anne-Marie's mother was to be prevented from embarking upon a hazardous and totally ill-advised course of action, a responsible family member had to be told, she related all she knew.

Emma listened, asking only a few salient questions, but she was deeply shocked by what she heard. She had had no indication that the situation between her brother and his wife had deteriorated to this degree.

Despite his promise to return to continue the discussion truncated by the news of Lady Catherine's death, Jonathan had not had the opportunity to do so.

On making some enquiries, Emma had discovered from her husband that Jonathan had begun work at Westminster and was being kept very busy with the negotiations between the opposition parties.

Emma was therefore completely surprised to learn of the bizarre behaviour of her sister-in-law and even more astonished at the involvement of Miss Caroline Bingley and her new friend, Mrs Arabella Watkins!

When Anne-Marie was quite recovered and had taken some food, Emma asked, "Who is this Mrs Watkins, and how does she come to have so much influence upon your mother?"

The question opened the floodgates of her frustration and she gave vent to her anger.

"She is a dreadful woman, Aunt Emma, a sycophantic hanger-on, who lives with your aunts, Mrs Hurst and Miss Bingley. I believe Mama only met her when she attended the funeral of Lady Catherine. Ever since then, she will not leave her alone; all these cards and letters and gifts keep arriving, and I am told Mama now treats her as a close friend and confidante!"

Emma was even more astonished when she continued, "And her only qualification for this role seems to be that she has been widowed twice! My dear Aunt, you should see her; she must surely be the merriest widow in England!"

"Is she young, old, or middle-aged?" asked Emma.

"It is impossible to tell, she wears so much powder and paint! I think she looks vulgar and wears flashy clothes to the most inappropriate places. Aunt Cathy said she came to church on Sunday with Mama and Miss Bingley wearing a yellow taffeta gown and a plumed hat! Can you imagine?"

Emma shuddered at the picture and asked, "How much of this does your father know?"

"Poor Papa, I doubt that he has any idea of their plans. I have sent an express to Longbourn, where he is visiting this week, telling him everything I know and urging him to return to Kent at once. They seem determined to detach Mama from us and take her back to Bath with them. Oh dear, what can we do? Aunt Emma, we must do something."

Emma Wilson, who had a strong bond of affection with her brother, took only a short while to decide that she would go to London with her niece. Her husband James would have to be told; he was probably the best person to help Jonathan deal with the ladies from Bath.

Having made the necessary arrangements and spoken with her children and the staff, reassuring them that she would be back with Mr Wilson on Friday, they set out the following day after both young women had enjoyed a good night's sleep.

Eliza Harwood was plainly keen to be home before her husband returned. They went first to Harwood House, where Anne-Marie alighted also to collect some things for her journey and, having begged Eliza to explain her absence to her superior at the hospital, returned to the carriage.

As they continued on their journey, she told Emma more details of the trying situation that had developed between her parents. It was plain that Anne-Marie was exceedingly distressed by it all. Despite Emma's gentle efforts to comfort her, she continued to look most unhappy and, though she kept a brave countenance for most of the journey, there were many occasions when Emma saw her bite her lip and hurriedly wipe tears from her eyes.

Several hours later, having stopped only for meals and to change horses, they arrived at the Wilsons' house in Grosvenor Street.

Once there, Emma proceeded to acquaint her husband with the events that had necessitated their journey to London. With Anne-Marie to provide the details, they were able to give him a complete account of what had transpired and some idea of what they feared might yet follow.

James Wilson was almost speechless with astonishment. While he had known of Amelia-Jane's objections to her husband's return to Westminster, nothing Jonathan had said had prepared him for such a turn of events as this.

"I cannot believe that Jonathan would have gone to Hertfordshire if he had any knowledge of Amelia-Jane's intentions. It is quite likely that he is as ignorant of all this as we are," he remarked.

"Has he given you no indication at all of the involvement of Miss Bingley and her friend, this Mrs Watkins, in Amelia-Jane's affairs?" asked his wife.

James was adamant. "None whatsoever; had he done so, I would have advised him to seek your father's help. Mr Bingley is far more likely to have some influence with his sister than Jonathan and may well have prevented matters going as far as this."

Emma was not so sure. "Papa has never had much influence with his sisters; they have always acted exactly as they thought fit, as a consequence of having been left their own quite considerable fortune by their father. I believe they used to have a much greater influence upon him until Mr Darcy took him in hand."

"Does that mean Caroline will not heed his advice?" asked James.

"I very much doubt that she will. Indeed, if what Anne-Marie says is true, the Bingley sisters appear to be well and truly under the influence of this Mrs Watkins—whoever she is!" said his wife.

"But, what is to be done?" asked Anne-Marie, feeling helpless and impatient as the conversation swirled around her. "How are we to prevail upon Mama that she must not go to Bath, leaving Tess and Cathy at the parsonage with Aunt Catherine, as if they were orphans!"

Her grief and anxiety moved James to speak more gently. "While it is a private family matter in which one generally ought not interfere, should Jonathan need my support to convince your mother, he will certainly have it," said James, but Anne-Marie was not comforted.

"But what about Miss Bingley and this dreadful Watkins woman? Who will confront them and ask them to stay out of our lives?" she cried.

James Wilson was not at all in favour of Anne-Marie's idea of confronting the three women at the Bingleys' house. "I do not believe that it will accomplish anything, except still more acrimony and embarrassment," he advised. "I cannot recommend it to you, Anne-Marie, and I do not think your father will appreciate it, either. He will probably feel that it is more than likely to inflame the situation between your mother and himself."

He did agree, however, that Jonathan should be warned and he promised to send a message to Longbourn by electric telegraph, urgently requesting his presence at Westminster.

Anne-Marie, though not entirely satisfied, was grateful for his help.

⚜

Jonathan Bingley would remember the Summer of 1859 to his dying day.

It was not a particularly remarkable Summer, as English Summers go, but he would remember it because it was the period when almost every aspect of his life changed radically. Some changes he had made himself, such as his decision to move back into politics, but there were others over which he seemed to have no control at all.

However, when he journeyed to Hertfordshire for his regular visit to the Longbourn estate, he had no hint of the volatility of the circumstances that surrounded him nor the events that were about to occur. The only change he could envisage, and which he would certainly welcome, was the one they had all been working hard to achieve since the election. Negotiations were leading to a point where the defeat of Lord Derby's government in the Commons was imminent. While the thought excited him, as it would be the culmination of their hopes, Jonathan did not dwell on it as he approached the end of his journey.

The countryside around Longbourn was so pretty and the early Summer weather so mild as to make one forget the clamour of life's demands on one's time. The gentle movement of the vehicle and the salubrious environment outside induced a most alluring mood of serenity, which was not necessarily related to reality at all.

Arriving at Longbourn, he found both Mrs Collins, his mother-in-law, and his aunt Miss Mary Bennet in good spirits. They were very excited that he had arrived early.

"Because it means you will be meeting the Faulkners, who are coming to tea with their daughter Anna, who is recently returned from Europe," said Mrs Collins who was obviously very proud of her young niece. "She is exceptionally talented and remarkably modest with it," she declared as the women, having attended to Jonathan, busied themselves preparing for their visitors.

"Indeed, she is," said Jonathan and surprised both Mary and Charlotte when he said, "I had the good fortune to meet Miss Anna Faulkner and her parents on the morning after Julian Darcy's wedding, when I called on my aunt Lizzie and Mr Darcy. The Faulkners were visiting Pemberley at the same time."

It seemed a long time ago, but he still recalled their meeting clearly and told Charlotte that he had found her niece charming and, from what he had heard of her work in Art and Music, it appeared she was very accomplished too.

Mrs Collins agreed completely and gave Jonathan a detailed description of her niece's accomplishments—the catalogue of which would have continued had they not been interrupted by the steward, who had arrived to take Jonathan on his regular inspection of the property.

He was eager to take a look at some new trees that had been planted in the orchard in the early Spring and went with the steward, promising not to be late for tea.

Although he had been exceedingly busy for almost all of the time since their meeting at Pemberley, Jonathan had not forgotten the Faulkners or their talented young daughter. Since he had been back at Westminster, he had met other people who had visited Paris and had spoken enthusiastically of the same French painters that Miss Faulkner had admired so much and he looked forward to telling her so.

Later, having returned to the house, bathed and changed, he came downstairs to find the Faulkners already ensconced in the drawing room, partaking of tea and a delicious array of cakes and pastries. He noted that Anna was talking quietly to his aunt Mary, who sat by the fire, while Mrs Collins was busy pouring out tea.

They all greeted him cheerfully and Mrs Faulkner made a point of coming over to the side table and condoling with him on the death of his former employer, Lady Catherine, and almost immediately afterwards congratulating him on the happy news that she had bequeathed him a substantial sum of money.

Even though she lowered her voice to a conspiratorial whisper, Jonathan was embarrassed and tried to dismiss it lightly, but Maria Faulkner was determined that he should know how happy she was for him.

"Your aunt Kitty mentioned it in her last letter," she said with a funny little smile that made her look almost child-like. "I just wanted you to know how very happy we all are for you. When I read Kitty's letter, I said to Dr Faulkner—'it cannot have happened to a nicer person than Mr Jonathan Bingley,' I said, and he agreed."

Jonathan thanked her and hurried back to join the others, hoping desperately to change the subject. As they helped themselves to cake, Dr Faulkner gave him the chance, with a remark about the value of properties in Hertfordshire.

"I believe," he said, as they stood beside the windows each balancing a cup of tea and a plate of cake, "Netherfield Park is vacant again and, this time, it is for sale."

Jonathan was so taken aback, he could not find anything to say at first, but as he recovered, he asked, trying hard to sound casual, "Is it really? Do you happen to know what price they are asking?"

Dr Faulkner did not know, but said he knew the agent in charge of the sale, a patient of his, and could make enquiries of him.

Before he could ask any questions, Jonathan added quickly, as if to explain his interest, "I was born at Netherfield, but the family moved to Leicestershire soon afterwards and I have never been back."

"Ah! I see," said Dr Faulkner in the sort of tone that implied that everything had suddenly become clear to him. "Well, I could give you Mr Armstrong's address, if you wish to call on him while you are here. His offices are in Meryton. I am sure he would be happy to let you look over the place. There have been some improvements made over the years."

Jonathan, though not wishing to proclaim his interest too widely, could not hide his excitement. He was glad Mrs Faulkner and her daughter had followed Mary into the library, which now served also as a music room; it allowed him to make a note of the address without drawing their attention. The last thing he wanted was to start some gossip in the town about his interest in Netherfield.

Thanking Dr Faulkner, he requested that the matter of his inquiry be treated as a confidence, to which the good doctor readily agreed.

"Of course, Mr Bingley, you may rely on me. I am accustomed to keeping matters confidential, and not all of them are medical matters! You'd be surprised at the confidences with which people trust us," he said as they moved out to join the ladies and admire the splendid display of Summer flowers in the garden.

Charlotte Collins was very proud of her achievements in the grounds of Longbourn and wished to show them off. As they walked along the flagged path bordering the lawn, Jonathan found himself between Miss Faulkner and Mrs Collins.

When they reached the terrace, he helped his mother-in-law down the shallow steps and turned to help his younger companion, but she was already there before him, smiling at his look of mild surprise.

"You are very sure-footed, Miss Faulkner," he said with a smile, to which she replied that she had done a lot of walking in Europe and had learned to watch her step, since many of the lesser roads and country lanes were in very poor condition.

"My friends the Armandes are great walkers. Every Sunday, after we had been to church, the entire household would walk miles, in every kind of weather, too," she said, "and when we got home, usually with our arms full of wild flowers from the fields and meadows, there was always steaming hot soup and fresh baked bread. The scent would fill the house!"

"You make it sound truly delightful," he said, amused by the obvious pleasure she took in recalling the experience.

Anna laughed. "Oh, it was. I must say, the Europeans know how to enjoy every simple experience. Things we would regard as commonplace, like collecting mushrooms in the woods, picking fruit in the orchard, or even just baking bread, I cannot explain it, but somehow, they seem to gain a new, more pleasurable quality over there. It's very much like the work of the new French painters, who render very ordinary things—a basket of fruit, a jug of milk, many homely articles luminous and extraordinarily beautiful."

Jonathan wanted to tell her of his friends at Westminster, who had seen and admired their work, but was reluctant to interrupt her. She spoke with so much feeling and enthusiasm and her eyes and voice were so expressive, he wished she would go on, but suddenly, as if conscious of her own voice, Anna stopped.

They had reached the end of the terrace. This time they had several steps to climb to the drive and she gladly took the hand he offered and thanked him for his help.

The others had stopped to admire a rose bush, of which Charlotte had added several to the garden at Longbourn; Jonathan, conscious of the warm afternoon sun slanting down upon them, led the way indoors.

"And have you been doing any drawing recently?" he asked and was surprised when she replied with obvious pleasure, "Indeed, I have. We visited Hatfield House a week or two ago. My father has an abiding interest in historic houses. When we were in Derbyshire, it was difficult to drag him away from Chatsworth and Pemberley. Well, he wanted to show me Hatfield House and the old Palace where Queen Elizabeth lived as a girl, when her horrid sister Mary Tudor sat on the throne and persecuted everybody who disagreed with her."

Jonathan laughed, amused by her irreverent view of history. He had often driven past the great mansion built by the Earl of Salisbury in the grounds of the palace where the young Queen Elizabeth had been told of her accession to the throne, and he wished now he had stopped to visit. It would, at least, have made this conversation easier for him.

"And were you impressed?" he asked.

"I most certainly was, but I think I was more excited by the buildings and the architecture than their historical significance, and my father was a little disappointed. I did make a few preliminary sketches and would love to go back and do some more, perhaps later in the year, when it is not quite so warm in the sun."

He was about to ask if he might be permitted to see her drawings when an express arrived at the door. The maid collected it and brought it directly to him.

It was a letter from Anne-Marie. Jonathan, a little surprised that his daughter should be sending him an express letter, excused himself and, as the others came indoors and fresh pots of tea were brought in and placed on the table, he slipped away to read his letter in the library.

No one seemed to notice when Jonathan Bingley did not come back into the drawing room soon afterwards. He had intended to read his daughter's letter quickly and rejoin their guests, but the contents so disturbed him he felt unable to return to the drawing room immediately and had gone upstairs instead.

Entering his room, which used to be Mr Bennet's bedroom, overlooking the park and shrubbery on the eastern side of the house, Jonathan read the letter again, unwilling to believe the words on the page.

She wrote, providing alarming information about her mother's present state of mind, and implored him to take her seriously.

Dearest Papa, I assure you I am not exaggerating the situation. We are in danger of losing Mama to the tender mercies of Miss Caroline Bingley and her dreadful friend, Mrs Arabella Watkins! I do not know if you saw her at Lady C's funeral; if you did, you will not have forgotten her for she is, I promise, quite the most insufferable woman I have ever met! ... It is beyond belief that she has so much influence upon Mama.

Papa, I beg you to return as soon as possible ...

… and so it went on, detailing all that had taken place in his absence.

Clearly, Anne-Marie had been in a desperately unhappy state when she wrote. Her usually neat, rounded hand was at times illegible, and the words almost leapt off the page at him, so passionately did the writer seem to feel the outrage she expressed.

Her father, who knew how deeply she could be moved, wondered at the distress she must have endured to write in such a vein.

Some twenty minutes later, conscious of his duty to their guests, Jonathan tucked the letter into his pocket and went downstairs. The Faulkners appeared to be preparing to leave and as they gathered in the hall; only Anna seemed to have noticed that he had been missing for a while.

Perhaps recalling the express communication he had received, she said discreetly, "Not bad news from home, I hope?"

Jonathan hardly knew what to say; taking the easy way out, he smiled and said, "No, it was my fault. I have not written all week and Anne-Marie has been anxious. I shall have to send off an express tonight."

Anna smiled and seemed as if she was about to ask a question when Mrs Faulkner came over to invite Jonathan to dine with them at Haye Park, on the Monday.

Even as he thanked her, Jonathan was unsure if he would be able to attend. Then Anna said, "You could look at my sketches of Hatfield House and tell me if you think they are worth working on," and the question was settled at once.

He smiled and declared that it would be a pleasure he would look forward to, even though he confessed he was not qualified in any way to give such an opinion on her drawings.

Like his father, Jonathan Bingley had been blessed with good looks and good humour, happily combined with a degree of modesty that usually endeared him to his companions and friends. It was no different on this occasion.

After the Faulkners had gone, Jonathan decided that he would write immediately to Anne-Marie, to reassure her and say he was arranging to return to London as soon as his business at Longbourn was done.

He wanted very much to go to dinner at Haye Park and calculated that it would probably delay his departure by a day and a half at the most. It was very unlikely, he decided, that his wife, with or without the malign influence of Mrs Arabella Watkins, would do anything extreme in the meantime.

The following morning, having returned from his early canter around the park, Jonathan changed, breakfasted, and went to Meryton to see Mr Armstrong.

He introduced himself as a friend of Dr Faulkner and was immediately told he needed no introduction; the name of Bingley was well known and respected in the district. Moreover, Mr Armstrong revealed that Dr Faulkner had called on him but a short time ago and asked him to pay very special attention to Mr Jonathan Bingley, who was interested in the property because he had been born at Netherfield House.

Mr Armstrong was so excited; he was all of a twitter at meeting Jonathan and would take him immediately to view the property.

Jonathan could not fail to be impressed by what he saw. The house was not too large nor too small, with a handsome exterior that was dignified without being pretentious and several fine rooms within. Improvements had been made to lighting, plumbing, and the landscaping of the grounds, all of which, as Mr Armstrong did not fail to mention, added value to the property.

The furniture, drapes, and fittings were in good order if a little overpowering in style and colour. A small number of trusted servants and a caretaker, who came highly recommended, might be retained if the new owner wished to do so, Armstrong explained.

They briefly discussed prices and Mr Armstrong was kind enough to say that Mr Bingley could have the privilege of first refusal before he considered any other buyers, "on account of your family's very intimate connections with the property, sir," he said, clearly intending to please.

Satisfied with his efforts, Jonathan saw an opportunity to restore his family to their own home, make Amelia-Jane happy again, and settle most of their current problems.

He was very confident that his wife would love Netherfield Park, just as his mother had done. It had elegance without affectation, which he found very acceptable. A modest gentleman of conservative taste, it suited him well.

Returning to Longbourn, he wrote and despatched another note, this one to Amelia-Jane at their house in Grosvenor Street, describing the property, expressing his enthusiasm for it, and urging her to come down with him to inspect it at the earliest opportunity.

His letter, though short, was affectionate in tone and gave sufficient information to demonstrate the seriousness of his intentions:

Dearest, I am sure you will adore the house and the park, which, though not as grand as Rosings or Pemberley, are both exceedingly handsome and perfectly maintained. It is a fine Georgian manor and should suit our family well.

We shall also be close enough to London—a mere twenty odd miles—and the neighbourhood is quite charming. Indeed, this part of Hertfordshire seems to grow prettier each time I visit …

… and so on, hoping with his appreciation to enthuse her as well.

That evening, the two ladies from Longbourn and Jonathan Bingley dined with the Faulkners at Haye Park, arriving with plenty of time to look around the place. Here again was another recently "improved" Georgian residence, which impressed Jonathan with its simple, uncluttered elegance.

Mrs Faulkner showed them around some of the rooms, which were very handsome, and the remarkable conservatory filled with tropical blooms. She was keen to point out that the interior design and choice of colours for pelmets, drapes, and rugs were the work of her daughter Anna, whom she credited with greatly improving her own appreciation.

"I myself had very little understanding of artistic matters, but Anna has been a patient teacher," she explained modestly.

Anna herself, charming and friendly, was the perfect hostess—attentive without being fussy.

At dinner, Jonathan found he was to sit between her and Dr Faulkner's mother, who was very quiet and concentrated upon her food, except when her son was speaking, when she would stop eating and give him her undivided attention.

They had been seated a while, making no more than small talk about the weather, when Anna said, "Mr Bingley, I was about to ask you last afternoon, when Mama interrupted us: how old is your eldest daughter?"

Surprised that she had remembered and taken the question up, he replied, "Anne-Marie is twenty, but she is very grown up and responsible for her age," he replied.

"And she lives at your home in Kent?" she persevered.

"No, indeed, she lives at Harwood House, just outside of London, with my cousin, Eliza Harwood. She used to be Elizabeth Courtney. Anne-Marie is a trained nurse," he explained. "She, too, was inspired by the example of Miss Nightingale. She works now at the military hospital, which stands in the grounds of Harwood House."

Miss Faulkner's eyes were wide with surprise, as she expressed her admiration in no uncertain terms. "Mr Bingley, forgive my astonishment, but I have no words to tell you how much I admire the selflessness and determination of such women. Nursing the sick and wounded, especially soldiers, must be the noblest of professions. Yet it must also be one of the most difficult and hazardous occupations."

She proceeded to relate a most touching story. "During the war in the Crimea, Monsieur Armande's two sisters volunteered as nurses to tend the French soldiers. They joined a group of fine French women, who could no longer bear to see the neglect and suffering of the men at the front. Unfortunately, Jeanette, the younger sister, contracted typhus and died. Poor Monsieur Armande was distraught, especially when Marie-Claire, her elder sister, insisted on carrying on her work until the war ended."

Jonathan was moved by the story and her quiet, deeply felt words. He was glad of yet another subject in which they shared an interest. He was finding it easier to converse with her each time they met.

After the meal, they repaired to the drawing room and Anna brought out her sketches—those she had made at Hatfield House and another of an old stone bridge—and laid them on one of the card tables.

Having declared that he knew very little of Art and drawing, Jonathan pronounced the sketches of Hatfield House to be "very good, indeed."

It was a considered and moderate response, which in fact did no more than imply that he found them very pleasing.

But then he saw the drawing of the bridge, with its arches spanning a river and the merest suggestion of mountain peaks against the sky.

"That bridge," said Jonathan immediately, "that is at Matlock, in Derbyshire, is it not?"

Anna laughed. "Of course it is; the drawing just happened to be amongst the others in my folio. I sketched that on the afternoon following our meeting with you at Pemberley after Julian Darcy's wedding. We visited the Gardiners, and Mrs Gardiner simply had to show us her favourite prospect in the Peak District. So off we went to Matlock and there was this lovely old bridge."

Jonathan was delighted. "That is the bridge over whose walls I used to hang as a boy, watching the fish in the water and the dragon flies in the reeds, while my sister Emma, terrified that I would fall in and drown, would hang on to my boots!" he reminisced with a smile, adding, "Miss Faulkner, that is a beautiful drawing and seeing it has brought back all those happy memories, I thank you." He was truly pleased he had accepted the invitation to dinner that night.

"Would you like to have it?" she asked, and when he protested that he could not possibly take it, it was her picture, she added unaffectedly, "It would give me far greater pleasure to know that you had it on your wall and enjoyed looking at it, than if it stayed locked up out of sight in my folio."

Faced with this disarming proposition, Jonathan could say no more than a heartfelt "thank you," promising to have it mounted and framed for his study.

"I shall show it to Emma when I see her. She will remember the bridge, I am sure, and the days we spent in Derbyshire as children with the Gardiners at Lambton and my aunt Lizzie and Mr Darcy at Pemberley. They were such happy times," he said again with a smile, and Anna could not help wondering why he spoke in such nostalgic terms of his happy childhood. She had no knowledge at all of Jonathan's present troubles, but could not help thinking he was not entirely content.

After a very pleasant evening, they returned to Longbourn, with both Mary Bennet and Charlotte Collins singing the praises of Miss Faulkner.

Her artistic talent, excellent taste, charming manners were itemised again and again as were her good looks and elegant European gown.

Jonathan remained mostly silent, except when applied to for an opinion and then he found it easy to agree with them.

On their return, there was a telegram awaiting him from James Wilson. It requested his immediate return to Westminster for urgent consultation.

Taking it to mean that something had gone wrong with the political negotiations he had been involved in, Jonathan made plans to leave very early the following morning.

He explained the situation to Charlotte and begged her to apologise for him to the Faulkners.

On learning that Jonathan had never been inside the old palace at Hatfield, John Faulkner had offered to take him there and personally point out the features of the historic building. When Jonathan had protested that he could not put him to all that trouble, Dr Faulkner had insisted that he had to take Anna so she could do more sketches, and having Jonathan for company would be an added pleasure. When seen in that convenient light, the proposition had seemed a very acceptable one indeed and they had agreed to set a mutually convenient date for their excursion.

Unhappily, James' telegram had arrived to change his plans altogether.

Even as he left, with very genuine regret, Jonathan urged Mrs Collins, "Please be so kind as to make my apologies to Dr and Mrs Faulkner and Miss Faulkner, for I had promised to collect the drawing of the Matlock bridge today and take it for framing. Please explain that urgent business has recalled me to Westminster immediately. I shall write as soon as I am able. Thank you very much, Mrs Collins, this has been a most enjoyable visit."

And he was gone, in the very early dawn, leaving Charlotte thinking how unhappy he looked.

Charlotte Collins, though a careful and attentive mother when her daughters were little, was far less involved in their lives, since they were all married, than either of her friends Jane or Elizabeth were with their children. She was therefore quite unaware of the extent of her youngest daughter's problems.

Although the distance that separated them was not great, she had so enjoyed her liberation, since the death of Mr Collins, from the stuffiness of Rosings that she was not easily persuaded to travel there.

She did, however, see Jonathan frequently, whenever he visited Longbourn and on this occasion, she had noticed that he had not seemed very happy.

So concerned was she that, shortly afterwards, she sat down at her desk and wrote to her friend Elizabeth Darcy.

> *My dear Eliza,*
>
> *If I remember correctly, I do not owe you a letter, having answered yours some days ago.*
>
> *This comes, therefore, because I am rather uneasy about a certain matter and being a selfish creature, wish to unburden myself upon you, my dear friend.*
>
> *We have just had our regular visit from Jonathan Bingley; a visit*

he has pronounced to be "most enjoyable." And it undoubtedly was, for we had the Faulkners to tea and then dined with them last night at Haye Park and on both occasions dear Jonathan seemed to enjoy himself a good deal.

Notwithstanding this, I have an uneasy feeling that something is wrong.

I cannot put my finger on it Eliza, but he does not appear to be happy in himself. I feel there is something troubling him and while I had neither the time nor the inclination to ask him outright, I wonder if you or Mr Darcy could try to discover the source of his discontent.

I have no way of discovering whether it has to do with his work or with his marriage.

Eliza, my dear, please write and advise me if there is anything I should know and have overlooked. I know that my Amelia-Jane has been unhappy since she lost her two little boys—who would not be? But I cannot help feeling that there is a deeper problem here than grief and it is hurting both of them. However, neither Amelia-Jane nor Jonathan has in any way confided in me.

Your help will be greatly appreciated, Eliza, and I trust you are all very well and enjoying your Summer at Woodlands.

Yours affectionately,

Charlotte

Elizabeth was sitting out in the garden at Woodlands with Jane when Charlotte's letter was delivered. Their husbands had decided to go into Guildford that morning, leaving the sisters together.

Since it was a fine, sunny morning, it had seemed like a good idea to take their writing materials outside. Jane claimed she had letters to answer, while Elizabeth was completing some notes for her diary.

When Charlotte's letter arrived, Elizabeth was delighted, if a little surprised.

"Two letters from Charlotte in one week! I cannot believe it; it must bring some news that could not wait until she had my reply," she declared, opening it up, never expecting to find the news it contained.

Jane had moved closer in order to read the letter together with her sister.

When she saw what Charlotte had written, she was very upset.

"Lizzie, what on earth does she mean? Why does she believe Jonathan is so unhappy? Do you think he is? He has said nothing to us. I know he has been very busy with his work and I do know he wants to do well at Westminster, but Emma tells me he is very well regarded by his colleagues. What ever could have happened to make him miserable?" she asked.

Elizabeth thought it unlikely that Jonathan's state of mind, if he were unhappy, would have anything to do with his work at Westminster.

"Dear Jane, if what Charlotte suspects is true, it is hardly likely that it is in any way connected with his work. When Darcy last spoke with him, he appeared delighted with the way matters were progressing and, as you say, he is well regarded in the party."

"What then?" Jane was bewildered. "I know he is very pleased with Longbourn, he has said so repeatedly, and Bingley says the place is better run than ever before. Lizzie, is it possible he has money troubles?"

Elizabeth smiled and shook her head. "No, Jane, I could never see your Jonathan having 'money troubles,' as you call them. He is far too sensible and careful a man. No, I am inclined to think that it has more to do with matrimony than money, Jane."

Jane looked exceedingly anxious. "Do you mean there is a problem with his marriage?" she asked. It was a subject that had caused her some concern, and her sister knew it.

Elizabeth nodded, and Jane continued, "Do you suppose it is to do with Amelia-Jane? I know she has been miserable since losing her little boys, and she was against him returning to Westminster, of course, so it is possible that she could be unhappy, and that would upset Jonathan," she mused.

"Indeed, it would, Jane, but we must remember also that Jonathan has been very busy and his wife may be feeling rather lonely and neglected," said Elizabeth. "I did notice, at Lady Catherine's funeral, that she was very much with the Bingley women, Louisa and Caroline and that other rather extravagantly dressed woman, who seemed very attentive to her. Do you remember her name?"

Jane could not; but she did remember her hat!

"It was the largest hat in the church, and I did not get a good look at her face. What do you suppose she has to do with it?" she asked in some confusion.

"I do not know, Jane, but if there is any matter that has added to Jonathan's woes, by making Amelia-Jane less amenable, I would wager London to a brick

Miss Bingley is involved. Jane, she has never forgiven you for marrying her beloved brother and thereby foiling her own plans in relation to his best friend," said Elizabeth so decidedly that her sister was shocked.

"You cannot mean that she is still smarting over that disappointment? Not after all this time?" Jane was unsure, but Elizabeth was quite certain.

"Caroline Bingley will never get over it. She wastes no love on either of us and if she were able to discomfit us in any way, she would gladly do so. Mark my words, Jane, she is involved. Ask Jonathan when you see him."

On arriving in London, Jonathan Bingley went directly to James Wilson's place at Grosvenor Street and, there, discovered that the urgency of Wilson's message owed little to the political situation and rather more to his own domestic problems.

His sister Emma was there, too, and together they gave him details, dates, and places of all the circumstances related to them by Anne-Marie and Eliza Harwood, both of whom had since returned to Harwood House.

"Jonathan, your daughter, who is not generally given to flights of fancy, was certain that Caroline Bingley and this new friend of hers, Mrs Watkins, intended to take Amelia-Jane back to Bath with them," said Emma. "I was not entirely convinced that this was the case, but seeing how upset Anne-Marie was, I travelled up to London with her and saw James."

"Which was why I sent you that telegram," said his brother-in-law.

Jonathan thanked them both profusely for their concern and, more particularly, for the care they had taken of his daughter, but he was equally sure that his wife would not be easily persuaded to leave her home at Rosings Park and travel to Bath.

Nevertheless, he was determined to see her as soon as possible and, despite their efforts to persuade him to stay and take some refreshment, he left almost at once and went directly to the Bingleys' town house, where he found Amelia-Jane at home, alone, and feeling very sorry for herself.

On seeing him, her expression changed from a somewhat petulant one to a rather injured, unhappy look. When he approached her with his usual affectionate greeting, she flung herself into his arms and made a great scene. Jonathan, though not always understanding his wife's recent tantrums, had tried to comfort her and he did so again, reassuring her and trying to allay her fears.

Clearly, she was insecure and unhappy and even his most loving and sincere expressions of affection did not entirely calm her anxieties. However, he did discover that she had arrived in London with Miss Bingley and her friend Arabella Watkins, who had tried to persuade her to go with them to Bath.

But, she told him, she had not had the heart to go because, as she put it rather quaintly, "I could not bear to leave my dear ones behind."

The fact that her "dear ones"—if by that she meant Teresa and Cathy—spent most of their time with either their aunt Catherine Harrison or their grandmother, Jane Bingley, seemed to have quite escaped her notice.

Wisely, Jonathan did not point this out, judging correctly that this was not the time for recriminations. Instead, he continued to soothe her hurt feelings and suggest it was probably all his fault.

"I know I have been away, dearest, far more than I should, and you have been on your own, which is not fair. Well, I have a plan that will help us solve all those problems. Tomorrow, after you've rested, I shall tell you all about it. I am sure you will love it."

She was impatient to be told, cajoling and pleading for more information, but he was firm and insisted that she should get a good night's sleep first.

"Tomorrow, I shall tell you all you want to know, I promise. We are both too tired to talk about it tonight."

Amelia-Jane had been feeling lonely and depressed and appreciated the genuine warmth of his concern for her. As she had done many times before, she abandoned her tantrums and, taking the path of least resistance, gave in and did exactly as he asked.

It was a tactic she had perfected over several years of marriage to a kind and amiable man who, she knew, could not resist her in a compliant mood.

The following morning's mail brought the letter he had written her from Longbourn. Jonathan waited until after breakfast had been cleared away then placed it before her.

At first, she was surprised and confused.

"Jonathan, this letter is from you. Why are you writing to me? Why can you not tell me what it is about?" she asked.

When he insisted that she read it first and then ask questions, she adopted a rather arch manner and tried to play games with him.

"Were you so displeased with me that you would not speak with me?" she joked, and, when finally persuaded to read it, she did not understand the point of it.

She thought he wanted to purchase Netherfield as a good investment—a place to be leased to tenants. Only when he took the letter from her and told her in simple terms what he proposed to do did she admit to understanding its true import. That he intended they should move to live at Netherfield Park when he had finished his work at Rosings seemed, at last, to sink in.

Jonathan had been prepared for astonishment and even displeasure, but he had not expected the violence of her reaction and the bitterness of her words.

"Move to Hertfordshire? Jonathan, are you mad? How can you suggest such a thing? What on earth would I do there? Who would I visit? Who would call on us, other than your aunt Mary and my mother? And I suppose, when you come to Westminster for days and weeks together, I will be expected to keep house and knit and sew."

Her fury was so great, it silenced him altogether. It was as if nothing he could say would matter or persuade her to change her mind. He knew it would do no good at all to suggest that there were many useful and interesting things to engage the mind of the woman who would be the Mistress of Netherfield Park. It was of no account to her that the Bingleys had been well liked and regarded in the district and she would have a respected position in her own right, unlike the situation at Rosings, where they had been dependent upon the patronage of Lady Catherine de Bourgh.

After the splendour of Rosings, even though she had only occupied the humble Dower House, Netherfield seemed déclassé, like a profound social demotion. She refused even to contemplate it.

Jonathan did not pursue the matter further, still hoping she might be persuaded to visit Netherfield and confident that if she did, she would be won over.

The signs, however, were not hopeful.

That evening, Amelia-Jane insisted that she intended to return to Rosings Park, where she declared she would occupy the Dower House "until they throw me out" rather than move to Hertfordshire. So saying, she retired to her room to pack for her journey and could not be persuaded to venture downstairs even for meals.

Her husband's disappointment was so profound he said nothing all afternoon. Having dined alone, he went out to his club and returned to sit in his study until nightfall. When a note was delivered by hand from Westminster, he opened it and had to read it twice before realising that it contained the news he had been waiting weeks to hear.

An historic political alliance had been formed, and the nation was on the verge of seeing a new government take office. A straight vote of "No Confidence" was set to bring down Lord Derby's government and, in the culmination of all their work, Lord Palmerston would form the new ministry.

Excited and immensely pleased, Jonathan ran upstairs to collect his papers and his coat, taking a few minutes to look in on his wife and tell her the news before racing out of the house.

Amelia-Jane received the news without excitement; she had long ceased to be interested in his political work and, indeed, blamed much of her unhappiness on his continuing interest in it. Significantly, Jonathan did not notice her indifference. He, too, had long since forgotten to feign disappointment at her lack of enthusiasm.

It was late when Jonathan returned to Grosvenor Street, and if he were to be quite honest with himself, he would have had to admit that he was somewhat relieved to discover that his wife had already retired to bed. His undeniably elated, even euphoric state would not have pleased her, nor was it conducive to logical argument about their future home.

The housekeeper advised him that Mrs Bingley had asked for her two maids to be packed and ready to travel to Kent on the morrow, stating that they would be making an early start.

Jonathan, who had spent several hours celebrating the prospect of bringing down the Tory government and restoring the Whigs to office, did not quite appreciate the full import of her words until he came down to a late breakfast on the following day to find that his wife had already left for Rosings Park.

"Mrs Bingley left very early, sir, and asked that you should not be disturbed, but she left this for you," said Mrs Giles, the housekeeper, handing him a sealed letter.

After breakfast, Jonathan opened it to find a curt little note in which Amelia-Jane reiterated her desire to return to the Dower House and her total opposition to any move to Hertfordshire, saying rather melodramatically, "I would rather die!"—after which she was able, surprisingly, to wish him well and urge him to "mind that you do not let James Wilson and the rest of those wretched Whigs take advantage of your obliging nature."

Jonathan was sad and confused. Sad that she had set her mind so firmly against a plan that meant a good deal to him, and confused because he could not understand why she had done so.

Not being privy to the snobbery and pretentiousness with which Caroline Bingley and Arabella Watkins had filled her head, he could not know how badly advised she was. Singing the praises of Rosings and Bath, whose constricting social mores were upheld as the epitome of upper class behaviour, they had consistently referred to places like Woodlands and Netherfield as provincial and lacking in style. When the first suggestions had come that Jonathan might want to move from the Dower House at Rosings Park, both women had urged her not to leave, but to attempt to reach an accommodation with the new manager of the Trust.

Miss Bingley had even suggested mischievously that, with Mr Darcy and Colonel Fitzwilliam on the board, they would surely not evict her and her children if she stayed.

"They would not want the embarrassment, my dear," she had declared, all the while entertaining the hope of seeing the family embarrassed by just such a contretemps!

Elizabeth was right about Caroline Bingley.

So deeply mortified had she been by her brother's determination to marry Jane Bennet and, to add insult to injury, by Elizabeth's marriage to Mr Darcy, that she sank into deep resentment, which she hid beneath a veneer of civility. Every so often, however, it broke through in the kind of petty spitefulness that Elizabeth and her sister had long since learned to treat with contempt.

On this occasion though, by being instrumental in the destruction of Jonathan Bingley's peace of mind, if not his marriage, she had reached a new level of malice. In this vicious exercise, she had been ably assisted by her newfound friend, Mrs Arabella Watkins.

A woman of mean understanding, little learning, and no taste, who had made her way in the world by ingratiating herself with those she considered to be her superiors, Arabella Watkins had money, but no other means to gain entrée into Bath society.

By the merest chance, she had been at the home of a Lady Gertrude _____, widow of a well-known Admiral, whither she had gone to seek a position as a paid companion, advertised in the local journal.

Mrs Watkins was being interviewed for this situation when the two Bingley sisters had called on Lady Gertrude.

Recalling a previous meeting with Caroline Bingley in London, sometime before the death of her second husband, and seeing a valuable social opportunity, she had introduced herself and, thereafter, used every occasion to consolidate her acquaintance with them.

Caroline Bingley, being single and without the contacts that enabled titled women to trawl the social scene for useful hangers-on, had welcomed, with but a few reservations, the egregious attentions of Mrs Watkins. She was certainly useful, being quite free with her money and time, whenever the Bingley women required her company.

Caroline had spoken highly of her to her sister Mrs Hurst, who had by now reached an age when she was disinclined to expend much effort or time on any person or activity that did not directly benefit herself.

Caroline promoted the value of Mrs Watkins to her sister.

"Arabella Watkins is the type of person who is genuinely obliging and helpful. Nothing is too difficult for her nor too tedious, if it will please a friend," she said and, in that instant, sealed for her worthless protégé another niche in Bath society, as the preferred companion of the Bingley sisters, who would accompany them wherever they went, ever ready to aid and abet in all their schemes, without actually imposing upon them.

When Amelia-Jane had first visited them in Bath, there had been no Arabella Watkins, and Caroline Bingley had made much of her nephew's wife, introducing her to all her friends and taking her to what she claimed were all the right places, where a woman of fashion and consequence would wish to be seen. Young enough to be gulled by the show of influence, Amelia-Jane had thought Caroline a kind woman who wanted to be her friend.

When she next visited the city, for the funeral of Lady Catherine de Bourgh, the indefatigable Arabella Watkins had joined the Bingley sisters, and young Amelia-Jane had no chance of escape.

Already depressed and unhappy after the loss of her sons, she had been ripe for picking, and the efforts of Mrs Watkins paid off handsomely, as she became to young Mrs Bingley a friend and confidante who would provide a sympathetic ear for all her complaints.

It was the very last thing that Amelia-Jane needed.

None of this was known to her husband, who still hoped for a late conversion to his way of thinking. He loved and cared for her and hoped she would finally see that they had no other practical alternative; they had to leave Rosings by Christmas. Too interested in Netherfield to be easily deterred, Jonathan had decided to seek his parents' opinion.

On the following day, he travelled to Woodlands to see them and to convey the good news regarding the imminent return of Lord Palmerston to government to Colonel Fitzwilliam and Caroline.

Arriving at Woodlands, he was greeted effusively as some sort of hero by the Fitzwilliams and more soberly, though with no less affection, by the rest of the family.

His mother was especially pleased because she had been very anxious ever since reading Charlotte's letter. She was truly happy to learn that Amelia-Jane had returned to Kent and was even now with her children at the Dower House in Rosings Park, where she would spend the rest of the Summer.

"And what about you, Jonathan?" she asked. "What will you do now?"

Jonathan replied quickly that there was still much work to be done at Westminster. "I shall be busy all week, Mama, and will continue to stay at Grosvenor Street, but I do intend to go down to Kent as often as possible," he declared, trying to set her heart at rest.

During and after dinner, he told them of his plans for Netherfield Park. He intended to use some of his savings and the money left to him by Lady Catherine to make an offer for the property, he explained.

They were all interested. Bingley declared that he had heard the new owners had made several improvements, and Darcy expressed the hope they had not destroyed the character of the early Georgian house.

Jonathan was happy to be able to assure them that yes, there had been much good work done with modern plumbing and lighting, and no, since it had been carefully and sensitively done, it had certainly not ruined the character of the place.

"Indeed, sir, while Netherfield House looks much like it always did, the lawns, walks, and shrubbery have been incorporated into the new plan of the park with great naturalness. The interior, too, looks most impressive, with new drapes and rugs; Armstrong tells me it has greatly enhanced the value of the property. However, I do not wish to rely upon his word alone, and I wondered if you and Mama would drive down with me and give me the benefit of your opinion," he said, pointing out, furthermore, that once they gave up the Dower House, they would need a country residence, not too distant from London.

"And where better than Netherfield Park, where my parents fell in love and I was born?"

Both Jane and Bingley, whose romance had been a matter of great moment at the time, engrossing not just their families, but the whole village, smiled at his words. Netherfield Park held a very special niche in their hearts.

Jane thought this was indeed a happy chance for Jonathan to acquire the place for his family.

"Everyone I speak with agrees it is a valuable property, and the asking price seems reasonable," said Jonathan, and his father broke in, "Well, Jonathan, it's Darcy who can tell you if it's worth the money. He's the best judge of these matters. I have always relied on his opinion."

Jonathan turned to his uncle. "Mr Darcy, will you advise me, sir? I really must decide or I may lose it."

Darcy and Elizabeth looked at each other and smiled and, as if on the spur of the moment, a decision was made that they would all go to Netherfield Park, except Fitzwilliam and Caroline, who were returning to Derbyshire.

There was general excitement as they confessed to having a sentimental attachment to Hertfordshire. A date was agreed and, when Jonathan returned to London, they had arranged to meet at Grosvenor Street, where they would stay overnight before leaving for Netherfield Park.

Jonathan had been delighted with their response to his plans. If only he had been able to persuade Amelia-Jane to see it in a similar light, he thought, wistfully.

❦

Back in London, he wrote three letters.

The first, to Armstrong the agent, advising him of the date of their proposed visit to inspect the property.

The second, to Dr Faulkner, apologising for failing to keep their appointment and expressing a hope that they could meet when he visited Longbourn the following month.

"And perhaps if you had some time to spare, we could arrange to see Hatfield House then," he added hopefully.

In a postscript, he asked that his apologies be also conveyed to Miss Anna Faulkner for his failure to collect the drawing of Matlock Bridge, and promising to collect it the very next time he was in the district.

The last letter was to his mother-in-law, Charlotte Collins, informing her that Amelia-Jane had returned to Rosings Park with the two youngest children, Tess and Cathy.

He did add a little hint that they might welcome a visit from her.

I know it is difficult for you to travel in Winter, but should you wish to make the journey in Autumn, when the weather in Kent is still very pleasant, I could arrange to send the carriage to convey you to London and thence to Rosings. Do let me know if you wish me to make the necessary arrangements.

As it happens, I expect to be in Hertfordshire with my parents and Mr and Mrs Darcy early next week, to look over a property. We will probably stay overnight at Longbourn, if that is convenient to you and Miss Mary Bennet.

Charlotte was a little puzzled at Jonathan's letter, since it had only been a day ago that she had received one from Elizabeth Darcy, urging her not to worry about Jonathan and Amelia-Jane.

Elizabeth had written:

Jonathan has been here only yesterday and he seems very happy. Jubilant about the Whig–Liberal victory in the Parliament, he certainly did not seem at all miserable ... Perhaps, dear Charlotte, you saw him after a long spell of hard work, with all those late sessions at Westminster. He tells me he intends to spend more time with his family in Kent, in the future ...

But despite both letters, Charlotte's feeling of unease persisted.

Much as she disliked interfering in her children's lives, she decided to write to her daughter Catherine Harrison and discover how things were in Kent.

Meanwhile, Jonathan had already called on his daughter at Harwood House and reassured her that all was well, or at least, it was soon going to be.

"Anne-Marie, your mother is safely back in Kent and so are Tess and Cathy," he declared. "As for this nonsense about Bath, she has told me that she was invited but refused to go because she could not leave her dear ones behind—those were her very words," he said.

Anne-Marie smiled but remained unconvinced. Her father had always been an optimist. She still had serious doubts.

❧

The visit to Hertfordshire was a great success.

Late Summer weather had clothed the woods and fields in gold and green, while the hedgerows and meadows were richly sown with flowers.

They were all agreed that the countryside had the appearance of great prosperity.

"I have never seen it look so well," said Bingley, admiring the wide enclosed fields as they journeyed towards Netherfield, where Mr Armstrong waited for them.

"It grows more prosperous every year, sir," said Jonathan, and Darcy reminded them that in some parts of England, the enclosure of fields had contributed to prosperity without necessarily pauperising the landless tenants.

"I cannot remember ever seeing it look so pretty," said Jane, with a touch of nostalgia for the place, "not in all the years we lived here."

Elizabeth teased her sister, suggesting that long absence might have something to do with her appreciation, and Jane protested that this was certainly not the case.

"Indeed, no, Lizzie!" she cried, "for we have been back on many occasions, but this time it is truly the best I have seen it."

Her husband was quick to support her, as usual.

Even Elizabeth and Darcy had to admit to a few sentimental memories as they drove past familiar landmarks and favourite walks which they had not seen in some years. The country around Netherfield had certainly gained a new degree of charm in their eyes.

Mr Armstrong was waiting for them at Netherfield Park and, as they alighted from their vehicles, everyone, including Darcy, who had remained rather sceptical about the "improvements" had to agree that the work done around the grounds and the house was excellent.

Jonathan was eager for Elizabeth's approval. Like his mother, he had always depended upon her good taste in such matters.

She did not disappoint him on this occasion.

"It has certainly improved the appearance of the place, Jonathan; it shows up the graceful lines of the house to better effect," said Elizabeth, as they surveyed the grounds before going indoors.

Once inside, they were all quick to express satisfaction with the improvements that had undoubtedly added convenience with style to the solid old house. Jonathan was soon convinced this was exactly what he wanted for a country residence for his family.

Bingley and Jane were happy to endorse his judgment.

Elizabeth was delighted with some superb detailing on the architraves over the doors and windows, which all had fine new drapes. She and Jane went upstairs to inspect the bedrooms and indulge in more nostalgia, while the gentlemen stayed to discuss more mundane matters, like the price, with Mr Armstrong.

Looking out of the windows upstairs to admire the view of the park, Jane and Lizzie saw a carriage turn into the drive.

"I wonder who that could be," said Jane, not recognising the unfamiliar vehicle that had drawn up in front of the house.

"It's Maria and her husband, Dr Faulkner," said Elizabeth and added soon afterwards, "and they have their daughter Anna with them."

Jane was rather puzzled. "They are at Haye Park, are they not? I wonder, could they be interested in this place, too?" she asked and her sister, declaring there was only one way to find out, led the way downstairs.

Meanwhile, the Faulkners, seeing Jonathan and the others, were quick to assure them that their visit was merely the indulgence of a nostalgic whim.

They had been passing, on the way home from visiting a sick relative, and decided to take a last look at Netherfield before it was sold.

"Dr Faulkner and I have been to dinner here on many occasions," said Mrs Faulkner, explaining the extent of her interest in the house. "We knew the previous tenants well; they were Dr Faulkner's patients."

Dr Faulkner declared his interest, too. "It's a fine place, Mr Bingley," he said, and with his knowledge of historic buildings, he was able to point out some unique and attractive features, which increased Jonathan's conviction that he was making a very good purchase.

"Haye Park is not as impressive a building, as houses go, I grant you," he admitted, "but it suits us well. It is just the right size and accommodates the three of us very comfortably. There is plenty of room, too, for either of our elder children and their families when they visit us."

By this time, Mrs Faulkner had come over to them and invited their entire party to dinner at Haye Park on the following day.

When Elizabeth and Jane expressed some disquiet about putting her to so much trouble to accommodate so many guests at such short notice, Maria laughed and dismissed their concerns, saying simply, "It is so rarely that we have the pleasure of having all of you down here together, you must come."

Her husband added his voice. "Pray do not concern yourselves; it will be no trouble at all and the pleasure will be ours, I assure you, Mrs Bingley."

Although they had not intended to stay over two nights, they allowed themselves to be persuaded and agreed to attend the Faulkners for dinner on the following day.

Having completed their discussions with Armstrong, they repaired to Longbourn, where Charlotte Collins and Mary Bennet welcomed them cordially. Tea and other refreshments were soon served in the parlour, and the rest of the afternoon was spent in light-hearted conversation, involving everything and everyone from Mary's music pupils to the newcomers into their neighbourhood, opening up a veritable Pandora's box of memories.

Some of them had been embarrassing at the time, but now were no more than remembered follies. Others, like recollections of Mr Bennet and Sir William Lucas, were more melancholy, but they were determined not to be sad on such a pleasant evening.

One piece of information, however, was new and Charlotte was happy to recount it for their entertainment.

A few days ago, they had had a sudden visit from Lydia Wickham and Jessie Phillips, their aunt Phillips' daughter, both of whom lived a short distance outside of Meryton. They had come bearing what they called "very exciting news" and were determined that Charlotte and Mary should hear it forthwith.

"As Lydia told it," said Charlotte, "a certain Mr Bingley is said to be interested in Netherfield Park! Not just interested, but has made an offer to buy the place and, said Jessie Phillips, 'the whole town is talking about it.'"

Charlotte could feel a ripple of amusement pass through her listeners as she continued, "Lydia was sure we would not be able to guess who this mysterious Mr Bingley might be and, in her usual excitable way, made a great to do about it, pretending that it was such a big secret, which she had heard quite by chance," said Charlotte, and they were all agreed that age had certainly not changed Lydia.

"Of course, we pretended we knew nothing at all," said Charlotte, adding, "and indeed, we did not, to tell the truth."

"Though we might have guessed, of course," said Mary, "but we thought it best that we say nothing to Lydia and Jessie, else it would have been all round the town in half an hour!"

Charlotte went on, "But, of course, it came out that Lydia knew it because her housemaid's mother is the sister of the caretaker at Netherfield Park! So, having been around and about a few times to tease us, she declared, 'Why, Charlotte, it is your son-in-law and our dear nephew, Jonathan Bingley! He is going to purchase Netherfield Park and move his family to Hertfordshire. There, now what have you to say?'

"Well, of course, we said nothing, and she then took the opportunity to utter such abuse against poor Mr Bennet for having cut her son Henry out of his inheritance and leaving it all to your Jonathan, who she said would now own both Netherfield and Longbourn and was that not selfish and greedy? Dear me, she was very cross indeed," said Charlotte, and while the others laughed, she added, "I had no wish to give her any encouragement, Eliza, so I said straight away, 'Well, Lydia, if it is indeed true, I shall be delighted. Nothing would give me greater joy than to have at least one of my daughters and some of my dear grandchildren within calling distance of Longbourn.'"

Seeing the smile on Jonathan's face, she said, "But I have not, of course, had any confirmation of this story."

Jonathan was happy then to confirm that it was indeed true and Lydia's gossip had, for once, been well founded.

There was no mistaking Charlotte's pleasure. She missed her grandchildren terribly. Jonathan did ask, however, that his plans be kept confidential for a while yet, until the legal formalities had been concluded.

On the following day, the entire party dined at Haye Park as arranged, for Miss Faulkner had called that morning at Longbourn to extend the invitation to Mrs Collins and Mary.

During a very pleasant evening, they admired Miss Faulkner's drawings, enjoyed her father's tales of his boyhood in India, and were taken on a conducted tour of his remarkable conservatory, which held an amazing collection of tropical plants. Mr Bingley was very interested indeed and asked many questions, wondering whether they would survive in his own hothouse at Ashford Park.

After dinner, they were entertained by Anna, who played the harp. It was an instrument that neither Elizabeth nor her sister had ever attempted to learn. Mr Darcy, whose sister Georgiana had mastered the harp, was most favourably impressed by Anna's performance, and Jonathan was as much charmed by the sweetness of her playing as by the music.

When they were taking coffee, Mrs Faulkner revealed that Anna was to travel to London on the coach the following day.

"She is going to stay a while with the Armandes, the Flemish couple whose school she attended in Brussels. They have recently arrived in London and have taken an apartment in Belgrave Square," she said.

Anna, feeling some explanation was required, said, "Monsieur Armande is to conduct some classes on the French painters, and I am to assist him with some of the teaching."

Jane, who had been standing with Jonathan beside the coffee table, said, "But why must you go by coach, Anna? We leave for London tomorrow, and you could travel far more conveniently with us. Mr Darcy and Lizzie are going on directly to Woodlands, but we shall be travelling with Jonathan to Grosvenor Street, which is not at all far from Belgrave Square. Should you come with us, we could take you to your friends."

Anna was, at first, taken aback by her offer, but was soon persuaded by her parents to accept.

"Oh, my dear, I should be so much happier to know you were travelling safely with friends, rather than on a public coach," said her mother, and Jonathan, noting her apparent reluctance, pointed out that it would be far quicker as well as safer.

"The public coaches tend to stop more often—to set down and pick up passengers; we would be in London in half the time," he said.

When Anna explained that her friends would not be expecting her until the evening, Jane solved the problem by inviting her to dine with them before going on to Belgrave Square.

With both her parents keen for her to accept, Anna agreed and it was arranged that she would be ready to leave early on the morrow.

As they drove back to Longbourn, Mr Bingley said he wished more young women of today were like Miss Faulkner. His friend and mentor agreed.

"Indeed, she is all a young woman should be," he said, "intelligent, accomplished, and handsome as well."

From Mr Darcy, this was high praise. She had already gained his approval by her conversation at dinner, where she had sat next to him, and later delighted him with her performance on the harp.

"Her proficiency in French and German is remarkable," he continued, "and yet she remains modest and unassuming. Throughout dinner she was able to carry on an interesting conversation about the time she spent in Europe, without once being boastful about her achievements."

The ladies had to agree. "Rarely does one meet a young woman who combines talent and beauty with an unpretentious manner," said Elizabeth, and Jane, whose sweetness of disposition had triumphed over every possible exigency, went further.

"Anna Faulkner is surely one of the most accomplished young women I have met and yet she is thoroughly unspoilt and charming," she said.

Jonathan, who was travelling in their carriage, remained silent for most of this conversation. Surprisingly and unaccountably, Lizzie thought, as she wondered what could have caused him to be so thoughtful.

She could not know that he was thinking of both his wife and his daughter and pondering how it had come about that a young woman of modest birth and background like Anna Faulkner had acquired the style and proficiency that she had in both Art and Music, while neither his wife nor their daughter Anne-Marie, to whom far greater opportunities had been available, had ever been interested to do likewise.

It seemed to Jonathan that, each time he met Miss Faulkner, her fascination increased, though neither had done anything to foster it. In her manner there was no archness or flirtatiousness, nor had his conduct towards her been anything but proper. Yet, he could not deny that of all the women he had met in recent years, he had not enjoyed the company of anyone above that of Anna Faulkner.

He was clearly in a quandary and could not explain it. It was no wonder that Jonathan remained mostly silent as they returned to Longbourn.

On the following day there would be more time and opportunity to appreciate her intelligence and charm, as she joined them on their journey to London. The Darcys had left early, since they were returning to Woodlands, while the Bingleys, having collected Anna and her luggage, took a more leisurely route to London.

For most of the journey Anna remained quiet and listened to their conversation, except when she was called upon to participate, and then her enlightened opinions and lively mind impressed, just as her charming manners and musical skill had pleased them on the previous evening.

Always sensitive to these matters, Jane thought Jonathan seemed especially charmed by their companion. But, as usual, she kept her counsel.

On reaching Grosvenor Street, Anna was grateful for the comfort and privacy of a room in which to rest before dressing for dinner. She was urged to stay overnight, but was determined to go to her friends. "If I do not arrive tonight, they will worry, since I had not the time to advise them of the change to my travel plans. They may think I have missed the coach or had some mishap," she said.

Impressed by her commendable sense of responsibility and concern for her friends, Jonathan offered to drive her round to Belgrave Square.

"Have no fear, Miss Faulkner, it is not at all far from here. You will soon be with your friends," he said, trying to reassure her.

Before leaving, she thanked them all for their kindness and hospitality, and on reaching Belgrave Square and locating their apartment, she invited Jonathan in to meet her friends.

The Armandes, who proved to be a charming Flemish couple, were most relieved to see her and pressed Jonathan to stay for coffee. But he, though sorely tempted, did not stay.

"Perhaps another day, Monsieur? You will call again? Yes?" Monsieur Armande asked, and Jonathan readily agreed. Yes, he would be happy to call another day, he said.

Anna, he had learned as they drove from Grosvenor Street, was to stay with them until the end of Summer, at least. It was a piece of information that made him inexplicably happy.

When he returned to Grosvenor Street, he found his parents talking together over coffee, in the sitting room. There was nothing unusual in that except the subject of their conversation was still Miss Faulkner.

On joining them and taking a glass of port, he was immediately appealed to for an answer to a conundrum.

Did he have any explanation, his father asked, why Miss Faulkner, charming, handsome, and accomplished, was as yet single?

"We cannot decide if she remains unwed by choice," said his mother.

If only to quell their speculation, he retold, albeit with some degree of reluctance and without too much detail, the story that his aunt Kitty had narrated at Pemberley those many months ago. His parents, being both kind and warm-hearted, were saddened by the tale, and Jane said she hoped Anna would not remain single forever.

"She is far too handsome and charming for that. I am sure that now she is in London for a few months, she will meet someone suitable."

"I certainly hope so," said her husband. "She deserves to be happily married. She is an admirable young woman."

Jonathan made no immediate reply. Strangely, the thought of Anna Faulkner meeting "someone suitable" in London disturbed and filled him with anxiety.

"London," he said, suddenly, "is full of totally unsuitable men. Miss Faulkner seems perfectly content with her situation. I believe she is happy as she is, Mama," he said, trying to sound casual, but his mother was surprised by the firmness of his tone.

"Did she tell you this?" Jane asked.

"Of course not. I would not be so presumptuous as to ask such a question of a young lady. But I did gather that this was the case from something Mrs Collins said," he replied, and soon afterwards announced that he was very weary and would go to bed. Collecting the picture of Matlock Bridge, which lay on the table in the hall, he retired to his room.

The following day, Jonathan discussed his plans for Netherfield Park with his father and confirmed his intention to proceed with the purchase.

"I think I have decided it is the best thing I can do," he said.

Significantly, he did not reveal to either of his parents that Amelia-Jane had flatly refused to move to Hertfordshire. His parents gave him their blessing. It was clearly a good investment, and they felt sure he would not regret it.

His father had assured him that the only reason he had not purchased the property all those years ago was that "your aunt Lizzie married Darcy and moved to Derbyshire. I could not then have your dear mother in Hertfordshire, pining for her sister, could I?"

Jane was especially pleased, taking it to mean that her son and daughter-in-law would be able to bring their family together at Netherfield.

"You had better see your attorney and have the matter settled," advised Bingley, as they left to return to Woodlands, where they were to spend the rest of the Summer.

After his parents had left, Jonathan went out to his club. On his return, he found a letter waiting for him. It was from his sister-in-law, Catherine Harrison, who wrote in rather urgent terms, very different to her usual measured and sober words.

Dear Mr Bingley, she wrote:

You will, no doubt, be surprised to receive this letter, but it is an indication of the extent of my concern about my sister.

Amelia-Jane has been over to Hunsford twice this week, and on both occasions, spent almost all of her visit—the better part of two hours—complaining bitterly of your decision to move to Netherfield Park in Hertfordshire.

She claims this is a decision which she opposes and she is determined that she will not go. When I explained to her that it may soon be impossible for her to stay on at the Dower House—(I believe the new manager will be in residence before Christmas)—she declared, without any hesitation, her intention to appeal to him to provide her with a small cottage on the Rosings Estate!

I need not tell you how mortifying such a request by her would be to the rest of us, especially Mr Harrison, who has a respected position in this community, not to mention yourself. My sister does not see it that way. She declares that if such a request were refused, she would rather go and live in Bath!

Jonathan was more alarmed by the idea of his wife begging for a "little cottage" than the prospect of her going to live in Bath. The idea seemed impractical and unrealistic, until he read a little further.

On her second visit, she brought along a letter from your aunt, Caroline Bingley, in which it was suggested that Amelia-Jane could do with a holiday in Bath, away from all the aggravation of London. She had come hoping to persuade me to have Cathy and Tess to stay. She pleaded with me to agree but I had to be firm.

I insisted that if the girls are to stay with me, while she goes alone to Bath, she must have your permission. I am unwilling to be a party to any deception or any scheme that may cause conflict between you and my sister and probably upset the children as well.

Mr Harrison, who arrived, fortuitously, in the middle of our discussion, also advised her against any rash plan to travel alone to Bath, where she will have no family and few friends and be totally dependent upon the goodwill of Miss Bingley.

We can only hope that she will not do anything foolhardy ... etc etc.

Jonathan was exceedingly grateful to his sister-in-law for her timely intervention and advice. He was also sufficiently perturbed by her news to sit down immediately and write to his wife, begging her to be cautious.

Indeed, he went so far as to warn her to beware of those who may urge her to act in an indiscreet manner, neglecting her own and her family's interest.

He was thinking specifically of Mrs Arabella Watkins as he wrote:

Do not trust these women; they are a tribe of persons who enjoy the discomfiture and embarrassment of others and spend much of their lives in gossip, creating disharmony and unhappiness. Please, dearest Amelia-Jane, believe me, those who will urge you to leave your children do not have your interest or theirs at heart.

He pleaded with her to return to Grosvenor Street. He told her he missed her and their children and longed to have them all with him again.

He hoped she would be moved, but even as he wrote and sealed the letter, he felt in his heart that she was unlikely to pay any attention to his appeal.

Jonathan's letter to Catherine Harrison expressed his heartfelt appreciation.

I thank you from the bottom of my heart, my dear sister, for your concern and sincere desire to help Amelia-Jane and prevent any action that may place her reputation in jeopardy.

My earnest desire has been to find the means to bring us all back together and to that end, I have tried assiduously to persuade Amelia-Jane to take a look at Netherfield Park, but to no avail. Perhaps your advice may be more acceptable to her than mine. I hope and pray that, with your help and that of Mr Harrison, we may succeed where, clearly, I have failed to convince her where her interest lies.

He concluded with more sincere thanks and, having despatched both letters by express, went out again, this time, to walk around the square for half an hour or so in a very melancholy mood.

On his return, he was informed that a Monsieur Armande had called and left his card. Since their lodgings were not far from Grosvenor Street, Jonathan decided to return the call. The Armandes were genial and friendly; Monsieur Armande had called to invite him to dinner to meet the man who was organising their Art School and exhibition. He was an expatriate Frenchman—a Monsieur Du Pont, who had lived most of his life in London.

"He will be here within the hour," Madame Armande said. "We thought you might be lonely now that your parents have returned to the country. Would you care to stay and have dinner with us?"

Jonathan was delighted to stay.

It was exactly what he needed after the depressing news contained in Mrs Harrison's letter—he enjoyed the delicious meal and the company very much indeed.

Du Pont turned out to be an exceedingly suave and elegant Frenchman of about forty, who entertained them with his witty and intelligent conversation and his fascinating anecdotes about social life in Europe.

Later, Anna was persuaded to play the pianoforte and Monsieur Du Pont was quite effusive in his praise. He had already waxed lyrical about her drawings and the two small still life paintings, which the Armandes hoped to include in the exhibition.

Jonathan, in his rather more reserved way, had been careful not to embarrass Anna with excessive praise, but it was difficult when she demonstrated such a high degree of skill and excellence of taste.

Her own modesty and reticence only increased his esteem, and he soon came to understand why the Armandes loved her dearly.

While Anna accompanied their two young daughters upstairs after dinner, Madame Armande recounted for Jonathan's benefit examples of her generosity and kindness.

On one occasion, in Brussels, Madame had been taken seriously ill. There had been no one to help with the housework or mind the children. Monsieur Armande had been away in Paris with a group of students.

"Monsieur, I cannot find the words in English to tell you how good she was. She gave up her holiday to stay with me and look after me better than a daughter. I shall never forget her kindness; she is an angel!" she declared.

Jonathan smiled and nodded. He could see now why they were so devoted to her. It was easy to like her. He had himself felt drawn to her, not only because she was amiable and accomplished, but because she seemed to have a genuine goodness as well. No other woman had held his attention as Anna had done and all without making any conscious effort to do so.

Jonathan Bingley was a very proper gentleman and had no intention of indulging in a pointless flirtation, but he could not deny how very highly he regarded her and how much he enjoyed her company.

He told himself firmly that his interest was an innocent and simple friendship, no more. He had no evidence that the lady wished for anything more either. She clearly enjoyed his company and shared with him her enjoyment of the Arts. Indeed, she even listened with some interest to his political anecdotes and laughed when he told tales of the foibles of his colleagues at Westminster, but there was never any flirtatiousness or dalliance in her words or manner.

She was unvaryingly open and frank in her conversation and made no attempt to draw him into any inappropriate familiarity. It had made their association pleasant, easy, and completely guiltless.

It was, Jonathan told himself as he walked home on that mild, Summer night, exactly what a good friendship between two intelligent people should be.

Though Jonathan was unaware of it, the Armandes seemed to find rather more to say about their beloved Anna and their new acquaintance, Monsieur Bingley.

They had noticed the easy relationship that seemed to exist between them and the way he watched her when she was playing the pianoforte or simply talking to someone else on the other side of the room.

Much as they would have liked to indulge in some Gallic romancing, they were discreet and sensible people and said nothing that might embarrass their guests.

The couple had also been the subject of discussion between Elizabeth and Darcy, for quite another reason.

On their journey back to Woodlands, the issue of Longbourn had arisen because Elizabeth had noticed that her sister Mary seemed rather frail and wondered how much longer she could go on teaching her music pupils.

Agreeing that Mary Bennet did look somewhat less well than when he had last seen her, Darcy revealed that the matter had already concerned Jonathan, who had spoken to his father about it some time ago.

"He has realised that Mary was growing more frail each year, and the respiratory problems that had plagued her as a child seem to have returned recently. I believe Dr Faulkner has advised that she take a holiday by the sea, but Mary has been unwilling to leave her pupils," Darcy explained.

Elizabeth, who knew nothing of this, asked, "And what does Jonathan propose?"

"I believe he has not spoken to Mary yet, because he has no wish to upset her, but he proposes to let her take an annuity from the estate, in addition to her present income, so she would not have to continue teaching or, if she prefers, she could reduce the number of pupils she takes. Knowing how much pleasure she gets from her work, he is reluctant to suggest that she give it up altogether."

Elizabeth was not surprised to hear of her nephew's proposals. He had always been a compassionate and generous young man. However, her husband's next statement did cause her some astonishment.

Speaking very casually, Darcy said, "Bingley asked if I thought it was a good idea to invite Miss Faulkner to take on some of Mary's pupils. It seems Jonathan thinks she may be interested. She would certainly have the necessary competence to do so."

"Miss Faulkner? Take over Mary's pupils?" Elizabeth was amazed. "And what did you say?" she asked.

Darcy continued in the same casual vein, "That it was a sensible idea. Do you not agree? Look at it this way, my dear: Charlotte Collins, who is still remarkably fit and active, is Anna Faulkner's aunt. She is unlikely to object. With Haye Park being in the near neighbourhood, it may suit all parties rather well."

Elizabeth's eyes were wide with astonishment. "Now, you have truly surprised me. Jonathan's concern for my sister I can well understand and I applaud it. But involving Miss Faulkner? Do you believe it can work? How is it to be arranged?" she asked.

He smiled and took her hand. "That, I am sure we can safely leave to the ladies to work out amongst themselves, Lizzie. I believe Jonathan will not rush into this, but means to put the idea to Mrs Collins first and then through her to the Faulkners and finally, if everyone is agreeable, he will talk to Mary."

Elizabeth suspected that Darcy had probably given Bingley exactly that advice and said with a teasing smile, "Was that your advice to Jonathan? Through his father, of course."

And he laughed, knowing she had found him out. "How well you know me, Lizzie," he said, though admitting nothing. "Had I given Jonathan advice, I believe that is what I would have said."

They were almost at the turn-off to Woodlands when a thought struck her and, on an impulse, she asked, "Darcy, do you believe Jonathan is just a little partial to Miss Faulkner?"

She half expected him to scold her for gossiping, but he, having taken a moment to think, nodded. "Yes, I do. Quite clearly, he finds her an engaging young woman. But I also know that he is a man of honour and will always behave with utmost propriety. Of that I have no doubt whatsoever," he said very firmly.

The carriage came to a halt before the house; Darcy alighted and helped Elizabeth out.

Later, unable to rest until she had spoken with him further, Elizabeth sought out her husband.

"I have been thinking about what you said about Jonathan and Anna Faulkner ... that you have also noted his partiality towards her. I cannot help being concerned; it will do neither of them any good at all were it to be thought that they were ..."

Darcy interrupted gently, "My dear Lizzie, I think you and I both know Jonathan Bingley well enough to say that there is not the slightest chance that he would do or say anything that will jeopardise the reputation of the lady, much less his own. He is not some irresponsible, selfish young buck around town—he has a strong sense of family loyalty and public duty. What is more, if he does have some special regard for Miss Faulkner, as he may well do, he will certainly not want her to be compromised in any way."

Elizabeth looked uncertain, but Darcy was very sure. He believed absolutely in Jonathan's integrity and would not concede that there was any danger in the association.

"I may be mistaken, Lizzie, but all I have observed is their shared enjoyment of Art and Music, in the completely innocent and acceptable context of a dinner party. One senses that there is a certain warmth, a special rapport perhaps, but no more," he said.

Elizabeth had to agree that their conduct had given her no cause for concern at all.

"You are right, I have seen no coy behaviour or archness on her part, nor anything in his conduct that could give rise to gossip."

"Exactly. So, I would not be too concerned, Lizzie," he said, and yet she was unable to rid herself of a nagging fear.

She could not be as sanguine as he was and so persisted a little longer.

"You do know that Jane has some grave concerns about Jonathan and Amelia-Jane, do you not?" she asked.

She knew that if there was a serious problem that Bingley knew of, he would seek Darcy's counsel on it.

In spite of that, she was unprepared for his reply when he said, frankly, "Yes, I do. Bingley is exceedingly concerned, too. But that has nothing whatever to do with Miss Faulkner. Indeed, the situation existed well before her return to England. Amelia-Jane has not been herself for almost a year now, and the problem has been compounded by Jonathan's desire to purchase Netherfield Park."

Elizabeth had had no idea.

"How do you know this?" she asked.

His reply left her incredulous. "Caroline Bingley has written to her brother, to warn him that if Jonathan goes ahead with the purchase, his wife will in all likelihood refuse to move to Hertfordshire. Bingley has not told Jane; he fears she will be very upset."

"And yet, Bingley has encouraged Jonathan to proceed with the purchase."

"Certainly he has. It would be stupid to indulge Amelia-Jane's whims on such important matters as the purchase of an estate. He hopes her fears may be allayed and she may come round, in time."

"Do you think she will?" Elizabeth asked anxiously.

"I cannot be sure. She is being childish and unreasonable. A great deal will depend on the influence that is brought to bear upon her. I believe she is very dependent upon Caroline Bingley and some new friend of hers, a Mrs Watson."

"Watkins—it's Arabella Watkins, she's a recent arrival in Bath and a friend of Miss Bingley, who appears to have taken a liking to Amelia-Jane," said Elizabeth, deciding to find out more about Mrs Watkins, but it was late and time to change for dinner.

Darcy put his book away and asked, "And Mr Watkins, what does he do?"

Elizabeth laughed out loud, a merry laugh. "Very little, if anything at all," she said and, seeing the look of bewilderment that crossed his countenance, she added, still laughing, "He has been dead for some years."

Her infectious laughter drew him in, too, and for the moment, at least, the tension was gone.

Elizabeth sighed gently. "Poor Jane. First it was Emma, and now Jonathan is unhappy, too."

Darcy tried to comfort her.

"Yes, it is hard for Jane; she and Bingley have been so happy, she cannot believe that her children have not been similarly blessed. Clearly there were hasty decisions and unfortunate choices made," he said as they went upstairs.

"Thankfully, Emma was given a second chance at happiness; I fear it may not be so for Jonathan," said his wife, but Darcy was more hopeful.

"I agree it will be difficult for him, especially if his wife continues to behave like a spoilt child; but have faith, my dear, Jonathan Bingley is one of the finest young men I know. I am confident that he will prevail."

꒰ꔛ꒱

When Jane and Bingley arrived a few days later, it was difficult for Elizabeth to believe that Bingley, knowing so much, had successfully concealed it from her sister, for surely he must have done, else she could not look as happy as she did. For Elizabeth, accustomed to the close intimacy of her relationship with Jane, in which they had few secrets from each other, this was a difficult time. Darcy had made her promise solemnly to bite her tongue if need be and not blurt out anything that would betray the confidence placed in him by Bingley. While Darcy abhorred deception of any kind and would have preferred frankness, he respected his brother-in-law's determination to avoid aggravating Jane's anxiety about their son's marriage.

This, however, seemed furthest from Jane's thoughts when they returned to Woodlands. Once alone with Elizabeth, resting and enjoying a cup of tea, Jane gave a lively account of their journey from Longbourn to London.

Elizabeth was quite surprised to find that Miss Anna Faulkner appeared to figure very prominently in her sister's conversation. Her dress, her demeanour, conversation, and manners were all deemed to be charming and admirable.

"Truly, Lizzie, I cannot recall when I have last met a young woman for whom I have developed such a liking. There is nothing about her that irritates or offends, even unwittingly, as most young women might do; she is a truly refined young lady. Do you not agree, Lizzie?"

Elizabeth had been so astonished by this paean of praise that she had been taken unawares, but she hastened to concur.

"Oh, yes, indeed," she said quickly, but before she could ask Jane if she knew what Jonathan thought of the young lady, Mr Bingley entered the room and, pouring himself a drink, followed up with even more praise of Miss Faulkner.

Elizabeth could hardly believe her ears; it seemed there was not a flaw to be found in her, as far as he was concerned.

"I've just been telling Darcy what a fine young woman Miss Faulkner is," he declared. "She is the pleasantest person and so talented, Lizzie, I shall be absolutely astounded if she is not engaged by Christmas."

"My dear brother, you astonish me; are you not rushing to judgment?" asked Elizabeth; even for her amiable brother-in-law, this was generous.

"No indeed, Lizzie. Mark my words. What is more, the man who persuades her to marry him will be a very fortunate fellow, and Darcy agrees with me."

Mr Darcy nodded, smiled, and succeeded in avoiding his wife's eyes, for he knew she was wanting to discover what he thought of this glowing account of the young woman they had all been speaking of in the last few days—a young woman whose very existence had hardly mattered to many of the family until her return from Europe a few months ago.

Further conversation was suspended when the servants arrived to clear away the tea things, and the ladies, realising that it was already half past five, withdrew upstairs to change for dinner.

❦

Later that week, Jonathan Bingley was invited by his brother-in-law James Wilson to attend an informal meeting of the Reform Group at Westminster. He found them very appreciative of the hard work he had done during the drawn-out negotiations with the Peelites and Liberals.

They urged him to consider returning to the Commons as an MP at the next election.

James Wilson, in whom Jonathan had already confided his plans for Netherfield Park, suggested that he could be fortunate enough to be given a constituency in Hertfordshire, should he decide to reside permanently in the county.

A diverse coalition of Whigs, Peelites, and Reformists had joined together and were seeking to establish a foundation for their new party. Much later it would be known as the Liberal Party and produce men of the calibre of Gladstone, but at the moment, they had to work hard at being united.

Keen to develop some momentum on issues they had been pushing for years without success, they were looking for experienced, politically astute candidates to swell their ranks and promote their policies.

Chief among them were freer trade and the extension of the franchise to give the vote to working men. Jonathan was invited to come on board.

"With your family's long and successful involvement in Commerce and Trade and your own unswerving commitment to the Reformist cause and the improvement of the lot of the working poor, you would be an ideal candidate," James Wilson said, and several others agreed.

Jonathan was flattered and interested, but wary. He asked for time to consider it, which, seeing the election was years away, seemed a reasonable request.

But in his heart Jonathan knew that with his wife's present attitude, there was very little chance that he would be able to accept. Indeed, he knew the idea of his ever returning to Parliament would be anathema to her and might well bring about the end of their troubled marriage.

Returning to Grosvenor Street, following the meeting at Westminster, he found a letter waiting for him from Amelia-Jane.

It was a reply to his urgent appeal, but had little to satisfy the urgency of his own plea. It was a cold and unfeeling letter; in it she predictably refused to even consider moving to Hertfordshire.

The tone was one of an injured party, put upon and ignored.

Surely, you cannot expect me to leave all my friends and most of my family and move to Hertfordshire, where I have never lived before.

I know no one there. I know you will point out that Mama is at Longbourn, by your invitation, but having her a few miles away, while I live at Netherfield with only Cathy and Tess for company, will not make amends for all the advantages I shall lose by leaving Rosings.

I do not object to your plan to purchase Netherfield Park. I do not doubt that it is a good investment, but it is not where I choose to live for the rest of my life.

Please Jonathan, do not ask me to reconsider—I have already done so, and it is useless to ask Catherine to press me to agree, for I shall not buckle.

It is all very fine for Catherine, who has a lovely home at the parsonage at Hunsford, with an entrée at all times to Rosings, to advise me to bury myself in Hertfordshire. But I am quite determined that I shall not move to please her or anyone.

Please do not believe that any threats will make me change my mind either. It is quite made up.

Jonathan could not believe his eyes as he read the words.

The language and tone were certainly not his wife's. He wondered whether Miss Bingley may have been responsible; or perhaps it was Mrs Watkins, who was fast becoming his bête noire. Determined to discover the truth, he decided to travel to Kent, arriving late in the afternoon at the parsonage in Hunsford.

There, he found Catherine, who was not entirely surprised to see him. It was a rather blustery afternoon, with short intermittent showers, and he was glad to be indoors, in front of a good fire in the parlour.

Waiting until the maid had left, Catherine poured out his tea and handed it to him, saying simply, "I suppose this is about Amelia-Jane, again."

Jonathan nodded and, putting down his cup, extracted the letter from his pocket and handed it to her.

"I received this yesterday," he said.

Catherine read it and returned it, sceptical and angry at its contents.

"That is not written by Amelia-Jane—oh, I know it is in her hand, but the language, all those pompous phrases … the entire tone of the letter, it is not her at all. She is not sufficiently well read to compose such a letter. It is clear to me that my sister has been put up to write this ridiculous piece."

Jonathan was relieved to have his suspicions confirmed even if it was unthinkable that an outsider, a person wholly unconnected with them, was influencing his wife in her communications with him, dictating the words and phrases she used.

"Is it Miss Bingley?" he asked. "Has she been here recently?"

Catherine shook her head. "No, she has not, but her good friend Mrs Watkins—an astonishingly vulgar woman, who has a man friend they call Alexander—has been here and is staying at the Dower House."

Jonathan was quite shocked.

"Do you mean they are staying in our home?"

"Indeed, my maid had it from their housekeeper that the visitors had occupied the main bedroom, while Mrs Bingley had moved in with Tess."

Jonathan was outraged. That rank outsiders should not only be influencing his wife to defy him but abusing his hospitality while they did it was beyond belief. It was the kind of situation he had never faced before.

He turned to his sister-in-law for advice. "Catherine, what can I do? Should I drive over now and confront them?"

She understood his helplessness; he was not a man accustomed to confrontation nor was he the type to seek it, if it could possibly be avoided.

Catherine, who had already discussed Amelia-Jane's recent conduct with her husband, knew well that in such open conflict, Jonathan Bingley would not win. His genteel manner and amiable nature did not fit him for dealing with the kind of contest he faced.

"Mr Bingley, Jonathan, you may not like what I am about to suggest, but it is the best advice I can offer you. I truly do not believe that any action you may take to confront your wife's newfound friends will help you solve the problem that faces you. Indeed, it is more likely to drive her away from you.

"Is it asking too much to suggest that you appeal to my mother to come to Rosings, stay at the Dower House, and help both of you to find a way out of this unhappy situation?" Seeing his dubious expression, she insisted, "You cannot let it go on, Jonathan, it will ruin your marriage and ultimately destroy both of you as well. I would be prepared to write to Mama and ask her, if that was your wish."

Bereft of any other ideas and unable to find another way, Jonathan was immensely grateful to his sister-in-law and agreed to let her write to Mrs Collins immediately.

Not long afterwards, he left and drove past the turn-off to the Dower House, disconsolate and with very little hope.

Leaving Rosings, he was far too depressed to return to London, and with a storm blowing in, he decided to make for Standish Park, where he knew his sister Emma would make him welcome.

It was Friday, and James would probably be back from Westminster, as well.

He recalled a similar visit, several years ago, when he had been the unhappy bearer of bad news, informing first James Wilson and his mother and then Emma of the disgrace and suicide of her first husband, David Wilson.

He, together with James Wilson, had attended to all the arrangements and coped with the consequences that flowed from that hideous event.

Concerned for his sister and outraged by David Wilson's behaviour, Jonathan had not suffered personal grief at the time. All he had felt was a deep sadness for his unhappy sister, who had concealed much of her suffering for years. At all times, he had been at pains to protect his sister and her two young daughters from the distressing consequences of his irresponsible brother-in-law's actions.

Now, when his own life was in turmoil, it was to Emma he turned for help. Emma, who, with her subsequent marriage to James, had finally found the happiness she deserved.

Emma Wilson was not entirely surprised to see her brother arrive, unannounced, at Standish Park late that evening.

She had heard from her husband of the proposal put to him by the Reform Group and had anticipated a visit, which she had expected would be occasioned by his desire to discuss the possibility of re-entering the House of Commons and the consequences that might flow from it.

They had grown closer over the years and frequently consulted each other on business and family matters. Though he had no real taste for business, Jonathan had a head for figures and sound judgment, which she had often appreciated.

Her parents had hoped that Jonathan would take over his father's role in the family business, but when he had become seriously interested in politics, he had been unable to find the time. Emma knew they were disappointed and had hoped to persuade him to take some share of the responsibility for the business.

It was therefore with a cheerful smile but a rather troubled heart that she greeted him as he alighted from his vehicle and came indoors.

"You are very fortunate to have escaped that storm, Jonathan—as you can see there is some very nasty weather blowing in," she said as he divested himself of his coat and followed her into the saloon, where the drapes had been closed against the gloomy weather and the candles had been lit for the evening.

Keen to ascertain whether they were likely to be disturbed, Jonathan asked after James and the children.

"James will be here tomorrow morning; he is staying overnight at Rochester; Victoria and Stephanie are gone to a ball for their cousin at Sevenoaks and will not return until Sunday, and both Charles and Colin have dined and gone to bed," said his sister, "so we are quite safe from interruption."

He seemed relieved. But when she sat down and waited for him to join her, he remained standing, clearly ill at ease, walked about, put down and picked up his drink, until she said, "Jonathan, while I am truly happy you are here, indeed, I am delighted not to be dining alone this evening, with James and the girls away, I should be even happier were you to tell me why you are here, for I cannot believe that you would have arrived in such haste and without warning unless there was something serious afoot. Now, tell me, am I right?"

Jonathan had stopped walking around the room while she spoke and then, quite suddenly, drew up a chair and sat down beside the sofa on which she was seated.

"Yes, you are, Emma. I need to talk to you," he said, with such a look of misery on his face that she relented and regretted her words, which she feared might have been too censorious.

"My dear brother, I am sorry, I did not mean to lecture you at all; please forgive me. I can see that you are troubled and unhappy, and I do want to help. Is it to do with this business of standing for Parliament again?" she asked and, when he shook his head, she was confused ... what could it be?

"If only it were as simple a problem as deciding whether to return to the Parliament," he said, in a low, unhappy voice. "No, my dear Emma, I fear I have all but lost Amelia-Jane. She has turned away from me and intends to leave me. She seems to have set her mind upon it and will not hear a word I say ... What is worse, she appears to have fallen into the clutches of some people who are intent upon destroying our marriage. Emma, I am completely at a loss as to what I can do."

Even as he spoke, he saw the expression of surprise and concern on her face change to one of disbelief and shock.

Emma had known from previous conversations with Jonathan and from her mother's letters that all was not well between her brother and his wife.

But nothing had prepared her for this!

She heard him blurt out with some difficulty, often without much clarity, the sorry tale of the problems that presently beset them. It was clearly painful for him to relate. Finally, he thrust into her hand the note he had received from his wife. She could see how deeply he had been hurt.

On reading it, Emma Wilson's outrage was plain. She could not believe that Amelia-Jane could have penned such a cruel message.

Very soon, she had reached the same conclusion as Catherine Harrison—that it was the work of either Miss Bingley or her new friend and confidante, Mrs Watkins, of whom she had heard not one favourable report!

Generally of a mild and easy-going nature, Emma surprised her brother with an outburst of anger. As she stood up and walked up and down the room, he felt the need to urge her to be calm, but Emma was not to be silenced.

"Jonathan, this note is outrageous! You cannot take this as a genuine expression of your wife's wishes. It is clearly not composed by her. Why, I cannot imagine such words from her lips, much less her pen. Obviously, she has been coached and directed to write this and we have to discover by whom. If it is, as Catherine Harrison thinks, the work of this Watkins woman, what right has she to interfere, and why do you have to accept it?"

Jonathan was amazed to see her so indignant. Clearly, she had been provoked by the letter, but he felt responsible for her state of agitation and begged her to be calm.

He told her of Catherine Harrison's suggestion that they invite the intervention of Amelia-Jane's mother, Mrs Collins.

While Emma thought this was probably a good idea, she was still determined that Mrs Watkins, in her role of confidante and conspirator, could not be permitted to influence her young sister-in-law unchallenged. She was already working on a plan.

"When James returns tomorrow, we shall tell him—not all the details perhaps, but sufficient to make him understand the urgency of the problem. He will be able to advise us objectively on the best course of action. My own inclination is to travel to the Dower House at Rosings Park with you and talk to your wife without this woman, Mrs Watkins, present.

"I would not stand on ceremony—it is your house, after all; I would simply ask her, politely, to remove herself, because we have private matters to discuss."

Jonathan explained that Catherine Harrison had warned against open confrontation. Emma agreed.

"It is not confrontation we seek, Jonathan, only an opportunity to talk to Amelia-Jane and put a point of view. What can be fairer?"

She sounded so reasonable that, by the time dinner was served, Jonathan had been persuaded to his sister's way of thinking and was feeling a good deal better than when he had arrived.

Emma was confident that if she could talk to her sister-in-law, she could persuade her at least to return with them to Standish Park, where they could talk over their problems in private, in a calmer atmosphere removed from the pernicious influence of her decidedly strange new friends.

Perhaps, Emma thought, Amelia-Jane might see things differently.

Jonathan was not confident of success, but at least Emma intended to try, and for that he was grateful.

They talked late into the night about the strange way in which their two lives had run on parallel and similar courses. It was uncanny. Neither had an explanation for it, but both their marriages had foundered; yet both had been undertaken in sincerity and love.

Emma was honest in her appraisal of her own poor judgment. "You must admit we were both of us young, and I had never had my feelings seriously engaged before. I was seventeen and very naïve. David was the toast of the town, the youngest member of Parliament; I must have been insane or very stupid to believe that he loved me to the exclusion of every other woman and that he would accord me some dignity when we were married, which he denied to others of his acquaintance.

"He treated me as if I were a doll he had purchased for his entertainment," she declared, and the sadness and hurt in her voice roused Jonathan to anger as he recalled her ill-starred first marriage.

Going over to her, he sat down and took her hands in his. "My dear Emma, he treated you abominably. David was a disgraceful blackguard. You need never make excuses for him, nor blame yourself.

"You may well have been innocent and naïve, but these are not criminal offences. David Wilson was a man of the world, a Member of Parliament, yet he deliberately betrayed your trust and that of his friends and family."

Jonathan's voice was rough with anger. "I shall never forget James Wilson's face when he was told of his brother's behaviour, nor his mother's grief at his suicide. They were all deceived, as you were. You have nothing for which to blame yourself."

Of his own actions in marrying Amelia-Jane Collins after an exceedingly brief courtship, he was more critical.

"For my part, I have no excuses to offer. We were all still stunned by the deaths of William and Edward in the Autumn of '34, and in the midst of the wretched, gloomy Winter that followed, with Emily's husband dying of tuberculosis, Amelia-Jane came to spend Christmas at Ashford Park. She was like a ray of sunshine, some hope for a little brightness in my life. She was very pretty, exceedingly good-humoured, and got on very well with my mother. I knew she was not as well educated as her two older sisters nor as well read as you and Sophie, but that did not seem to matter very much then. I always assumed that she would learn to value reading and music as she matured.

"I confess that, at the time, I was charmed by her bright temperament, which I hoped would rescue me from my dismal state of mind. She also said she loved me," he said wistfully, pulling a self-deprecating face as if to mock his own naïveté.

Then, as if to remind himself as well as his sister that it had not all been a dreadful mistake, he added quickly, "But Emma, I must be honest. She did change my outlook on life. She was a good, affectionate wife for many years and we were very happy. I cannot believe, after reading her recent letters, that she is the same Amelia-Jane I married."

Emma interrupted him. "Ah, but that is exactly where you are mistaken, Jonathan. Amelia-Jane is not the same young girl you married all those years ago; she could not be, no more than I am still the ingenuous innocent who married David Wilson.

"She has lived in the world, experienced life, and is no longer the compliant creature who adored you and never questioned why you spent so much time at Westminster. Now she is an attractive woman who is aware—or has been made aware—of her own power as your wife, and she intends to use it to get her own way," Emma explained.

"But Emma, she could have had her own way in most things, without threatening to wreck my career and destroy our marriage," he protested.

Emma agreed. "Yes, I do realise that it is not your wife we have to fight, but those who wish to influence and use her."

Jonathan nodded and said his wife had appeared to lose interest in their marriage, regarding it as a burden which deprived her of her freedom.

"It is as if she no longer cares. Even the children feel it," he said sadly.

Emma understood. "Yes, it does seem as if she has grown more stubborn and less considerate. But again, I am more inclined to blame those who encourage her whims and fancies. It is they who are culpable. They are happy to use her weaknesses," she said. Then, in an attempt to give him some hope, she added, "Jonathan, I truly believe that if we could speak with her alone, perhaps persuade her to return with us to Standish Park, we should have some chance of changing her mind, at least regarding this preposterous plan to move to Bath!"

Her brother seemed less hopeful. "I hope she will listen to us," he said.

"Indeed, Jonathan, so do I," she replied.

Whereupon, noting how very late it was, being almost midnight, she suggested they retire and await her husband's arrival on the morrow. Buoyed by Emma's optimism, Jonathan retired to bed, a little more hopeful than he had been before.

James Wilson, on being told by his wife of Jonathan's difficulties, was very concerned. Having been totally immersed in the political developments within his party and the Parliament since the election, he had not had the time to discover how his brother-in-law had resolved his personal problems. He was disappointed to hear that far from being resolved, they had escalated to breaking point.

When Emma revealed her plan to accompany her brother to Rosings, he was wary and cautioned her against confrontation.

"Consider this, my love," he said in that unfailingly logical way he had, "Amelia-Jane may want time away from her family, to think."

Emma was unconvinced. "Dear James, do you really believe poor Amelia-Jane is going to be allowed to think for herself, with Caroline Bingley and this dreadful Watkins woman filling her head with nonsense?" she asked, and he agreed it was unlikely.

"All I ask is that you do not attempt to compel her; that will only send her into the arms of her new friends."

Having given him their word that they would in no way attempt to coerce Amelia-Jane, Emma and Jonathan set out for Rosings Park.

Their journey was not long, since both estates were within the same county and the roads between them were in excellent order. On reaching Rosings Park, they proceeded directly to the Dower House.

To their astonishment, they found the house closed and the servants all gone except for a caretaker, who informed them that Mrs Bingley and her children had left for London very early that morning and did not expect to be back.

The servants, except for her personal maid and the children's companion, had gone home and the keys had been handed over to the housekeeper at Rosings, to be passed on to the new manager. He was expected next week, they were informed.

Shocked, Emma and Jonathan drove to the parsonage at Hunsford, where Catherine Harrison told a similar story, showing them a note from her sister advising of their departure for London.

"There was no mention of Bath, I am happy to say," said Catherine, who had also been informed by the man who delivered the note that the servants had been asked to report to the new manager.

"Was there any message for me?" asked Jonathan, and Catherine told him, with some difficulty, that there had been none.

His disappointment was plain to see.

After taking some refreshment, they had no alternative but to return to Standish Park, all their plans of the previous night thrown into utter confusion.

James Wilson was surprised to see them return earlier than expected, with no Amelia-Jane. When he was told what had transpired, he became very concerned, even alarmed.

Clearly, Amelia-Jane, upon some irrational impulse or under a malign influence, had taken to acting unpredictably. For the first time, he was genuinely anxious for her safety and that of her children.

He suggested that Emma and Jonathan should travel to London with him, and go to the Bingleys' house, where, presumably Amelia-Jane would be staying.

"If she has given up the Dower House, she must intend either to live in London or move to Bath. Perhaps, Emma, you may be able to persuade her that the latter is not in her interest."

This time, neither Emma nor Jonathan was confident of success.

On the journey to London, despite James' efforts to involve him in conversation over Parliamentary matters, Jonathan remained disconsolate and uncommunicative. On reaching London, they went directly to the Bingleys' house in Grosvenor Street and, once again, disappointment was their lot. While Cathy and Tess were at the house with the servants, Amelia-Jane and her friend Mrs Watkins were not home.

Both girls greeted their father warmly, yet neither knew where their mother had gone, except that she had "gone out in the carriage with Aunt Arabella."

So enraged was Jonathan, he had to fight back tears as he embraced his children and left, promising to call again. They were to tell their mother he would be back and wished to see her.

Emma and James were at pains to console him, pointing out that the two women could have gone out to the shops or something equally innocent, but it was easy to see he was deeply disturbed.

Before returning to their own apartments, the Wilsons had to turn down Spender Street and pick up some books and stationery for James.

While they were waiting for the packages to be placed in their vehicle, a familiar figure appeared on the other side of the street. Jonathan, recognising Madame Armande, crossed the street to greet her. Even as he did so, Monsieur Armande emerged from a shop which stocked artists' supplies, followed closely by Miss Faulkner, her arms full of parcels.

Jonathan hastened over to assist her and there was a great flurry of greetings and kissing of hands as they stood on the pavement.

Watching from across the street, Emma could only guess at the identity of the older couple, but realised immediately that the handsome young woman in a very stylish gown must be Miss Faulkner. Her mother's description had been very accurate, indeed.

Presently, Jonathan escorted the young lady and her two friends over to be introduced to his sister and her husband, who were waiting beside their carriage. The Armandes were delighted. Cards and invitations were duly exchanged and the two parties went their separate ways.

Emma could not help noticing, however, that subsequently, Jonathan appeared much less discomposed than before. He seemed generally more animated, and she wondered whether it might not be a good idea to have a dinner party, at which they could all talk of matters other than the problems of Amelia-Jane, which had monopolised their conversation for days on end, to the exclusion of anything pleasurable or amusing.

When they had reached their apartment and had unpacked, changed, and taken tea, she put it to her husband and Jonathan.

James thought it was an excellent idea.

"It might do all of us some good to turn our minds to other things," he said and urged Emma to proceed with her plan.

Jonathan was even more enthusiastic. He was certain the Armandes would love to come and would prove very interesting company.

Indeed, he offered, with unusual alacrity, to take an invitation round to their apartment at Belgrave Square, saying he had a couple of books on English painters in his case which he had promised to lend Monsieur Armande. Emma did not fail to notice how very keen he was and had the invitation written out for him to deliver when he came downstairs later in the day. She was even more amused at the obvious pleasure with which he undertook the errand.

When he returned almost two hours later, Jonathan seemed quite cheerful, light-hearted even.

"It is as I said it would be," he reported. "Monsieur and Madame Armande declared they are honoured, Miss Faulkner is delighted, and they all thank you very much indeed for your invitation," adding, "They have heard a great deal about you and James."

Emma, who was sure that his own pleasure was enhancing his account of theirs, teased her brother, "I do hope, Jonathan, they will not have been frightened into silence by your account of us."

He was quick to deny this. "Certainly not! You will not find either the Armandes or Miss Faulkner wanting in this. They are not intimidated by company, however distinguished, being all well-read and cultured people with an excellent knowledge and understanding of the Arts. Their school in Brussels is highly recommended by Mrs Collins and is patronised by many well-connected families in England and France.

"As for Miss Faulkner, she has the genuine savoir faire of a young woman of good education who has lived and travelled in Europe. She speaks French and German with great facility, and her understanding of the Fine Arts and the high standard of her accomplishments in Art and Music are quite remarkable. As my father and Mr Darcy have both noted, she has all these qualities and is modest as well," he said.

His sister was quite astonished at this catalogue of praise.

"And when did Mr Darcy and Papa meet this paragon?" she asked with a smile, meaning to tease him a little.

He did not rise to her bait. Jonathan had had no occasion to tell her of their visit to Netherfield and their meeting with the Faulkners.

Her question, though lightly put, prompted a comprehensive answer, complete with more descriptions of Miss Faulkner's talents and his plans for Netherfield Park. That started another subject running and accounted very nicely for the rest of the evening.

Emma could not fail to notice how, in the space of a few hours, her brother had lost his dismal outlook.

Unfortunately, mention of his promise to call at the Bingleys' house again rather dampened his mood, as did the heavy rain that was drenching the city. It was certainly not conducive to going out, and Jonathan was able to persuade himself quite easily that the visit could be postponed.

The arrival of a Parliamentary colleague to see James opened up an entire Pandora's box of political possibilities, which left Emma free to escape to her room.

By the time James came upstairs, Jonathan had gone to bed.

Emma was still uneasy about him, but was convinced by her husband that there were times when people's lives were best left to work themselves out.

"Even if it may not seem like the best solution," he said, "it may be better left alone. I believe, my dearest, your brother is reaching just such a point in his life. Whatever we—that is, you or I or any others of his friends and family—may advise, I fear there is a momentum in the series of events set in train by Amelia-Jane that will be difficult to resist. Whether either of them can salvage something at the end of all this depends upon what they each want from life. I am firmly convinced that intervention will only make matters worse."

Emma, who set great store by the mature judgment of her husband, the man to whom she owed her present happiness and the well-being of her two daughters, agreed that he was probably right.

She was even more certain he was right when, on the following day, an express was received for Jonathan from Charlotte Collins.

It brought news that his mother-in-law, having received her daughter Catherine's letter, was making arrangements to travel to London by coach and asked to be met at the inn, from where she proposed to set out with Jonathan for Rosings Park.

Clearly, Mrs Collins had no idea of Amelia-Jane's latest actions; she had assumed they would find her daughter in residence at the Dower House in Kent. Jonathan did not look forward to telling her otherwise.

That evening, despite a threatening storm, the Armandes and Miss Faulkner arrived at the appointed time. Simply but charmingly dressed in a silk gown, Anna Faulkner was the cynosure of all eyes.

Throughout the evening, Emma was intrigued by the effect that the visitors—and in particular, Miss Faulkner—seemed to have upon her brother.

Gone was the gloomy countenance, replaced by an amiable manner which was both welcoming and attentive to their guests.

Since they were only a small party at dinner, there was little formality in the arrangements at table, and Emma saw how naturally and easily Jonathan and Miss Faulkner entered the dining room together and were seated next to each other at the dinner table, leaving the Armandes to occupy the places next to James and herself.

Not that this presented any difficulty, for Madame Armande was most loquacious and spoke well, despite her protestations of inadequate English, while Monsieur, whose English, though accented, was excellent, had no difficulty communicating with their hosts at all, and there was much to talk about.

Their conversation was of Art and Music and the glories of Paris and Florence, which the Wilsons had visited on their recent tour of Europe. The Armandes hoped also to visit some famous English galleries and expressed great admiration for the work of Turner.

Then, there was the Art School and exhibition, to be held in the Autumn. They had been busy planning for it, Monsieur said, "and Miss Faulkner is helping me; she is so good, I could not do it without her."

Madame Armande agreed enthusiastically, reminding her husband that "Monsieur Du Pont has declared that Mademoiselle Faulkner was *magnifique!*"

Hearing her name spoken, Anna paid some attention and said, "Pray do not believe all that they say of me, Mrs Wilson; Madame Armande is too generous with her praise."

But Emma protested that she was quite ready to believe everything she had heard.

"Indeed, Miss Faulkner, I cannot believe that any amount of praise is too much for one as dedicated to the Arts as you are."

To which Jonathan added with an unusual degree of enthusiasm, "You are absolutely right, Emma. You see, Miss Faulkner, as I have told you, my sister is always right about such matters."

With much protestation and even more laughter, complementing the good food and excellent wines, the conversation was lively and entertaining.

After the meal, they withdrew to the larger drawing room, which boasted some elegant Regency furniture and a fine Italian *forté-piano*. Emma was happy to demonstrate the sweetness of its tone to her guests, but having completed a couple of short compositions, she turned to Anna and said, "Miss Faulkner, now we must hear you, please. My brother has told me how well you play."

It encouraged the Armandes to urge their star pupil and beloved friend to sing and play, a request earnestly seconded by Jonathan, who was seated beside the lady and rose at once to escort her to the instrument. With her usual lack of fuss, Anna obliged, playing first a favourite Chopin and then proceeding to sing a pretty French song.

The Armandes were in near ecstasy, but in truth, her performance was so fine that even James abandoned his usual reticence and applauded, demanding an encore! Jonathan, who had not heard her sing before, was enchanted not just by the quality of her performance, but by the unpretentious simplicity of her manner.

Totally charmed, he forgot the task he had been entrusted with and had to be gently prompted to turn the pages by the performer herself. It was a rebuke he seemed almost to enjoy, so readily did he apologise and make amends with greater attention.

Looking on, Emma wondered whether her brother realised that he was in grave danger of falling in love with Miss Faulkner.

Admittedly, he behaved with great decorum and propriety at all times, but everything about him, his attentive stance, his obvious appreciation and delighted expression, all revealed how deeply impressed he was with their guest. Surprisingly, Miss Faulkner gave no indication of being affected by all this admiration; if she was, she did not show it.

Emma guessed that she might well have been pleased, as any young woman might have been, but she certainly did nothing to encourage it.

As she remarked to her husband, she could not recall when she had last seen her brother in such good spirits.

When their guests prepared to leave after thanking them for a wonderful evening, Jonathan was heard making arrangements to call on them the following day. The Armandes asked him to take coffee with them, and while Anna smiled and looked pleased, the only word to describe Jonathan's expression was "blissful." Not long afterwards, refusing more port and still looking unusually pleased with himself, he retired upstairs.

Later that night, Emma wrote to her dear friend Emily Courtney.

I cannot tell you how grateful I am for the presence in London, at Belgrave Square—no more than a brisk walk from us—of the charming Monsieur and Madame Armande. They are here to conduct an Art School and

Jonathan has become very attached to them, which is such a blessing, since it distracts him from our present vexing problems.

Staying with them for the Summer is Anna Faulkner. You will recall she is Maria Lucas' youngest girl, who is recently home from Europe. Handsome and very accomplished in the European manner, she is much admired by everyone, including Jonathan. There is no trace of manipulation on her part, no deliberate encouragement or archness of manner. She is absolutely exemplary in her conduct and so, to all intents and purposes, is my dear brother.

But if you saw them together, Emily, only a fool or a blind man would fail to read the signs.

I wondered whether I should warn Jonathan. Here he is a married man with a wife who is threatening to destroy all they have built up as a family, and yet clearly he is in danger of losing his heart to a lovely young woman, who is probably unaware of the problems their friendship could cause.

Should there be some gossip, should Amelia-Jane or the vile Arabella Watkins hear of it, the consequences for all of them will be catastrophic. The reputations of both my brother and Miss Faulkner may well be sullied.

And yet, my dear Emily, recalling his previous misery and seeing his unusual happiness this evening, I had not the heart to spoil it all. Perhaps I was being too indulgent with my brother, but who can tell what lies ahead for him? This was a moment of innocent pleasure, and who was I to take it from him?

Charlotte Collins had been deeply distressed by her eldest daughter Catherine's letter. She had brought it with her, reading it often on her journey from Longbourn, and when Jonathan met her at the coaching inn, she got it out and demanded to know how he had permitted things to get to such a pass.

With some difficulty, Jonathan persuaded her that the parlour of the inn was not the best place to discuss the matter and urged her into his carriage, which then set off for the Wilsons' apartment.

Mrs Collins expressed some surprise. "Jonathan, where are we going? Are we not going directly to Rosings Park?" she asked.

Jonathan informed her that they were expected at his sister's apartment in Grosvenor Street, where she could take some refreshment after her overnight journey from Longbourn. Charlotte was anxious to see her daughter and her grandchildren and was keen to ask about arrangements for travelling on to Rosings, when he started to explain the reason for the change of plan.

As he spoke, in his usual quiet, restrained way, Charlotte reacted at first with shocked silence, and then, as it became clear to her that Amelia-Jane was proposing to leave her husband and family, she could not hold back the tears.

To see his mother-in-law, for whom he had a great deal of affection and respect, a woman who had maintained her quiet dignity under exceedingly difficult circumstances while being married to one of the silliest men in Christendom, and to watch her weep, moved Jonathan deeply.

It was of no use to try to offer comfort; he was just as miserable as she was about the situation in which they found themselves. Indeed, he could not trust himself to say much more and was very grateful when they arrived at the Wilsons' and found Emma waiting for them.

Though she tried with tea and refreshments to calm her anxiety, Charlotte would not be put off. She was determined to go to her daughter as soon as possible.

"I must see her and speak with her, Jonathan. She cannot know what she is doing, she has no understanding of the consequences for herself, her children, and all her family of this behaviour. I must see her and make her understand," she insisted and they all knew it was useless to argue.

Fearing confrontation, Emma offered to accompany them.

It was unlikely, she thought, that Amelia-Jane would remain recalcitrant in the face of her mother's appeal, but if the Watkins woman was present, she thought it might help Charlotte to have an ally with her.

When they reached the house, once again they were told that Amelia-Jane was out, but there to greet them in the sitting room, for all the world like the lady of the house, was Mrs Arabella Watkins.

With an insolence that was quite breathtaking, she introduced herself, welcomed them into Jonathan's own house as if he were a casual visitor, and offered them tea and cakes!

Charlotte, refusing both the refreshments and the chair that was offered, demanded to know where her daughter was.

"Mrs Watkins, I am here, having travelled overnight from Hertfordshire, to see my daughter. Where is she?"

At this, Mrs Watkins, became rather officious and, affecting an air of specious self-importance, declared in an irritating, high voice, "Mrs Collins, Amelia-Jane is a very dear friend and I could not possibly betray a confidence. I can only say to you, she is out about her own business and ..."

Impatient, Emma spoke up. "Mrs Watkins, are you suggesting that my brother has no right to know where his wife is? I would remind you that this is his house."

The Watkins woman was clearly stung, and, being rather florid in the face, she looked very angry indeed.

"My dear Mrs Wilson, I would not consider it the act of a friend to inform a lady's husband of her whereabouts, if she were anxious not to have it known to him." Turning to Charlotte, she continued, "And while I am deeply sorry for you, ma'am, and appreciate your concern, I fear I am not in a position ..."

Aggravated beyond bearing, Charlotte Collins interrupted her. "Oh, do stop talking such arrant nonsense, Mrs Watkins! Whatever claims you may make for your friendship with my daughter, my claim as her mother and Mr Bingley's as her husband are far superior to yours. We are concerned for her safety, the interests of her children, and the good name of her family. I must speak with her and I demand to be told where she is, if she is not here in this house."

Though initially shaken by Charlotte's attack, Mrs Watkins appeared to harden her resolve. Clearly determined not to oblige them, she changed her tactics.

Softening her voice and speaking in a less pompous manner, indeed becoming almost obsequious, she offered to pass on a message to Amelia-Jane and urge her to see her mother.

"Far be it from me, Mrs Collins, to try to come between you and your daughter, who is become such a dear friend to me in so short a time. I give you my word, ma'am, I will convey your message the very moment she returns and beg her to see you on the morrow."

Charlotte's anger was obvious, but she was careful to control herself. "Can you not, at least, tell me when you expect her to return?" she asked.

Mrs Watkins was even less helpful. "Alas, I have not that information. Indeed, the only person who knows is Mr Alexander and the driver of the hansom cab, who conveyed them to their destination," she intoned somewhat dolefully.

At the mention of Alexander, Jonathan walked out of the room. He felt himself quite unable to cope with the information that his wife had gone out in a hansom cab, to an undisclosed destination, in the company of a Mr Alexander, of whom he knew nothing at all!

Emma asked, "And who is this Mr Alexander?"

Arabella Watkins smiled, a simpering, coy smile, and said in an arch voice, which left no one in any doubt of her relationship with the gentleman, "Mr Alexander is a gentleman of my acquaintance, who is assisting my friend Mrs Bingley with some of her problems."

"Assisting her? In what way and with what problems?" asked Charlotte, sharply, astonished by this new revelation.

Mrs Watkins immediately resumed her role of confidante. "I cannot say exactly … I mean, I have no knowledge of the details. Mr Alexander is an attorney and he is very clever, indeed," she declared.

It was with the greatest difficulty that Charlotte restrained herself, and Emma said afterwards that she felt as if she would explode with pent-up fury at the sheer stubbornness of Mrs Watkins.

With a final withering remark about the possible consequences of her behaviour, Charlotte Collins and Emma Wilson left the house, vowing to return the following day.

They found Jonathan standing on the pavement, his face a study in abhorrence. So dejected did he seem that when they related the rest of their conversation with Mrs Watkins, he appeared not to react at first, almost as if he had lost all hope.

Emma had felt her own expectations disappear as she realised that nothing they said would have any effect upon the obstinate woman with whom they had been confronted.

Only Mrs Collins remained hopeful. "I intend to get my daughter out of the clutches of that woman even if it is the last thing I do," she said with the kind of determination that had characterised most decisions in her life. In many instances, they had been very successful—like the occasion, after the death of Mr Collins, on which she had turned down Lady Catherine de Bourgh's offer to employ her as a companion, deciding instead to open her own school for young ladies.

This time, however, while there was no lack of determination on her part, the result would depend largely upon circumstances beyond her control.

Emma, feeling unhappy and frustrated, continued her letter to Emily:

Dear Emily, I do wish you were here, for we are all so wretched, we can do nothing to improve each others' spirits. James is indeed fortunate to be away all day at the Commons, for we would not be good company at all.

Jonathan and Mrs Collins are too miserable on their own to be any comfort to each other, and I do not know how I can do anything to help. It is too horrible to contemplate that Amelia-Jane will remove herself and the two girls, Cathy and Tess, to Bath, where she will continue to be under the influence of this appalling woman!

Who would have expected such conduct from Amelia-Jane? Jonathan, I think, has had some inkling of this, but poor Mrs Collins is utterly distraught.

I wonder, Emily, at the coincidence. Can it be possible that both Jonathan and I were so naïve in our judgment, that we both misread utterly the characters of the persons we married? I know we were young, but we were surely not both so foolish?

I paid for my mistake for many years, as you know, and it is only thanks to my dear James that I retained my sanity. It seems that poor Jonathan is only just starting his purgatory …

The appearance of her brother at the door of her sitting room caused Emma to stop writing.

He had only looked in to advise her that he was expected at the Armandes' that afternoon and was just leaving.

"I have promised to give Monsieur Armande my opinion on a few of the items he hopes to include in the display they will have at the Art School next month. I expect to be back in time for dinner," he said, and Emma could not help wondering how Jonathan's opinion was likely to assist someone like M. Armande, who was himself a teacher of Art! However, she said nothing, glad that he could find something to occupy himself at this anxious time.

Continuing her letter to Emily, she said as much:

I confess I cannot find it in my heart to begrudge him the obvious and, up to now, innocent pleasure he seems to get from his visits to the Armandes and Miss Faulkner.

While we await whatever developments tomorrow may bring …

She was interrupted here by the doorbell and the sound of voices in the hall. On going downstairs, she found Mrs Giles with one of the servants from the Bingleys' place.

An hour or so later, her brother returned, in the teeth of a gale which was stripping the leaves from the trees in the street and driving every traveller indoors. A sudden squall had whipped up the worst weather they had seen this Summer, and Jonathan, entering quickly to get out of the biting wind, found the house in uproar.

A message had been received only an hour ago, relating that Mrs Bingley, Mrs Watkins, and her "friend" Mr Alexander had left London for Bath, leaving the two girls, Teresa and Cathy, in the care of the maid and housekeeper at Grosvenor Street.

Mrs Giles, who was an old trusted housekeeper, had been very distressed and, having waited until the coast was clear, she had written a note to Mrs Collins.

It had given very little other information, except to express her hope that "Mr Bingley or Mrs Collins or someone would pay attention to the needs of the two children, who have had no governess for over a week and are very lonely with only the maids for company—poor dears! It is not right that they should see neither their mother nor their father, ma'am, and they have not set foot outside the house since arriving in London. It is cruel indeed, for they are not to blame for all the goings on." She concluded with a request that Mr Bingley should do something at once, for the sake of the children.

Mrs Collins, who had opened and read the note, was shocked.

Standing ashen-faced in the hall, she had cried out that they must go after them at once and bring Amelia-Jane back. It had taken a great deal of patient explaining to persuade her that no one could possibly chase after the travellers bound for Bath in this foul weather.

Emma had to point out that, in any event, they would have to wait until either Jonathan or James returned, since the gentlemen had both carriages.

When her son-in-law arrived and was told the news, Charlotte immediately appealed to him. "Jonathan, you must go after them and bring her back. You cannot let her do this. She must be saved from this dreadful widow Watkins."

To her astonishment, Emma heard her brother say, "Mrs Collins, I have no intention of following Amelia-Jane to Bath or anywhere else. She has chosen to leave me and the children to join her friends. I shall not attempt to force her to return. It is her choice."

There was a disbelieving silence in the room as Mrs Collins began to weep, and he continued calmly, "In the last few weeks, I have tried by every means I know to persuade Amelia-Jane not to take such a step. Yet despite my efforts and those of her sister Catherine, she has preferred to follow her newfound friends. They cannot possibly have her interests at heart, but my duty now is quite clear; I have to ensure that Cathy and Tess are safe and that Anne-Marie and Charles are informed of this unhappy situation.

"I shall also secure the house at Grosvenor Street against further intrusion by persons who have absolutely no connection with my family and no right to be there at all."

Emma had not seen her gentle brother in such a mood ever before.

Begging her to look to Mrs Collins' health, he insisted on leaving, in spite of the driving rain, to visit his children.

When he returned, James Wilson met him in the hall.

"Jonathan, I am shocked and appalled! Emma has told me the unhappy news," he said as Jonathan divested himself of his sodden coat.

Hearing him come in, Emma had rushed downstairs to enquire after the girls, and they were all relieved to hear they were well and were sleeping soundly.

"They have very little understanding of what has happened," he said. "Mrs Giles tells me that they spent all afternoon reading in the old nursery; they have not come downstairs since their mother left and have not asked for her at all."

"Poor darlings," said Emma, thinking immediately of her own two daughters and how difficult it had been to conceal from them the activities of their father, her first husband.

"Jonathan, I think I shall go with Mrs Collins tomorrow and bring them over here, if this wretched weather has eased," she said.

He nodded, grateful for her concern, and then asked after his mother-in-law. Emma was glad to be able to say she had eaten and was resting.

"I think you should come up with me now and reassure her. She has been very anxious about the girls," she suggested, and he was happy to do as she asked.

While Charlotte was relieved to hear that the girls were safe and well, she could not agree with Jonathan about Amelia-Jane. She tried again to persuade him that he ought to go to Bath; indeed, she offered to accompany him herself, but to no avail.

Jonathan had decided that if his wife had made a decision to leave her family and go to Bath, he would not interfere; he would certainly not follow her and either order her or beg her to return.

Coming downstairs, Emma asked, anxiously, "Jonathan, dear, are you sure? I mean, to leave Amelia-Jane to the tender mercies of Mrs Watkins and her friend—do you really believe it is the right thing to do?"

Jonathan did not give her a direct answer. "It may or may not be, Emma; all I know is I cannot see any other honourable course of action for me, in the circumstances. Tomorrow, I shall write to my father and ask him to speak to his sisters; perhaps they may have more influence upon her than I have had. After all, it was through them she was introduced to the Watkins woman; if anyone should attempt to influence her, they should."

At dinner, of which Jonathan hardly ate anything and Emma very little, James Wilson strongly supported his brother-in-law's stand.

He had recently told Emma of his belief that there were times when inter-ference in the lives of people did no good and could possibly do harm.

This was one such instance, and James was quite convinced that for Jonathan to get in his carriage and chase after his wife, who might very well refuse to pay any attention to him, was the very worst thing he could do.

"Quite apart from the indignity you would suffer, should she refuse to return with you, there is the possibility that she may well claim that she is only taking a temporary holiday in Bath at the invitation of her friends and turn the tables on you, making you seem overbearing and ridiculous."

Emma had not thought of that and was now inclined to agree with them. "Let us hope and pray she will realise her mistake and return," she said, and though James said "Amen to that," Jonathan bit his lip and remained silent.

Emma left them together and went upstairs. Too exhausted to finish her letter, but unable to sleep, she lay awake for the best part of an hour. When her husband came upstairs, he found her still awake, standing at the window, gazing out at the dark street below.

When he tried to take her to bed, she turned to him and said, "James, do you believe Amelia-Jane will ever return to us, of her own free will?"

He was touched by her obvious sadness. "I cannot say, my love, I never did get to know her very well; she was always rather distant with me. I do know that Jonathan believes she will not return."

"Is that what he told you?" she asked, incredulous.

James nodded and said, "I think he is at the end of his patience, Emma, and I cannot say I blame him. As for trying to recover her and bring her back, I do not believe it should even be attempted."

Tears filled Emma's eyes. She had known great unhappiness herself and felt deeply for her brother.

"Poor Jonathan, gentle, kind Jonathan. Life is simply not fair," she said.

They had each gone to bed speculating, hoping, perhaps praying that a way might be found for Jonathan's fractured family to be brought together.

They were never to find out whether their prayers would be answered because, just before dawn, they were awakened by a loud knocking at the front door.

On going downstairs, James found in the hall a manservant from the Bingleys' house at Grosvenor Street, together with an officer of the local police. The news they brought would destroy all their hopes and throw many lives into chaos.

George, the Bingleys' butler, had driven over with the constable, who had initially called at the Bingleys' place.

James took the two men into the sitting room and sat them down so they could tell their story. He called a servant in to light the fire and the candles in the room, which was dark and cold. By the time Emma, who had been awakened by the sound of voices, had come downstairs and, reluctant to go into the sitting room, sat at the foot of the stairs, many of the servants had crept up quietly from their quarters below. They stood around in the dark doorways or lingered in the back hallway, whispering, anxious to discover what had occurred.

The story was told mainly by the police officer.

There had been a serious accident. It had happened not more than twenty miles out of London on the road to Bath, somewhere between Salt Hill and Maidenhead, just before the road crosses the bridge over the Thames and runs downhill towards the dreaded Maidenhead Thicket, a patch of scrub frequented by footpads and villains.

The small, light vehicle had apparently lost a wheel and rolled off the road and down an embankment. The constable put it down to the stormy night, a poor road, and possible exhaustion of the driver.

"He was the only one to escape with his life, albeit with severe injuries. The passengers—a gentleman, two ladies, and a young maid servant—were all dead when they were found by a mail coach doing the night run to Bath," he said, as gasps and cries went up from all around.

Emma, sitting at the foot of the stairs, began to weep.

She could not believe what she had heard. Her sobs brought James out into the hall and to her side. Her cries and the voices of the servants awakened Jonathan and Mrs Collins, who came downstairs and so the entire story had to be retold for them as they stood in shocked disbelief.

The constable explained that it had been difficult to discover the identity and address of the passengers, since no one carried any papers; only the name and address on the lid of the maid's tin trunk had led them to the Bingleys' house at Grosvenor Street.

Now they wanted Mr Bingley to identify the bodies of his wife and the maid servant, Annie Ashton, a young girl not yet eighteen.

Later, Emma could not clearly remember what had happened in the next few minutes, except that she was holding Mrs Collins, whose body was shaking with violent, heartrending sobs. Charlotte had never dreamed she would face such a disaster.

Jonathan, walking as if in a nightmare, turned to his mother-in-law and embraced her and his sister, but seemed unable to say a word.

For the second time in his life, he was observing the harrowing sorrow of a family following an accident. Somehow, as on the previous occasion, he had the dreadful feeling that he had not done enough to prevent what had happened.

As they helped Charlotte up the stairs and to her room, James came to tell his wife that he would go with Jonathan and the police officer. He did not know how long they would be; he urged her to get some rest and ensure that Charlotte did the same.

Inconsolable, Charlotte could only recall the little girl, her youngest daughter, the one Mr Collins used to spoil. "He always spoilt her … she was his favourite, not just because she was the littlest and prettiest, but because he could never say no to her. She used to know exactly how to wheedle favours out of him," Charlotte said, as they sat together trying to sip hot tea, even as the sky outside glowed red and the sun rose over the still sleeping city.

Emma's first thought had been of the two girls—Teresa, not yet sixteen, and little Cathy, whose lives had been shattered. As the sky grew lighter, she determined to go and fetch the children, so they would have their aunt and grandmother to comfort them. Mrs Collins did not feel strong enough to travel the short distance, so Emma went with her lady's maid Lucy, who was known to both girls.

She found them shocked and dry-eyed, apparently unable to fully understand what had occurred and how it affected their lives. Emma hugged them both to her, and gradually her own emotion seemed to bring their feelings to the surface; first little Cathy and then Tess began to weep softly.

As Emma held them close, Lucy went upstairs to pack their things.

When they were back at her house, Emma let them spend the morning with their grandmother, making sure that they were left undisturbed, with plenty of refreshments and time to themselves.

Emma finally concluded her letter to Emily Courtney.

Oh dear God, Emily, did I ever dream I would complete this letter in these circumstances? I shall send it express, so you get the news as soon as possible. I suppose Jonathan will send telegrams to Papa and Mr Darcy.

We do not know all the details of how the dreadful accident happened, the police and the magistrate will be investigating, but what good will it do?

Amelia-Jane is dead, together with her two friends. We think the other woman was Mrs Arabella Watkins and the gentleman, an attorney by the name of Alexander. They at least went by choice on this ill-conceived and dangerous journey. Not so, young Annie Ashton, Amelia's maid, not yet eighteen and her parents' only daughter!

She was dragged away from Kent, where she had lived all her short life in the country and taken first to London and then to Bath! A young, innocent life snuffed out because of the stupidity of her mistress and her fine friends! How can this be fair?

Please Emily, pray for them all and for us, especially Jonathan, who seems like a man in a nightmare. He is not yet returned from the police office, where he has gone with James. A terrible task awaits him on his return. Anne-Marie and Charles must be informed of their mother's death!

You can see why he needs your prayers.

I hope we shall see you soon. I have no information about the funeral arrangements; I expect you will hear from Jonathan in due course.

All is confusion at the moment.

Yours etc

Emma.

When the gentlemen returned, Jonathan set about immediately sending out telegrams and express letters to close friends and family in many parts of England.

He had already written to his son Charles, but with his daughter Anne-Marie, a journey across town had to be undertaken.

Funeral arrangements had to await the completion of the police enquiries.

Charlotte Collins had asked that Amelia-Jane be laid to rest in Hertfordshire, in the churchyard where the Lucases had rested over several generations. Jonathan agreed immediately. He could see no reason for refusing her mother's request, nor did it seem appropriate to insist upon having Amelia-Jane interred among strangers in the North, where his father's family lay.

Another painful duty awaited him.

Young Annie Ashton had to be returned to her grieving family in Kent.

It was a task Jonathan intended to perform himself; having already sent for her uncle John Ashton, who was the caretaker at the Hunsford Church, to accompany her body. Jonathan would bear the cost of her funeral, of course, and travel to Kent to face her family.

James Wilson offered to arrange for the announcements in the newspapers, and Emma, having seen the expression on her brother's face and feeling his pain as if it were her own, dressed appropriately and went downstairs.

"I'm ready, Jonathan; I think we have to go to Anne-Marie without any further delay. It will not do that she should hear it from someone else or read of it in the *Times.*"

His gratitude was expressed wordlessly, in the warmth of his acknowledgement of her concern, as he collected his things and followed her out to the carriage.

To Harwood House they went, Jonathan determined to do the right thing by his daughter and Emma anxious to do all she could to help her brother at perhaps the worst moment in his life.

Eliza Harwood was tending the roses when Jonathan and his sister alighted from their carriage in the driveway of Harwood House.

The bright smile with which she prepared to welcome them faded and her cheerful greeting died upon her lips as she took in the significance of their mourning clothes.

They had come with grave news, she was sure of it.

"Mr Bingley, Emma, I am so happy to see you, but surely … there must be something wrong … please tell me, what has happened?"

They went indoors and into the sitting room, where Jonathan asked, "Is Anne-Marie home?"

Eliza nodded. "Yes, but she was very tired, having been up all night with a difficult patient. I sent her upstairs to rest a while," she explained.

Jonathan decided to tell Eliza the reason for their visit, and, omitting the personal details of his troubled marriage, he told her of Amelia's ill-fated journey to Bath and the accident that had taken her life.

Jonathan had no knowledge of how much of his wife's unhappy story was already known to Eliza Harwood, but he assumed that his daughter may have divulged some but not all of the unfortunate circumstances.

However, when the death of four persons including Amelia-Jane was revealed, Eliza cried out in horror and covered her face.

"Oh my God! Mr Bingley, I am so sorry, oh dear! What will Anne-Marie do? It was but a short time ago that she wrote to her brother, begging him to come to London and help her convince her mother not to move to Bath.

"But Charles is busy with his medical studies in Edinburgh, as you would know, and can spare very little time. Does he know of this terrible accident?" she asked.

Jonathan nodded gravely. "Yes, I have written to him by express," he replied.

After asking some more questions and taking a little time to calm her own feelings, Eliza dried her eyes, ordered some tea for her visitors, and went upstairs to break the news to her friend.

When they came downstairs, Anne-Marie went directly to her father and clung to him as she sobbed, tears spilling down her cheeks.

For several minutes, she didn't say a word; then asked, "Did you see her, Papa?"

Jonathan knew exactly what she meant. "I did. Your uncle James and I went with the police to identify your mama and poor little Annie Ashton." He paused and tried to compose himself before saying, "Your mama was not disfigured in any way, nor was Annie. The fall must have caused instant death; we can only hope they did not suffer," he said, as she wept inconsolably for her unhappy mother and young Annie, too—they had played together as children and attended Sunday School at Hunsford.

Then, to everyone's surprise, she said, "I must return with you to Grosvenor Street. Cathy and Tess will need me," and went directly upstairs to pack her clothes.

She returned in less than half an hour, before they had finished their tea, packed, changed, and ready to leave. Embracing Eliza and thanking her for all her help, she asked her to explain her absence to the matron at the hospital.

"Please tell her I am sorry to let her down; I hope it will not be for too long," she said, and Eliza's eyes filled with tears as they said goodbye.

Emma and Jonathan were astonished at the calm, measured, and responsible way in which Anne-Marie had organised everything.

On the journey between Harwood House and Grosvenor Street, Anne-Marie said very little, but she sat close beside her father and held his hand in hers, as if to comfort him, while seeking to draw from him some strength to help her cope with what lay ahead for both of them.

When they arrived at the Wilsons' apartments, she ran upstairs to her two young sisters and found them reading to each other. Her arrival triggered both tears and joy, for the girls had longed for their sister.

She embraced and kissed them and told them they were going back to their own home and their grandmother was coming, too.

Emma watched, amazed at the way she got them packed and ready, and thanked both James and herself and all the servants for their kindness to her sisters, as they prepared to leave. It was hard to believe that this young woman had been told of the death of her mother a couple of hours ago.

What neither Emma nor Jonathan knew was that Anne-Marie had spent many days agonising over a letter she had received from her mother the previous week, a letter in which she had hinted at a journey and a new home with kind friends. While she had made no mention of Bath or Mrs Watkins, it had been plain to Anne-Marie that her mother was planning to leave London and her family.

> ... I shall write to you, my dearest Anne-Marie, and I hope you will come and see me when I am settled in my new place. I know I can depend on you to look after Tess and Cathy for me.
>
> They will not be short of money, of that you can be certain, for your father is very generous with allowances; indeed, if he were as generous with his time and affections as with his money, we should have all been a good deal happier.
>
> Remember, dear Anne-Marie, when you marry, whether for love or money is not the important matter, but whether your husband has time to spare for you ...
>
> If he has not, it is a lonely life indeed ...

The sad little message had lain hidden, even from her friend Eliza, while she had fretted about it, wondering whether she should acquaint her father with its contents. Now her poor unhappy mother was dead, it was unlikely to see the light of day again. The news of her death, even though it had come as a terrible shock, had been almost a relief after that letter, a cry of despair, more sharply poignant than before.

At least now, Anne-Marie knew what she had to do.

After Jonathan, his three daughters, and their grandmother had left, Emma and James Wilson found themselves alone in their own apartment for the first time in several days. They were, neither of them, strangers to pain and death, and felt great sympathy for Jonathan and his children. Discussing the circumstances surrounding Amelia-Jane's death, they were forced to the conclusion, in the absence of any evidence to the contrary, that she had been foolishly misled by her friends into leaving her husband and children for no apparent reason. Her own agony and sense of helplessness was unknown to them.

Emma, who, for the sake of family loyalty and her children's security, had borne many years of mistreatment and humiliation in her first marriage, was more severe on her sister-in-law than James, who was willing to allow that there may have been extenuating circumstances that explained Amelia-Jane's unhappiness; but neither would admit that any level of discontent could justify what she had done.

As to any thought that Jonathan, by some act of omission or commission could have contributed in any way at all to the problems that beset his wife, nothing could have been further from their thoughts.

"Jonathan has always been a good husband and father; no one could doubt that he loved Amelia-Jane and the children and has always provided for them most generously," said Emma, of her beloved brother. "He is devoted to his family, loyal, kind, and hardworking to a fault."

James agreed. "He brings the same estimable qualities to his work for the Party and I have no doubt that, should he choose to re-enter Parliament, he will fulfil the duties of a Member equally well."

They went upstairs in complete agreement that Jonathan Bingley had been singularly hard done by. Life, they agreed, had not been fair to him.

The following morning brought even more evidence of this.

They had risen late, since James did not have to attend the Parliament and Emma was weary from several days and nights of anxiety, and had just finished breakfast when Jonathan arrived. This time, he brought with him a letter from his son, Charles.

It had arrived that morning and was a short, sharp, hurtful letter, in which he appeared to censure his father for not doing enough to prevent his mother's death.

Clearly, Sir, your unwillingness to take a strong stand against Mama's notion of moving to Bath has contributed to this disaster. I cannot believe that she would have acted as she did had you made it clear to her you desired her to remain in London with you because you needed her at your side.

I have often felt that, just as you did not always indicate to me what you expected of me, neither did you let Mama know what you expected of her.

She was, as a result, frequently bewildered, as I was, by what we took to be your indifference and, in such a state of confusion, she would have been easily misled and used by others, as she undoubtedly was.

Perhaps she was persuaded that there was more satisfaction to be had in the social round of Bath, where she had friends, than by staying in London, when you spent most of your waking hours at Westminster.

Reading the letter, written as it was in the plainest of terms, Emma and James both felt that young Charles Bingley had obviously misunderstood the situation completely.

Jonathan was hurt and confused. "He thinks I am solely to blame. How am I ever to convince him otherwise?" he asked.

Seeing his anxious, unhappy expression, James urged him not to despair. "Emma and I will talk to Charles when we meet. I assume he will come direct to Longbourn for the funeral. We will meet him and persuade him to return with us via London. Have no fear, Jonathan, we will ensure that he learns the truth. He is mistaken. No one who knows you can doubt that."

Jonathan was grateful but insisted that they must not try to salvage his reputation by damaging that of his late wife.

"I will not have you do that under any circumstance; if my son or anyone else wishes to hold me responsible, I will bear that burden, rather than see Amelia-Jane vilified in death. She was, for most of the years of our marriage, a loving wife and mother. Those who encouraged her discontent are far more culpable than she ever was. As for Charles, any attempt to censure his mother will only harden his heart against me," he declared with great firmness, eliciting from his brother-in-law an immediate assurance that they would do no such thing.

"You can trust me, Jonathan, I will do no such thing; but I hope to help Charles to understand the facts," said James, and Jonathan, being somewhat comforted, was persuaded to stay and take tea with them.

Some minutes later, the doorbell rang. A servant answered it and presently announced Monsieur and Madame Armande and Miss Faulkner to see Mr Bingley. They had heard news of the accident that morning and had come as soon as they could to offer their condolences.

The Armandes, who were completely ignorant of the strains that had beset Jonathan's marriage, attributed the tragic accident to the dreadful weather on that night. They could not know that it had only hastened the end of a marriage that neither partner could sustain much longer.

Miss Faulkner, on the other hand, though unaware of the details, had nevertheless, a more intuitive understanding of the situation. Though not a single word of criticism of his wife had ever passed Jonathan Bingley's lips during their conversations, his reticence about her, his apparent reluctance to speak of her even in response to the most innocuous enquiries, had led Anna to believe that all was not well.

Amelia-Jane was her cousin, and Anna was not entirely ignorant of her immature and frequently self-indulgent behaviour. It had occasioned comment within the family, and she knew it had troubled her aunt.

She did not know if any blame attached to Jonathan, but on this occasion, she could see enough of the pain reflected in his face and the downward drag of the usually upright attitude of his tall figure to understand how he must feel. Everything she said and did revealed her sincere compassion and concern.

"If I can be of any help, if there is anything we can do, please do feel free to call on us," she said, and the Armandes added their voices, too. Jonathan was touched by their genuine solicitude.

They stayed to take tea, but left soon afterwards, having received a promise that they would be informed of the funeral arrangements as soon as a firm date was known.

At Woodlands, the news, received by express letter, had come like a bolt of lightning out of a Summer sky.

The morning had been bright and inviting, cloudless, with a light breeze to soften the warm breath of late Summer. "An absolutely perfect day for a drive into the country," Bingley had said at breakfast.

"And an easy walk through the woods," added Elizabeth, while Jane proposed, "Why not a picnic in a shady meadow, beside a stream?"

"I cannot think of anything better; do you not agree, Darcy?" asked Bingley, and Darcy had replied with some degree of enthusiasm, "Certainly, and if you will have all that and a delightful old inn as well, where we might retreat should the weather change, I suggest we make for the country around Horsham. We could take the open carriage."

"Do you mean The Black Horse Inn in the village below Monks Gate?" asked Bingley.

"Indeed, I do—the very place. There are woods and streams enough to satisfy us all," his friend replied, and soon they were all agreed that it was the perfect spot.

Preparations were afoot when an express had arrived for Bingley.

He had opened it in the midst of a lot of light chatter about their plans for the day, not for a moment expecting what was found within.

"This is probably Jonathan confirming that he has closed the Netherfield deal," he had said, and Darcy, commenting that it was a pretty good deal too, had added that Jonathan was a fortunate fellow.

Minutes later, unable to believe his eyes, much less take in what he had read, Bingley handed the letter to Darcy, without explanation, save for a quiet exclamation, "Oh, my God! Darcy, I cannot believe this."

Jane and Elizabeth, who were packing a picnic basket in the kitchen, had just been laughing over a silly mistake, when Darcy, his face pale with shock, came in and took them aside.

He had Jonathan's letter in his hand, and without too much ado, told them there had been some bad news. Amelia-Jane had been travelling to Bath with friends and her lady's maid; they had been caught in a storm and there had been an accident, just below Maidenhead, he said and he stopped, unable to continue.

He did not need to say another word; Jane knew in her heart and cried out as Elizabeth plucked the letter from her husband's hand and read it aloud.

As the truth dawned upon them, Jane wept; she could not understand it.

"Oh, Lizzie, she must have been going to Bath as Caroline Bingley said she would. How could she do it? How could she leave them?"

Elizabeth tried to talk to her, to console her, to tell her they did not have all the facts, but Jane would not be comforted.

"Lizzie, is it possible that Amelia-Jane thought so little of her husband and her children, even the littlest one, that she was prepared to leave them? What did she hope to achieve?" she asked, thinking only of her son and her grandchildren and the effect of this tragedy upon their lives.

Elizabeth would have liked to comfort her by saying otherwise, but she could not, for all the evidence seemed to confirm her fears.

It did seem as though Jonathan's wife had decided to carry out her threat to move to Bath if he did not abandon his plans for Netherfield.

"I am sorry, dearest Jane, but it does seem, shocking though it is, that you are right. Indeed, I cannot find any other explanation. One cannot explain her behaviour on the grounds of youth, ignorance, or stupidity, as was the case with Lydia. All we know is that she has been very depressed since she lost her two little boys, but that is insufficient reason for such an act as this."

"Poor Jonathan, how he must suffer, and poor dear Charlotte, what a terrible blow this must be for her," said Jane, whose concern for others outweighed, as ever, her own feelings.

Mr Bingley, who had gradually recovered his composure, came in to ask what they wished to do. Following a brief discussion, it was decided they would travel first to London and thence to Longbourn for the funeral.

The gentlemen went to make the necessary preparations for the journey and Elizabeth, seeing Jane's distress, took her sister upstairs to rest a while. They gave instructions for their things to be packed, unsure how long they would need to stay in town or indeed at Longbourn. There had been no date fixed for the funeral, as yet.

"We shall have to get our gowns for the funeral made in London," said Lizzie. "All my sober clothes are back at Pemberley."

Jane had nothing suitable, either; they had brought only light Summer gowns to Woodlands. They would have little use for them now, as pretty floral gowns would give way to the darker tones of mourning clothes.

The picnic basket was unpacked and the light, open Victoria returned to the stables, where the groom was preparing the carriage and horses for the more arduous journey to London.

The Summer of 1859 was all but gone.

❧

Meanwhile, Jonathan Bingley, together with Annie Ashton's uncle John, had accompanied young Annie's body to Hunsford, where her family, despite their desperate sorrow, thanked him sincerely for his kindness and thoughtfulness. They appreciated the genuine goodness of the man who, as manager of the Rosings estate, had been their Master for many years, during which time they had regarded him with affection and esteem.

His fairness and generosity were well known, frequently tempering the brusqueness of Lady Catherine de Bourgh.

That, in spite of his own terrible loss, he had seen fit to acknowledge their loss by his presence and his genuine grief at Annie's death, had touched their hearts, even more than his benevolence in paying for all of the funeral arrangements.

When Elizabeth and Jane arrived in London, they went directly to the Bingleys' house at Grosvenor Street.

Jonathan had not, as yet, returned from Kent. They found Anne-Marie with her two young sisters, all attired in deep mourning, sitting in the front parlour, with Emma Wilson and Miss Faulkner, who had come to keep the girls company while their father was away.

All day long, there had been a stream of visitors.

The younger girls, especially Cathy, seemed unable to comprehend what had happened, and Anne-Marie, despite her best efforts to be brave, looked tired and tearful. Teresa's eyes were red with lack of sleep, and when Jane put her arms around her, they wept together, and Emma soon followed suit.

It was left to Elizabeth and Anna Faulkner to try to console them. Elizabeth was grateful to have someone who could help with the girls. Anna Faulkner seemed to manage well. She appeared to have a way with children, and her gentle, unfussy manner put them at ease.

At first, Elizabeth and Jane did not know that Charlotte Collins was also in London. It was only when one of the girls mentioned their grandmother that they asked, "Charlotte is in London? Where is she?" asked Elizabeth and, on being informed that she was upstairs, in this very house, but was so distraught she had not left her room all day, Elizabeth went at once to her friend.

She was shocked by her exhausted state, for not only was she grief-stricken, as any mother would be, she was also beset with feelings of shame and guilt. Unaware of all the circumstances surrounding Amelia-Jane's ill-fated journey, Charlotte felt she had to bear the opprobrium for her daughter's conduct, and it seemed as if the burden was too heavy for her. Always a devoted and proper mother, who had raised her daughters with sound instruction and by good example, she was at a loss to understand how her youngest child had gone so far astray.

Charlotte had believed that of her three girls, Amelia-Jane had been the most fortunate in marriage, for not only had Jonathan Bingley been regarded as eminently eligible, handsome, and well educated, with a good income and excellent prospects, he was by far the most amiable young man one could hope to meet. There had not been a mother in town during the season of 1835, who had not congratulated her on the good fortune of her youngest daughter in becoming engaged to Mr Jonathan Bingley.

She could not think of a single reason to change that judgment. Yet, the excellent marriage lay in ruins and her daughter was dead.

Elizabeth went to her, her arms outstretched. "Charlotte, my dear friend."

They embraced and could not help the tears. Charlotte could barely speak and when Jane followed her sister into the room, her sense of guilt was heightened further.

"Jane, what can I say? How can I apologise for this dreadful thing?"

But Jane, despite her sorrow, was not about to countenance such sentiments.

"Apologise? Charlotte, you have no apology to make to me. You are not to blame, dear Charlotte. Amelia-Jane was surely old enough to know her own mind and make her own decisions, wrong though they may have been. She was responsible and whatever the matter was, it was between Jonathan and herself, not between you and me," she said, firmly.

Elizabeth looked on, somewhat surprised, as she went on, her voice, though steady, betraying the strain of emotion.

"As for those who may have contributed to this terrible tragedy by their constant urging and encouragement of her discontent, some have already paid a high price for their efforts. And Caroline Bingley, my sister-in-law, can add the memory of all four deaths to her book of remembrance.

"They will not be easily forgotten or forgiven."

Jane was shaking by the time she had finished and Charlotte went to her at once, grateful for the kindness of heart that had caused her to speak as she had done. Charlotte claimed she'd had no knowledge of the extent of Miss Bingley's influence over her daughter, but Elizabeth did know and was determined that her friend should be made aware of the truth.

She told her of the letter Bingley had received from Caroline, which had contained a threat that Amelia-Jane would leave Jonathan and, presumably, move to Bath if he persisted with his plan to purchase Netherfield Park.

"She has undoubtedly encouraged Amelia-Jane to believe that it would be right and proper for her to refuse to move to Hertfordshire, with her husband, if she did not wish to go," Elizabeth explained.

Charlotte was astounded and hurt. "Eliza, why should she do such a thing? Jonathan is her nephew! What could she hope to gain?"

Elizabeth was scathing in her criticism of Miss Bingley.

"Ever since her brother first met Jane and fell in love with her in Hertfordshire, all those years ago, Caroline Bingley, who, as you know, imagined herself to be the object of Mr Darcy's matrimonial plans, did everything in her power to thwart their marriage and, when she could not, proceeded to make things difficult for Jane and myself, whenever an occasion presented itself," she explained and, as Charlotte listened in some astonishment, continued, "My marriage to Mr Darcy clearly drove her to desperation, and though we have attempted to treat her with politeness at all times, she has never forgotten. Having failed to find a man sufficiently rich, fashionable, and of a suitable status to satisfy her ambitions, she has remained unwed and embittered. With very little to occupy her, except gossip and an empty social round, she has time enough for the sort of mischief that she made with Jonathan and Amelia-Jane."

"But why did she pick on my poor daughter?" cried Charlotte, who had very little understanding of Miss Bingley's machinations.

"She probably saw in her someone young and a little naïve, perhaps, whom she could influence. I do not pretend to know very much about Miss Bingley's mind, but I was convinced her influence on Amelia-Jane would not be benign. I recall clearly the words of Mrs Reynolds, who was our housekeeper at Pemberley, about the influence of Miss Bingley on Georgiana Darcy; she was very unhappy, felt it did her no good at all."

Charlotte was still unconvinced.

"But surely, Eliza, is it likely that Miss Bingley would try deliberately to harm either Amelia-Jane or Jonathan?"

"I do not mean to suggest, Charlotte, that she set out to harm them physically; I do not believe that even Caroline, arrogant and proud though she may be, would have advised anything as foolhardy and dangerous as travelling to Bath, at night, in an unsuitable vehicle, in the midst of a thunderstorm. For that particular piece of stupidity, we have to thank Caroline's friend Mrs Arabella Watkins and the mysterious Mr Alexander. But, remember it was Caroline Bingley's meddling, her interference that had Amelia-Jane involved with Mrs Watkins and God knows with what silly notions they filled her brain. No, Charlotte, Miss Bingley is going to have to live with this catastrophe on her conscience for quite a while," she replied.

Charlotte had not seen Elizabeth in such a mood before, nor heard her speak of anyone with such anger and passion. Not since Wickham's elopement with Lydia had there been reason to do so.

Jane, despite her own reluctance to single out her sister-in-law for criticism, had to agree.

"Yes, Charlotte, I do agree with Lizzie that Caroline must carry some of the blame. Emma has told me today that Mrs Watkins encouraged Amelia-Jane's complaints and led her to believe that what she was doing was correct. She has had this from the housekeeper, Mrs Giles, who has expressed outrage at the liberties taken by Mrs Watkins and her gentleman friend while they were at Grosvenor Street."

Emma, who had come upstairs to inform them that Jonathan had returned from Annie Ashton's funeral, heard the comment and felt impelled to add her own opinion. "Indeed, Aunt Charlotte, you would be astonished at some of the things we have heard. Jonathan is still unaware of all this, but I intend to acquaint both Jonathan and my father with the facts. I do not believe either of them understand the extent to which Miss Bingley and her friends are responsible for this tragedy. It was they who fostered an atmosphere of discontent and supported her constant complaints about what was in many ways a most advantageous and happy marriage to a good man, whose love for her and their children has never been in question. Papa should know that his sister contributed to the destruction of that marriage and the death of poor Amelia-Jane, even though Miss Bingley will never admit to it."

Charlotte was incredulous. "Jane, Eliza, I had no knowledge of this," she said.

Jane, usually a reluctant participant in recrimination, confirmed that Mr Bingley had responded to his sister's letter with a rather curt note, quite unlike his usual affable style, urging her to stay out of her nephew's marital problems.

"He suggested that they should be encouraged to resolve their difficulties themselves, since her interference could only aggravate them," said Jane, recalling that her husband had read his letter to her before despatching it.

"I was quite surprised at the sharpness of his tone and said so, but he was adamant that Caroline should be warned to mind her own business. He was very angry," she said, and even in the midst of their sorrow, they smiled at the idea of a very angry Charles Bingley! No one could imagine it!

Emma and Jane went down to the parlour and found Jonathan with Anne-Marie and Miss Faulkner. Teresa had taken a weary little Cathy to bed.

Jonathan thanked both Emma and Anna Faulkner for their invaluable help with the children.

"I cannot thank both of you enough for your kindness and help. Miss Faulkner, it is hardly fair that you should give up your time to sit with the children, I really do thank you very much indeed. Emma, I know how tired you must be and yet, tomorrow, we must all travel to Hertfordshire."

He told them then of the arrangements for the funeral, to be held at the church in Longbourn, as Charlotte had wished.

Soon afterwards, Bingley and Mr Darcy arrived and went with Jonathan into the study, where they spent some time together. Both father and son looked so anguished, it was with relief that Elizabeth and Jane went out to acquire their mourning gowns, even though there was no pleasure to be had in the task.

Emma and Anna Faulkner stayed on with Jonathan for a while longer, awaiting the carriage that was to call for them, during which time he told them of the heartrending funeral he had attended in Kent that morning.

"Annie Ashton was a bright, happy girl; I remember her when she would come over to play with the girls, always cheerful and lively. She was devoted to them and to Amelia-Jane. The Ashtons have lost their only daughter, because she was Amelia-Jane's maid and was taken on this ridiculous journey, and yet, they were so civil to me. I expected some resentment, hatred even, but there was none of it. Not a harsh word, no resentful stares; they thanked me for coming … I could not believe it. I have never been so disconcerted … I felt so utterly unworthy of their regard and gratitude!" he said.

Emma was quick to comfort him. "My dear brother, you really must not take all this upon yourself; how are you to blame for any of what happened? I feel for the Ashtons, we can understand their pain, but they must know it was an accident, something over which you could have had no control," she declared.

"Indeed," he said, nodding as if in agreement, but adding with a tinge of sarcasm in his voice, "but, no doubt they would have expected me to have some modicum of control over the activities of my wife."

When she looked uncertain, he added, "No, Emma, you are very kind, but I know how they must feel. It is common knowledge in the village of Hunsford and around the Rosings Estate that Amelia-Jane had decided to leave me and move to Bath.

"The servants at the Dower House knew it; Annie Ashton's family knew it, too. Mrs Harrison's servants told her of it. It seems, I was the only person who did not know."

His voice seemed to break and a sudden, involuntary gasp from Anna, who had been sitting quietly by the window while Jonathan and Emma talked, lest her presence should embarrass them, drew his attention to her and he was immediately apologetic.

"Miss Faulkner, we have embarrassed you with these unhappy details of our troubles, I am truly sorry. We should not burden you with these particulars … please pay no attention, it was thoughtless of me."

Anna was startled into speaking out at once. "Mr Bingley, pray do not apologise, you are surely entitled to speak your own mind on any subject in your own house, even more at such a time as this. My presence here is purely incidental; I am truly happy to be of any assistance at this time and do not wish to cause you the slightest inconvenience. Please let me assure you that anything I may have heard in this house will go no further than myself. Though we were never very close, Amelia-Jane was my cousin."

He was most appreciative of her words and as she and Emma rose to leave, took her hand and thanked her again for her kindness.

Embracing his sister, he asked that James Wilson and the Armandes be informed of the funeral arrangements and escorted them to the waiting carriage.

As he handed them into the carriage, first Emma and then Miss Faulkner, he thanked them once more and, as they drove away, Anna observed him standing on the pavement, looking at the vehicle as it proceeded down the street, and wondered if he were thinking of that other, ill-fated vehicle which must have left this place just as theirs had done, on another journey but a few days ago.

How utterly had his life changed since then, she thought, feeling in her heart deep sympathy for his anguish.

The prospect of a further half day's journey to Hertfordshire on the following day, and perhaps another night or two at Longbourn, did not please Elizabeth, but there was nothing they could do. Charlotte had asked for her daughter to be laid to rest amongst her family, and Jonathan had agreed.

Bingley and Jane decided to remain at the house in Grosvenor Street with Jonathan and the girls, while Elizabeth and Darcy went on to Portman Square.

It was the first time they had been alone since they had received the news of the accident. When they retired to their room, Elizabeth asked, "Do you suppose Amelia-Jane really meant to leave Jonathan and her children?"

It was a question that had engaged her thoughts for some time.

Darcy was unsure. "Who can say, my dear? It certainly seems that way. It is indeed difficult to believe she would depart in so unceremonious a manner, in such an unsuitable vehicle—I believe the police have told James that it lost a wheel on the downhill run from Maidenhead!—with no reason or plan in mind. It is an extraordinary thing to have done."

"It appears she gave Jonathan no warning," said Elizabeth. "She left no letters, said no farewells, not even to the children. Emma says when Jonathan heard she had left, he was so shocked, he could not speak for several minutes."

"I can well believe it. Jonathan has such a strong sense of family loyalty and self-discipline, it would never occur to him that anyone, however distressed, could behave in such a way. It seems an act of reckless self-indulgence," said Darcy, whose affection and respect for Jonathan was of the highest order.

Apart from their son-in-law, Richard Gardiner, Jonathan Bingley was, in Mr Darcy's book, the very best of men. He could not accept that so terrible a blow had fallen upon such a man of honour and integrity. And yet, he knew, as did Elizabeth, that disappointment and sorrow could strike without warning or logical reason, destroying dreams and inflicting deep wounds.

Elizabeth and Darcy had suffered the loss of their eldest son in just such a circumstance, where Death like a thief in the night steals the core of one's happiness and nothing, no matter how many other joys may follow, ever restores the loss.

During a long and weary night, they relived those terrible hours and days, as they thought of Jonathan and his children and sought to comfort each other before sleep would finally come.

꧁꧂

It was a cold, crisp morning when they attended the funeral service at the village church, which was filled with neighbours, friends, and family.

Charlotte Collins' mother, father, and eldest brother lay in the same churchyard where no doubt Charlotte herself hoped to rest one day.

It had been a grim, painful day for everyone, most of all for Charlotte.

Proud of the achievement of bringing up three young daughters single-handed and seeing them all well married, Charlotte had been ravaged by the shame and guilt she felt on her daughter's behalf.

Even though it was not yet generally known that Amelia-Jane had been killed while leaving her husband and children in a senseless and wilful act, Charlotte knew and, in her heart, felt deep remorse.

She saw Amelia-Jane's actions as a betrayal not only of her husband and children, but of all she had believed in and taught her children by both precept and example.

Furthermore, Charlotte regarded Jonathan Bingley so highly; he combined qualities of goodness and generosity with an engaging disposition inherited from his excellent parents. To have to live with the thought that her daughter had caused him so much grief was almost too much to bear.

Over and over again during the past week, she had expressed to Jonathan her personal sorrow and regret and, each time, he had patiently assured her, with great generosity of spirit, that she must not take on the guilt of her daughter's actions.

"My dear Mrs Collins," he had said, "were I to look for someone to blame for this misfortune, other than myself or my late wife, you would be the very last person I would choose. I beg of you, do not distress yourself and do not take on the burden of our guilt, it will be a fruitless and bitter load," he had advised.

He had sought, then, to comfort her by assuring her that he and Amelia-Jane had enjoyed many years of happiness and he would never regret their marriage, nor permit her name to be dishonoured because of her recent indiscretions. Charlotte knew he spoke sincerely, for indeed, at no time had she ever had reason to doubt his feelings for Amelia-Jane and had long regarded them as happily and success-fully married. She'd had no indication that there was any serious disharmony between them, which was why the last few days had seemed like a nightmare.

For Jonathan, the entire week had been so appalling, that the desolation of the final day was merely an added tribulation that had to be endured.

He had been surprised by the large numbers of people who had travelled to Longbourn, including many Parliamentary colleagues who joined family and friends at the church.

He was grateful for the support of all his family, who stood with him and Anne-Marie as, heartsick and grieving, they had struggled through the ceremonies. Astonishingly, Charlotte Collins and her two elder daughters, Catherine Harrison and Rebecca Tate, seemed calm and demonstrated great strength as they joined him at the graveside.

Charles, his son, stood apart from his father and sisters, while Caroline Bingley did not attend. Her sister, Mrs Hurst, arrived and was heard to say that Caroline had suffered a seizure on hearing the news of the accident and the deaths of Amelia-Jane and her friends.

Cassandra Darcy had overheard her say that Miss Bingley had been confined to bed since then. Her mother Elizabeth, on hearing this piece of news, remarked abruptly that it might be best for all concerned if Miss Bingley were permanently confined!

Even Jane, who was hardly ever heard to utter a harsh word against anyone, could not resist expressing her gratitude that indisposition had prevented Miss Bingley from attending Amelia-Jane's funeral, for, she declared, she was quite sure no one, not even her nearest and dearest, would have welcomed her presence.

It was a sentiment echoed by almost everyone there.

Finally, it was all over and Jonathan, free at last of the need to maintain a brave exterior, left the gathering at Longbourn and drove alone to Netherfield, where he could give vent to his own feelings, without fear of exposure. It was there that Mr Darcy and Richard Gardiner found him an hour or so later, walking aimlessly in the park.

While understanding his desire for solitude, they encouraged him to return to Longbourn, where Emma Wilson and Anna Faulkner had spent all afternoon comforting Anne-Marie and her younger sisters.

"You must come back, Jonathan. The girls need you with them at this time," said Richard, and Darcy added that he and Fitzwilliam had succeeded in fending off the queries of most of his friends from London.

"I think you can assume quite safely that they accept it was an accident and will leave you alone; there will be no gossip," he said as they persuaded him to return with them.

While most of the family returned to their respective homes, Mr and Mrs Bingley stayed on at Netherfield with Jonathan and his daughters.

Young Charles Bingley, however, in an uncharitable act that no one could understand or condone, returned to Edinburgh without a word to his father.

Jane and Bingley had tried hard to persuade him to stay, but he had remained intransigent, saying only that his father had never had a great deal of time for him and he did not believe things would be any different now.

Returning to the house in Grosvenor Street some weeks later, having first accompanied Anne-Marie to Harwood House and the care of her friend Eliza Harwood, Jonathan Bingley found several calling cards and messages of condolence awaiting his attention. He spent an hour or more responding to them. Most were from colleagues and friends who had been unable to travel to Longbourn for the funeral.

Having finished the rather tedious task, he decided to walk up the street and call on the Wilsons. Since the funeral, after which they had returned to London, he had missed their company. He yearned for Emma's kindness and her husband's unvarying generosity of spirit.

Disappointed to discover that they had, that very morning, left London for Standish Park, he was at a loss, not knowing what he would do with his time. His two younger girls were with their grandmother at Ashford Park and he was on his own, alone for the first time in weeks.

In no mood to face the camaraderie of his club, he was about to retrace his steps, reluctantly, facing a lonely evening at home, when a cab slowed down and Monsieur Armande, leaning out, called to him.

He could tell from Jonathan's smile that he was exceedingly pleased to see him. Stopping the vehicle, he opened the door and invited him to "join me for a drink." Jonathan climbed in, clearly happy to accept.

Madame Armande was delighted to see him.

"You will stay to dinner, yes?" she asked, and he did not need much persuasion to agree.

It was certainly a far better prospect than dining alone.

Monsieur Armande got their drinks and, as they talked, he brought out some of the material he planned to use in the Art School, the opening of which was fast approaching. Indeed, it was less than a fortnight away. Monsieur Armande was anxious to have Jonathan's opinion on the program he had drawn up and though his friend protested that he was not, by any means, qualified to pass judgment on such matters, Monsieur had too high an opinion of him to pay much attention to such a little matter.

They had been involved in their discussion for some time when the front door opened and Miss Faulkner came in. Rising to greet her, Jonathan noticed that her complexion glowed and her eyes shone with the exercise of walking in the brisk Autumn air.

She explained that she was returning from Evensong. She had enjoyed the walk across the park, she said

"You've been at the Abbey?" asked Jonathan, who had heard the Abbey's celebrated choir often, on ceremonial occasions.

Anna smiled. "Oh no, nowhere as grand as the Abbey; at St Margaret's, where they sing just as sweetly and with much less fuss. I find it more restful than its larger neighbour. Have you never been?" she asked, and Jonathan confessed reluctantly that he had not.

"For shame," she said with a little laugh that indicated she was only teasing and was not seriously censuring him, "You do know it is the parish church of the Parliament?"

"Indeed, I do," he said, with a self-deprecatory smile, "I know I ought to attend more often."

She was so enthusiastic about the beauty of the young voices that Jonathan promised to come along and hear them one day, very soon. When she assured him he would not regret it, he said, "You have certainly persuaded me, Miss Faulkner, but, while I admire and enjoy fine singing, I must confess I am a mere novice in the appreciation of church music."

As if emboldened by her initial success, she promised that it would give her great pleasure to instruct him, since choral music was surely one of the most sublime of human achievements.

Jonathan then declared that he would no longer delay his enjoyment of such a singular pleasure and an appointment was made to attend the church of St Margaret at Westminster the following Sunday.

Clearly pleased, she went upstairs to put away her bonnet and wrap and returned to find them discussing the program for the Art School.

Monsieur Armande had already told him that Anna would be assisting him with the teaching. Now, he revealed that she had been entrusted with a set of lessons in Still Life studies, which she had been busy preparing.

When Jonathan expressed an interest, she brought out her folio and let him see her work, in the same unpretentious manner in which she had played for them when he had first dined at Haye Park.

Jonathan genuinely admired her work and admitted he was looking forward to the exhibition.

"It would do no good to try to teach me," he said modestly. "I could never draw, but my lack of skill has made me an even greater devotee of the work of those who can and I do look forward to seeing your work and that of your students, of course."

Madame joined them as they went in to dinner and revealed that there had been a great deal of interest in the classes; Monsieur Du Pont was very pleased.

"We have already enrolled twenty-seven, mostly young ladies, but one or two gentlemen also," she explained as they sat around the table.

Monsieur Armande expressed great pleasure and declared that he had not hoped for half that number.

Jonathan, sitting next to Madame and opposite Anna, could not help noticing how well Anna looked. She had removed her outdoor coat and wrap and wore a simple gown of deep blue silk, which seemed to highlight her eyes and brilliant complexion. As they talked, she spoke eagerly and without affectation on matters that interested her, remaining silent when the conversation drifted to other subjects.

He was not given to paying compliments, being, for all his time in London and at Westminster, rather shy and afraid of giving offence.

On this occasion, however, he was a little less diffident and, taking the opportunity afforded by the absence of both Armandes from the room for a few moments, he told her how well the colour suited her and was rewarded for his courage with a smile that lit up her face and a sincere expression of thanks.

The rest of the evening was spent in such various and interesting discussions as absorbed all of the hours between dinner and midnight, when Jonathan, alerted by the chiming of the clock, leapt up, apologised for keeping them so late, said goodnight, and left rather abruptly.

Refusing Monsieur Armande's offer to accompany him, he set off to walk to Grosvenor Street.

The distance was certainly not great, and it was a fine night. Though the trees had begun to shed their Autumn leaves, he enjoyed the clear, cold air as he crossed the Square and chose deliberately to walk through St James' Park, instead of taking his usual route.

It had turned out to be such a satisfying evening, he could scarcely believe how depressed he had felt at the start of it, facing the prospect of a solitary supper. How fortuitously Monsieur Armande had appeared just as he had decided to return to Grosvenor Street.

Jonathan was very grateful to the Armandes. Their company and their generous hospitality had made a great difference to his life.

And of course, there was Miss Faulkner, in whom he found more to admire and esteem each time they met. He looked forward to their next appointed meeting at St Margaret's Church, with a keen anticipation of pleasure.

For the first time in months, Jonathan Bingley felt liberated from the melancholy that had afflicted him.

It was an exhilarating feeling.

End of Part One

NETHERFIELD PARK REVISITED

Part Two

IN THE LATE AUTUMN of 1859, the government of Lord Palmerston was almost totally obsessed with the questions of Italian freedom and unity. The Prime Minister, with his able Chancellor Gladstone and his enlightened Foreign Minister Lord Russell, believed it was in England's interest to take up the Italian cause and did so most assiduously throughout the year and into the next.

In the lobbies and corridors of Westminster, the names of Count Cavour and Garibaldi were heard more often and spoken with greater regard than were those of the working class leader John Bright or the champion of individual liberty, John Stuart Mill.

It appeared as though neither the improvement of the conditions of the artisans and their families nor the freedom of the individual had for Palmerston the same urgency as the need to gain for Britain an advantage in Europe, through the support of Italian unification.

Jonathan Bingley, whose interest in foreign affairs was far outweighed by his desire to press for Reform of the electoral laws, which still prevented most working class men and all women from voting, found little to interest him in the matters that absorbed the time and effort of the Parliament.

In fact, since the death of his wife and the purchase of Netherfield Park, he had felt even less enthusiastic about returning to Westminster as a Member of the House of Commons. On several occasions, he had turned over in his mind the idea of standing down from the position he had taken with the party, but had postponed the decision out of consideration for his brother-in-law, James Wilson.

In the course of the following week, when the Parliament was not sitting, he took the opportunity to attend to a number of outstanding matters.

Initially, he had, with Anne-Marie's help, gone through Amelia-Jane's things, keeping some of her personal trinkets and ornaments for either the children or their grandmother Mrs Collins and sending most of her clothes away to a charity that Eliza Harwood ran for widows of the war.

In the process, he'd had a rather unpleasant surprise, discovering a large number of unpaid bills that had come in. In the present unhappy state of his family, Jonathan did not feel inclined to speak of it to Mrs Collins; instead, he took them down to Netherfield, where he could peruse them in private.

They were, for the most part, bills from shops and warehouses, mainly for clothes, food, and wine, though in one or two cases, even Jonathan was unable to decipher what they were for. There was, however, no doubt that they were genuine and would have to be paid.

Then, there was the matter of his wife's will.

Perhaps the final irony lay in the revelation that she had recently changed her will, to leave almost all her valuable jewellery and some small number of gold sovereigns to Mrs Arabella Watkins. Indeed, to do so, she had taken them away from Miss Caroline Bingley, who for some unknown reason seemed to have suddenly lost favour with her.

The lawyers, an old and trusted family firm, explained that they had tried their best to dissuade Mrs Bingley, but to no avail. Now that Mrs Watkins was no more, they had informed Jonathan that his eldest daughter, Miss Anne-Marie Bingley, would inherit it all. Mercifully, she would never discover that she was her mother's third choice, receiving her inheritance only "in the event of Mrs Watkins' earlier demise."

It was almost too bizarre to contemplate, especially in view of the fact that most of the items so bequeathed had been gifts to her from her husband or his parents.

Jonathan decided to tell no one except Charlotte Collins, to whom he handed over several of her daughter's trinkets and a few pieces of jewellery not itemised in the will. He believed, rightly, that she would appreciate them for their sentimental value. Mrs Collins was grateful for her son-in-law's thoughtfulness. The little velvet case he brought her contained a bracelet of coloured stones, an ivory brooch, and some rings—all dating from the early years of their marriage. Charlotte could not wear them, they were far too youthful for her, yet they had a greater value as keepsakes.

She thanked him sincerely and invited him to stay to dinner. She was dining alone, she said.

"Unfortunately, Miss Bennet is not feeling well enough to come down tonight. She has been rather poorly since the funeral. Sarah has taken her a light dinner. She eats very little," she explained.

Jonathan was most concerned and, before leaving Hertfordshire the next day, he called again to enquire after his aunt's health.

Mrs Collins reported that she was feeling a little better but still too weak to leave her room.

Perturbed by her news, Jonathan proceeded to Standish Park to visit Emma and James. He wanted to thank them for their unfailing support during the dreadful days and weeks just past and consult them about the situation at Longbourn.

Under the terms of his grandfather Mr Bennet's will, when Miss Mary Bennet died, Jonathan would inherit the entire property, including the house. He had begun to wonder about the position of Mrs Collins in such a situation. He was well aware that, although she would be welcome to stay with either of her daughters, Rebecca Tate in Derbyshire or Catherine Harrison in Kent, Charlotte Collins had a strong preference for continuing to live independently in Hertfordshire.

For his part, Jonathan wished to do his best to accommodate her, especially since Lucas Lodge, the family home in which she had grown up, was now occupied by her brother's children and virtually closed to her.

"What would you suggest, Emma?" he asked, as they sat in the drawing room after dinner, on the evening of his arrival.

His sister was unwilling to even consider the prospect of another death in the family so soon after Amelia-Jane's funeral.

"Surely, my dear Jonathan, it cannot be such a pressing problem. I know our aunt Mary is not as well as she used to be, but I do not believe it is a life-threatening condition. I hope she will recover soon and live on for many more years. It is quite distressing to consider it at this stage," she protested.

Jonathan understood and did not press the matter, which was clearly upsetting his sister.

"Dear Emma, pray do not upset yourself, I asked only because of the position of Mrs Collins at Longbourn. I have no objection at all to her staying on, but it may be best to have it clearly understood in what capacity she stays. It would save her any embarrassment in the future," he explained.

James Wilson, himself a lawyer by profession, agreed with Jonathan, even though he hoped it was a problem that they would not have to face for a while yet if Miss Mary Bennet recovered from her present illness, as they all hoped she would.

Amelia-Jane's unpaid bills, however, were quite another matter and had to be given immediate attention.

Emma was shocked to discover how much money was owed to how many tradesmen, shopkeepers, and merchants. In a few cases, it was not clear who had placed the orders and then, there was even some housekeeping money owing to Mrs Giles!

"Poor, silly, misguided Amelia-Jane. It is quite clear now that her so-called friends Mrs Watkins and Mr Alexander were exploiting her and she, poor thing, was none the wiser," said Emma, outraged by the information Jonathan had put before them.

Her brother agreed, adding that despite some very good advice from her mother, his wife had never taken money matters seriously.

"At first, it was something of a joke between us, when she used to run through her allowance midway through the month, but gradually it became more embarrassing and less funny," he said and, turning to James, asked, "James, would you please instruct your clerk to attend to these bills? You can draw on my account with you to settle them. Anne-Marie has already written to some of them and I have settled Mrs Giles' account and paid the caretaker at the Dower House, who was owed two months wages!"

James was happy to oblige, relieved that the financial obligations had not been greater.

As Jonathan prepared to return to London, Emma and James were eager to discover when he intended to move permanently to Netherfield Park. He smiled for the first time that evening and Emma noticed a look of real satisfaction upon his tired face as he anticipated the pleasure.

"Quite soon, indeed, as soon as I have had a few changes made to some of the rooms. I find the main bedroom too ornate and dark, and the drapes in the study and drawing room may have to be changed; the colours are rather over-powering—all that heavy plum-coloured velvet!" he said with a grimace. "I intend to get some sound advice on the matter while I am in town and get the work started very soon."

He bade them farewell and, before getting into his carriage, said, "You must all come and stay at Netherfield when I have settled in there, bring the children too, there is plenty of room. Mama tells me it is quite beautiful in Spring!" and he was on his way, leaving Emma hopeful that her brother was, finally, recovering from the shock and distress of the last few months.

❦

He made the journey to London in good time, stopping only a few hours at Rochester to rest the horses and snatch some sleep.

The following day being Sunday, he rose late, read the papers, wrote some letters and, in the evening, went out to St Margaret's Church in the shadow of the great Abbey at Westminster, where he was to meet Miss Faulkner at Evensong.

Alighting from his carriage and crossing the road to the church, he had an irrational feeling that she may have forgotten their appointment or changed her mind, leaving him alone in the unfamiliar church. He could not explain it to himself, but a disconcerting feeling of panic assailed him as he entered the church and did not immediately see her there. But it was only momentary, for as his footsteps sounded in the nave, a young woman in a bonnet of lilac and grey turned around, and he saw his fears had been groundless; she was here already.

He joined her in a pew some distance from the chancel, where the priest was reading from the Book of Common Prayer. After the reading, the priest and his attendants retired to their seats below the altar steps, and the choir sang, first a psalm and then a glorious anthem. As Anna softly explained the order of service, the sublimely beautiful young voices rose, creating an almost ethereal sound that Jonathan found profoundly moving.

After the closing hymn, they left the church and stepped out into the late evening light. She turned to ask if he had enjoyed the music but did not; seeing the unmistakable expression of pleasure that suffused his face, she knew he had clearly been deeply moved.

He spoke before she did. Taking her hand in his, he said, "Thank you, Anna. I can say quite sincerely that was one of the loveliest experiences of my life. Thank you for asking me. I am very grateful."

She had not expected such a deep response and did not know quite what to say—except that she was happy it had brought him so much pleasure.

They had by now crossed the road and he was about to hand her into the carriage, when he stopped and said, as if on impulse, "It is such a beautiful evening and there is still so much light in the sky, shall we walk back through the park?"

When she agreed without any hesitation, for she was very fond of walking, he looked pleased and gave instructions to his driver to take the carriage round to Belgrave Square and wait for him.

Turning to Anna, he offered her his arm.

As they walked, he asked after the health of Monsieur and Madame Armande and, being assured they were well, there followed other questions about preparations for the Art School including her own classes.

Was everything in readiness for the opening? She said it was and he was happy to hear it.

Then it was her turn to ask if he had left Mrs Collins and Miss Mary Bennet in good health. He mentioned his aunt's indisposition and she was concerned at her continuing ill health, pointing out that the onset of Winter was not far away. On hearing he had visited Standish Park, she wanted to be told about Emma Wilson. Was she well, and how were the children?

These queries filled up the time as they walked, each seeming reluctant to stop, lest the silence between them became awkward.

They had reached the lake and, as they made to walk around it, a flock of migrating birds flew in and wheeled across the water; they stopped to watch them.

In the silence that followed, Jonathan spoke, "Anna,"—he broke off. Self-conscious and a little awkward, he asked, "May I call you Anna?"

She smiled at the question.

"Of course you may, you have known me since I was a child. We are almost cousins!"

"We are indeed, thank you," he said and added, "Then you must call me Jonathan, I should like you to; besides, there are at least three Mr Bingleys in the family and what is the use of a name if no one ever uses it?"

Anna laughed and indicated that she would be happy to oblige him.

Returning to his original opening, now they were walking around the lake, he said, "Anna, please let me thank you from the bottom of my heart, no, not just for the pleasure of this evening, though that has been rare and lovely, but for all your kindness to me and my family, especially my young daughters.

"You gave of your time and attention so generously, and your willingness to comfort and help them … I fear I have no words to express my thanks. Please accept my heartfelt gratitude on their behalf and for myself."

His words took her by surprise. There was no doubting his sincerity.

Anna was silent at first, unable to respond; then recovering her composure, she urged him to accept everything she had done, even as she insisted it was very little, as part of the friendship and regard that she and her family had for him, his children, and all their family.

"Mr Bingley, Jonathan, you must believe me when I say it was a pleasure marred only by the sad circumstances in which it occurred. If the situation had been different, it would have been wholly enjoyable. Quite apart from the sense of duty I must feel towards them as my cousin Amelia's children, both Teresa and Cathy have such gentle, affectionate natures and are so well taught, I had no trouble keeping them occupied," she declared.

Jonathan, proud of his two young ones, said, "They are good girls, certainly. They were raised mostly by my mother and, as you know, she is the gentlest of women. Forgive me, I do not mean to speak ill of my late wife, but it is Mama I have to thank for Teresa and Cathy turning out as they have, and might I say, Anna, that they speak very warmly of you. My mother writes that Teresa has not ceased speaking of you since they returned to Ashford Park. She cannot wait to meet you again—something about a promise you made to her... ." He was smiling, and Anna laughed.

"A promise? Ah, I see Teresa has a good memory as well. Yes, I did promise to teach her to draw. She told me she did not like drawing, only colouring in outlines drawn for her by her teacher; so I promised to teach her how to draw, because that way, she will really be making her own pictures."

"That is indeed true and I am indebted to you for convincing her. She has been a little headstrong about learning to draw, not wanting to try."

"I am sure she will learn to enjoy it, if I have the opportunity to show her how," said Anna and then asked, "Do you expect to have them with you at Netherfield by Christmas?"

They were almost at Belgrave Square, and as he helped her across the road, he said, "It has not been decided yet, but I should like to. Anna, there is a related matter on which I need your advice, but there is not sufficient time today to discuss it. We shall talk about it very soon."

They were almost at the door, and his carriage was waiting. Although the Armandes both pressed him to stay and take tea with them, he had an appointment to dine with a colleague, he said, and promising to see them again soon, he climbed in and was driven away.

Anna Faulkner said nothing to her friends, but held close to her heart the delight she had felt in sharing with him the music at St Margaret's and their conversation during the walk through the park. She wondered what was the "related matter" upon which he would seek her advice. Could it possibly involve the girls, Cathy and Tess? She was impatient to know.

But, circumstances did not favour her; with the Armandes so busy with their preparations for the Art School, there was no opportunity for them to meet in the next few days and, with Parliament in recess, Jonathan Bingley did not remain long in London. He had work to do in Hertfordshire.

The school and exhibition of modern French Art conducted by the Armandes opened the following week, and while Jonathan avoided the formal opening by Monsieur Du Pont and a celebrated French woman, Madame Roussard, he did go round on the third day.

To his delight, he found Miss Faulkner taking a class of seven young ladies, who were trying to draw and presumably learn to paint in the French mode—a bowl of fruit, artistically tipped on its side, with its contents spilling out onto a crisp white napkin. On the wall above the subject was a similar painting—one of Anna's, which he had seen before in her folio. Framed and hung, it looked quite beautiful to his untutored eye.

Permitted to stand at the back of her class, Jonathan watched as Anna described and explained the difference in painting styles between the old classical artists and the avant-garde painters working on the tree-lined boulevardes and in the cafes of Paris.

He was fascinated by her knowledge of the work of Manet, Degas, and Latour, whose names he had not heard mentioned among the traditional Art circles in London.

She spoke and drew with unself-conscious ease as she showed her students how they could capture form and texture, and he could not help being drawn in and sharing their enthusiasm.

Later, while her students worked at their task, she joined him at the back of the class.

"They are so keen and work so hard, it is a joy to teach them," she said, smiling. "I think I could teach Art for the rest of my life."

He smiled and teased her, "And give up your music?"

"Oh no, never that, but much as I love my music, I am finding so much pleasure here … these young girls, they get such enjoyment out of doing this. I do not pretend that they will all develop into brilliant artists, but at least some of them will have improved their understanding and appreciation of Art, and perhaps one may produce a work worth hanging," she said, and he could see how eagerly she would help them as they worked to get the right effects of line, colour, and texture in their pictures.

"And through you, they will have all learned to take delight in the beauty of form and colour," he said, paying a tribute to the teacher.

She blushed, but acknowledged the compliment politely, expressing the hope that such appreciation was the aim of every artist.

Having further admired the work of pupils and teacher, he thanked her and left the room. An idea had occurred to him, one he was sure would work well, but judging that this was not the right time or place to advance it, he said nothing for the moment.

On his way out, he met Monsieur Armande, who had just completed a drawing class using a live model. Several keen-looking young men dressed in the kind of dishevelled style that art students seemed to affect, were admiring each other's work.

"Ah, it is so exhausting," declared Monsieur, as he stepped outside for a breath of fresh air and a cigar, "but so rewarding, Mr Bingley!"

Jonathan took the opportunity to congratulate him on the excellence of the display and invite them all to dinner on Friday night, an invitation that was happily accepted.

He was at pains to ensure that they had a good though not unduly extravagant meal ready when the Armandes and Anna Faulkner came to Grosvenor Street. Mrs Giles, having been advised that the Armandes were Catholic and ate no meat on Fridays, had instructed the cook, who had procured some excellent trout and salmon and plenty of fresh vegetables. These were turned into delectable dishes, which drew much praise from the guests.

Since there were no classes on Saturday, they could all relax after dinner in the drawing room, where coffee was served. They talked of the week's work and Anna's love of teaching Art. Monsieur Armande's generous praise of her work gave Jonathan the opportunity he had been waiting for.

"Miss Faulkner, when your work here is done, when you return home to Haye Park, would you consider doing some teaching of Art, Music, that sort of thing?" he asked.

When Anna looked puzzled and raised her eyebrows in surprise, he explained.

"My aunt, Miss Mary Bennet, has, as you know, a number of pupils, who attend for classes in Music at Longbourn. Recently, she has been ill and is, I fear, still rather weak. She may appreciate some help; if you were free to take on some of her pupils, you could perhaps let it be known that you would teach Art as well—or would you find that a dreadful chore?" he asked, a little uncertainty creeping into his voice.

"A dreadful chore to teach Art and Music?" she exclaimed. "Certainly not. Do you mean I could teach them at Longbourn?"

"Yes, if you agree, I would suggest it to my aunt. I know she is distressed at having to miss lessons; Mrs Collins has said so. I do realise that teaching young people can be exhausting—not everyone is equally talented; however, they will all pay a fee, of course," he said.

"And I could have my own Art students at Longbourn, as well?" she asked eagerly.

"Certainly, there is plenty of room; indeed, there is a back parlour which the ladies once used as a sewing room; it is spacious and well lit, but little used these days. It may suit you well as a studio."

"And my Aunt Charlotte would continue to live there?"

"Of course, that was part of my plan. I have been concerned of late, should anything happen to my aunt in the future, I would hope that Mrs Collins would not feel obliged to leave Longbourn. I know she would rather stay on in Hertfordshire than move to live in Derbyshire or Kent. Now, if the music school were to continue, and you were teaching there, I am sure she could be persuaded to stay on in some capacity," he explained.

Even as she listened, Anna was amazed at his generosity.

It was well known in the district that Longbourn had prospered under his management. Yet, instead of looking forward to a day when, as its owner, he could lease the valuable estate for profit, he was proposing a scheme that would accommodate her Aunt Charlotte.

"And would you continue to manage the estate?" she asked.

"Oh yes, that would remain unchanged, and it would be a good deal simpler once I moved permanently to Netherfield Park," he replied.

"And will that be soon?" asked Madame Armande, who had been listening with interest.

"I certainly hope so, Madame," said Jonathan. "I wish to have Teresa and Cathy over at Christmas. They are with my mother at present, and I miss them very much. Anne-Marie will come too, I think."

The Armandes, who were returning home to Brussels for Christmas, were sympathetic, and Anna's eyes lit up.

"That would be wonderful for them," she said, and Jonathan saw that this was his best opportunity to speak up.

"Yes, it will, but it does depend on whether I am able to get some things done in time."

This injected a note of uncertainty, and everyone was disappointed and demanded to know what could possibly delay the return of his daughters to their home.

Jonathan explained. "I need some advice on a few changes that are needed at the house," he said, and went on, as they listened, to detail his objection to the plum-coloured velvet drapes and some ornate accessories in the rooms. He thought the girls' rooms were rather gloomy, he said.

"I should like them to have a lighter, more welcoming appearance."

Monsieur Armande smiled and declared, "If that is all, Mr Bingley, you have not a problem. Anna here has a superb sense of design and colour, as well as excellent taste, so you have an artistic adviser on the spot, as it were."

Jonathan had not expected this windfall in the way of an introduction but, determined not to let the opportunity slip, turned to Anna Faulkner, "Will you be willing to advise me, Miss Faulkner?" he asked.

Anna's smile revealed she was very pleased to be asked, but she held back a little, not wanting to appear too eager or presumptuous.

Jonathan wanted to reassure her.

"I am not trying to make great changes," he said. "I should just like the house to look a little more … somewhat more like …"

As he struggled for the right words, she suggested, "A little more like a home, perhaps?"

"Exactly," he said, "it is rather more of a showplace at present. I think the interior designer took his commission very seriously and set out to create a perfect Georgian environment. The girls and I could do with a little less ornamentation and a little more homely comfort."

They all thought it was a splendid scheme.

Then Jonathan had an even better idea.

"How would you all like to come down to Netherfield Park with me? Next Saturday, after your Art School is over, we could travel down together, and you could all give me the benefit of your advice," he suggested.

Anna appeared more comfortable with this plan and agreed that it was a good idea to go and look at the house and its environs before discussing the changes he wished to make.

Jonathan guessed that her reluctance was the result of modesty, for he knew, having seen the interiors at Haye Park, which she had designed, that she would be well qualified to advise on such matters.

Without more ado, dates and times were arranged for their "grand expedition to Netherfield Park," as Monsieur Armande put it, and by the time the visitors left, there was an air of anticipation surrounding the project.

Jonathan did not wish to acquaint anyone in his family with the reason for his journey to Netherfield with the Armandes, but seeing that Anna Faulkner was to be of the party, it was bound to get about that they were arriving. While the Armandes were to stay at Netherfield as his guests, Miss Faulkner had written to inform her mother that with the Art School ending, she was returning to Haye Park.

Almost two days prior to their arrival in Hertfordshire, Lydia Wickham and Jessie Phillips arrived at Longbourn with the news.

"Charlotte! Mary! You'll never guess what we have just discovered. Mr Bingley is arriving from London with a large party to stay at Netherfield and Miss Anna Faulkner is with them," Lydia announced and, having waited a moment or two for the desired effect, added with a degree of archness that quite belied her age, "Now, can you think why Miss Faulkner would be coming to Netherfield with Mr Bingley?"

Charlotte Collins, who'd had very little patience with Lydia in her youth, had even less tolerance of her silliness now, when her vacuous mind held little more than local gossip, which she happily retailed to all and sundry.

"Lydia," she said rather sharply, "are you sure? I cannot believe that Mr Bingley would come to Netherfield without informing us. He is a most meticulously polite gentleman and his inspection of the property is not due for a fortnight."

Lydia was completely unmoved by Charlotte's doubts.

"Well, that's as may be, Charlotte, but I can assure you it is a fact, because the servant from Netherfield was at the butcher's giving orders for meat and poultry to be taken up to the house on Thursday, and Jessie's maid is the half-sister of the gardener's boy at Netherfield, and she had it from him that the Master was arriving, so you can depend upon it," she boasted, proud of the authenticity of her information.

"What of it?" said Mary, who regarded servants' gossip as unreliable anyway. "Surely if Jonathan Bingley wishes to bring a party to stay at Netherfield, he may do so without half the village being informed of it. He has bought the place, has he not?"

"Indeed he has, Aunt," Jessie Phillips declared, not to be outdone by Lydia, "but the question is, what does Miss Anna Faulkner have to do with it?"

This pointless argument could well have gone around forever, had a note not been delivered for Charlotte from her sister, Maria Faulkner.

Charlotte excused herself and retreated to her room to read it, unwilling to let their visitors discover who it was from or what it contained.

Once in her room, she opened up her letter.

Maria, who was a good deal younger than her sister, still treated Charlotte with great respect and in her note asked if Charlotte and Mary would dine with them on the following Sunday, when Anna would be returning home from London, where she had spent most of the Summer.

> *She is coming down with her Belgian friends, the Armandes, who are very charming and I know you will enjoy meeting them again after all these years.*
>
> *Mr Jonathan Bingley is coming also, since he has invited the Armandes to see Netherfield House, before they leave England.*
>
> *Dr Faulkner and I thought it would be nice to have a little dinner party for our Anna and ask them. If you and Miss Bennet would like to join us, we would be just the right number for a very nice party …*

Charlotte was delighted.

She had met the Armandes some years ago and been very impressed with them. It would be pleasant indeed to meet them again, she thought.

But she was quite determined that Lydia and Jessie Phillips would not have this news from her, to spread around the village.

She was sure Mary would not wish to go and thought she would have to write to Maria and ask her to send their curricle for her early in the evening.

Pondering how this might be arranged, she went downstairs and was relieved to find that the two women from Meryton had left.

Mary was happy to be rid of them, too. She had very little time for her silly younger sister, especially since age had brought no improvement at all in her understanding or conduct.

When Charlotte told her of the Faulkners' invitation, she was surprised to find that Mary was quite determined to attend.

"I have heard very good reports of the Armandes from your sister Maria," she said. "I must meet them. Please thank Maria, Charlotte, and accept for me, as well. I am looking forward to seeing Anna again, too; she is such a talented young woman and yet so modest, unlike most of the foolish creatures in society today," she declared, and Charlotte agreed that her niece Anna was the very model of an accomplished young lady.

So it was arranged they would go to dinner at Haye Park on Sunday and both ladies looked forward to the occasion with much anticipation.

When Jonathan Bingley and his guests reached Netherfield Park, they were welcomed by his new housekeeper, Mrs Perrot, a very capable and pleasant woman, who had once served his parents as a parlour maid and came highly recommended from her last employer.

Having had their luggage taken upstairs, she proceeded to serve them a splendid afternoon tea in the saloon, where a lively fire kept them warm.

The room, which used to serve as an informal parlour, had been refurbished and was now a well-proportioned space, handsomely fitted up with elegant Regency furniture, of the type Anna particularly admired. Light and welcoming, with a pretty prospect from its windows, which opened to the floor, of the northern part of the park extending to the woods beyond, it was indeed a happy choice as a reception room for visitors.

While Jonathan had no recollection of the original interiors, Mrs Perrot was a veritable mine of detailed information on this and other parts of the house for, as she explained to the ladies, she had spent almost eighteen months at Netherfield with the Bingleys, before the family moved away to Leicestershire.

Anna and her friends were especially interested, and since she was to advise on changes to drapes and accessories where necessary, she had extracted from Mrs Perrot a promise to be available to accompany her through the rooms on the following day.

"I think it will be best to see them in daylight," said Anna, and Mrs Perrot agreed enthusiastically.

"Oh indeed ma'am, the rooms upstairs are too dark to be seen at their best after four o'clock at this time of year."

After tea, Miss Faulkner was conveyed to her parents' house, a few miles away, escorted by Mr Bingley, while the Armandes were shown up to their rooms, where they could rest a while before changing for dinner.

"We must have you home before dark, Anna," said Jonathan, "or your parents will begin to worry."

The Armandes noted his solicitude with some amusement, and so must the housekeeper. What Mrs Perrot thought of all this is not known, but one could be confident that, while she was not the type to gossip about her employer, she would certainly share her knowledge with her sister, who just happened to be the cook at Longbourn.

It was not long, therefore, before Charlotte Collins and Mary Bennet heard of the unusual arrival at Netherfield of Mr Bingley and his small party of friends, including Miss Faulkner, and the even more remarkable fact that they appeared to be inordinately interested in the furnishings and accessories of his recently purchased home.

The information, which by the time it reached Charlotte's ears had become somewhat garbled in the retelling, caused some confusion among the ladies of Longbourn. They could not imagine why the Armandes would be advising Jonathan Bingley on the interiors at Netherfield, unless they intended to rent or lease the place.

Not privy to Jonathan's plans, they were beginning to speculate wildly, when at a most opportune moment—in the middle of their morning tea—the gentleman himself arrived on Sunday morning. He was, he said, on his way home from church and had come by to acquaint them with his plans and apologise for not writing to advise of his visit.

"There was just so much to do, with all the legal matters to be settled, and I have been very busy; I do apologise for not writing. Indeed, at this very moment, I believe Monsieur and Madame Armande and Miss Faulkner are being shown around the house by Mrs Perrot, so they can advise me on the redecoration of some of the rooms," he explained and added, "I am truly indebted to Monsieur Armande and his wife, who have offered to help Miss Faulkner, else I would not have the work finished by Christmas. The rooms must be made ready for Tess and Cathy, who together with Anne-Marie will be joining me for Christmas, and I hope both you ladies will spend Christmas Day with us at Netherfield."

This approach so charmed the ladies of Longbourn that they were no longer concerned at the invasion of Netherfield by "foreigners."

As for the involvement of Miss Faulkner, her mother had already been over to tell them how delighted she was that Anna's artistic talents were being recognised.

"She has been asked to advise Mr Bingley on the refurbishment of Netherfield, just as she did for us at Haye Park. Mr Bingley was extremely impressed with our interiors when he came to dinner, and I told him our Anna had done it all herself, choosing the colours and materials, designing the pelmets and everything. So you see, sister, when he needed some advice about Netherfield, he turned to Anna, of course. And why should he not? She is as good as any professional, Dr Faulkner says," declared Maria Faulkner, with the confidence of a proud mother.

If Charlotte had had any reservations about the Armandes, they were soon cleared away when she met the Belgian couple at the Faulkners' that evening.

During a particularly good dinner and the very pleasant evening of music and conversation which followed, both ladies were agreeably impressed with the charm and competence of the Armandes.

By the end of the evening, Mrs Collins and Miss Bennet were agreed that they could feel quite confident that the refurbishment of Netherfield was in good hands. Being undertaken under the artistic supervision of Miss Faulkner, with the help of the Armandes, they had no doubt the work would make the old Georgian place more comfortable for Mr Bingley and his daughters. The prospect that they would all be there together at Christmas added enough excitement to make it all worthwhile.

For Anna, the evening had been much more than a homecoming. At dinner, she had been seated next to Jonathan Bingley, and all their conversation had been on subjects that brought mutual pleasure and accord, for it seemed they were at one on many matters.

It had been many years since she had felt so at ease and in harmony with a gentleman, especially one who was some seventeen years her senior. She was conscious of his age, yet there was in no sense any feeling that he was patronising her or indulging her whims because she was a young woman.

At every point in their conversation, he paid attention to her opinions and frequently asked for information on matters where he freely admitted to being less well informed than herself.

Speaking of her Art class, which he had visited the previous week, he had expressed an interest in the unique styles of the new breed of young French painters, about whom she had been so enthusiastic and of whom he knew very little.

"I am probably not the best judge of artists, Anna, having spent most of my life viewing the work of classical painters in the collections at Pemberley and Rosings, but to me the pictures in your exhibition had a charming naturalness, a spontaneity which was quite new. It seemed a very fresh approach to painting," he said, as they waited for the dishes to be removed and the fruit and cheese to be placed on the table.

Anna, pleased that he had noticed the essential quality of the new art, congratulated him. "Indeed, you do yourself an injustice, you have noticed the very essence of the new art. It is spontaneous and fresh—there is a greater desire to capture an atmosphere or a vivid impression before it has fled, rather than spend hours upon the perfection of detailed line drawing. I find myself drawn to their work because it seems to express so much feeling for their subjects, whether they be portraits, landscapes, or still life. There is a personal warmth in them which I love."

"And do you have a favourite among them?" he asked, pleased to have her approval.

On this subject, she was less forthcoming. "It is not easy to pick out one amongst the many young men and indeed one or two women painters. Some have been refused entry to the Ecole des Beaux Arts because they were judged to be too modern and lacking the classical discipline; others do not even apply, wishing to be free of the strait-jacket of the school's teaching. If you press me to select one, I suppose I must pick Manet—he is a pupil of the great Thomas Couture, a most enlightened teacher of Art. But, I confess that I find the brilliant colours of Pierre Renoir enchanting, too," she said, her eyes sparkling.

Jonathan, though fascinated, did not wish to burden her further with questions, but vowed to take the very next opportunity to visit Paris and acquaint himself with the work of these remarkable new artists.

Monsieur Armande joined them as they left the dining parlour and, hearing Jonathan's words, invited him to call on them whenever he visited Europe, promising to show him the brightest and best stars of the new age.

"Miss Faulkner has been telling me of their struggles with the traditional schools," Jonathan said, and that set Monsieur Armande off, raging about old men who refused to see the beauty of anything new.

"Anna will tell you all about these young artists, she has studied them with great dedication; she has a wonderful sensitivity. Mr Bingley, I have taught many young Englishwomen in the last ten years, but never one with so much feeling for the art as Anna. When she speaks of a painting, be it a Corot landscape or a portrait by Rembrandt, she looks for the heart of the artist. Ah, if there were more students like her, there would be greater pleasure in being a teacher of Art," he said, wistfully.

Seeing the subject of their discourse approaching, Jonathan tried to change the conversation, to spare her any embarrassment, but Monsieur would not be diverted. Indeed, drawing her towards them by the hand, he told her she must "teach Mr Bingley to look at pictures as you do—not only with the eye, but with the heart. It is not always easy, but it is the right way," he declared.

Anna coloured as she met Jonathan's eyes, but smiled and said softly that she thought it would not be difficult, because it was clear to her that Mr Bingley had both a keen eye and a good heart.

So saying, she slipped away to attend to her Aunt Collins who needed help with getting her tea, leaving Jonathan feeling very happy indeed.

It was generally agreed at the end of the evening that it had been a most satisfying occasion for everyone.

Driving back to Netherfield with the Armandes, Jonathan was, for the most part, silent, while they were full of praise for Dr and Mrs Faulkner's hospitality and their daughter's charm and skill.

Bidding them goodnight, he retired to his room, not the elaborately finished master bedroom, which he found somewhat overpowering, but a smaller room at the end of the long corridor. He kept turning over the events of the evening in his mind and found himself enjoying the recollections. He looked forward very much to the coming week and anticipated the pleasure of seeing Anna again, soon. Recalling their long and interesting exchange during the evening, he acknowledged to himself that he had rarely enjoyed a conversation more.

Most of the women he met socially, outside of his family, were either wives or friends of colleagues. Their topics of conversation ranged from serious to silly, but rarely would they become involved in a discussion that could hold his interest for longer than a few minutes.

With Anna, it was very different, and Jonathan was becoming conscious of his appreciation of that difference. That she was also remarkably handsome merely enhanced his interest in her.

Maria Faulkner and her husband had retired to bed well pleased with the success of their modest dinner party. Being affectionate and proud parents, they were especially happy to have their daughter back at home.

They heard her come upstairs and, as she walked down the corridor, they could hear her singing softly a little scrap of music, the charming song from *Figaro*, which she had sung for them after dinner.

"It is nice to have our Anna home again, is it not, my dear?" Maria remarked, and her husband agreed.

"Indeed, it is, my dear, and especially to see her so happy. She seems almost light-hearted. If I did not know her better, I would have said she was in love," he said, regarding his wife over his glasses.

Maria was about to retort, when Anna looked in to say goodnight.

Both her parents, seeing her lovely smiling face in the doorway, said good-night and waited only till she had closed the door, before turning to each other and saying almost at once, "Perhaps she is!" But neither of them would speculate any further.

Monsieur and Madame Armande had no such qualms.

They had observed both their friends, for they had come to regard Jonathan Bingley with a high degree of respect and affection throughout the Summer and were quite convinced that it was inevitable that they would fall in love. They had no doubt about it at all.

Of course, there had been the terrible tragedy of Mrs Bingley's death and, while they had no knowledge of the details, they had drawn their own conclusions about the nature of their marriage.

Since then, however, they had watched, with barely concealed delight, the unmistakeable pleasure that Anna and Jonathan had in each other's company. They shared many interests and seemed so much at ease with one another. For two elderly romantics like the Armandes, there was only one possible conclusion to be drawn. They did caution each other, though, it was bad luck to anticipate another's happiness before the event, so they would say nothing.

As for Anna, she completed her toilette and went to bed.

She had admitted to herself, as she brushed her hair, that the evening had left her with a very special feeling of felicity, but being a young woman of discretion, she took care not to advertise her state of mind.

She did not lie awake long, but just before she fell asleep, she made a little mental note to ask Jonathan Bingley if he preferred Wedgwood blue drapes or mossy green ones in the main bedroom.

They had all agreed that the existing crimson brocade had to go. "Too much like Royalty," she had joked, and he had agreed absolutely.

Two days later, work began in earnest at Netherfield, and over the following fortnight, since time was of the essence, a feverish level of activity was reached.

The Armandes, who had no urgent need to return to London, were happy to accept Jonathan's hospitality at Netherfield, while advising on the redecoration. Jonathan had his steward organise a team of tradesmen and labourers, while Mrs Perrot gathered together a group of young women to do the sewing. The yard and back parlour began to resemble a manufacturing establishment, as they worked to carry out the changes required. Anna and Madame Armande measured, mixed, and matched, drawing innumerable sketches and trying out a range of ideas until they were satisfied they had the right one.

As to designs and colours, they had been given a free hand and, though the new Master of Netherfield was often consulted, he rarely found himself in disagreement with the ladies.

Some things, it was generally agreed, had to go.

First to come down, with not a single dissenting voice, were the "Royal Brocade" curtains in the main bedroom. Jonathan had confessed that he could never sleep in there while they remained. Together with the plum velvet in the drawing room and the rather gloomy grey and maroon stripe in the study, they were consigned to a basket in the attic.

"They'll do for charades and pantomimes," said Jonathan, firmly.

When the question arose of choosing colours for his own rooms, Anna insisted it was his choice since he had to live with them. He picked a very acceptable Wedgwood blue for the bedroom and a cream with deep green drapes for his study.

The Armandes praised his choice as being "far more modern" than the drab colours they had replaced.

The drawing room and library, which occupied the long spaces on either side of the main staircase and hallway, were both transformed by the use of ivory and cream, increasing the impression of light and air, since both rooms opened onto terraced gardens. Simplicity and good taste predominated throughout.

In the girls' rooms, which opened into each other, Anna had been reluctant to proceed without having them choose the colours, but they were in Leicestershire and the work had to be done before Christmas. When it was completed, however, her choice of soft French beige with rose printed drapes was applauded by all.

But the pièce de résistance was the inspired creation of an informal upstairs sitting room, much like the one at Haye Park, out of a rather cluttered space at the top of the stairs, where a tall window let in plenty of light and admitted a most attractive view of the park.

By banishing two formidable Chesterfields that had occupied most of the space, and replacing them with elegant Regency lounges taken from two of the unused bedrooms, adding some chairs, a table, and a writing desk, the area was changed dramatically into an inviting and useful sitting room.

So pleased was Jonathan with the result that he declared he would further enhance its appeal by purchasing for the walls two pictures he had admired in Monsieur Armande's display. Monsieur was delighted to oblige. The result would surely be a room that was a triumph of imagination and good taste—destined to become a favourite family retreat.

The weeks spent in redecoration and rearrangement at Netherfield would be remembered by all of them as some of the happiest days they had spent together. While they worked very hard, and, for Jonathan and Anna, there was no privacy and little time alone to permit any further exploration of their feelings, it did afford them opportunities to discover the many ideas and aspirations they shared.

For Jonathan, this was a novel experience. His courtship of Amelia-Jane had been so short and intense, his decision to propose marriage to her so precipitate as to surprise even himself. It had caused his usually calm, even-tempered mother some degree of consternation and provoked her to question his judgment in a most unusual way.

He recalled her anxious questions about Amelia-Jane's tender age and her ability to be certain of her feelings, "She is not yet sixteen, Jonathan, how can you be so sure she knows her own mind?" she had asked. Even his father had abandoned his generally disinterested approach to the matrimonial plans of his children to counsel caution.

"It would be wise, since you intend to stand for Parliament, to be quite certain you are marrying a lady who understands the responsibilities of the position," he had said.

Yet Jonathan recalled also how, captivated by the beauty and exhilarating energy of young Miss Collins, he had felt no qualms. He had believed that her unquestioned good character was insurance enough; her mind would improve with association and maturity.

Of his own affection for her, he had had no doubt at all.

The feelings he had begun to recognise stirring within his heart for Miss Faulkner seemed to have developed over the many months of their recent acquaintance, each occasion providing scope for their enhancement. It was a sensation completely different to the rather desperate ardour of his earlier wooing of Amelia-Jane.

The Armandes had noted their increasing intimacy with much pleasure, for they had a deep affection for both of them. To their partial eyes it seemed the pair were ideally suited, and they would dearly love to see them engaged.

Each evening, it appeared to them that Anna, having taken tea, left more reluctantly than before in the carriage that took her home to Haye Park. While every morning, after breakfast, Jonathan seemed restless and impatient until he heard the curricle from Haye Park come up the drive.

While in all their dealings, there was perfect decorum and propriety, they could not conceal their genuine enjoyment of each other's company. To be with them was to share that pleasure.

When most of the work was done, Jonathan, prior to leaving for London with the Armandes, who were soon to return to Europe, wrote to his mother and daughters at Ashford Park.

A letter he had received earlier that week had said the girls longed to see their father again and hoped they would be together at Christmas.

His mother urged him to let the children know when he would come for them.

"While it would be no trouble at all to have them stay over Christmas, I know they long to be with you," Jane wrote.

Replying, Jonathan promised he would soon be there to collect them and bring them home to Netherfield.

Dearest Mama, please assure Cathy and Tess that I share their longing for us to be together again. Indeed, it is to this end that we have all worked so hard these last few weeks, getting the house and especially their rooms ready for them.

Netherfield, thanks to the wonderful work of many people, including Monsieur and Madame Armande, Miss Faulkner, and a whole team of tradesmen and staff who have worked tirelessly to finish the job, has been transformed from a rather dull though solid Georgian manor house into an elegant and comfortable home for us all.

I look forward to having all three of my dear daughters home at Christmas and I know they will want me to thank everyone on their behalf.

Indeed, Mama, I can hardly wait until Spring, when you and Papa, Aunt Lizzie and Mr Darcy, Emma and James are all to join us at Easter.

It will be a pleasure we shall look forward to all Winter long.

He concluded with an assurance that, having collected Anne-Marie from Harwood House, he would soon be travelling to Ashford Park.

After despatching the letter to the post, he said his farewells and drove with the Armandes to Haye Park.

Expecting to be away for a fortnight at least, returning only a few days before Christmas, Jonathan had hoped for a private word with Anna to thank her for her help and perhaps obtain from her a promise to visit Netherfield when he returned with his daughters.

But, there was never an opportunity. Whether by accident or design, there was always someone around to engage them in conversation whenever he tried to see her alone.

Only at the end, as they waited for his carriage to be brought round to the front door, was he able to say a few words. They mainly reiterated his appreciation and added the hope that they would meet again soon.

It was she who reminded him of her promise to teach Teresa to draw and he eagerly took the chance to invite her to dine with them on their return.

"I know the girls will be looking forward, very much, to seeing you again, Anna, and so will I," he declared, with as much feeling as he could express, as the carriage rolled up to the door.

It had been said so quickly and with so little warning, she had no time to take in the significance of the words, much less to respond to them. The others were waiting and before she could say more than a brief "thank you," he had kissed her hand and was gone.

On reaching London, the Armandes prepared to leave almost immediately for Europe, but Monsieur was as good as his word and ensured that Jonathan was able to make his choice of paintings for Netherfield and another very special item, which he selected and had carefully packed and stored at Grosvenor Street. The Armandes, loathe to part from their new friend, urged him to visit them. Jonathan, though he had no immediate plans to visit Europe, assured them that he had hopes of seeing them again, soon.

Anne-Marie was seeing her father for the first time since the two weeks they had spent, following her mother's death, undertaking together a series of melancholy tasks. It had not been a pleasant time. Going through her mother's things and writing to all the friends and relations who had to be thanked and, even worse, finding the right words to apologise for the delay in settling the many bills she had accumulated over two or three months, had been difficult.

But much worse was the task of explaining, haltingly, to her younger sisters what had taken place, without destroying their image of their mother. Teresa, being rather slight and fragile since her premature birth, had spent most of her childhood with her grandmother Jane Bingley. She was less likely to miss Amelia-Jane than Cathy, who was a sturdy, cheerful girl, who had lived most of her life in Kent. She had been closer to her mother than any of the other children. Her little world had changed utterly overnight, and while Anne-Marie had done her best, there were questions she could not possibly answer.

To some, she did not know the answers herself, while others were best left unanswered, seeing that most of the participants were dead. No one could explain to Cathy why her mother had decided to leave for Bath in Mr Alexander's light carriage, which she had criticised only the previous week as being unsafe for the girls to ride in.

Cathy had recalled and retold the incident when Mrs Watkins and Mr Alexander had been visiting and Mr Alexander had offered to take the two girls for a drive around the park. Cathy had been willing, but Teresa, cautious as always, had wanted her mother's approval, which had not been forthcoming. Indeed, she had been quite cross with Mr Alexander for even suggesting it and had ordered Cathy to get out of the carriage and go upstairs at once.

"She was very cross," Cathy had said, and Teresa had claimed she would never forget the sharpness of her mother's voice as she rebuked first her daughters and then Mr Alexander for what she had called a "stupid idea."

"Clearly she did not approve of him driving the girls around the park, and yet, she was willing to make the much longer, more hazardous journey to Bath with him and Arabella Watkins in the same vehicle, careless of her own reputation and safety," Anne-Marie had said to Eliza Harwood, who had agreed there appeared to be no logical reason for her behaviour.

It was something that had concerned Anne-Marie, but she had never been able to talk to her father about it, feeling he had borne enough pain and needed no more.

When they set out on their journey north, having stopped off in London to purchase Christmas presents for the family, Anne-Marie seemed cheerful enough. But as they journeyed on, her father became aware that she was unusually restless and yet remained silent for most of the time.

At first, he put it down to tiredness and hoped she would recover her spirits after they had broken journey for the night at Cambridge.

But the following morning, at breakfast, she was still very quiet and appeared out of sorts. Determined that she should not travel all the way to Ashford Park in such a state, Jonathan decided to bring the matter out into the open by asking her directly, "I can see you are not happy, Anne-Marie, and it grieves me. Will you not tell me what is the matter? Is there not something I can do or say to help?"

She was startled by his question and appeared, at first, unwilling to let him see what it was that troubled her.

But when he persisted, she turned to him with tears in her eyes and told him of the letter she had received from her mother, just two days before her imprudent journey to Bath. It started slowly, but as she talked, it all poured out, the grief and strain of keeping it all to herself for so many months exacerbating her distress.

Jonathan was shocked and remorseful about her solitary suffering.

"Why did you not tell me, my dear?" he asked. "Why did you choose to keep it to yourself, all these months? It cannot have been easy. You have suffered unnecessarily and for too long."

Taking the letter out of her pocketbook, where it had lain hidden, she gave it to him and watched, tearfully, as he read it through.

His face drained of colour, Jonathan looked devastated.

Gradually, painfully, she explained.

"What good would it have done to expose it, to give you even more pain? Why would I wish to add to your suffering, Papa?"

He held her hands in his, trying to comfort her, but realised that it was not the kind of emotion that could be easily explained away.

For himself, Jonathan had never fully understood the extent to which his wife had blamed him for the failure of their marriage. Always a loving father and husband, he had not regarded his absence from home in pursuit of his Parliamentary career a matter for disapproval. This was especially so since Amelia-Jane had admired and encouraged his dedication to his constituency when they were engaged.

After they were married, she had enjoyed the early excitement of being the wife of a promising and popular Member of Parliament. That it had caused so much aggravation between them later had surprised and disappointed him; he had always hoped that she would in time come to understand the value of his work for the community.

He had the examples of women like his sister Emma Wilson and his cousin Caroline Fitzwilliam—both married to dedicated Parliamentarians, both Reformists with a strong commitment to improving the lot of the working people and extending the franchise to all.

He tried to explain to Anne-Marie. "It is not as if I was indulging myself, as David Wilson did for many years, keeping poor Emma in ignorance, while he enjoyed the high life in London. I was just a hard-working MP, pressing for reform, trying to help the people who elected me to Parliament," he said.

It had been increasingly difficult for him to comprehend his wife's antago-
nism to his work.

"I could not imagine why your mama thought it was such a waste of time;
I thought I was doing well," he said sadly, and Anne-Marie was sympathetic.

"Of course you were, Papa. I knew that and so did many other people.
But poor Mama—after she tired of the London scene, she lost all interest in
the work of Parliament. She was not like Aunt Emma or Cousin Caroline,
she felt no personal loyalty to the Party as they did, nor did she understand
very much about the reforms you were struggling to introduce. She was bored
and annoyed that you were always away doing things in which she had no
part and no real interest."

Then, seeing the stricken look upon his face, she took his hand. "Poor Papa,
you did not know and no one told you, but, after our two little brothers died,
she even lost interest in the rest of us. She had very little time for Teresa and
me, and even Cathy spent a lot of her time with Aunt Harrison. I think Mama
was lonely and sad, but whenever she tried to speak of Thomas or Francis,
someone would try to cheer her up, tell her to dry her tears, and I think that
made things much worse. She thought that you and the rest of us did not feel
their loss as deeply as she did."

Jonathan shook his head in bewilderment.

"What did you think?" he asked, wondering how his wife could have been
so mistaken, and astonished also at Anne-Marie's understanding of her
mother's sad and confused state of mind.

She held fast to his hand as she spoke.

"It matters little what I thought. For the most part, I agreed with Mama
that you worked too hard, but I do not censure you, for I know what dedication
means. In my own work, I have learnt the value of single-minded commitment
to a cause, and I know the satisfaction it can bring."

"You do not blame me then, as your brother does?" he asked, anxious to
discover her opinion.

"Not at all, except that I would have wished you were home for us more
often; we missed you, Charles and I. We had no real grown-ups to talk to. But
I cannot blame you for your desire to work hard at your chosen profession, nor
can I agree with Mama's demand that you give it all away and stay home, like
the landed gentry do."

Jonathan had to smile as she continued.

"As for Miss Caroline Bingley, nothing will make me forgive her for introducing Mama to Mrs Watkins and Mr Alexander. The two of them filled her head with such foolish ideas, ideas that bore no relation to reality and led ultimately to her death. My only consolation is that justice was served when they died with her in the accident."

Jonathan was surprised by the harshness of her judgment, yet he understood how, having borne the frustration and sorrow, she was not ready to forgive and forget. She held those who had misled and deluded her mother into a calamitous course of action duly culpable.

Presently, they approached the village of Ashfordby, a few miles before the turn-off to the Bingleys' estate.

She spoke more gently, urging him to remember that Cathy and Tess would be waiting, seeing him after a long separation. They would notice his mood if he was upset, she warned.

"We must try to be a little more cheerful, Papa, for their sakes; they are too young to understand our continuing sorrow, and we have no right to add to theirs."

Jonathan was proud of her selflessness and maturity. Clearly, she had acquired, at an early age, the qualities her poor confused mother had never learned. He suffered again those feelings of remorse that had assailed him directly after his wife's death, when he assumed that he might have been able to prevent it in some way.

They were approaching Ashford Park and the journey would soon be over. He turned to her and asked anxiously, "Anne-Marie, tell me truthfully and do not try to spare my feelings, do you not believe that I, had I been more vigilant, paid greater attention to the character of her friends and perhaps exposed their true nature, that I might have averted this disaster?"

She was absolute in her denial.

"No, Papa, I do not accept that for one moment. While I was sympathetic to Mama's complaints that you were frequently from home and she was often lonely, I do not believe that anything you could have said or done would have separated her from her new-found friends," she declared.

"They set out to ingratiate themselves with her in every possible way. Had you tried to warn her against them, she would have concluded immediately that you were trying to detach her from them for some sinister, selfish reason. It is likely to have made matters worse rather than better."

Seeing his troubled expression, she added, "I tried too, Papa, I did everything I could think of and so did Aunt Emma and Aunt Catherine, and every one of us who tried must have suffered as you did, feeling we had failed or could have done more to prevent Mama acting as she did, so do not judge yourself too harshly. You must not take on all the blame."

The gratitude he felt was too deep to be expressed in a few words, and, in any event, the carriage had already turned into the park. As they drove up to the house, their eagerness to see the children and the Bingleys again lifted their spirits.

Despite the cold November day, everyone came out to welcome them as they drove to the door, and Jonathan was left in no doubt of their feelings as his mother and two daughters greeted him warmly, with smiles and tears combining as he enfolded them in his arms.

Standing to one side, it was a while before Anne-Marie was similarly received, first by her grandparents, and then by the two young sisters who owed much to her courage and compassion.

For Jonathan Bingley and his daughters, happiness came not only from being together again at last, but from the warmth and comfort of what was, in the words of his eldest daughter, "without any doubt, the happiest home in all England."

The Bingleys—Jane and Charles—enjoyed a degree of conjugal felicity that was the envy of many others and, while they had not been spared the sorrow of life's vicissitudes, they seemed better able than most to rise above them.

They were both blessed with an evenness of temper and a capacity for compassion that enabled them to cope with their own afflictions while understanding the concerns of others. Jane's affectionate heart and her husband's amiable nature endeared them to many, and where it was needed, they gave of their time and shared their good fortune gladly.

The year just past had brought them more than a fair share of tribulation, as they had watched Jonathan's family disintegrate and then endured the disastrous consequences of Amelia-Jane's needless death. With courage and generosity they had taken on the task of comforting the two youngest children. Uncomprehending and desolate as the two girls had been at the time, it had not been easy. But they had persevered, and here they were, welcoming their father and elder sister and planning a happy reunion.

Jonathan planned to spend a week or ten days at most in the area, during which time he hoped to see as many members of his family as he could, visiting his sisters, Sophia and Louisa, who were married and settled in the district, as well as his former political mentor and friend, Colonel Fitzwilliam.

No sooner had the Fitzwilliams become aware of his arrival in the area, than an invitation to dinner was despatched and happily accepted.

Anne-Marie wanted to stay home with her sisters, but was persuaded by Jane to accompany her father. Though not as interested in matters political as her father, she nevertheless enjoyed the stimulating conversation that always flowed at any occasion hosted by the Fitzwilliams. She had enormous admiration for Caroline Gardiner, who at a very tender age had married both the handsome Colonel and his political causes, working assiduously and with great conviction to help him promote them.

Both the Colonel and Caroline still retained an interest in Parliamentary matters, though he had given up active politics many years ago. They looked now to Jonathan—a protégé of whom they were very proud—for information about developments at Westminster.

Congratulating him on the role he had played in the important negotiations leading up to the defeat of the government of Lord Derby and the return of the Whigs to the Treasury benches, Fitzwilliam was eager to discover when the next Reform Bill would be brought into the House of Commons.

Fitzwilliam had always been a great admirer of Lord Palmerston, and though occasionally disappointed in the pace of change under his administration, he still hoped for great things from the man.

"With Russell and Gladstone in Cabinet, surely Palmerston will take the initiative on reform. What is your opinion, Jonathan?" he asked, and to his great disappointment, Jonathan replied, "I wish I could confidently predict that he would, Colonel Fitzwilliam, but I fear that the very fact that Mr Gladstone is encumbered with the Treasury and Lord Russell has been drafted into Foreign Affairs suggests that Palmerston has put the Reform agenda aside for at least a year. Sadly, there will be no Reform Bill this session, nor in the next, I fear."

Fitzwilliam and Caroline were astounded. Caroline spoke for both of them, "I cannot believe that, Jonathan. Surely if there was one thing the people expected to see, it was the extension of the franchise. As it stands, the middle class and the working people, if they have no property, have no vote," she protested.

"Indeed, ma'am, you are quite right, and I imagine that many of the Liberals who joined the Whigs to defeat Derby would have expected it, too. I believe Lord Russell is eager to see the matter dealt with, but Palmerston has never been very enthusiastic about it and he is too obsessed with the question of Italy to pay any heed to the matter of extending the franchise," he explained.

Fitzwilliam looked bitterly disappointed.

"Jonathan, are you quite sure? Does that mean we can expect no change at all?" he asked, half hoping to be proved wrong. But Jonathan had little joy for him and went further by suggesting that, unless and until the question of Italian Unity was settled, there was probably no hope of Parliamentary Reform.

"What about the conditions of workers?" Caroline asked. "Is that to be set aside as well?"

Jonathan, who had a very particular interest in the subject, on account of complaints received from his sister Emma regarding workshops in the east end, had slightly better news for her.

"I believe we are somewhat better placed here, ma'am, with the influence of Mr Gladstone on the rise within the government. He has been building bridges with John Bright, the best hope for the working class yet, and I do believe we shall see some results. However, Lord Palmerston will not let anything get in the way of his European campaign; he believes this is Britain's best chance to secure her influence in Italy. It is possible that Mr Gladstone, with the support of the Liberals, will push for reform, but one cannot be certain of his success."

"And, when you return to the Commons, Jonathan, will you join with the liberal Whigs and take up the cause of reform?" asked Fitzwilliam, pouring out more wine and passing a bowl of fruit across to Jonathan.

He had spoken lightly, having taken for granted that Jonathan had accepted the Party's offer to place him in a safe constituency and enable his return to Parliament at the earliest opportunity.

Jonathan's answer shocked him.

"I am not sure I will be returning to the Commons, Sir," he said, quietly, peeling a tangerine with some care.

Caroline and her husband responded as one, "Jonathan! What do you mean?"

NETHERFIELD PARK REVISITED

Anne-Marie, who had listened in silence except for the odd, inconsequential remark, was roused out of her reverie by the vigour of their reaction. She saw her father smile and put down his knife and wipe his fingers meticulously, before he spoke.

"I have not yet decided to accept the Party's offer, sir. I am conscious of the great honour they have done me, but I am not certain that my own interests and those of my children will be best served by returning to Parliament," he said very deliberately and firmly.

Fitzwilliam could not believe his ears. To be offered a seat by the Party, when most others had to struggle to get preferment, was a singular honour and this young man was turning it down!

"Jonathan, what has brought about this change of heart?" he asked, unable to hide his disappointment.

"You are right, sir, for it is indeed a change of heart, rather than a change of mind. I cannot give you a logical argument to justify it. Indeed, I cannot be certain that such a decision can be justified logically. But there are many circumstances, some too painful to discuss here, which have affected my thinking on this matter. As you know and Anne-Marie will agree, I was for some years a dedicated Member of Parliament and afterwards a conscientious adviser to my brother-in-law James Wilson and other members of the Party. I have given unstintingly of my time."

No one at the table doubted this for one moment.

"However, my circumstances have changed and I am inclined to believe that my children, especially my daughters, must now have the right to expect that same dedication and conscientious attention to their cause."

"Does James Wilson know of your changed position?" Fitzwilliam asked, and Jonathan had to confess that he had not had the opportunity to speak to Mr Wilson on the subject.

"However, I do intend to visit them and tell him personally. I know he will be disappointed," he explained, apologetically.

There was a very long silence, during which Fitzwilliam looked rather disapprovingly into his glass, before Caroline sighed and said, "And what do you think, Anne Marie?"

Anne-Marie looked at her father and smiled before replying in a very quiet but firm voice, "If I thought that by returning to the House of Commons, Papa could achieve what he believes in, what he and others have worked for, I would urge him to return. He has been a most hard working Member and I am proud of what he has been able to do. But if he has not that certainty, it will only cause him more aggravation and discontent. I should not like to see that happen, Papa."

Her father leant across and touched her hand, a gentle, intimate gesture of understanding and gratitude that seemed to answer the questions the Fitzwilliams had raised far better than any words.

The mood changed when they rose to move into the drawing room for coffee and began to talk of other things, of farming and Netherfield and, somewhat surprisingly, of the Faulkners.

Caroline was a friend of Anna Faulkner's cousin Rebecca Tate, whose husband owned several newspapers in the Midlands and, meeting her at a function in Derby recently, she had heard of Anna's return from Europe.

"I understood from Rebecca that she was spending some time in London working at an Art School," said Caroline, looking to Jonathan for confirmation.

Jonathan confirmed that Miss Faulkner had indeed spent the Summer in London, helping her friends the Armandes run their Summer school on French Art, but had since returned to the country and was living with her parents at Haye Park where, he had been told, she was very happy.

Caroline recalled meeting her as a very young girl visiting her cousin Rebecca some years ago.

"I think it was Josie's birthday or it might have been Walter's, and Anna was here with her parents. Even then, she was remarkably pretty and exceedingly talented. I understand she has since studied Art and Music in Europe these three years," Caroline remarked.

Jonathan had to agree.

"Yes, ma'am, I believe she has. I have seen some of her work and it is quite beautiful to look at, though I must confess I am no great judge of Art."

"Ah, but you are a good judge of beauty, Jonathan, I'm sure. After all these years, is she still as pretty?" asked Fitzwilliam.

Jonathan answered without hesitation, "Indeed she is, sir, I would regard her as one of the handsomest, most elegant ladies of my acquaintance."

Fitzwilliam and Caroline exchanged glances and smiled.

"Now that is high praise," said Caroline, and Anne-Marie added her voice.

"Indeed it is and well deserved," she said. "Miss Faulkner is not only an elegant and handsome woman with many accomplishments, she combines these qualities with the kindest and most generous of hearts. Were it not for her and our dear Aunt Emma, I do not know how we would have survived the dreadful days following Mama's accident. She came to us day after day, frequently rising early and walking the distance from Belgrave Square to help comfort Cathy and Tess, and often, when I could no longer cope with the unending stream of callers at Grosvenor Street, she would step in and let me get some rest.

"I think we are all very grateful to Miss Faulkner, are we not, Papa?" she asked, turning to Jonathan, who had remained silent during this passionate tribute, trying, not very successfully, to conceal his pleasure.

Forced by her question to provide an answer, he was delighted to agree.

"Oh yes, indeed we are, all of us, very appreciative of Miss Faulkner and her wonderful friends the Armandes, who have only this week returned to Europe. They were most helpful, nothing was too much trouble for Monsieur Armande and as for Madame, she was a tower of strength when we needed it most," he added, not wishing to speak only of Anna.

Caroline heard all this with interest and declared, "Indeed, I must tell Becky when we next meet. I am sure she will be very happy to hear it. She was becoming concerned about her young cousin, wondering if she would ever get over her early disappointment. I believe she was very young at the time …"

Jonathan, sensing the direction of her conversation and being unwilling to become involved in a discussion of Anna, for whom he was beginning to feel a far deeper affection than would permit him to speak of her with impartiality, sought to divert it.

"From what I could observe, ma'am, she seemed very content, and Dr and Mrs Faulkner are delighted to have her back home at Haye Park."

This brought the conversation to a close and gave him the opportunity to rise and suggest that it was time to leave. They parted, promising to meet again before Jonathan and his daughters left for Netherfield. In the carriage, Anne-Marie asked her father whether he had really believed that returning to Parliament was not in his children's interest.

"Are you sure it was not seeing Mama's letter that made you feel that way?" she asked. Jonathan was quite certain.

"I am; my dear, I have been contemplating this change for almost a month or more—ever since I moved to live at Netherfield. It may be that it is the first time I have had a place of my own. I would like us all to make our home there and to do that, I must decide that it is where I spend most of my time. I would go up to London from time to time, of course, but Netherfield will be my home. I should like to think that you would come and stay with us, Anne-Marie. Would you?" he asked.

Hearing the anxious plea in his voice, she replied, "Of course I would, Papa. I should love to have a place to go home to. Eliza is very kind, but Harwood House is not my home; I am a guest there and it is not the same. I shall certainly come to Netherfield, I cannot wait to see it after all the work you have had done," she declared, and he smiled, happy to find her so agreeable.

"Does that mean you would approve if I decided against returning to Westminster?" he asked.

The maturity of her answer belied her tender years.

"Papa, it is not for me to approve or disapprove. You must do what is right for you. But I can say this: I think you would make both Tess and Cathy very happy if you remained at Netherfield. They do miss Mama terribly and it would help them cope, should you be there with them. I wish I could stay, but I must do what I am doing, it's work I cannot turn my back on. We are saving lives, literally, and they depend upon us. It is very good to come away like this but I must return after Christmas," she said.

"And do you intend to continue your work at the hospital?" he asked, and she answered with eyes bright and a voice firm with conviction.

"I do, Papa. Believe me, there is no nobler, more satisfying work for a woman. I am completely committed to it. Miss Nightingale, who has been our inspiration, has recently written a book about nursing and she proposes to start a school for nurses, very soon. I dare not expect to be fortunate enough to be selected as one of her first students, but I intend to keep trying. I have already spoken with Eliza Harwood, and she has promised to seek a good recommendation for me from the military hospital in Harwood Park."

Suddenly, seeing his expression, she stopped.

"Papa, you are not going to object, I hope?" she cried, an anxious frown upon her face.

Jonathan laughed.

"Object? Of course not, my dear Anne-Marie, why should I? If it matters so much to you, how could I object? However, I do believe you are not strong enough for all the hard work it entails. It is an arduous job, as you well know. I shall have to nag you about eating more nutritious food."

She was smiling now, knowing she would not have to fight his disapproval.

"As for Tess and Cathy," he went on, "you are not expected to play nursemaid to them, even though you are their elder sister. I intend to ask Mrs Collins to recommend a suitable governess, who will take over their education, and I hope Miss Faulkner may be persuaded to give them lessons in Music and Art."

It was something he had thought about, but had not had the opportunity to discuss with anyone. This, he decided, was as good a time as any to discover what Anne-Marie thought of his plan.

"So you see, I have it all planned and you need never feel guilty about returning to your beloved wounded soldiers. They are fortunate, indeed, to have such a dedicated nurse."

Anne-Marie almost hugged him with delight.

"Thank you, Papa, you have made me so very happy. I have been meaning to tell you, but there it is—it's all out now and I am so glad you do not object."

"Would it have made a difference if I had?" he asked, only half serious.

She looked crestfallen.

"Of course it would. I should still have gone on with nursing, but without your blessing, I should have been most unhappy, even doing what I loved."

He was glad they had no cause for such unhappiness.

"When you have decided about Westminster, what will you tell Aunt Emma and Mr Wilson?" she asked, assuming he would have to break the news to them soon.

Jonathan bit his lip.

"I shall tell them the truth when the time comes. I have decided that I do not think it is possible for me to do my duty by my constituents and care for Cathy and Tess as I should. I may, however, continue in my role as adviser to James' group until the next election. That may alleviate some of the disappointment he will undoubtedly feel. But in the end, they will both understand my children must come first."

❧

Two days later, they were dining at Pemberley together with Jonathan's parents and Richard and Cassandra Gardiner when the subject came up again. No doubt Darcy had heard it from his cousin Colonel Fitzwilliam and Cassy had been told by Caroline. Jonathan knew the questions would be forthcoming and braced himself, expecting the same look of disappointment, perhaps even disapproval, he'd had from Fitzwilliam.

When the question came, as they were finishing dinner, he saw Elizabeth look at him across the table, and both his parents appeared rather apprehensive, as Mr Darcy asked, "I understand, Jonathan, you may not be going back into Parliament after all?"

His reply was cautious, not wishing to start an argument all over again.

"I have not quite decided, sir. I am inclined to believe that my place, at the moment, is with my children, especially Tess and Cathy. They miss their mother desperately and I think my first duty is to them."

He was quite unprepared for Darcy's reply.

"Of course it is, you are right to consider carefully what you must do. It will be difficult enough to raise young children on your own, without taking on the responsibilities of a Member of Parliament, which are becoming increasingly burdensome."

Jonathan smiled broadly. He had a great deal of respect and affection for Mr Darcy and was delighted to have his support.

"It is very kind of you to say so, sir," he said. "I realise I shall be disappointing several people in the Party, but I do have to think of the girls."

"Of course you do," said Darcy, adding, "The Party will be disappointed, certainly. I know from James Wilson that they had great hopes for you, but you have given them excellent service both in and out of Parliament. Fitzwilliam has told me of your valuable work after the election, negotiating with the Peelites and Liberals to secure the alliance that defeated Derby. That alone must be cause for gratitude, but no one, however dedicated, can be expected to put the interest of their Party above their family forever. Your children are entitled to expect you to look to their future as well."

Jonathan was exceedingly pleased. Anne-Marie, knowing he placed a great deal of value on Mr Darcy's opinion, realised that this would help fix his resolve. No one else said anything more on the subject.

Mr Bingley, who was in the happy position of agreeing with both his son and his brother-in-law, decided it was time to change the topic.

"Jonathan, do you intend to keep all the farm land at Netherfield together, or do you expect to lease some of the fields?" he asked, which was surely the beginning of a discussion from which the ladies could politely withdraw to the drawing room to talk of other matters.

Elizabeth was keen to discover Anne-Marie's opinion of her father's decision and to find out how she was coping with her work at the hospital. They had not met since her mother's funeral. She had lived for many years in the shadow of a beautiful if rather empty-headed mother; now she was on her own, and a very independent young woman had emerged.

"Anne-Marie, I know that you must work very hard at the hospital; tell me, are they looking after you well at Harwood House?"

"Oh, Aunt Lizzie, they certainly are. Eliza is very kind and I want for nothing. I do pay my board, of course, but they will accept nothing for my lodging. Mr Harwood is such a generous man, you cannot believe how good he is. Why, shortly before I left to come to Ashford Park, we were collecting donations for the hospital's Christmas dinner," she explained. "There are many men who are either too ill or too badly disabled or disfigured to return home, and we intended to get them each a little gift. Well, we were short of about twelve pounds in all and, would you believe, when Eliza happened to mention it over breakfast, Mr Harwood took twenty pounds out of his wallet and gave it to her; it was his donation to the men's Christmas dinner. We could not believe it, but Eliza says, although he is a business man and cares about money, he is also very generous and gives it away to charities all the time. Well, now the men at the hospital will have their Christmas dinner and there will be plenty of money for presents."

Judging from her excitement as she told the tale, Elizabeth realised that Anne-Marie had very different enthusiasms and values to those of her unfortunate mother.

"And do you intend to continue your work at the hospital?" she asked.

"I certainly do, Aunt Lizzie. It is most rewarding work. Besides, we have heard that Miss Nightingale is soon to start a training school for nurses. I should love to train with her."

Cassandra, who had heard a great deal about Miss Florence Nightingale and her amazing organisation of medical services during and after the war in the Crimea, added her voice in praise of the woman who had become the heroine of the Crimean War, leaving no one in any doubt of the validity of Anne-Marie's claims.

"I do believe she has been invited to visit the Queen, who has expressed great admiration for her work," she said.

"Oh, I do not doubt it, she is regarded as a heroine by the soldiers, who worship her. Many know they owe their lives to her work and the fight she put up to improve their conditions in the Crimea and afterwards in many hospitals in England. She is an inspiration to us all," Anne-Marie declared, her eyes bright with enthusiasm.

"And will you spend Christmas at Netherfield?" asked Cassy.

"Oh yes," she replied, "it is good to get away from London occasionally, and I am very happy to be spending Christmas with Papa and the girls."

Jane remarked that Jonathan had told her of the changes he'd had made at Netherfield since moving there.

"I believe Miss Anna Faulkner and her friends from Europe have been very helpful with their advice on colours for drapes and furnishings and things; Jonathan tells me the changes have greatly improved the appearance of the old place. I cannot wait to see it at Easter."

Anne-Marie was warm in her praise.

"Indeed, Miss Faulkner is very artistic. Papa speaks very highly of her work. He has seen it at the Art School in London and at Haye Park, her parents' home."

"Anna Faulkner is a very talented young woman," said Elizabeth.

"She certainly is," said Anne-Marie, "and kind. She was like a sister to me when Mama died and we had to break the news to Cathy and Tess, and everyone was feeling so dreadful. Poor Papa had so many things to do and Mrs Collins was unable to leave her room. There was only Aunt Emma. Anna was wonderful. Being Mama's cousin, she understood how we felt. She was so patient and strong, I could talk to her about anything at all," she said, and there were tears in her eyes.

Jane and Elizabeth looked at one another. They had not realised how deeply Miss Faulkner had become involved in the lives of Jonathan Bingley and his daughters.

The gentlemen rejoined them, and at first there was much talk of the readings given by the celebrated Mr Dickens, who having completed his novel about the French revolution, *A Tale of Two Cities*, was touring the country again.

A visit to the Midlands had afforded Richard and Cassy the opportunity to hear him read his own work, and as usual, everyone agreed that there was no writer in England today as good as Charles Dickens.

The usual request for music followed. This brought yet another favourable mention of Miss Faulkner when Anne-Marie, having played for them, rose and closed the instrument saying, "I wish I could play and sing as Miss Faulkner does. She has the softest touch on the keyboard. She has studied in Europe, of course, and has the advantage of it."

This lavish praise of Anna Faulkner did not go unnoticed by Elizabeth.

Before retiring for the night, she mentioned it to her husband, who was less surprised than she had expected him to be, pointing out quite reasonably that Anne-Marie and Miss Faulkner had a lot in common.

"I would have thought they would be ideal companions for one another, Lizzie," he said. "It will be good for Anne-Marie to get away from that dreadful hospital of hers and cultivate an interest in the Arts. She is an earnest and sincere young woman and needs to broaden her mind, else she will fall into the error of living a narrow, confined existence. She may well be dedicated, but not every woman can be a Florence Nightingale."

His wife agreed.

"I think you mean she needs to widen her horizons and take an interest in things other than nursing?"

"Exactly, and Miss Faulkner, who is clearly a woman of taste and good sense, is probably the right person to encourage her in that endeavour. She will benefit from the association in the same way that my sister Georgiana was advantaged by her friendship with you, my dear Lizzie."

Touched by his tribute, she sat down beside him and asked, "So you see a long association between them, do you?"

"Indeed, I do," he replied with some enthusiasm. "They share similar backgrounds and values already. They are both intelligent young women with remarkable skills. One is involved in the care of the sick and wounded, while the other is an accomplished student of the Arts. Now Lizzie, surely they can only benefit one another. Their association is to be encouraged. I can see no disadvantage in it."

Elizabeth was wide eyed with surprise.

"Now that is praise indeed—from you."

"Do you not agree, Lizzie? On what grounds do you disapprove?" he asked, teasing her, and Elizabeth threw up her hands in mock surrender.

"Oh no, I do not disapprove! Indeed, I have no arguments to bring against your proposition. I am only intrigued at its coming on so quickly," she replied. "A year ago, they had barely a nodding acquaintance, yet now here is young Anne-Marie quite unable to stop singing the praises of Miss Faulkner on every occasion."

Darcy laughed, a rather light-hearted laugh and said, "I see, so it's the mystery of this sudden attachment that intrigues you. Well, my dearest, there are moments in our lives when we are particularly miserable and grateful for the kindness of someone we may fortuitously meet and make the focus of our warmest appreciation. If you recall what Emily came to mean to us, you and I, when we lost William, I think you will better understand how Jonathan and his daughters regard Miss Faulkner with such affection."

Elizabeth knew exactly what he meant and fell silent, recalling sadly the days and nights of unremitting sorrow, during which her cousin, Emily Gardiner, had come to mean a lot to them, starting a friendship that continued to this day.

Having contemplated her deepest memories, she turned to him and said, "You are quite right, my love, I can see why Anne-Marie, reeling from the shock of her mother's death, must have found comfort in Anna Faulkner. She is kind, and sensible as well; she must have been a Godsend at such a dreadful time. I know Charlotte was close to collapse. Poor Jonathan, Emma wrote to say, he bore it all with heroic fortitude. Emma did speak very highly of Anna in her letter, too."

Then, in a quieter voice, in which changed inflection he detected the direction of her thoughts, she asked, "But do you entirely discount the possibility that some part of Anne-Marie's enthusiasm for Miss Faulkner may stem from her father's attitude? Do you not detect in Jonathan some degree of partiality to Anna Faulkner?"

Darcy smiled, amused that he had, at last, flushed out the question at the heart of their discussion and though, in the dim light of the room, she could not see his face very clearly, the laughter in his voice betrayed him.

"No, Lizzie my dear, I do not discount it, and yes, there may well be some attraction there. Indeed, if he is so inclined, then surely, the good opinion of his daughter must be a decided advantage," he said, and she realised that he had probably known all along the true purpose of her questions, but clearly was unwilling to speculate any further on Jonathan's private life.

Meanwhile, unaware of these discussions, or even of the interest his affairs were arousing among members of his family, Jonathan Bingley went to bed well pleased with Mr Darcy's remarks on the matter of his decision not to stand for election to the House of Commons.

At least, he thought, he had one strong ally.

Just moments before he fell asleep, he wondered what Anna's response might be and decided he would speak of the matter to her when they next met, which he hoped would be soon.

It was a meeting to which he was looking forward, very much.

When they set off from Ashford Park, after a week that had been restful and restorative to both body and mind, there were but a few days to Christmas. Travelling via London, where they spent the night at Grosvenor Street, and ensuring that their thoughtfully chosen Christmas gifts were stored with care in the carriage, they left to make the last twenty-five miles to Netherfield Park.

The weather in the south of England remained fine and in Hertfordshire they were even favoured with some hours of Winter sunshine.

By the time they approached Netherfield Park, however, at the end of a tiring day, it was almost dark and lights glowed in all the windows to welcome the travellers home. Passengers, coachmen, and horses were all weary, and the three young ladies asked for no more than hot baths and warm beds. But there was much more, for the staff at Netherfield House were determined that the Master's daughters would receive a warm welcome to their new home.

As they drew up before the house with its wide, impressive flight of steps leading to the front doors, the housekeeper Mrs Perrot and the butler came out to greet them. When they were shown their rooms, there were genuine gasps of pleasure, even from Teresa and Cathy, who had become accustomed to the relative luxury of Ashford Park.

As for Anne-Marie, as the young Mistress of the house, she had the privilege of having a beautifully appointed Regency suite all to herself, with fine linen, fresh flowers, and a superb view of the park and the woods beyond. When her father entered the room some time afterwards, to say "Welcome home," she turned to thank him with tears in her eyes.

For the first time in many years, she really felt she had a home.

No one was surprised when all the young ladies slept late the following morning. Mrs Perrot had given orders that they were not to be disturbed. Jonathan alone had risen early and left for his usual ride around the park. Returning later, and finding the girls still upstairs, he changed his clothes, partook of a light breakfast, and went out again, this time in the carriage, for he was visiting Longbourn, some three miles away.

Once at Longbourn, to call on Miss Bennet and Mrs Collins and offer them the use of his carriage to transport them to church on Christmas day, he was impatient to be on his way again.

At Haye Park, he called on the Faulkners, expecting to see Anna. However, disappointment awaited him when he arrived, for while Dr and Mrs Faulkner were delighted to see him, Anna was not at home.

"Anna is gone to her sister in Hampshire," said Mrs Faulkner, urging him to stay and take tea with them, it being around eleven o'clock.

His disappointment was so great that he almost refused, but then realising that it was his only means of obtaining any information about Anna, he thanked her and stayed. Presently, tea was ordered, and Mrs Faulkner proceeded to give him the news.

"It was not two days after you had all left for London, we had a desperate letter from our son-in-law, Mr Martyn,—he farms in Hampshire," she added by way of explanation, "begging us to send Anna to them as soon as possible. You see, my elder daughter Sarah, who is married to Mr Martyn, had been taken ill suddenly with a severe respiratory condition and could hardly breathe, he said. They have three children and my son-in-law was finding it impossible to manage. They do not keep many servants," she explained and added, "as soon as Anna read the letter, she was eager to be gone to her sister. She was packed and ready within the hour, and Dr Faulkner took her to meet the coach at Meryton."

Jonathan expressed some concern.

"Have you heard from her since her arrival in Hampshire? I do hope your daughter Sarah's condition is improving," he said, hoping desperately for a favourable answer, but none was forthcoming.

Maria Faulkner was not hopeful. She was a pleasant enough woman, but she had never been a very practical person. She knew little or nothing of what she referred to as "serious matters," by which she generally meant politics, health, or money—all of which she considered to be strictly the province of her husband.

She could give him no information at all, except to reveal that they had received a short note from Anna, hastily penned between attending to her sister and getting the younger children to eat their dinner.

She said Sarah had been very happy to see her and begged her to stay as long as possible. Anna thought her sister was improving, with proper care and better food, but could not say when she would be well enough to be left on her own. Anna feared Mr Martyn was not very good attending upon his sick wife and organising his several children.

"He is a farmer, a very good one by all reports, but a farmer none the less," said Mrs Faulkner, as if that explained everything.

Jonathan could not comprehend why a man who was a good farmer could not care for his sick wife or organise his young children, but tactfully said nothing. There were only four days to Christmas and Anna had been gone just above a week.

"Do you expect her home for Christmas?" he asked, a little anxiously.

"Oh dear, I do hope so," replied her mother, but added as an afterthought, "I wonder how the Martyns will cope when she leaves."

Jonathan was beginning to lose patience with the Martyns, a family he had never met but continually heard of, chiefly on account of their inability to do anything for themselves.

Anna had previously told him how her father was called upon to travel to Hampshire each time one of the children fell ill, to reassure them the child would recover.

Rising to leave, he thanked Mrs Faulkner for the tea and invited them to Netherfield House after church on Christmas morning, so they could meet his daughters. Mrs Faulkner was very appreciative and promised to convey the invitation to Dr Faulkner and Anna, when she had returned from Hampshire, assuring him they were all looking forward to meeting his daughters.

Sadly, that was all the consolation Jonathan had from her that day.

Returning to Netherfield, finding it difficult to conceal his disappointment, Jonathan found his daughters in a state of high excitement and was glad of the distraction. A party of carollers had turned up at the house to ask if they might come around and sing on Christmas Eve.

There was a new, rather strict young rector at the village church, they explained, who had insisted that they must not go round to people's homes uninvited.

Cathy was determined that they must be welcomed at Netherfield.

She had never encountered the traditional carollers before.

"Papa, please can we tell them they may come round and sing for us?" she asked and, having consulted Mrs Perrot, who promised to have some food and drink ready for the party, Jonathan gave his permission. The three sisters then set off to tell the carol singers, who were practising at the church hall, the good news.

Jonathan watched them go, all eager and laughing together; only Anne-Marie continued to wear the traditional dark mourning gowns. Her young sisters had been dressed in shades of blue and lavender since leaving Ashford Park. His mother had pointed out that it was past six months since their mother's death and surely the children could put aside their mourning clothes. Jonathan had agreed and had suggested to Anne-Marie that she should also get herself some lighter gowns while they were in London, but she had replied quietly that she would "wear these out until Christmas."

While they were out, Jonathan retired to his room, disappointed, unable to concentrate on anything. He had so looked forward to bringing the girls home and asking Anna round to meet them in happier circumstances than when they last saw each other. It was as if Fate had conspired to cheat him, and his plans had come to naught.

He was beginning to understand how closely she had become involved with his hopes of happiness. He was missing her at every moment and on every occasion.

His depression worsened considerably when a short note arrived from his son Charles, to whom he had written, inviting him to spend Christmas with them at Netherfield.

Charles wrote to wish them all a blessed Christmas, but asked to be excused from joining the family this year.

"I have but a few days before I must return to the hospital at Edinburgh, and since it is only half the distance to Ashford Park as it is to Hertfordshire, I intend to join my grandparents at Christmas, this year," he wrote.

Clearly, thought Jonathan, his son had not stopped blaming him for his mother's death. It was a bleak prospect.

Though his mood was sombre, the weather, at least, remained fine, though some snow was predicted on Christmas Eve. Mrs Perrot and the rest of the household went briskly about their business, making all the usual preparations. Puddings were boiled, hams smoked, and geese plucked, while throughout the house the maids were busy hanging up wreaths of holly and little sprigs of mistletoe.

In deference to the Master's wishes, there was not to be the traditional Netherfield Ball and supper this year; however, a party was to be given on Boxing Day for the children of the tenants and servants, and doubtless Mrs Perrot would ensure that everyone was well fed and there was plenty of hot punch and ale for the grown-ups. Very few of them had known the late Mrs Bingley, who had spent no time at Netherfield, a fact that made it easier for all of them to cope.

As the family waited for the carriage to be brought round on Christmas morning, Jonathan noticed that Anne-Marie was wearing a gown of pale blue silk with a warm cashmere over-garment in deeper blue. It was the first time he had seen her out of her mourning attire, and though she looked rather pale, it suited her well.

In the carriage, Cathy could not stop talking about the carollers, who had come by last night, and Tess commented on how blue the sky was, in spite of the Winter cold. Delicate and pretty, Teresa resembled her mother most of all the girls, though they had not been very close. Indeed, as they chattered on, they seemed not to notice her absence at all.

Anne-Marie did notice, however, that none of this seemed to gladden her father's heart and assumed that he was grieved by Charles' note, which he had shown her the previous night.

Arriving at the church, they noticed the Faulkners' carriage ahead of theirs, and presently, it drew up at the door to let the occupants alight. Jonathan watched as Dr Faulkner climbed out and helped his wife to step down and then turned back to the vehicle and there, alighting from the carriage, was Anna Faulkner herself.

Even before she saw her, Anne-Marie noticed the change in her father's expression and when she turned and looked, following his eyes, she was not surprised to see Miss Faulkner, who was being greeted by the Rector, before accompanying her parents into the church.

She was left in no doubt at all that the pleasure reflected in her father's face was caused, at least in part, by the presence at the church of Miss Anna Faulkner.

In a gesture that demonstrated her maturity and insight, she took her father's arm as they went into the church and, as they took their seats, whispered quietly to him, "I am so happy to see that Anna is back. It means her sister must be quite recovered."

Jonathan turned and, meeting her eyes, realised that his daughter had seen and comprehended the feelings he thought he had concealed so well. Grateful for her understanding, he smiled and said, "Yes indeed," as the organ heralded the Rector's little procession moving slowly up the aisle.

After church, Anne-Marie was again her father's best ally; taking her sisters out to greet the Faulkners and engaging Dr and Mrs Faulkner in cheerful chatter about the sweetness of the singing, the colour of their gowns, and the relative warmth of cashmere and wool, while Jonathan found Anna standing just inside the side door and, despite the cold, he succeeded in conveying in the warmest terms his pleasure at seeing her again as well as his hope that her sister was fully recovered.

She had arrived home, she said, barely twelve hours ago, after a long and boring journey from Hampshire, and despite being tired, she was glad she had come to church.

"I had to come, I have never missed church at Christmas; I love the music," she said as they stepped out into the shelter of the porch, where several families were busy greeting one another and their new Rector.

Reminded by Mrs Perrot, Anne-Marie prompted her father to invite the Rector to Netherfield for sherry and Christmas cake later. The Faulkners were coming too as were Charlotte Collins and Mary Bennet and a few other neighbours. Cathy was very excited. It was the first time she had been in her own home at Christmas in many years. It was a day that promised much.

For Jonathan, there was not only the joy of seeing Anna again, and that was considerable, but it now seemed likely that Anne-Marie was probably aware of his feelings and may well favour their friendship. Her gentle little hint in the church had indicated as much. Her father, who had been apprehensive about her probable reaction to such an association, had been delighted, but contained his pleasure well, not wishing to appear too eager.

Noting that there were many miles to be travelled before the desired destination may be reached, he decided to proceed with some caution. There were, in addition, questions of decorum and etiquette involved, since it was not quite seven months since his wife's death.

He would do nothing that might involve his family in village gossip, of which he was sure there would be plenty. Acutely aware of the need to spare Anna any embarrassment, he determined that at this time, it would be best if their association continued as a friendship, whose warmth would be known only to the participants.

While Anna's greeting had been friendly and cordial, she too had been discreet, unwilling to lay herself open to prattle, conscious, no doubt, that some members of the congregation like Miss Jessie Phillips may have had their eyes upon them.

It was, for Jonathan, sufficient happiness that she was here, within calling distance, and he had plenty of time on his hands.

While he had never had to play the part himself, Jonathan Bingley was familiar with the role of the country squire, having seen his father and uncles carry out their duties at Ashford Park and Pemberley over many years. Since taking over the management of Longbourn, after the death of his grandfather Mr Bennet, he too had been called upon to meet some of the obligations that his Aunt Mary Bennet and her guest and companion, Mrs Collins, were unable to fulfil. These responsibilities he had accepted conscientiously and with a certain amount of pride.

It was therefore without trepidation and with some degree of personal satisfaction that he looked forward to the first such occasion at Netherfield on Boxing Day, when the tenants, servants, and their families would arrive to greet their squire and attend their customary Christmas party. Jonathan, like his parents, had been well liked, and his arrival at Netherfield with his three daughters after his wife's sudden death had resulted in a wave of neighbourly sympathy and thoughtfulness.

The Bingleys had a good reputation in the village, thanks mainly to memories of his father's kind, amiable nature and his mother's sweetness of disposition. Expectations of their son, who had been born at Netherfield, were therefore high. Jonathan knew he had to ensure that they were not disappointed, and his family and staff would be striving to do just that.

Christmas morning was, however, quite another matter.

A small group of guests—mainly family and close friends—placed no strain on anyone, and consequently everyone was able to enjoy the occasion.

Everyone that is, except the new Rector, Mr Griffin.

Obviously unaccustomed to the roads and unfamiliar with the district, having taken up his living just a fortnight ago, he became lost and it was quite some time before he arrived at Netherfield House, suffering from cold and feeling very sorry for himself.

Jonathan's guests had been busy entertaining themselves and each other and hardly noticed that a good hour had passed and the Rector had not arrived. This was not surprising, since the three Misses Bingley were spending their first Christmas at Netherfield, and everyone was determined to help them enjoy it.

There was plenty of excellent festive fare and there were gifts for everyone, including the staff. Jonathan's daughters were delighted. Their father's gifts were opened last and with much ceremony and many exclamations of pleasure and disbelief. Anne-Marie had helped him choose for her two sisters, and they had chosen well, for both Teresa and Cathy loved their gifts of jewellery. Her own, which her father began by pretending he had forgotten to collect, was delivered to her after much teasing.

Judging by her response, it was clearly a gift worth waiting for. An exquisite ivory cameo brooch, edged in gold, featuring the profile of a young girl, it brought cries of delight and enthusiastic approval from everyone. Anne-Marie was ecstatic.

While the family gathered around her, Jonathan brought out another package, one that had waited almost a month to be delivered.

"This is not just a Christmas present, Miss Faulkner," he said, trying to explain away the size of the item, as he handed it over, "it is a gift from all of us, to thank you for your wonderful work in helping to make this house such an elegant and comfortable home for us all. Without your advice and help, it would have been quite impossible. My daughters have been delighted with their rooms and I shall be eternally grateful that you helped me rid myself of the 'Royal Brocade' in mine. We hope you will like this just as well."

Anna was completely surprised, unable to say a word as she accepted it except a quiet thank you. She opened up the package to reveal a perfectly executed Japanese woodblock print of wisteria in bloom, spilling out over running water—the work of a famous Japanese artist, whose influence over some of the avant-garde French painters was considerable.

Her response left him in no doubt that she was absolutely enchanted.

"I wondered where that had gone … I asked Monsieur Armande and he said he had sold it," she cried. "I am delighted to see it again."

Indeed, she did not say he was too kind or that he ought not have done it, nor did she protest that she could not possibly accept such a valuable gift. Instead, she let everyone admire it, and when they had all acknowledged its beauty, she thanked him once more, protesting only that Monsieur Armande, from whom it had been purchased, had hidden the truth from her and pretended that it had been bought "by some young man about town with more money than sense."

"'He's probably a collector' he told me," she said to their general amusement, then turning to Jonathan, expressed her heartfelt thanks, "Mr Bingley, this is one of the loveliest gifts I have ever received. I thank you and your daughters from the bottom of my heart. I adored it when it was in Monsieur Armande's collection. Now, it shall hang in my room, where I can see it at any time of the day or night. Thank you."

Both Dr Faulkner and his wife were very impressed with the beautiful gift and Mr Bingley's excellent taste.

While admiring their various gifts, no one heard the knock at the door until Anne-Marie, alerted by the sound of a neighing horse outside, ran to the window and, seeing the Rector's pony cart in the driveway, rushed to open the door and let the man in.

"Oh my goodness, Mr Griffin, there you are," she cried, "please do come in, you must be freezing, come in and sit by the fire. Papa, I think Mr Griffin would like a sherry," she said, as she took his coat and handed it to the servant, but her father and Dr Faulkner were both quite sure that a large brandy was what the frozen Rector needed "to thaw him out."

It transpired that he had been an hour or more in his pony cart, traversing the country in the cold, until a passing farmer set him on the right road to Netherfield Park.

Anne-Marie's kind heart was touched by the unfortunate man's plight and she rushed around to make sure he was warm and then was plied with food and drink, until gradually, the frozen Rector began to look normal again.

Mr Griffin was not by any means a man one would call personable or good looking, being rather gaunt with unfortunate features that in repose took on a somewhat lugubrious expression.

Cathy had already decided that he resembled a character from her favourite tale by Charles Dickens, *A Christmas Carol.*

"Which one?" teased Tess. "Ebenezer Scrooge—or was it Marley's ghost?"

"He has such a doleful face," said Anna, and Jonathan, who had joined them at the piano, agreed.

"Not the kind of face you expect to see spreading the good news at Christmas! But I did note that he does have a strong voice, of a somewhat disembodied kind. It does not seem to proceed from that slight frame!" he said, and Anna could not contain her laughter.

Finally Anne-Marie came over and begged them not to make fun of the poor man.

"He's frozen half to death and he is our guest," she reminded them in a tone of mock severity, which both her father and Anna Faulkner took to heart. But even Anne-Marie could not resist a smile when he was heard to declare to Mrs Faulkner, who had suggested that he ought to return to his home and go directly to bed to avoid catching a bad cold, "Your concern is appreciated, ma'am, but I believe I must set aside my own comfort and attend to my flock; the shepherd cannot take account of the weather."

The vision of Mr Griffin as an intrepid shepherd was too much even for Anne-Marie's kind heart.

Meanwhile, a man servant had taken the unfortunate horse and its cart into the shelter of the stables, and Mrs Perrot had the Rector served with plenty of hot food. Clearly pleased with all the attention he was getting, Mr Griffin stayed much longer than expected.

Anne-Marie, feeling that her duty as hostess required her to be attentive to him while the rest sang, played, or simply listened, seated herself beside him and listened while he talked endlessly of his parish concerns.

Mr Griffin, having told Anne-Marie how much he enjoyed church music, proceeded to urge her to join the choir, and it was with the greatest difficulty that she succeeded in convincing him that it would be of very little use, since she would soon be returning to London.

At this piece of news, he looked dismayed and sank back into his rather mournful mood until it was time to leave.

Anna, who had been observing Anne-Marie, found herself standing beside Jonathan as they took tea. She said, softly, "Is it not remarkable how Anne-Marie has helped comfort her sisters? Both Tess and Cathy seem a good deal calmer."

Jonathan agreed. "Indeed they do," he said. "Anne-Marie has been wonderful. I cannot tell you how strong she has been, nor how much I have depended upon her. I was very apprehensive about bringing all three of them down to Netherfield, and in truth, my mother did offer to have Tess at Ashford Park over Christmas. But I decided that if the children were going to live at Netherfield, it was best that they come down together, at Christmas."

Anna's face had been grave, but she smiled, reassuring him, as she said, "I think you have done the right thing; you have given them a beautiful home here and, most of all, a sense of belonging to a family, which they must have longed for. There is no better way to heal their hearts."

He turned to her as though she had said exactly the right words.

"Do you really think so? I am very glad to hear it, Anna, I am grateful to you for your kindness to them. As for your advice and help with redecorating this place, it has made a world of difference," he said with great sincerity. With equal candour she assured him that it had brought her much pleasure, too.

"And you do not think they will find life in Hertfordshire dull?" he asked.

"Of course not," she replied, her eyes sparkling. "I have lived most of my life here and I would not like it to be thought that it had been a dull life."

Jonathan assured her that he had not meant that at all, and she laughed as she said, "I know you did not, but I must affirm that dullness is more a state of one's mind than a condition of the county," a proposition with which he agreed completely.

Shortly afterwards, the Faulkners, who had another call to make at Lucas Lodge, left, having invited Mr Bingley and his daughters to dine at Haye Park the following evening.

Mr Griffin, who was then the very last to leave, rose to make his farewells and took so long over them, especially with Miss Bingley, trying again to persuade her to join his choir, that Cathy asked Mrs Perrot if he was staying to dinner, a prospect that appeared to horrify young Teresa!

Grateful when he had finally gone, the family came together for their own little celebration in the cosy upstairs sitting room, which was fast becoming their favourite room in the house.

It had been a very special day, and later that night, when the girls had gone to bed, Jonathan found time to write to his sister.

Would you be astonished, my dear Emma, if I were to say that this has been the best Christmas I have had in many years? I realise it may sound unfeeling to say so, but there was nothing contrary to spoil a simple family occasion.

The girls have taken over their home with great enthusiasm, and Anne-Marie has surprised us all with her poise and sensibility as she played hostess today. You would have been proud of her, Emma; I certainly was.

Miss Faulkner, who was here with Dr and Mrs Faulkner, remarked on her amazing ability to help her younger sisters recover, and yet it was Anne-Marie who seemed most distraught when it all happened last Summer.

I can scarcely believe it is less than seven months ago since that dreadful day, and yet, so much has happened since then, it seems as if years have passed. While my memory is clear enough, the painful consequences of that day have been diluted by many small pleasures, especially since moving to Netherfield.

I sincerely wish you and James the very best of health and look forward to seeing you in the New Year.

God bless you all

He was about to put his pen down and fold up the letter when, hearing a sound in the corridor, he went to the door and opened it.

Standing there, wrapped in her coverlet, was young Cathy.

"Why Cathy, my dear, what's wrong?" he asked.

She looked up at him and said softly, "I wish Mama was here too, Papa. I miss her." Sensing her sorrow, Jonathan scooped her up in his arms and carried her to her room, where Anne-Marie, awakened by the sounds, came swiftly to his aid and took her young sister to bed, comforting her and staying with her until she fell asleep.

Some days later, she wrote to her friend Eliza Harwood:

My dear Eliza,

If you had told me a month ago that I would be writing to you from Netherfield, at Christmas, in a mood that is for the most part happy and content, I would probably have declared you to be a cruel, unfeeling creature, even though I know you to have a heart of gold!

Yet, here am I, a few days after Christmas with Papa and my two young sisters, and hardly a care in the world. I am being rather selfish, I confess, for I have at Netherfield not only a lovely home, but, for the moment at least, I am the lady of the house and may give whatever orders I please and entertain who I choose.

Not that we are doing much in the way of entertaining this year.

On Christmas Day, we had some friends and relations over after church and then on Boxing Day, there was the party for the children of the tenants and servants of the estate. This was a very jolly occasion organised by Mrs Perrot—our wonderfully capable housekeeper and Papa's steward. A very good time was had by all.

That night, we dined with the Faulkners at Haye Park and after an excellent meal, we were treated to a feast of music. Miss Faulkner plays the pianoforte and the harp. I must admit to being completely fascinated by Anna Faulkner's harp. It is a beautiful, statuesque instrument, and she plays it with such ease and sweetness, we were just spell bound.

She sings too and while I lay no claim to being a judge of these things, Papa has lived in London and travelled often to Europe, yet he says he has not heard so fine a voice as hers. I do hope you will come to Netherfield one day soon and hear her sing and play. It is a pleasure I can promise you with confidence.

My sisters and I have enjoyed our stay at Netherfield and Papa seems very happy too. In fact, his spirits have lifted considerably since he moved here and I am hopeful he has begun to recover from the dreadful depression he has suffered from since last Summer.

Meanwhile, my sisters will have me help them with a curious undertaking—a pantomime. Our local church hall is the venue and Miss Faulkner and the Rector, Mr Griffin (of whom you shall hear more when we meet!) are to direct the performance.

Our Teresa is to play the Sleeping Beauty, and since she discovered that the princess does more than sleep, indeed, she sings and dances, she has begun to worry about playing the part. Fortunately, Miss Faulkner, who is marvellous with all the children, has promised to help her. I am to be general factotum and help Papa with the stage business, while Cathy is to be Prince Charming's helper!! Prince Charming himself is a girl!—our steward's daughter, Alison.

Papa is very pleased to see us all involved.

I trust you and Mr Harwood had a happy and blessed Christmas, dear Eliza, and look forward to seeing you soon. I hope to return to you and my work at the hospital in the second week of January, if that is convenient

God bless you,

Anne-Marie Bingley.

When the pantomime was over, and it was generally agreed to be a success, Teresa Bingley, who had just made her debut in amateur theatricals, had to write to her grandmother.

She was very excited about her role in the pantomime:

I was the sleeping princess, but when I discovered I had to sing and dance as well as sleep on stage, I was rather anxious about doing the part, but Papa said I would be all right and Miss Faulkner taught me the songs and it was really fun after all. She has been very kind to all of us.

Papa says she is going to teach us to sing and play the piano as well as draw and paint in the new year. Cathy and I both think it will be good fun.

Grandmama, we have had a good Christmas. No one has quarrelled or wept as we did last year, when Mama was away in London and we were at Hunsford. Everyone is trying to be really good for Papa's sake and cheerful.

Anne-Marie believes that we will all be happier, now we are at Netherfield. She is certainly right about Papa, for we have not seen him so pleased in many months. He smiles more.

She concluded her letter with affectionate greetings to her grandparents and expressed a desire to see them soon.

> *It is far too long to wait until Easter. Could you not come to us sooner? I am longing to show you my room, for which Miss Faulkner chose the colours. She is very artistic and it is beautiful. Grandmama, I am sure you will like it too ...*

... and so on for a page or more.

When Jane Bingley received the letter, she did not know quite what to think. While they were only the words of a young girl, some of what Teresa wrote appeared to confirm her own impressions. It was clear the girls and their father shared the same opinion of Anna Faulkner.

On New Year's Eve, they were all expected at Pemberley for the customary end of year celebrations.

The Bingleys arrived well before nightfall and, as soon as Jane found a moment when her sister was free, she took her aside and showed her Teresa's letter.

"Lizzie, I want you to tell me, what do you make of this letter?" she asked.

Elizabeth, who had received a letter from Charlotte Collins covering most of the same ground, seemed unsurprised by the contents. This was due in part to her recent conversation with Mr Darcy on the same subject. She did not wish her sister to know that they had been discussing her son's private life and in order not to make too much of the hints in Teresa's innocent little note, she said casually, "I am very glad to see that it confirms what I have gathered from Charlotte's letters—the girls are clearly settling in well at Netherfield. Jonathan must be pleased."

Jane looked at her sister as if she had not heard a word she had said.

"Lizzie, of course he must be pleased. So am I. What I want to know is, does he intend to marry Anna Faulkner?"

With the question so bluntly put, Elizabeth had no hope of avoiding it.

"Jane! How have you reached this conclusion?" she asked, quite astonished by her sister's words.

"I have not," Jane protested. "But if you read Tessie's letter, you will have to agree that something is afoot."

"All she has said is that her father seems very happy and Miss Faulkner has been very good and helpful to them. There is nothing untoward in that, is there?" asked Elizabeth.

"No, but I am sure his happiness is not simply the result of a move to Netherfield and the success of the children's pantomime," replied Jane.

"You clearly believe it has more to do with the presence of Anna Faulkner?"

"I certainly do, Lizzie. Do you not think so?"

Elizabeth shrugged her shoulders.

"If it were, would you mind? Jonathan is a grown man, a widower with three young daughters. It is hardly surprising that he may consider marrying again," she said, reasonably.

"Of course he may, I have no quarrel with that idea. But, Lizzie, I do hope and pray that for his own sake and that of the girls, he will take longer to consider his decision this time around."

Elizabeth was surprised at the vehemence of her sister's words, but understood her concern. Jane had seen the marriages of her two eldest children break down, having been made in haste. Emma, after a miserable decade, was now settled happily, while Jonathan's whirlwind courtship of Amelia-Jane Collins had masked the lack of depth and understanding in their marriage, which had subsequently crumbled.

Elizabeth sought to reassure her sister.

"Dear Jane, I think you can rest assured that Jonathan, some twenty years later, is far less likely to rush headlong into another marriage. Besides, unlike Amelia-Jane, Anna Faulkner, should she be his choice, is an intelligent and mature young woman. Indeed, she may well prove to be an ideal companion for him and his daughters."

"But do they love each other, Lizzie?" Jane asked, and Elizabeth was taken aback by the question. Before she could speak, Jane went on, "I know, from everything I have seen over the years, that where there is love and respect, most other difficulties can be overcome; however, if a marriage is not built on true affection and understanding, it will fail when beset by problems. With Amelia-Jane, of whom I was very fond at the time of her marriage to Jonathan, it was easy to see that she had become bored with his work. She had very little understanding of its value, and the more engrossed he became in it, the greater was her annoyance with him. Yet, he had no indication at all of the nature of her feelings."

It came as no surprise to Elizabeth that her sister, whose marriage was one of the most felicitous she had ever seen, should be anxious about her son.

She tried again to set her mind at rest.

"Jane, Jonathan is a responsible man with a far greater understanding of these matters now. You should not be too anxious on his account," she said, but she could see her sister was not altogether convinced.

Jane had hoped for a chance to take up the matter with Jonathan. The opportunity she sought would arise a few weeks later, when several members of the family travelled to Oxford, to attend a recital by young William Courtney, who was a student of Music there.

His parents, James and Emily Courtney, travelled with the Darcys, while the Bingleys went directly to Oxford with their daughter, Sophia. They had rooms reserved at a local inn, the same one at which Jonathan and his daughters were to be accommodated.

Jane planned to speak with Jonathan after the recital.

Unbeknownst to her, however, Jonathan had already visited his sister Emma a fortnight ago, to seek her counsel and, en route, he had received some unsolicited advice from his eldest daughter.

Travelling together to London, they had dined at the house in Grosvenor Street and, as they took tea after dinner, she had surprised him when she remarked, gently but with the clear certainty of youth, "Papa, may I speak plainly with you about a matter that concerns all of us?"

Though somewhat taken aback, Jonathan was quick to declare that she should feel free to speak her mind.

"Of course, Anne-Marie, but what is it that has you so worried?"

"I am not worried, Papa, but if I did not speak now, I would not rest for fear that I would have let you down by keeping silent."

Even more astonished than before, he hastened to reassure her.

"My dear Anne-Marie, you need have no such fear, you could never let me down. Have I not told you how much I have valued your help with your sisters, at a most difficult time for all of us?"

"Papa, I do not mean to harass you, please hear me out. I speak only out of concern and great affection for both you and Miss Faulkner," she said.

"Miss Faulkner? How is she involved?"

Anne-Marie stopped and took a deep breath before continuing. Placing her hand on his, she said rather quickly, "It matters not if she is or is not, Papa. What I have to say concerns you most of all. Should you decide some time in the future to marry again, I merely ask you to be certain that it is because you love and value her, whoever she may be, and not because you feel that Teresa, Cathy, and I need a mother." Seeing his shocked expression, she hastily added, "Forgive me, Papa, I have no right to speak to you in this way, but it would break my heart, should you take such a step and suffer more unhappiness. I shall never forgive myself."

Jonathan was speechless for a few minutes. He was not angry, merely astonished. Yet, he had to ask, "And may I ask why you have mentioned Miss Faulkner in this context? Did you suppose I could involve her in such a cold and cynical arrangement?"

Anne-Marie had tears in her eyes; she had not wanted to hurt or annoy him and now she feared she had done both.

"No, Papa, I did not suppose that. I was only afraid because I have much respect and affection for her and I could not fail to see how close you have become over the past few months, since moving to Netherfield. I would be delighted if Miss Faulkner and you could find happiness together. But, having seen how much you suffered over the years, trying to please Mama, while your work in Parliament consumed so much of your time, I was afraid that it might happen all over again. I am sorry, I did not intend to distress or anger you."

Her father leant forward and took her hands in his.

"Anne-Marie, please do not upset yourself; you have neither distressed nor angered me. I should be churlish indeed, were I to take offence at the words of my daughter, when she was attempting to secure my happiness.

"I was, at first, surprised, but no more than that. My dear child, let me assure you, I believe that no woman, not Miss Faulkner nor anyone else, deserves to be married merely to provide a substitute for a mother. I would never ask any woman to marry me unless I cared deeply for her and was certain she could love me and my children. On that score, I can give you my absolute word.

"As for Miss Faulkner, I am very pleased to hear that you regard her with affection and esteem. I have far too much admiration for her to even contemplate the sort of unfeeling arrangement you fear."

"But you do like her, Papa?" she asked, quietly.

"Yes I do. I like her very much," he replied. "She is one of the most enlightened women I have ever met and I enjoy her company immensely. But, I have no indication what her feelings are; it is a matter for the future."

He then stood up and moved to the window and said in a somewhat matter-of-fact voice, "There is something else I want you to know. When I have conveyed you to Harwood Park, I shall proceed to Kent to see Aunt Emma and Mr Wilson. The visit is not purely for pleasure, though I am sure it will be that; I intend also to inform James Wilson that I shall not seek re-election to the House of Commons."

Seeing her startled expression, he held up a hand.

"Before you say anything, let me tell you that I have made this decision on my own, because, since moving to Netherfield, I have realised the value of my time and my children. I am responsible for Tess and Cathy; I want to stay with them and be a good father to them. I cannot do that if I spend most of my time at Westminster."

Anne-Marie sighed, "Are you sure, Papa? Are you not giving up your life's work?"

Clearly, she was troubled by the prospect.

But her father was not.

"Indeed, no. I shall not be giving up on anything important. I intend to continue working on causes that matter to me, but outside the Parliament. I could make speeches, persuade people, lobby Members of Parliament, and be generally useful, whilst remaining at Netherfield," he explained.

"Do you think Mr Wilson will be angry?" she asked, apprehensively.

"No, I do not; disappointed perhaps, but not angry. Not when he understands my reasons."

Anne-Marie went to him and put her arms around him.

"Papa, if it is what you want, I am very happy you have decided. I pray that everything will work out well and we will all be happy again."

And he assured her that it was his wish as well.

Later that afternoon, having seen her safely returned to her friends at Harwood House, Jonathan left for Standish Park. Emma and James Wilson were very glad to see him, though they were disappointed that Anne-Marie was not with him.

Over the years Jonathan Bingley had become not just a brother-in-law to James, but a dear friend and trusted colleague. They had known one another since their college days, developed an interest in politics, entered Parliament, joined the Reform Movement, and fought diligently to promote the same causes.

A dedicated Reformist, James had consistently supported the extension of the franchise beyond the rich and powerful. Jonathan had worked with him to persuade their colleagues and negotiate with their opponents.

Personally, too, James, whose errant brother David had been married to Emma until his death ended their wretched marriage, had reason to be grateful for Jonathan's discretion and sensitivity. It had been his swift action that had spared the family the scandal that might have engulfed them following David's suicide.

James' subsequent marriage to Emma, whose years of anguish had ended only with her husband's death, had been welcomed by the family and especially by Jonathan.

Brother and sister were very close and often turned to each other for advice. It was not surprising, then, that before telling James of his decision, Jonathan sought out his sister.

Emma was alone, missing her daughters Victoria and Stephanie, who were touring Italy with their governess; when her brother entered the sitting room, she greeted him warmly, glad of his company.

She did not notice the gravity of his expression and chatted on for a few minutes about the girls' departure and how much they were missed.

A maid brought in tea and cakes, and Jonathan waited until she had left the room before he spoke.

"Emma, pardon me for intruding upon you …" he began, but she interrupted his apology.

"Jonathan, you know you have no need to apologise. You are not intruding and I am very happy to see you."

Jonathan smiled and tried to continue. Initially, he had hoped to explain in clear and logical terms the reasons for his decision not to stand at the next election, but when he began, he appeared to become confused and blurted it all out at once and not very coherently, either. He told her of his distress at discovering that Amelia-Jane had blamed him, specifically, in a letter to Anne-Marie, for the breakdown of their marriage.

"She blamed me for spending time at Westminster and leaving her at home to manage the household and raise the children. Emma, I had no idea she felt so strongly about it, she had always encouraged me to seek ministerial office and seemed disappointed when I did not," he said and proceeded to tell her more about the letter his daughter had received a few days before her mother's death.

Emma listened to him without further interruption and, when he had finished, spoke quietly.

"Jonathan, of course, you must do what you believe is right for you and the girls, and should you honestly feel that you cannot do your duty by them while being a Member of Parliament, then you must do as you suggest. There can be no argument about that, but I implore you not to do anything out of a sense of guilt because Amelia-Jane or anyone else believed you were to blame for her problems. That would be wrong.

"You were not to blame. I know you and I knew how things were at the time, you had told me yourself, and at no time have I or anyone I have spoken with since that dreadful day—not James or Mr Darcy or Aunt Lizzie or Catherine Harrison—ever suggested you were to blame. Others were culpable; some of them are gone with her and some remain. It is they who should carry the burden of guilt, not you."

He was touched by the sincerity with which she defended him and said, "Then you will not censure me for deciding that my place is at Netherfield?"

"Censure you? Why, Jonathan, surely you cannot believe that I expect you to abandon two girls who have lost their mother in the most tragic way."

"And James? What will he say?" Jonathan asked.

"He will be disappointed, of course. He has set great store by your ability to argue and persuade, and was looking forward to your returning to the Commons. But he will not blame you, I do not think," she replied.

Then noting that he still appeared rather troubled, she asked pointedly, "My dear brother, will you forgive my impertinence if I were to ask you a very personal question?"

When he made no objection, she went on, "Jonathan, do you intend to ask Anna Faulkner to marry you?"

Never having expected such a direct question, he could not answer her at once. Seeing his confusion, she continued, "Perhaps I should rephrase my question. Are you in love with Miss Faulkner?"

This time, having recovered his composure, Jonathan answered, but cautiously.

"Emma, do you ask because you believe this may have something to do with my decision?"

"Does it not? Have you given no thought to the effect your standing for Parliament may have on Miss Faulkner, were you to ask her to marry you?"

Jonathan looked embarrassed. Her questions were forcing him to confront his own feelings.

"I cannot deny that I have thought of it. I realise that, quite apart from Miss Faulkner, it would be unfair to any woman."

"Let us not speak too generally, Jonathan," said his sister. "How do you think Miss Faulkner may respond, should you ask her? Have you spoken of this to her?" she asked.

"No, I have not. But Emma, I will be honest with you, I do admire and respect her very much and so do the girls. She is, without any doubt, the most amiable and intelligent young woman I have met in years. She is probably aware of my appreciation—I have certainly not hidden it—but I have not mentioned any of this to her simply because it may have seemed indelicate, being too soon after ..."

Emma was sympathetic.

"I understand. But if it were possible, would you wish to?"

"If I thought she loved me, yes, I would," he confessed, a little reluctant to admit to her what he had not as yet admitted to himself.

"Well, Jonathan, there is only one way to find out. You must ask her."

"And, does that mean I have your blessing?" he asked.

Emma smiled and nodded.

"If you love her, of course. Anna is a most affectionate and generous hearted woman, and if she agrees to marry you, she will be a wonderful influence upon your daughters, and I believe she will make you very happy. Are you certain of your feelings?" she asked.

He responded sincerely, "I am, Emma; I think I have known it for many months now."

They spoke together of love and marriage and their own experience of both. Emma recalled their mother telling her of their Aunt Lizzie's determination that "nothing but the deepest love will ever persuade me to marry."

"It is a good philosophy," she declared, adding, "I think you will find Anna willing to listen to you."

The sound of James returning brought their conversation to an end.

James Wilson greeted his brother-in-law cheerfully, very glad to see him again. They always had a great deal to discuss, and their conversations usually went late into the night.

After dinner, Emma left them together, knowing Jonathan needed time to tell his brother-in-law of his decision.

Jonathan had expected it would be a difficult undertaking, but strangely, it turned out very different indeed. James was disappointed, of course, but he comprehended and sympathised with Jonathan's grave concerns. He realised, he said, that the death of his wife and the subsequent move to Netherfield Park had materially altered Jonathan's circumstances.

Nor did he argue with the need for a father to put the interest of his young daughters first.

"I will not try to hide my disappointment, Jonathan," he said, after he had listened to his reasons. "I had hoped we would have your voice to support our push for further electoral reform. Lord Russell is eager, but Palmerston is not. Darcy is quite right, he is very much the Tory he was in matters of electoral reform. And of course, we intend to work for a policy on Public Education, including education for girls. We have the Prince Consort's support on this, but nothing worthwhile is being done." James seemed very frustrated.

"Then there is the matter of Lord Shaftesbury's Bill—yes I know he is a Tory, but he alone has fought for laws against the exploitation of children. I understand he plans another assault on the chimney sweeps—he wants to outlaw their use of children as young as four and five to clear chimneys and put out fires! It is a subject very close to Emma's heart. The charity she works with in the east end of London can produce dozens of cases of children hurt or even killed by this reprehensible practice. It is truly appalling that we permit it to go on in England, yet the only person who has shown an interest in stopping them is Shaftesbury. I have promised him my full support.

"I should have liked very much to have you on our side in the Parliament, but I cannot cavil at your desire to devote your time to your daughters; they probably need you even more than the little chimney sweeps," he said.

Jonathan protested that he would not turn his back on the little chimney sweeps or any of these causes; they were far too dear to his heart.

"James, I give you my word, I shall work outside the Parliament, in the councils and the community, wherever I can, to make people aware of these dreadful injustices. I shall not abandon you and my friends in the Reform Group, I promise."

James Wilson was very touched and thanked him, but then asked, "And does Miss Faulkner share your enthusiasm for reform?"

Jonathan responded, without stopping to think, "Indeed, she does, James, very much so," realising only after the words were spoken the true import of his reply.

His stumbling efforts to correct the impression he may have given of an unusual level of familiarity with the views of the lady amused his brother-in-law. But James was kind in his response.

"My dear fellow, you do not have to explain, I am not entitled to question you about your private life. Your sister Emma and I have wondered, for some time now, when you and Miss Faulkner would come to a realisation that you are well suited and, if you loved each other of course, would make an excellent match."

Jonathan tried once more to explain that while he had always admired the lady, he had not approached her with any proposal.

James smiled and said, "Perhaps you should, Jonathan; do not leave it too long, she is a very attractive and accomplished young woman."

And with that he rose and they moved into the drawing room, where Emma joined them for coffee.

She was eager to discover more about Netherfield and how his daughters were settling in. Jonathan was beginning to feel very tired. He had done a great deal of travelling in the last few days, and it was taking its toll upon him. Emotionally, he felt drained and exhausted.

Fond though he was of his sister and happy to answer all her questions, he was very glad when James, who had returned from London just that afternoon, suggested they could all benefit from an early night.

~❦~

Waking up the next morning, Jonathan Bingley went for a long walk in the park before breakfast. It was cold and the leafless trees were stark against the sky, but even in this bleak wood, a dawn chorus of birds had begun as the first rays of the sun lit the horizon. Jonathan had always preferred living in the country, enjoying its changing moods and colours, as well as the variety of work the different seasons brought. It had held, for him, a far greater appeal and a more interesting challenge than the prospect of an office in town.

At no time, however prosperous the business, had he considered going to work for the Commercial Trading Company, in which the Bingleys had a lucrative interest. At first, his parents had been disappointed, but they had never attempted to compel him to take it up.

Here in Kent, as in Hertfordshire, the land had a gentler profile, clothed in softer woods and pastures than the rugged Midlands with which he was familiar. It was a landscape in which he was always comfortable, with a rural charm that had persisted through many centuries. He had been surprised at the ease with which he had slipped into his role at Netherfield Park and the extent of his enjoyment of it.

After his conversations with his sister and her husband, Jonathan had decided that he would, on returning to Netherfield, call on Anna Faulkner. He was keen to discover what her feelings were, since he now had no doubts at all about his own.

The weather in Hertfordshire was still wintry when Jonathan returned to Netherfield, but a few green buds had begun to burst upon the grey boughs of the old trees in the park. The early rain had soaked into the earth, and the fields looked ready for the plough in Spring, he thought, as the carriage approached the house. Mrs Perrot greeted him in the hall and informed him that Teresa and Cathy had gone with Miss Faulkner to Longbourn.

It was a windy afternoon with occasional gusts bringing more spattering rain. Riding out was not an attractive prospect, and Jonathan decided to stay in and await their return.

They came in time for afternoon tea, and Anna, seeing him in the hallway as they entered, was clearly pleased. He went forward to greet them, first the girls who embraced their father before running upstairs to change their shoes and then Anna, who followed him into the sitting room, where a fire had been lit and tea would soon be served.

They exchanged the usual pleasantries as the servants brought in the tea things. She asked after his sister at Standish Park, and he inquired if her parents were well and if the ladies at Longbourn were in good health. But, even as they talked of such inconsequential matters, seeing her there in the warm fire-light, knowing how easily she seemed to fit into his home, he knew that he loved her and had to know her mind.

Now, he needed only an opportunity to ask her.

Teresa and Cathy returned and were full of questions all through tea. How was their aunt Emma? Did Anne-Marie reach Harwood House safely? Did their father see anything of their cousins, Victoria and Stephanie? And a myriad others, besides!

Anna and Jonathan had little opportunity for private conversation before it was time for her to leave. She was alone and eager to be home before dark. Escorting her to the carriage, Jonathan asked if he may call on her the following day. He told her of some sheet music he had purchased in London and asked if she would like to try it.

She was immediately agreeable, and a time was arranged, convenient to both of them. He noted with pleasure that she had agreed with some enthusiasm, almost as if she had anticipated his request.

This, he thought, was a good sign.

That night, after an early dinner, when the girls had gone to bed, Jonathan planned what he would say to Miss Faulkner.

Best not to be too startling, he decided. She was not the sort of silly woman who would be impressed by dramatic gestures and extravagant compliments. That was not her at all.

Simple, sincere words were best, he thought.

Should he ask her father's permission first? he wondered.

Perhaps he should write to him … he pondered the question a while before deciding he would follow his brother-in-law's advice and ask the lady first.

The sheet music he had bought had been recommended by Emma, who declared it to be one of the loveliest compositions she had heard in recent days. Her own daughter Victoria had practised long and hard to master it, she had said. She was sure Anna would enjoy it, too.

It would certainly provide him with a good reason to spend some time with her, Emma had said, thoughtfully. He smiled as he recalled her words.

Jonathan spent a restless night, wondering how he would be received, but finally fell into a deep sleep—the result of physical tiredness rather than mental serenity.

When he awoke early on the morrow, he had been unable to resolve the questions that had engrossed his mind before he fell asleep. What manner of approach should he make to Miss Faulkner? How direct should he be? How much of his deeply felt attachment must he declare? Most pressing of all, how would she respond?

Looking out of the window, however, he found the rain had ceased and the wind had blown most of the clouds away, leaving a startlingly blue sky. He was eager to be on his way.

To Haye Park he would go, soon after breakfast, in much the same way as his father had gone to Longbourn to propose to the lovely Miss Jane Bennet, all those years ago. The romantic story of that proposal was a legend in their family.

At Haye Park, Anna Faulkner had been preparing for her visitor.

She had, when he asked permission to visit, agreed at once, because she had been genuinely pleased to see him after several days and always enjoyed his company.

Indeed, she was beginning to believe that, of all the men she knew and all those she had met over the last few years, Jonathan Bingley was the one gentleman whose company had given her the most pleasure.

With him, each conversation was as interesting as the last. Their mutual enjoyment of the Arts and his particular appreciation of fine music had set him apart in their circle of acquaintances.

The friendship that had developed between herself and his sister Emma, in the course of the previous Summer, had served to enhance their own understanding. It had become clear to Anna that Emma Wilson was sufficiently concerned for her brother's future happiness to hope that he would make a more felicitous marriage soon. She had as good as admitted to having had her doubts about the maturity and suitability of his late wife, Amelia-Jane, as a partner for her brother.

If Anna had been looking for encouragement, it was there to be found in the praise and affection she had received from his family. Since Christmas and the arrival at Netherfield of his daughters, there had developed a degree of closeness between herself and the girls, which was bound to increase as a result of her agreeing to teach them Art and Music.

As for the man himself, she had few reservations, particularly since observing his attentive and gracious hospitality to her friends Monsieur and Madame Armande. They had met with increasing frequency and on many pleasant occasions, before and after his move to Netherfield. Each time, he had been very gentlemanly and friendly towards her, often favouring her with special attention, yet maintaining a most particular decorum, while extending to the Armandes every courtesy.

This had delighted them and pleased her very much.

Still, as she waited for him to arrive at the appointed time, she experienced an unfamiliar sense of excitement and heightened expectation, which she could not entirely comprehend. It was as though she did not quite know what to expect from him and was therefore rather discomposed.

Anna was watching from the window of the upstairs sitting room, which afforded her a clear view of the park and the lane beyond, when the carriage swung into the drive leading to the house. She was halfway down the stairs before she realised she may need a handkerchief and sped back to her room to fetch one. The delay meant she was barely at the foot of the stairs, and was somewhat breathless from hurrying, when the bell rang and he was admitted into the hall.

As they greeted one another, a trifle more formally than usual, it was apparent that he was somewhat less at ease, too. Anna was very grateful that her mother, who had been reading in the parlour, was on hand to engage him in conversation upon some mundane matter, giving her time to compose herself.

Jonathan could not help noticing that Anna was looking particularly well, in a long-sleeved gown of sapphire blue, which perfectly suited her dark colouring. He recalled telling her, on another occasion, how well the colour became her and speculated for a moment before dismissing the thought that she may have anticipated his motives for calling on her and dressed to please him.

Fires had been lit in both the parlour and the adjoining room where her piano and harp stood. She was impatient to try the new music he had brought.

It was a composition by the French composer Gounod, and, as she played, while he took tea with her mother, he was very tempted to go over to the instrument. But a combination of nervousness and courtesy to Mrs Faulkner restrained him, and it was only after Anna had finished playing that he rose and went over to her.

She declared the piece to be complex but beautiful and worth working on.

"I shall practice diligently, Mr Bingley, and in a week or two when I have it well learned, you shall hear it again."

He was delighted and said he would look forward to the day. They were more at ease with one another now, after their initial nervousness.

Dr Faulkner was away in Watford, visiting a colleague, and Mrs Faulkner invited Jonathan to join them for an early dinner, which invitation he accepted with pleasure. Since there were many hours to dinner time, and it was such a beautiful day, Jonathan asked Anna if she would like to take a walk and enjoy the freshness of the morning.

"It feels almost like Spring," he said, and Mrs Faulkner, who had been out in the garden earlier, agreed that it was a very good idea.

"Now, if you were intending to walk in the direction of Lucas Lodge, my dear, I have a note to send to your uncle," she said tentatively. "It would save me sending a servant over, if you could call in and deliver it for me."

Anna, who knew her mother well, guessed this was a scheme to encourage her to walk out with Mr Bingley, but having no objection to it herself, she agreed and went upstairs to change her shoes and put on a bonnet.

"I have noticed," said Jonathan as they set out, "that the Spring flowers are out earliest in the meadows that lie to the south of Lucas Lodge. I think we may have the pleasure of seeing them first."

As they walked towards the old house where her uncle, now retired from Naval duties, lived with his son, they talked lightly of many things.

The New Year just begun and the prospects thereof, how swiftly the last few months had flown, and what astonishing changes were taking place around them, what with Mr Charles Darwin's new theory on the Origin of the Species and Miss Florence Nightingale's bold suggestion that women should have the vote, and of course, the rumours that were all over London, that George Eliot, author of the popular novel *Adam Bede* was none other than Miss Mary Anne Evans—the essayist! They were all grist to the mill.

"So much has happened in so short a time, one feels the time has flown," she said.

Jonathan remarked that his daughter Anne-Marie had told him being in London seemed to have sped up her life.

"She claims she is always rushing towards the next day or some goal she must reach, and though she says she loves her work at the hospital and is devoted to her patients, she misses the leisurely pace of country life."

Anna was instantly sympathetic.

"I know just how she must feel; the day seems twice as long in the country," she said, as they reached the old arched bridge halfway between Haye Park and Lucas Lodge. Anna peered at the water slipping noisily over the pebbles far below.

"When I was a little girl," she said as she leaned over, making her companion rather nervous for her safety, "the days were long and unhurried. I would wake up in the morning, and there, stretching before me, was the day—hours and hours of it, to do whatever I pleased, until nightfall." Her expression reflected the pleasures remembered, and Jonathan was reminded, too, of long warm Summer days at Ashford Park.

"I used to yearn for those long Summers all through Winter," he said.

"I remember most of all just waiting for Autumn," Anna declared. "'Oh Season of mists and mellow fruitfulness,' my most favourite time of the year; endless Autumn days in the country, with the woods ablaze with colour and the scent of ripening fruit everywhere; there can be few greater joys in life. I used to hate going to bed before it was dark, for fear that I might miss some small magic moment of the day."

She turned around, leaning against the parapet of the bridge, laughing as the breeze pushed her bonnet back and freed her hair, which then fell around her shoulders. Jonathan gazed, fascinated, as though he were seeing her for the first time, freer, lovelier than he had ever seen her before.

He wanted very much to speak, to remark upon her beauty, to tell her he loved her, but he was afraid to break the spell.

A sudden gust of wind caused her to draw her wrap closely around her; the moment was gone as she remembered they had an errand to run for her mother and should be moving on. They walked on and as the road deteriorated, he offered her his arm. She thanked him, glad of the support.

She continued, telling him of the time she had spent in Europe, "The Armandes have this wonderful place in the country, not very far out of town, where time seemed to stop. There was no clock in the house; you could do what you wished, at the pace that you wished to do it, whether it was painting, cooking, walking in the woods, or picking mushrooms. For me, it was close to heaven," she said softly.

"Could you not find that same feeling in England?" he asked.

Having paused to reflect, she replied, "I don't see why not. Not in London, though. I did enjoy the Summer school and the students, but I could not live my life in London. It is just too busy and I hate large crowds. You see," she added, laughing, "I need space as well as time to be content."

"And yet, you liked Paris," he said, and she smiled, remembering.

"Indeed, I did like Paris. I loved it. It is full of bustle and excitement and yet, you could always stop and step out of the crowd and do something quite different if you wished. We used to sit in the sunshine beside the river and watch the passing parade, while we drank coffee or watched the artists working by the river. It was possible just to dream as the rest of the world rushed past. Paris lets one do that."

"And does no part of England offer you similar pleasure?" he asked, a little sadly, at which she looked contrite.

"Now you are going to scold me for being disloyal to England, but truly, I do love England, there are parts of the country, mercifully still unspoiled, which are so beautiful, they move me to tears. But at home, much as I enjoy being here, with my father's profession, it has always been a rather busy place. I would give anything to have time and space to myself ..."

"To dream?" he asked, and she laughed again.

"Perhaps, but in truth it is to think or maybe to draw as I used to, when I was a girl. My old sketch-books are full of drawings, some only half finished, of trees, birds, and houses, anything that caught my eye. Yet now, there is so little time for all of that. I would like, I would very much wish to have more time to reflect and perhaps to paint."

They had reached the point in the road where it went down to Meryton, while a narrow lane turned away towards Lucas Lodge. Jonathan knew that if he did not speak now, he would not have another opportunity. Desperate to let her know how he felt and eager to discover her feelings, he broke in upon her musings.

"Anna, forgive me, but I must speak with you. Let us walk on along the road a little further and perhaps, we could deliver your mother's letter on the way back," then, seeing her bewilderment, added quickly, "My dear Anna, if I do not speak now, I fear you may never know how I feel. Please, do me the honour of listening to what I have to say."

Even though she had prepared herself for some approach from him, Anna was surprised at the suddenness and intensity of his declaration.

She indicated her readiness to do as he had suggested and took his arm. They walked further down the road, crossed a meadow where the first wild flowers of Spring were pushing up everywhere, and then passed through a patch of woodland.

He was silent at first, until they had passed a group of men gathering kindling, remarking only on the profusion of flowers.

Anna was quiet, waiting for him to speak.

Presently, he did, and it was a quiet, modest, almost diffident speech, from a man renowned for his eloquent powers of advocacy in the Parliament.

"Anna, forgive me if I do not do and say all the things I am traditionally supposed to do at this point, but please permit me to tell you how deeply I love you and how happy I should be, if you will agree to marry me."

Jonathan had little experience of this type of situation. His proposal to Amelia-Jane, made as they sat in a box at the theatre, had been so speedily and happily accepted, he had never worried about rejection.

With Anna, it was different. He felt the need to explain, to tell her how he had reached this point and he wanted above all to urge her to remember how happy had been the times they had spent together on many occasions over the past few months.

As he spoke, they had reached the end of the path, where, in a small clearing overlooking the river valley below, they found an old stone seat.

Rather weary from walking, Anna sat down and he sat beside her, keeping hold of her hand. He was encouraged by the fact that she had not drawn away or discouraged him at all. Indeed, she had heard him out with great courtesy.

He was concluding his speech as they sat together.

"Should I have had the opportunity, I would have spoken sooner, for my feelings and my thoughts have been preoccupied with you for several weeks now. But as we both know only too well, we are not always masters of our time, and I have not been afforded an appropriate occasion on which to address you, alone. Now, at last, I have the time and I must speak; dearest Anna, I admire and love you very much, will you be my wife?"

Anna had heard him at first with surprise and then with increasing pleasure. She had known he enjoyed her company; to be told she was admired and loved was quite another matter. That she was pleased and gratified, she could not deny.

He was a man she had long admired, and more recently her esteem had increased, as she learned more about him. She had known he was clever as well as principled and kind. From his sister, his daughters, and her aunt Charlotte Collins, she had gained such information as would convince her that his character was beyond reproach.

When he entreated her response, she knew she had to speak with care. She had no desire to hurt him, nor by any sign of caprice or indifference drive him away. That her own affections were engaged, she did not doubt. She wanted only to know their strength before accepting his.

She was, therefore, eager to ensure by her expression, her general demeanour and tone of voice, that he understood his proposal was in no way repugnant to her. Anxious to reassure him, she began with gentleness and sensitivity, to explain why it would not be possible, nor wise, for her to give him an immediate answer.

"Much as I would wish to do so, if only to ensure that you will not think ill of me, as one who would cruelly torment you with unnecessary deferment and delay, I cannot. Jonathan, please understand, that now I know your feelings and wishes, I need time to discover my own.

"The question is not whether I can marry you, for that may be easily answered; indeed if eligibility were the only concern, I would marry you, gladly. But, I need to know whether we share more than just the transient tenderness that is born of mutual fondness and sympathy; whether these feelings, to which we both admit, mean genuine love of the deepest, most enduring kind."

She continued, explaining in a most reasonable voice, "Because, dear Jonathan, if it is only the former, why then, there is no reason to marry, for we can remain good friends, who will always hold out a helping hand to one another, listen sympathetically, advise wisely, and enjoy each other's company. Why marry and risk this pleasant association for so little gain? For my part, I have no need to marry for mercenary reasons. Thanks to my dear generous grandfather Sir William Lucas and the prudent management of my parents, I am well provided for.

"I am certainly not wealthy, but should I remain unwed, I shall not be any less comfortable in the future than I am now. Indeed, should I choose to use such skills as I may have, as you have suggested, to teach Music or Art, I may well improve both my income and my satisfaction with life."

She proceeded then to provide him with an example of the kind of marriage that held no attraction for her.

"I have recently spent two weeks with my sister Sarah at her husband's farm in Hampshire, and nothing I saw convinced me that poor Sarah is happier or more satisfied with her life now than when she was at home with the rest of us. Indeed, she appears less able to enjoy the things we shared as sisters, so bound up is she with the material concerns of the farm. I saw little pleasure and even less love in their home.

"Your sister, Emma, on the other hand, strikes me as a woman who enjoys every moment of her marriage. Oh, I know about her first tragic experience, my aunt has told me of it, but to see her now with James and her children is surely to be reassured of the power of love, is it not?"

As he listened with interest, wondering where this was leading, Jonathan had to agree that his sister and brother-in-law were indeed a singularly happy pair.

She went on in a quiet but determined voice.

"Well, unlike my sister Sarah, who has made what can only be deemed to be a dull and passionless union, with little hope of mutual happiness beyond the most ordinary, I have decided that I shall marry only were I to be convinced that life without the man I wed will be unendurable."

At this point, convinced he could never match her ideal, he looked so crestfallen that she relented and, leaning forward, touched his face, gently, kindly, and said, "Dear Jonathan, please do not look so dejected; this is not a rejection of your proposal, which I was honoured to receive; I would not have you think otherwise. You have offered me your love and I am happy to confess my own feelings for you; I ask only that you allow me time to discover if we really love each other, so that if I marry you, you may be absolutely certain that I do so because the thought of living the rest of my life without you is unbearable. Now, need I say more?"

She looked and sounded so sincere, Jonathan had to believe her and though he was somewhat disconcerted at being left in limbo, with no definite decision, he agreed, albeit reluctantly, to wait.

As she smiled, relieved at his reasonableness, he asked, only half in jest, "And in the meantime, should some fine knight ride into your life, upon a white charger, and sweep you up in a wave of passion, will I lose you forever?"

She laughed then, a merry laugh that echoed around the clearing.

"Jonathan, there has been no knight on a white charger to sweep me off my feet in the last seven years, so I think one would have to admit that the chances of him appearing now are remote. But, if he were to appear, I promise to refer him to you, and you may deal with him as you think fit."

She was clearly going to be light-hearted about it and expected him to follow suit.

Having assured her once more that his own feelings for her were beyond question, he was keen to acquaint her with another matter, lest her ignorance should influence her decision. Quietly, he told her of his determination not to seek re-election to the Parliament.

She was genuinely shocked, almost sad, as she asked, "Why Jonathan, I had thought it was something you wanted very much to do. I know how important these reforms are to you. I had thought your heart was set on achieving them. Why have you changed your mind?"

She sounded disappointed, but as he explained in the same calm manner in which he had described his reasons to James and Emma, she understood and accepted his reasoning.

"I need to make a life for myself, with my children and, if you will accept me, dearest Anna, with you," he said, taking her hand in his.

The warmth and genuine affection in his voice broke down her reserve and she let him draw her into a close embrace, her smile making her complicit in the fond exchange that followed.

"How long must I wait?" he asked.

"Not long, Jonathan. Please do not believe that I am doing this to inflict the pain of uncertainty upon you. I am not, for I care too much for you to do such a thing. Nor is it a sign that I am being wayward or contrary."

She was keen to reassure him. "Ever since Christmas, I have known in my heart that this was likely to happen. Now it is out in the open, and I know how you feel, I want only to discover the truth of my own feelings. I ask no more than that.

"I wish you to know that I esteem and admire you more than any other man. Your daughters are precious to me, your sister Emma is a dear friend. All I need to know is my own heart. Once that is certain, there will be no further waiting, I promise. Please tell me, am I making an unreasonable request?"

He thought he saw tears in her eyes and said, at once, that it was no such thing. Though his heart was heavy with disappointment, he said firmly that she was not being unreasonable at all.

She continued, "Jonathan, we must remember that your young daughters may not as yet have fully absorbed the shock and pain of Amelia-Jane's death; Teresa and Cathy, especially, need time to let the memory of their mother become part of their past, if they are to accept me as part of their future. It will not do to hasten matters and find that they have turned resentful. I have their trust and affection now and could not bear to lose that."

At this, Jonathan had to agree, thinking how wisely and selflessly she had considered the risk. In the end, they were agreed, he however reluctantly, that they would wait a few more weeks.

As they rose to leave, he kissed her hand and embraced her with great tenderness, and she permitted him, knowing that in doing so, she was letting him see how deeply she cared.

As they retraced their steps, they were agreed on one more thing. So as not to appear to impose upon her parents, Jonathan would write to Dr Faulkner in confidence, while she would explain to both her parents that it was her wish to wait a while before making a final decision.

Meanwhile, only to Emma and James Wilson would he reveal the understanding they had reached.

Returning to Netherfield, Jonathan felt strangely ambivalent about the day just gone. When he set out that morning, he had expected to return elated or totally dejected. He was neither and, as he sat to write to his sister, he pondered his strange emotional state.

My dear Emma, he wrote:

I would have dearly liked to commence this letter with the good news I know both you and James expect to receive from me.

Unhappily, that news must be delayed. I have today returned from Haye Park, having dined with Anna Faulkner and her mother (Dr Faulkner is from home visiting a colleague in Watford). Prior to this very pleasant meal, I was given a rare opportunity of spending some time alone with Miss Faulkner, which I used to tell her of my feelings and ask her to marry me.

Emma, she has assured me of her regard and affection, but she will have us wait some weeks, while she delves into her own heart and decides if we may or may not marry!

Her reasons, my dear sister, which I will not weary you by quoting here, were all reasonable and impossible to fault. I had no option but to agree and must now consume my soul in patience, though I am deeply disappointed at not knowing my fate, as it were.

I doubt if either you or James would have disagreed with the logic and wisdom of her arguments. One in particular, relating to the children and the loss of their mother, shows a genuine goodness of heart, I think. I could not help but agree and admire her selflessness.

And yet, my dear sister, I feel so alone tonight, not knowing if the woman I love, who assures me that I am the man she most admires and esteems of all her acquaintances, will actually agree to be my wife.

Or will she, if some remarkable stranger crosses her path and declares undying love, depart and leave me bereft? (I do jest, of course, but I think you will understand how I feel.)

The next few weeks will move exceedingly slow for me, dear Emma, but I shall try to endure it with cheerful fortitude.

Your loving brother etc.

꧁꧂

Jonathan's mother Jane was not privy to any of these developments when, driven only by maternal affection, she decided to approach her son about the same subject.

They met, fortuitously, after the recital given by William Courtney and his fellow students at St John's Chapel, Oxford, whither several members of the family had travelled.

The recital over, many of the guests were invited to the Grantleys' house, where Dr Grantley and Georgiana were hosting a supper party. Light rain was falling, and Jonathan, who had intended to walk to the Grantleys' place, was taking shelter outside the chapel when the carriage bearing his parents approached and his father invited him to jump in.

He did, glad to be out of the rain, and when they reached the house, found that several guests had arrived already and there was quite a buzz of conversation in the parlour.

Young William and his parents were being congratulated, and there were requests for more music, which gave Jane an opportunity to take Jonathan aside into Dr Grantley's study, where they were sure to be undisturbed.

Jonathan assumed his mother had had some information from his sister. He was annoyed with himself for not insisting upon secrecy. But, as it turned out, it was not Emma but Charlotte Collins who had been Jane's informant.

Charlotte, whose letter was produced for his perusal, had written with the best of intentions. A couple of paragraphs on page three were drawn to his attention …

I hope, dear Jane, that I do not upset you by recalling unhappy memories of things past, when I say how pleased I have been to see the growing friendship between Jonathan and my niece Anna Faulkner. I know they met several times in London, before and after the dreadful days following Amelia-Jane's death, but in more recent times they seem to have been often together. I am aware that they are frequently in each other's company and, though my sister Maria says very little, I do believe she has hopes in this regard.

The other day, she was at Longbourn, the day after Jonathan had dined with them, and she seemed a little disappointed that nothing was said by either Anna or Jonathan that would give her any indication of their intentions.

"I can get nothing from Anna, sister," she said and added that she hoped "Anna would not be hurt again as she was some years ago."

I assured her then and there, dear Jane, that Jonathan Bingley, who was my own son-in-law, and a man of utmost integrity, would never deliberately hurt anyone, least of all a fine young woman like her Anna.

"He is an honourable and sincere gentleman," I said, *"and I am sure if he has any intentions, he will acquaint you and Dr Faulkner with them very soon."*

I hope, dear Jane, you will agree that I have been fair to your son, for whom I have great respect and affection. I know he has suffered a great deal of aggravation and misery, some of it on account of my poor foolish Amelia-Jane, who was so cruelly misled by her false friends, and I am sorry for all of that. But, Jane, neither you nor I could have foreseen what happened and I sincerely hope that this time, he will be truly happy, for Anna is a remarkable young woman, with quite the most charming disposition of anyone I know.

Jonathan read and returned the letter to his mother. He looked thoughtful and concerned. Sitting beside her, he took her hand in his.

"Mama, has this letter upset you? Have you been unhappy about the prospect of Anna and I …" She put a hand up to his lips to hush him.

"No, Jonathan my dear, it is not a matter of being upset or unhappy about you and Anna. Why would I be? She is accomplished and handsome and of impeccable character. Her parents are respectable and have been our friends for many years."

He was bewildered. "What then? What objection could you possibly have?"

"None," she replied, but then, she looked at him and sighed. "But, I will admit I have been concerned that in your sorrow and loneliness, you will rush into a marriage without giving it much thought. Jonathan, I could not bear the thought of you being miserable again. All I ask is that you give yourself sufficient time to consider your future. There is really no need to make a hurried decision, is there?"

She even had a practical proposition for him. "If you are anxious about the girls, perhaps I could stay with you a while at Netherfield until they settle in."

Jonathan was both relieved and touched. Relieved, because he knew his mother was not implacably opposed to Anna, and touched by her genuine concern for his happiness. He hastened to reassure her.

"Dear Mama, you need have no fears at all. There is not going to be another precipitate proposal this time, nor a hasty marriage. I confess I was both precipitate and hasty the last time, but in my defence, I was young and we were all suffering the effects of a terrible tragedy. I do not say this to excuse my failure of judgment, merely to explain it. But, Mama, it is almost twenty-five years later; I am no callow youth and Anna is a mature and intelligent young woman. You have no cause for anxiety."

"But Jonathan, tell me, is it true? Is Charlotte right? Have you been courting her?" she asked, searching his face for the truth.

He smiled. "Well, it is and it isn't," he said, and to allay her fears, explained some of what had passed between Anna and himself.

She listened, her face reflecting her changing response from surprise to relief.

"So you see, there is no reason to worry. I do believe I love her, very much. When you know her better, I know you will, too. I have asked her to marry me and I have written to ask her father's permission, but the lady herself wishes to have a little more time to be quite sure of her feelings and mine."

At that point, his mother bridled, outraged that any young woman could doubt her son, but was appeased when he assured her that Anna had a very high opinion of him. All the same, she smiled and remarked, "Of course she has. Why should she not?"

"Trust me, Mama," he said, putting his arms around her, knowing that her affection would always win out in the end, "When you come to us at Easter, you will meet Anna again and I hope we shall have settled all this business by then. I know you will agree that she is a most engaging and intelligent young woman," he said as they went to rejoin the rest of the party, taking comfort from the fact that his mother was smiling and content again, much more like her usual self.

❦

Returning home from Oxford, the Darcys and Bingleys travelled through Warwickshire, breaking journey at Leamington Spa, where the gentlemen had an appointment with a business acquaintance, who had recently shown an interest in the trade in Tea and Spices. Since Mr Gardiner's recent illness, which prevented him from travelling far from home, Bingley had taken on some of the work of dealing with clients and, with Darcy's prestige to substantiate his own claims, was making a very good fist of it.

Travelling at a leisurely pace, stopping to enjoy the singular beauty of tiny Warwickshire villages, of stone and thatch cottages, and neat lanes edged with a profusion of wild flowers, they reached the inn where they were to stay by late afternoon. The gentlemen were keen to be gone to their meeting at the Pump Room of the Spa, while their wives, disinclined to squander an evening, decided instead to take advantage of a well-appointed room with a blazing fire that the landlady put at their disposal.

Despatching the servants, who had never visited the town before and were eager to see the sights, the two sisters settled down to enjoy the evening. It had been a while since they had had time to themselves.

Elizabeth knew that Jane had intended to speak with Jonathan. Since receiving Charlotte Collins' letter, she had been impatient to discover how things stood with her son and Miss Faulkner. With all three daughters now happily settled, she worried only about the happiness of Jonathan and the well-being of his children.

"Well, Jane," said Elizabeth, "I know you have had your little talk with Jonathan, because I saw you come out of Dr Grantley's study together; indeed, I remarked to Darcy that it must have gone well, since you were both smiling. Are you going to tell me about it?"

Jane, who had never been able to keep anything from her dearest sister and best friend, blushed as she recalled how she had decided that Jonathan's private life was to be protected from idle gossip. Indeed, she had resolved not to discuss it with anyone, not even Bingley, until Jonathan had declared his intentions. But with Lizzie, it was different.

"Lizzie, of course I am going to tell you about it. But you must promise to keep Jonathan's secret, though I suppose you may tell Mr Darcy. I do not believe Jonathan would mind at all if Darcy were to know."

Elizabeth knew her sister well. She knew she would not have to press her for the details, but only if Jonathan had not asked that it be kept secret, for so delicate was Jane's sense of honour, she would not dream of breaking a confidence, even to discuss it with her sister.

Fortunately, this was not necessary, and soon, Elizabeth had heard all the circumstances that Jonathan had recounted to his mother regarding his friendship with Anna Faulkner.

"Lizzie, he says he loves her and has proposed to her; he has written to Dr Faulkner as well, so he does seem to have made up his mind quite some time ago," said Jane.

Elizabeth was eager for news; having had her own discussion with Darcy on the prospect of such a match, she was impatient to discover how the matter had progressed.

"And Anna, how did she respond? Has she accepted him?" she asked, expecting an affirmative answer, for it did not seem possible that her favourite nephew, her godson, Jonathan Bingley, once regarded as the most eligible bachelor in two or three counties, could be turned down.

When Jane revealed that Anna had insisted they wait a few more weeks, Elizabeth was totally perplexed.

"What has possessed the girl?" she asked, expressing her frustration and impatience, ahead of discovering the reason for Anna's request.

However, when Jane revealed her reasons, as Jonathan had explained them to her, including Miss Faulkner's commendable concern for the feelings of Jonathan's daughters, Elizabeth was immediately contrite and praised her sensitivity.

Jane's own opinion, quietly but firmly expressed, underlined her own satisfaction with the manner in which Jonathan and Miss Faulkner had arranged their affairs.

"I think, Lizzie, it reveals a most unselfish and thoughtful nature, to have persuaded a man as ardent as Jonathan to wait while she examines the strength of her own feelings and allows time for the children to overcome the shock of losing their mother. Of his own attachment, he has left her in no doubt, and Lizzie, I am sure that once she discovers her true feelings, they will soon be engaged," she declared.

Elizabeth had to agree, and she congratulated her sister on the imminent prospect of acquiring a most amiable and accomplished daughter-in-law.

Jane was more cautious. She had known disappointment before.

"Oh I do hope you are right, Lizzie, for I have no doubt at all that Jonathan is very much in love with her, and it would break my heart to see his hopes dashed. He has a tender heart, and I know how much mortification he suffered when Amelia-Jane turned against him. He has, for the sake of his children, shown such courage and forbearance, it is surely time he found some happiness. I wish there was something I could do to help."

Elizabeth put an arm around her sister, whose gentle nature and kind heart often caused her to suffer on behalf of others.

"Dear Jane, pray do not upset yourself, both Jonathan and Anna are mature adults and are surely not unaware of what marriage to each other can mean for both of them. I realise Jonathan has suffered greatly, and that is all the more reason why he will be especially circumspect.

"Anna has clearly wished to consult her own feelings more deeply before committing herself to a completely new life, with a husband and children, two of whom are close enough to her own age to be her siblings," she explained, adding, "You need not worry about them, Jane. Do you recall how concerned I was when Julian became engaged to Josie Tate?"

Jane recalled very well her sister's anxiety on that score.

"I do; you thought she was too young, not mature enough to appreciate his work at Cambridge or his future role at Pemberley," she said.

"Indeed, and Darcy convinced me that an intelligent young woman like Josie would learn, as she grew into her marriage, what her responsibilities were. I am sure he will be proved right. Julian seems very happy and they are both looking forward to their first child," said Elizabeth.

Jane smiled, a sad little smile, remembering her own reservations about Amelia-Jane, who had not been more than sixteen when she became engaged to Jonathan. Jane's initial anxiety had been soon pushed aside on seeing how much in love they were. Yet, as things had turned out, she had been justified to fear for her son's happiness.

"I suppose, Lizzie, the difference between Julian's situation and Jonathan's was that Josie Tate is an educated and intelligent young person, whereas poor Amelia-Jane remained as immature as she had been when he married her, with very little to recommend her except her beauty. I do hope you are right, Lizzie, for he surely deserves to be happy again."

The return of the gentlemen in time for supper brought their discussions to a close, for they wisely assumed that after an hour or more of business dealings, neither of their husbands would be in a mood to contemplate the complexities of Jonathan's love life.

Instead, they anticipated the delights of a day to be spent at Stratford upon Avon before returning to Ashford Park and Pemberley. The problems of today would be set aside while they enjoyed the drama and romance of the past. It was an experience they looked forward to with pleasure.

~~~

When Emma Wilson received her brother's letter and read the first two lines, she was saddened and shocked, thinking he had been turned down by Anna Faulkner.

But, reading on, she was delighted with the news and left the breakfast table to find her husband, who was in his study composing a speech.

James, seeing her expression, assumed she'd had good news from Jonathan.

"Are congratulations in order?" he asked and, even when she read out the parts of his letter explaining what had transpired, James remained optimistic.

"My dear Emma, Jonathan is a persistent young man, I am confident he will have her agreement by Easter," he said and, noticing that she seemed rather doubtful, added, "Now Emma, you are not going to fret about your brother, are you? Believe me, he is well placed in this matter. Miss Faulkner already admits to admiration and esteem, he is easily the most eligible man in the county; if she will not marry him, she must be more foolish than I had thought her to be."

His wife protested that Anna Faulkner was not at all foolish.

"Aunt Lizzie believes her to be very intelligent and sensible and my own knowledge of her confirms it," she said.

James smiled rather smugly, as if she had proved his case.

"Well then, your worries will soon be over, for I cannot believe an intelligent and sensible young woman would turn down a proposal from Jonathan Bingley," he said confidently.

Returning to Netherfield from Oxford, Jonathan found, among the letters waiting for him, one from his sister. Emma, having received his letter, which had conveyed an impression of dejection, had hastened to reply, urging him to regard the waiting time as a period in which he could perhaps prepare himself and his children for what Emma felt was his inevitable engagement to Miss Faulkner.

My dear brother, she wrote:

We were delighted to hear that you had found an appropriate opportunity to approach Miss Faulkner.

As for the rather delicate situation in which you find yourself, it is at least not one of hopelessness. I cannot believe that the conclusion to this story is going to be other than happy, for everything I know of you and Anna, as well as my understanding of the circumstances you have described, leads me to believe that she is being careful, cautious, perhaps, but nothing else.

Generally speaking, this suggests a prudent sensibility and a greatness of mind that does her credit. There is no hint of evasiveness or pretence, which requires to be persuaded with gifts and flattery etc.

It bodes well for your future life together that she has such excellent judgment, and I know how much you value such qualities.

All this is good news, dear brother, and you must not let the small aggravations wear you down to the point where you permit your sense of hurt to impinge upon your friendship with her. For it is in this manner that you will convince her that you are best suited to each other.

Believe me Jonathan, Anna loves you, and if you are not engaged at Easter, I shall be very surprised. And since we are to spend Easter with you, together with Mama and Papa, an engagement would be singularly pleasing!

She concluded with her usual affectionate felicitations, but in a brief post-script added almost as an afterthought what she called "a very good idea, which has just occurred to me."

She intended to write to Anna and invite her to Standish Park.

"Spring has arrived in the Weald of Kent and the park is an artist's paradise at this time. I am sure Anna will find many things to draw and paint. If she can make the time to spend a week or two with us before Easter, she will be very welcome.

"Perhaps, you may like to join us for a few days yourself, Jonathan," she wrote.

Her brother smiled as he read her letter.

"Dear Emma," he said, to himself, "you clearly intend to do your best for me. I hope and pray you may succeed."

Later in the week, he visited Longbourn and was happy to learn that Anna had already begun to take over the instruction of some of Mary's pupils, while Mrs Collins had directed that the old sitting room be made ready for her Art classes.

Riding over to Haye Park, Jonathan hoped to find Anna at home. Sadly, he was disappointed to be told by the maid that she had left for Hatfield House with her father and a couple of foreign visitors, who were staying in Meryton. She knew very little about them, except that they were foreign, she supposed from their accents; Jonathan was puzzled since Anna had not mentioned any foreign visitors.

It was on the Sunday, when they met at church and Jonathan accepted an invitation to dine with the Faulkners, that he learned that the "foreign visitors" had been none other than Monsieur Du Pont and Madame Roussard.

"Madame Roussard has a special interest in Architecture and Papa had offered to show them Hatfield House. Of course, I had to go along, too, because while Monsieur Du Pont speaks passable English, Madame Roussard has very little English and she asks so many questions, it would have driven poor Papa quite mad," Anna explained.

Apart from his disappointment at not seeing her on the day, Jonathan thought no more of it, attaching no particular significance to their visit. That was until Dr Faulkner re-opened the subject, when they were in the sitting room, taking tea.

"Monsieur Du Pont has invited Anna to participate in an exhibition—this one is to be held in Paris," he announced.

Mrs Faulkner, obviously proud of her daughter, added, "It is a great honour, Mr Bingley."

Jonathan, surprised, looked immediately at Anna, who was getting him a cup of tea. She put it down carefully on the table in front of him, before she spoke, quietly.

"And I have said no; I have no paintings good enough to exhibit in Paris, and in any event, I do not wish to go."

Her father sounded disappointed, pointing out that she ought not be too hasty, she may well regret not going.

"The gentleman was very keen and Madame was most enthusiastic after seeing Anna's drawings of Hatfield House and St Alban's Abbey. I think, my dear, they were both very impressed," said her father, but unaccountably, Anna remained less than enthusiastic about the entire scheme and somewhat embarrassed by her parents' promotion of it.

When he was preparing to leave, Jonathan was tempted to tease her about being invited to Paris, but she pre-empted him.

Speaking low, so her mother, who was dozing by the fire, would not hear, she said, "I have no interest in going to Paris, or anywhere else, Jonathan. I am very content with my life in Hertfordshire at this moment."

Jonathan was not entirely reassured by her remark, he wondered whether it was meant to indicate that she was too content to contemplate a change at all, but he made the only possible response.

"I'm very glad to hear it, Anna, very glad indeed. I should have missed you very much, had you gone away to Paris," he said softly, and having arranged to call again, later in the week, he left.

A spell of bad weather prevented him returning to Haye Park for some days. The streams were overflowing from the heavy rains, the fields were sodden, and the roads were getting to be rutted and dangerous. One was well advised not to ride out, if possible. Finally the sun struggled through and, in spite of threatening clouds on the horizon, Jonathan decided to travel to Haye Park.

He found Anna alone, practising at her pianoforte. When he was shown into the parlour, she rose and came to greet him.

"You find me alone this morning, my parents are gone to Lucas Lodge to visit my uncle, who is unwell," she said.

"I'm sorry to hear it, I hope it is not a serious condition. I am, however, very happy to find you in," he said as he kissed her hand. She smiled; clearly she was pleased to see him too. Having assured him her uncle's ailment was no more serious than a common cold made worse by his stubborn refusal to stay in bed, she proceeded to order tea.

He urged her to continue playing, which she did, to his great delight, for while he was not a practitioner himself, Jonathan had a fine appreciation of Music. Clearly, Anna had mastered the composition he had brought her; he was delighted with her performance.

Presently, she closed the instrument and came over to where he was seated. The tea had been brought in and she busied herself with dispensing it. They were a good deal less formal with each other now. Jonathan even plucked up the courage to tease her, asking if he should be jealous of the elegant Frenchman, Monsieur Du Pont.

At which, she laughed merrily.

"Jealous of Monsieur Du Pont! For shame, Jonathan, surely you do not mean to attribute such motives to him as should make you jealous? Why I had thought he was merely being very generous. Madame Roussard, his companion and patron, owns the gallery where the exhibition is to be held and they were kind enough to invite me to participate, that was all," she explained.

"And that was all?" he quizzed, looking a little sceptical.

"Indeed it was. Oh Jonathan, you are not going to be old-fashioned and imagine that every man who speaks with me or praises my painting is in love with me, are you?"

This time, his riposte was more audacious.

"I don't believe it would worry me at all, if he was. But if I thought his affection was returned, now that would make me very jealous indeed," he declared. She blushed, rose, and went to the window, looking out over the garden, returning only after she had composed her face.

Changing the subject as she sat down beside him, she said, "I have had a letter from your sister Mrs Wilson. She has very kindly invited me to stay at Standish Park for a few weeks before Easter."

He looked pleased.

"Will you accept?" he asked, a little anxiously.

She was thoughtful before replying.

"I think I shall. Mama and Papa go to Ramsgate for a fortnight fairly soon; I thought I might travel with them as far as Canterbury and take the coach to Standish Park. My maid Sally could travel with me."

"An excellent idea," said Jonathan, letting her see how pleased he was.

"As it happens, I have to be in London next week on Parliamentary business. If you would inform me of the dates and times of your journey, I could arrange to accompany you from Canterbury to Standish Park."

He was happy to see she seemed to find the prospect agreeable and, promising to call again to see her parents, he rose to leave.

As he kissed her hand, he could not resist one last gentle jest.

"And you are quite certain, Anna, that you would not prefer to be in Paris, instead? Not even the boulevardes in springtime can tempt you?"

She smiled as she expressed her exasperation with him, declaring that if he continued to tease her, she may well decide to travel to Dover instead of Canterbury and catch the packet boat to France, after all!

Feigning terror at her threat, he begged her forgiveness and beat a hasty retreat, leaving her laughing.

No sooner had he left than Anna sat down at her desk and wrote to Mrs Wilson, thanking her for the invitation and accepting it with pleasure. All her dealings with Emma Wilson had been exceedingly agreeable and she was certain this visit would be no different. She had just sealed it and was about to send it to the post, when her parents returned from Lucas Lodge.

Soon afterwards, her father called her in to his study, saying, "Anna, my dear, I am about to reply to a letter which I received last week, one which has pleasantly surprised me. I should like a word with you before I do."

Anna, who knew that Jonathan Bingley had intended to write to her father, applying for his consent to marry her, was not unduly concerned. She was, however, more intrigued by her father's claim to have been pleasantly surprised by the contents of the letter.

The pleasure apparently derived from the fact that Mr Bingley, a man of excellent character and reputation, and a member of a highly respected family, wished to marry his daughter.

"We all know him to be a man of intelligence and principle, and though I had not suspected any deep attachment between you, your mother claims she has known of it for some time. Is this true, my dear?" he asked, to which Anna replied that she had only recently become aware that his partiality towards her had involved a proposal of marriage.

Her father continued, "That brings me to the reason for my feelings of surprise, indeed one might almost say astonishment. You see, Anna, Mr Bingley, who is a man of considerable fortune, requests your hand, but seeks no marriage settlement of any kind. Rather, he proposes to settle upon you, when you are his wife, 'a sum sufficient to ensure her independence and comfort in the years to come, should some untoward occurrence bring about my early death or disability.'" He was reading from the letter before him.

An anguished cry escaped her lips, "Papa! pray do not go on."

Her father was immediately solicitous.

"Come now, my dear, there is no cause for alarm; he is merely being cautious and sensible. He needs to be, being several years older than you are. Do not upset yourself, my child, he simply wishes to assure me that you will want for nothing, even if he should …"

"Papa, please, do not repeat it. It has never occurred to me, and I do not wish to contemplate it. Why, Colonel Fitzwilliam is almost twenty years older than Caroline and he is perfectly well. Why should we even consider that it will be different with Jonathan?"

Dr Faulkner was smiling when he spoke.

"Ah, I see. Then, may I assume that you wish me to write to him giving my consent?" he asked, a distinctly humorous note in his voice.

But she was not to be so easily led. She asked, "Have you any objection, Papa?"

"None at all; it is by any measure an excellent proposal. I should be proud to have him for a son-in-law and, if you were to tell me you love him, I shall be delighted to give my consent."

"On that matter, may I ask what he says in his letter?" she asked.

Her father sounded sceptical.

"Anna, you do not expect me to believe that you are unaware of the nature of his feelings? I know, you merely want the satisfaction of seeing written down what he has already told you. You modern young women are very particular, you want to be quite certain. I do not blame you, but I am sure we can believe Mr Bingley when he says … wait, let me read it to you."

He read from Jonathan's letter, "'I can assure you, Sir, that the love I feel for Anna is deep and sincere, and I faithfully promise to do everything in my power to make her truly happy.' There, I think, Anna, we can assume he loves you dearly; the question is, do you want to marry him?"

When there was no immediate response, he seemed anxious.

"Why do you hesitate, Anna? Is something amiss? Is it because he is a widower and there are children to consider?" he looked at her, searching for an answer.

She replied at once, denying she had any such reservations.

"Oh no, Papa, not at all. I am truly honoured that Mr Bingley, whom I admire and respect, should wish to marry me. I have no reason to refuse him, but have asked only that I be permitted a little time to consider his offer and give him my answer."

Her father, though a little puzzled, agreed that it was a fair request.

"Very well," he said, "I shall tell him that your mother and I have no objection, indeed we are happy to agree to his proposal, but he must obtain your consent himself. When he has, he can count on our blessing. How will that do, my dear?"

Anna rose and embraced her father.

"Thank you, Papa, that will do very well," she said.

Later, in the privacy of her bedroom, she thought about the generosity and concern reflected in Jonathan Bingley's offer, which her father, a practical man, had seen as a sensible arrangement. While even the thought of his death brought tears to her eyes, it had also served to force the realisation that he meant a great deal to her. She was very close to acknowledging that life without him would be impossible to contemplate.

Jonathan Bingley called again that week, but while his visit was pleasant and friendly, it was also short, for he came to say that his brother-in-law Mr Wilson had summoned him to Westminster for a vital meeting. Unhappily, this would mean that he could not dine with them on the Sunday, as previously arranged. Mrs Faulkner, who had hoped to ask her sister Charlotte Collins to join them, was very disappointed.

Anna was curious to know when they would see him again, and if he would give her any indication of his plans. Did he expect to spend most of the Summer in Hertfordshire or in London, she wondered.

She received a part of the answer when he took the time to indicate to her that he had had a reply from her father to his letter. He gave her no details, but from the expression on his face and the tone of his voice, she was able to deduce that he was certainly not unhappy with the response.

Earlier, she had heard him thank her father for his letter. While she had not wished to appear as if she was eavesdropping on their conversation, she had lingered long enough to hear her father wish him success and warmly shake his hand.

Before he left, he had made a note of the dates for their journey to Ramsgate and had settled upon the place and time for their meeting in Canterbury.

He was clearly reluctant to leave, delaying his departure until the last possible moment, accepting a final cup of tea and standing in the hallway with Anna, drawing out their farewell for several minutes.

When he was gone, her parents heard her go slowly up the stairs to her room. She was never dismal, but it was quite clear that she was sad to see him go.

~⚓~

As the days passed, Anna, though she did not permit herself to be overcome with melancholy—it was not in her nature to do so—began to miss him. Increasingly, she had realised she had come to rely upon him to stimulate her interest in a whole range of new ideas. Without the expectation of his company, her days seemed endless and dull.

It was fortuitous that the time fixed for her parents' holiday was fast approaching and with it the day of her departure for Standish Park. Her mother had agreed to let their maid Sally travel with her, and the next few days were filled with the excitement of preparing for their journey.

On their way to Ramsgate, Dr Faulkner and his family stayed with his brother in London. The main attraction of this arrangement to Anna was the close proximity of her uncle's house to the Royal Academy's Exhibition centre, whither she would go, while her parents and their hosts spent their time in Bond Street or the shops of the Burlington Arcade.

They took time also to attend one of the popular readings by Charles Dickens and, while Anna and her father were delighted with Mr Dickens and enjoyed the performance, her mother did not at all, declaring in a loud whisper that she had heard so much gossip about Mr Dickens and his mistress, she wondered that he found time to write at all!

Soon afterwards, they left London and journeyed on to Canterbury, where they had rooms reserved for the night at the Bell, an excellent hostelry recommended to them by Mrs Wilson, who had written to Anna to confirm their arrangements.

You should find it very convenient and comfortable, she had said,

> *...the landlord is well known to James, so please feel free to mention his name and they will know you are friends of ours. We have stayed there on several occasions and have been very happy with the service.*
>
> *Mr Wilson and my brother Jonathan will be returning from London and expect to meet up with you at the Bell.*

Adding a personal note, she wrote,

Dear Anna, I am looking forward very much to your visit. It seems such a long while since we have spoken. I do hope you are bringing your brushes and paints, for there are a myriad sights and scenes in the park and the woods which you will surely want to paint.

Since reading her letter, Anna had been impatient to be gone to Kent. Jonathan had left for Westminster, and life in Hertfordshire, since his departure, had seemed flat and uneventful.

The Bell, which was situated a mile or two outside the town, turned out to be much more than a place which afforded rest and food to the traveller and a stable to feed and water the horses.

It was an impressive institution housed in a handsome Georgian building, set back from the main Canterbury road, with gracious interiors and comfortable rooms.

Dr and Mrs Faulkner and Anna were shown into a large, well-furnished parlour, where a fire burning in the grate and a table laid for tea welcomed the travellers. Here, they waited for Mr Wilson and Jonathan Bingley who, the landlord assured them, were expected within the hour.

They arrived as arranged and met with the Faulkners before repairing to their rooms to change for dinner. Jonathan, who had missed Anna terribly, searched her face for some indication that she had been likewise afflicted. Unfortunately, she was so pleased to see him that her countenance revealed no more than her present satisfaction, and he was almost disappointed. However, as they were waiting to go in to dinner, he approached her and asked how she had spent the past two weeks.

"Very impatiently," she replied. "I have rarely felt so restless, I must confess, and I was never keener to set off on a journey anywhere. Indeed, I could not wait to leave."

Encouraged by this declaration, he asked in a quiet voice, "May I be so bold as to ask if my absence from Hertfordshire contributed in some small way to those feelings?"

She smiled and turned to look out at the garden, so her reply would not carry to the others in the room.

"You may, Jonathan, and I shall answer you truthfully. I missed you very much and longed for your company, for I have had little pleasure in any conversation these last two weeks. I am very happy to see you again."

Since he was at least a foot taller than she was, his face, which reflected the delight with which he received these words, was not visible to her as they stood together by the window. Had it been, she would surely have seen how deeply her words had moved him.

When they went in to dinner, he moved without hesitation to sit beside her. While James Wilson ventured into a political discussion with Dr Faulkner, and Mrs Faulkner concentrated upon the excellent meal, for most of the time Jonathan and Anna were left to themselves.

It was during this time that he, aware there would be little opportunity for private conversation on the drive to Standish Park, decided to return to the response he had received from her father to his proposal.

She was not surprised and indicated, softly, that her father had spoken with her on the matter before writing to him.

"Did you see his letter?" he asked, a little taken aback.

She shook her head. "No I did not, but he did acquaint me with the sentiments expressed in yours and asked if I was already aware of your feelings and how I had responded."

"Am I to understand, then, that you told him you had not made up your mind about me?" he asked, with an expression so anxious that she was immediately concerned that her father's reply may have offended or hurt him. Could he have been more blunt than she had intended and given the wrong impression? she wondered.

Keen to ensure that Jonathan understood exactly what she had said to her father, she recounted most of their conversation, trying desperately not to speak in too conspiratorial a manner, yet having of necessity to lower her voice, lest her mother should hear.

Fortuitously, Mrs Faulkner, being tired from the long journey, excused herself after the main course and retired upstairs.

When Anna tried to follow her, she urged her to stay.

"I am not ill, my child. It is just that it has been such a long day. I think I will go to bed," she said and, bidding them all good night, withdrew.

Jonathan asked, "Anna, does your mother not know of my letter to your father?"

"She does, but I persuaded him to keep my response from her until I had decided, because I did not wish her to try to persuade me. I told Papa that you had spoken with me and had agreed that I could have some time to give you my answer, but that I was generally well disposed towards you; oh dear, this is so difficult—can you not spare me and tell me what he said to you in his letter?" she pleaded, now very embarrassed by the situation in which she found herself.

Jonathan was beginning to see some light at the end of this rather convoluted tunnel.

"If you wish me to, certainly, but it might be better to wait until we are back in the parlour."

It seemed that her father and Mr Wilson were about to rise and Anna was impatient to return to the parlour, where tea or coffee was taken.

Deep in discussion, Dr Faulkner and Mr Wilson did not notice that Jonathan had left the port to them and gone over to the table for a cup of tea, thereafter seating himself beside Miss Faulkner on the chaise lounge.

He revealed that Dr Faulkner had written that he had discovered from his daughter that she had asked for some time to make her decision. In view of this, he had said he would be happy to give them his blessing if and when she agreed to marry him.

The choice was hers, her father had said.

"Was that all?" she asked, disappointed at the brevity of her father's reply.

Jonathan was reluctant to say more, and it was only as she plied him with questions that he was persuaded to reveal the appreciation and pleasure her father had expressed at receiving his proposal. His characteristic modesty prevented him from telling her all, but sufficient was said to reassure Anna that her father had been neither blunt nor too deferential in his response.

The generosity of the proposal and the sincerity of the sentiments expressed had served to convince him that Mr Bingley was indeed a worthy suitor for his favourite daughter, he had said. He had needed only to know that her affections were genuinely engaged to give his consent.

Later, when she rose to go upstairs herself, Jonathan followed her into the hall. It was late and there was no one else about. They were standing at the foot of the stairs; she was about to ascend them when he reminded her of his hope that she would at least relieve him of the anguish of uncertainty.

"My dear Anna, I do love you so much, will you not give me some hope?" he asked, and she could hold out no longer.

"Forgive me, Jonathan, I have no right to do this to you. If I have hurt you, I am truly sorry. I do love you, I think you must know that already, and yes, I will marry you, but I ask only that we wait a while before announcing our engagement."

She was totally unprepared for the excess of joy this statement evoked as she felt herself enveloped in an embrace, which she could not easily resist even if she had wanted to, which in truth, she did not.

Still holding her close, he asked, "May we tell Emma?"

To his delight, she said, "Of course," causing an even greater outbreak of bliss.

After which, despite his reluctance to part from her, she insisted she had to go upstairs, or she would not be in a fit state for the early start they were to make on the morrow. Unwilling to let her go, but with that well-known capacity for endurance only those wholly consumed by love may boast of, he agreed to let her out of his sight until the following morning.

When he returned to the parlour and sought to pour himself a drink, he found the decanter of port empty, but no matter, Jonathan needed no wine to lift his spirits.

His brother-in-law and Dr Faulkner were still engaged in political debate, which he found easy to ignore. Tonight, very little mattered except the knowledge that Anna had agreed to be his wife. He would sleep well.

Anna, on the other hand, could not sleep at first, for worrying about not having told her parents what she had known for weeks. She determined to tell them as early as possible; as soon as she could get them alone on the morrow.

That she loved Jonathan Bingley she had known; indeed, in the course of the last few months, she had become aware that her feelings for him had undergone a remarkable change. She had moved from regarding him as an engaging and intelligent companion, whose interest in her was flattering and enjoyable, to discovering that he meant a good deal more to her. She had found herself thinking of him whenever they were apart and wishing for his return.

That she could not imagine life without him had dawned upon her gradually, and that evening, as they stood in the hallway and she saw the anxiety on his face, the thought that she could be the cause of his grief had become intolerable.

The following day brought a typical Spring morning in Kent and, after an early breakfast, they prepared to set off for Standish Park.

Anna had already been to her parents' room, for their journey to Ramsgate was not due to start for an hour at least. She had explained first to her father and then more carefully to her mother, who had not been privy to their earlier discussions, that she had accepted Jonathan Bingley's proposal, but, because it was as yet not twelve months since Amelia-Jane's death, they would not announce their engagement immediately.

Her father was pleased and, having congratulated his daughter, went down to find Jonathan, whom he sought out in the breakfast room.

"I respect your desire to wait a while before announcing it," he said and added, "but I do know you will both be very happy together. You have my blessing, of course."

Mrs Faulkner, however, was so overcome with joy that she could not get dressed fast enough and only just succeeded in getting to the hall to wish her prospective son-in-law every happiness before the party left for Standish Park.

Wishing them God-speed and waiting only till the carriage was clear of the drive, she rushed up to her room to pen a note to her sister Mrs Collins, to give her the good news. Only Dr Faulkner's timely intervention, reminding her that the engagement was supposed to remain secret, prevented her from rushing to have it despatched to the post!

For years to come, Mrs Faulkner would believe that her daughter's decision had been made in a few hours at the Bell. It took her husband a long time to convince her that it was only one chapter of a story which had started many months ago and that their daughter had given considerable thought to her choice.

The journey to Standish Park took them across the North Downs, traversing some of the prettiest country in England.

Spring had arrived rather early and the day was neither as windy nor as cold as it might have been. The Wilsons' property, a substantial one by any measure, had been in their family for over a hundred years.

It was early afternoon when they reached Standish Park, and Anna saw the house at its best, its russet brick glowing in the sun, the handsome building standing out against the gold and green of the new Spring foliage in the park.

Emma Wilson came out to greet them as they alighted from the carriage and took Anna, whom she embraced warmly, into the house.

Seeing the place for the first time, Anna was enchanted.

"This is such a beautiful house, Emma, I can see why you do not wish to leave it often. It is elegant, yet so warm and welcoming," she said as they entered the saloon, where refreshments awaited them.

Some time later, after she had been shown to her room and her maid Sally had been suitably accommodated, Anna had time to bathe and change. Coming downstairs, she was directed to the handsome drawing room, where Emma's piano stood open. It was a beautiful instrument, and Anna was tempted to try it, to the delight of Emma's two little boys, Charles and Colin, who had followed her downstairs and waited, a little shyly, to hear her play.

When Jonathan joined her and invited her to walk out into the garden, Anna could scarcely restrain her delight.

"I know, now, why your sister insisted that I bring along my paints; everywhere I look, there is some thing, a tree, a balustrade, or a vista, I want to sketch or paint. How wonderful it is to be surrounded by such beauty."

In the days that followed, she would spend a great deal of time, just as Emma had predicted, sketching swiftly an object or a scene that caught her eye and then filling in the colours, working until she was satisfied or, occasionally, casting it aside because it did not please her.

On her first evening, after she had retired to her bedroom, Emma came to see if she was comfortable. Anna knew that Jonathan had told his sister of their engagement, for she came to her and embraced her.

"Dearest Anna, you must know already, but let me tell you how happy I am that you and Jonathan are engaged. It has been my dearest wish, ever since I discovered how he felt. I know you will make each other happy. He loves you dearly and, Anna, he is without doubt one of the best men alive. I know he is my brother and you will expect me to say this, but believe me, had he been a stranger and you my sister, I would tell you no different, for I know him well and he is a good man."

"Indeed he is and, God willing, we shall be sisters, Emma," said Anna. "Much as I love your brother, I cannot deny how important you have been to my decision," for Emma was in her eyes one of the best women she had ever met.

The week that followed was almost idyllic. The lovers, having acknowledged their feelings to one another and confided in the Wilsons, were completely at ease now, enjoying the hospitality of their hosts, who afforded them all the privacy they could desire.

Amidst the elegant surroundings of the house and the rich natural beauty of its environs, they enjoyed each other's company, unhindered by curious neighbours or concerned friends, falling even more in love than before and free to express their feelings as they chose.

When Anna was not with Jonathan, she was claimed by Emma, who would drive her around the park in a little open carriage or wander down with her to the village, which lay across the river at the lower end of the valley.

"I could live out the rest of my days in a place as lovely as this," Anna declared. "You must love it dearly."

Emma admitted that she did, but then asked, "Tomorrow, I intend to visit the cottages which lie on the other side of the home farm. Would you like to accompany me?"

As Anna looked interested, she went on.

"They are some of the families who lost their homes and livelihoods when their landlords enclosed the farms and the commons, leaving them with nowhere to live or work."

Anna, who knew little of what had gone on at the height of the enclosure movement, said, "That must have been an awfully cruel thing to do. How did they live?"

"It was certainly cruel, but many did it at the time; it was the way to increase production and make more profit. They had no thought for the poor families who had been so deprived. James' father, who inherited this property, was a good man and a very dutiful landlord. When he realised what was happening, he took some of these people in and gave them the lower meadow, beside the river. It is not the best land and it floods from time to time, but it was better than nothing at all and they were very grateful. When he died, he left an instruction in his will that they were to be protected tenants, who could not be deprived of their living ever again."

Anna was amazed.

"And they are still here?" she asked.

"Indeed, they are. James has allowed them the use of the pastures in the valley for their sheep, and they have access to the river, so they are quite a thriving little community now," said Emma. "I shall be going over tomorrow, since it is almost Easter and we take gifts for the children at Easter. If you wish to come, I shall be happy to take you along."

Anna indicated that she would love to accompany her, and on the following day, they set off for the small village that was little more than a cluster of cottages and market gardens in the river valley below the home farm.

James Wilson and Jonathan, meanwhile, had several matters on their minds, matters which were as important as they were intractable.

The previous week had been spent with members of the Reform Group who were becoming increasingly impatient with the government of Palmerston.

The Prime Minister's obsession with Italy and his total concentration upon foreign affairs to the exclusion of any part of the Reform agenda upon which the original agreements had stood, were creating many problems within the government, as well as outside of it.

"It seems impossible to get through to him that the people of Britain are less likely to be concerned with the fortunes of Garibaldi in Sicily, than with the state of our own society," James complained, as he detailed the causes he had tried vainly to pursue in the last year.

"I know Lord Russell is keen on extending the franchise and Bright is impatient to see it done, but Palmerston shows no interest at all."

"There is the question of public education, too," said Jonathan, who was aware that Prince Albert himself had tried to interest the government in the idea. "With the recalcitrant churchmen being implacably opposed, it seems like a hopeless cause, does it not?"

James agreed. "Even less hopeful than that of the little chimney sweeps— though, on this I am determined I shall support Shaftesbury's Bill when it comes before the Commons. He plans to have the age lifted to ten or twelve, if the Lords can be persuaded to let it through."

"You will need to watch your back, James, there will be many among the Whigs who will resent your support for a Tory Bill," Jonathan warned.

"Indeed they will, but there are matters of conscience which go to the heart of my beliefs in our duties as representatives of the people. I cannot turn a blind eye to such appalling conditions as these children suffer."

James made his own dedication to the cause very clear.

"Jonathan, we legislated to stop the enslavement of adults when we banned the Slave Trade; how can we permit the enslavement of children here in England? Emma and I both feel very strongly about it."

Remembering Charles and Colin, his two young nephews, Jonathan could well understand the strength of James Wilson's commitment. That his sister Emma supported her husband totally was no surprise.

Their conversation was interrupted by a servant, who brought in an express that had just been delivered. It was addressed to Jonathan and came from Eliza Harwood.

Jonathan could not imagine why she would be writing to him, unless—and as he tore the letter open the only possible reason occurred to him—unless it had to do with Anne-Marie!

He was right; Mrs Harwood wrote:

Dear Mr Bingley,

I hope this finds you well and still at Standish Park. I had gathered from Anne-Marie that you were to spend a few weeks in Kent with the Wilsons.

I am sorry to be writing with news that will trouble and inconvenience you, but Anne-Marie is ill and I should feel that I have been negligent if I did not inform you at once.

She has had during this last week or so a persistent cough, which she has ignored except to take some medication to soothe her throat, and she has continued her work at the hospital.

Yesterday, however, the matron in charge found her feeling very low and sent her home, by which time she had a fever as well. I had the apothecary in immediately, but he could not give her any comfort.

Tonight, her fever was very high and I have sent for Dr Morton, who may be more help than the apothecary.

By the time he had read half of what she had written, Jonathan had leapt up from his chair and declared that he had to leave at once.

Ignorant of the content of the letter, James was immediately concerned for his brother-in-law.

"Jonathan, what is it? What has happened?" he cried and was handed the two carefully penned sheets to read, while Jonathan raced upstairs to make preparations for his journey.

James read on.

Eliza was apologetic:

Mr Bingley, I am truly sorry to trouble you, but my present condition prevents me from nursing Anne-Marie and I do believe she needs careful nursing over the next few days. Perhaps if Mrs Wilson could recommend a good, experienced nurse, you may wish to bring her with you. At this moment, I have a woman from the hospital who will stay overnight, but she is not a trained nurse.

She concluded with more expressions of regret and prayers for her friend's recovery.

James had by now realised the seriousness of the situation. He knew Jonathan would want to set out as soon as possible and, in view of the distance he had to travel, would probably need a different vehicle to the one in which they had arrived.

He was on his way out to the stables to see his steward when his wife and Anna arrived at the front entrance, having just this minute returned from their visit to the cottages. They were talking happily together as they came in, carrying bunches of flowers given them by the children.

James hated having to give them the bad news. But no sooner had she heard than Anna declared that she could nurse Anne-Marie; she had nursed Madame Armande through a terrible illness, and in any event, there was no time to find "an experienced nurse" who could leave her family and travel to London, she said.

She raced upstairs to find Jonathan, only to discover that he would not hear of it.

"Anna, I cannot allow it. It may be an infectious disease, some contagion she has caught at the hospital. Your parents would never forgive me if you were to be stricken with it, too. It is out of the question."

In spite of his seemingly unshakable opposition, she went away and packed her things and urged her maid to prepare to travel almost at once.

With Emma's support, she returned to Jonathan and begged to be allowed to go with him.

At first, it seemed he would not be moved. But as she persevered, explaining that she was old enough at twenty-six to make her own decisions and asking him to consider how important it was that Anne-Marie should receive the most devoted care, he softened and, finally, said, "I will only permit it if the doctor assures me it is not infectious and you will not be in any danger. Should he declare it to be some pestilential disease, you must promise me you will leave at once with Sally and return to Haye Park. I shall engage a trained nurse in London to care for Anne-Marie."

Anna agreed to all his conditions, praying meanwhile in her heart that it may not be as he feared. She felt Anne-Marie would recover sooner with the care of someone who knew and loved her.

Jonathan's anxiety to be gone meant that every other matter was set aside and arrangements were expedited for their departure, in order that they may reach Dartford by nightfall and be on their way to London in the early morning. There was general sadness at the manner in which what had been a near-perfect fortnight had been disrupted, and fervent hopes expressed for Anne-Marie's swift recovery. Emma and Anna embraced, each promising to write.

In the carriage, Anna sat opposite Jonathan, trying very hard to keep the tears which were stinging her eyes from spilling down her cheeks. His face revealed his own agony, and it struck her that she had never seen him look so downcast, not even when, a year or so ago, the dreadful news had broken of Amelia-Jane's accident and death.

Finally, unable to bear it alone any longer, she crossed over to sit beside him and took his hand in hers. The little gesture of kindness seemed to be the last straw and she saw him struggle with the tears, as he gripped her hand and gazed steadily out at the darkening landscape.

All the beauty that had surrounded them on their journey to Standish Park now receded from their sight as they thought only of Anne-Marie and prayed that her condition would not worsen before they reached her.

They were eager to get to their destination, and yet, when Dartford was reached, there was no comfort in it, for there was still more than half a day's journey to London. Neither Jonathan nor Anna could eat or sleep, and while she, with Sally for company, could at least speak of her fears, he suffered alone, wondering how it was that Fate had picked upon his daughter, just as it had done with Amelia-Jane.

When dawn came, they partook of a light breakfast and were soon on their way again. Fortuitously, it being a Sunday, the roads were almost deserted and with fresh horses, they made excellent time.

At Harwood House, Eliza came out to welcome them, and it was plain that, in her condition, she could not be expected to care for the sick.

Clearly, she would very soon be brought to bed with her first child, yet she greeted and welcomed them into her home and, having first reassured them that the doctor had declared that the condition, though serious, was not infectious, she sent her maid upstairs with them to Anne-Marie's room.

Because Dr Morton had insisted that Mrs Harwood should not enter the invalid's room, Eliza had not seen her friend since her condition had worsened, so was unable to give them an accurate account of Anne-Marie's state.

When they entered the room where she lay, with the heavy curtains closed lest the glare hurt her eyes, Anna could not suppress a gasp, and even Jonathan was shocked at the sight of the slight figure lying in the bed.

Having spent a restless and feverish night, Anne-Marie had a bad headache and had not the strength even to sit up, but lay there, weak and listless. If she heard them enter, she made no movement at all to indicate it.

Anna rushed to her side and Jonathan could not believe how languid and pale she seemed as he stood at the foot of her bed. Only when her father took her thin hand in his did she respond to their presence, with the merest pressure of her fingers as she clasped them around his.

Leaving them for a moment, Anna tried to discover from the nurse who had been tending her what potions and cordials had been administered and in what measure. The woman, who had merely carried out the doctor's instructions, knew very little. Determined to discover more, Anna went downstairs to find Eliza and found her in the hall with Dr Morton, who had just arrived to see his patient.

Mrs Harwood made the introductions, and Anna accompanied him upstairs, where Jonathan Bingley waited at the top of the stairs.

He was eager for information.

"Dr Morton, please tell me, what is this dreadful disease that has afflicted my daughter?" he asked.

Dr Morton had to admit, reluctantly and in many circumlocutory words, that he did not know the true nature of Anne-Marie's illness, except to say it was a condition whose symptoms were a high fever, headache, and aching limbs, all of which caused severe discomfort, but were unlikely to result in anything more catastrophic than temporary debilitation.

When Anna and Jonathan asked almost together, "In how much danger is she?" he answered that she was gravely ill, but she was also young and strong, and with good nursing care and the right medication, he was quite confident that she would recover in time.

Having been in to see the patient, during which time Anna was permitted to remain at her bedside, Dr Morton pronounced her to be "very little improved" on her condition of the previous night.

"But," he said, "her fever must be reduced further by taking more potions, which I shall prescribe, and she needs plenty of deep, restful sleep."

Asked if he had any particular instructions, he replied, "You must see to it, Miss Faulkner, that she has her medication on time and gets plenty of rest to restore her body's health," and, having doled out more pills and cordials, he left, promising to call again that evening.

All that day and most of the following night, Anna sat with her patient, who seemed to wander in and out of sleep, awaking suddenly and crying out, without knowing what she feared; then just as quickly falling into a deep slumber again. Around midnight, it seemed her fever had reached a frightening level, making her very restless and causing Sally to wake Anna, who had dozed off in her chair. They placed strips of damp, cold cloth on her forehead, gave her small sips of water to drink, pulled the bedclothes up around her, and waited for her body to sweat out the fever. They would then rub her down and change her sodden clothes. Thereafter, they knew she would sleep more peacefully.

Her father came and went, his agony unabated, waiting for the dawn and some change in her condition. Jonathan was extremely worried and twice pressed the need for a second opinion, but was prevailed upon by Eliza Harwood and her husband to trust Dr Morton.

"He has been a very sound physician, Mr Bingley; members of my family have been in his care on many occasions; if there is any need to call in a colleague, I am sure he will do so," Mr Harwood assured him, and Jonathan agreed to wait one more day.

"If there is no material improvement in her condition, I shall call in a man I know in Harley Street," he said, firmly.

Shortly after first light, Anna heard a carriage arrive and, parting the curtains at the window, she saw a man alight. He was an unfamiliar figure and she assumed it was Mr Harwood, returning from one of his business trips. However, soon afterwards, she heard footsteps on the stairs and in the corridor, coming down to Anne-Marie's room. The door opened and in the half-light, she could not at first recognise him—it was Charles, Anne-Marie's brother and Jonathan's only son.

While Sally went to find Mr Bingley, Charles greeted Anna briefly and explained.

"I came as soon as I heard. Aunt Emma sent me an express ... I had no idea she was ill. What is it? How long has she been like this?" he asked.

Anna remembered suddenly that he was studying to be a physician himself and answered his questions, which, though pointed and brusque, were sensible enough.

He checked the patient without disturbing her sleep, looked at the array of medications on the bedside table, and left the room.

In the corridor, he met his father, who had come upstairs, having been alerted to the arrival of his son.

The two men, who had not spoken in several months, stopped, looked at one another, and suddenly grasped each other's hands and embraced briefly, before going downstairs together.

Anna, seeing their brief reunion, smiled as she closed the door and returned to her patient's bedside. She prayed their disaffection may be resolved; she knew how deeply it had hurt Jonathan.

Later, Charles returned and was happy to find his sister awake. She seemed to recognise him and, though she did not speak, she let him sit with her and hold her hand until it was time to take her medication.

The arrival of Dr Morton gave him a further opportunity to discuss her condition, and it appeared he was familiar with similar symptoms in patients he had seen in Edinburgh. They had suffered from a virulent type of influenza, he said, many had recovered, albeit severely weakened by the illness, but some— notably the elderly and the very young—had died, mostly of pneumonia following neglect or a relapse.

Dr Morton, who claimed he had not seen too many patients who had died of the affliction, agreed with Charles that rest and good nursing were essential for a full recovery.

"I must congratulate Miss Faulkner," he added. "She has hardly left Miss Bingley's side since arriving here." Charles and his father exchanged glances and appeared to share an unspoken thought.

All day, Charles and Anna took turns at sitting with Anne-Marie until, at about 4 o'clock, Anna, relieved by her maid Sally and urged by Eliza Harwood, came downstairs to tea. Hitherto, she had taken all but her main meals upstairs, so as to be near her patient.

"How is she?" Jonathan asked, comforted to note that Anna seemed less fearful than before.

"I hope and pray I am right; I think I have noticed a small improvement since about two o'clock this afternoon. She has slept for almost four hours and her pulse is stronger, she breathes more easily and does not groan in pain as she used to. While I am almost afraid to hope and must await Dr Morton's verdict, I do believe she is past the worst."

"Is she awake now? May I see her?" asked Jonathan, and Anna agreed.

He was gone in a trice, running up the stairs to his daughter's room, where he found her propped up on her pillows, still looking wan and listless, but when she saw him, she managed a smile. A few minutes later, Charles followed his father upstairs.

When Anna returned to the room, she found them together, not speaking, for Anne-Marie was too weak to converse at any length, but both men were clearly pleased to find her looking much better than before.

Anna was about to slip out and leave them together when Anne-Marie looked up and beckoned to her. Slipping an arm around her neck, she whispered her thanks and stroked her hand, before lying back on her pillows. The gesture, however feeble, gave great hope to her family.

Jonathan, realising how tired Anna must be from three days of unremitting anxiety and exertion, sent her away to rest, which she did gratefully, in a quiet room that had been prepared for her further along the corridor.

So exhausted was she that she did not awake until Dr Morton arrived that evening and asked to see her, so he could congratulate her on her care of his patient.

That night, Jonathan sat with Anna in the drawing room after dinner, while upstairs, in her bedroom, Anne-Marie slept for the very first time without the aid of sleeping draughts or pain reducing potions. Her fever was at its lowest since they had arrived, and her body no longer ached unbearably. Her brother sat with her, having persuaded Anna to let him do some of the work.

Jonathan was keen to take her home to Netherfield Park, where she could rest and regain her health. He was well aware that they had already accepted the generous hospitality of the Harwoods for a week and was keen to leave as soon as it was safe to do so.

Meanwhile, in a gesture that further indicated the improvement in their relations, he gave Charles permission to use the house at Grosvenor Street for as long as he intended to stay in London.

When Dr Morton was applied to, he warned that the patient must not in any way be exposed to the risk of pneumonia and great care must be taken to ensure a continuation of the excellent nursing she had received.

"A relapse must be avoided at all costs," he declared, solemnly. "I cannot say it often enough, Mr Bingley," he said, "medication alone will not do. Your daughter owes her recovery, maybe even her survival, to the admirable way in which Miss Faulkner has organised her care."

Turning to Anna, he declared, "My dear ma'am, I am sure Miss Nightingale herself would have been proud of your selfless devotion to the care of your patient."

Anna said little except to thank him for his kind words, but she was pleased to have his approval, for she had no training at all and had used only her common sense and experience in caring for her sister in Hampshire, who had suffered a very similar affliction last Winter.

Jonathan took the opportunity to tell her how grateful he was for her devotion to Anne-Marie, as well as her support at such a critical time.

"I could not have managed without you, my dear Anna; your calmness and strength have meant everything to me."

Anna, though delighted with his words, was even happier that his problems with his son seemed to have been resolved.

"I am glad the difficulty with Charles has been settled. I can see it has brought you much relief, and he seems more contented, too," she said quietly.

"I believe you are right, Anna. Even better, he has expressed a very high regard and affection for you," he said, as he took her hand.

Anna, who had felt no hostility at all from Charles and had found him helpful and courteous, was pleased to have her impressions confirmed.

By the end of that week, Anne-Marie was sufficiently recovered to come downstairs, to the delight of her family and her friend Mrs Harwood, who, having been denied the chance to attend her when she was sick, lavished a great deal of attention upon her now she was convalescing.

It was still not considered wise for her to travel directly to Hertfordshire, but with Dr Morton's permission, she was allowed to be moved to Grosvenor Street. He promised to call in daily to see how she was progressing, and only after he was quite satisfied that she was out of danger, would she be permitted to undertake the twenty-five mile journey to Netherfield Park.

Charles Bingley, having acquainted Dr Morton with his own training as a physician, was entrusted with watching over his sister, and together with Miss Faulkner, he was confident they would ensure her safe passage home.

While at Grosvenor Street, they suffered some further disappointment.

It came in a letter from Mr Darcy, who wrote to say that Elizabeth's uncle and his business partner, Mr Edward Gardiner, had suffered another heart attack, and his son Richard, himself a physician, had warned that he may not recover from this bout of the disease, which had already weakened him considerably.

Elizabeth and I do not feel we can leave the family, especially Mrs Gardiner, at this time, in order to travel to Netherfield at Easter, as we had planned …

Darcy wrote, however, assuring Jonathan that they all prayed for Anne-Marie's swift recovery and promising they would visit them later in the year.

Jonathan, your aunt Lizzie and I are both delighted with your still secret news, of which we have had some intimation from your mother. We hope to see you before we travel to Woodlands for the Summer and to wish you both joy, personally.

Meanwhile, you may be assured of our discretion; we understand that it is not as yet generally known.

Aunt Lizzie sends her love to all of you and especially to Anne-Marie.

We look forward to seeing you before long.
God bless you,
Fitzwilliam Darcy.

With their plans for Easter now in some confusion, Jonathan decided that it would be best to travel to Netherfield as soon as Anne-Marie was fit enough to make the journey. Jonathan's parents, his sister Emma, and her husband were expected to make up the party.

For Charles, the visit to Netherfield would be his first. Anna had told him a great deal about the place and he was looking forward to seeing it.

"I understand you had an important role in advising on the redecorating of the old place," he had said, as they had sat with Anne-Marie one afternoon.

Anna had blushed, not expecting that he would have heard of her work, but then admitted that, yes, she had made some suggestions.

"They were mainly to do with changes in colours of drapes and shades, where Mr Bingley felt they were either too heavy or inappropriate for the room, as in the case of your sisters' rooms. The original drapes were heavy brocade in a dull gold and brown pattern; they have been replaced with something more cheerful, and you shall be judge when you see it."

Charles could not fail to be impressed by her confidence and charm. He was beginning to understand why his father seemed to find her indispensable to his happiness.

As the days passed and Anne-Marie's health improved, they made plans for their journey. A larger vehicle had to be procured to take them, since more room was required so Anne-Marie would be comfortable. Anna also insisted that they should break journey to allow the patient bed rest for a few hours before proceeding to Netherfield.

Unfortunately, the weather turned cold and miserable as soon as they had left London, and she was very concerned lest Anne-Marie should catch a cold or a chill and her condition worsen. Every possible effort was made to keep her warm and comfortable and, when they reached Netherfield, they were rewarded by a change in the weather, as the wind dropped, the showers eased, and the sun came out again. Charles noted with approval the constant care and attention that Anna Faulkner devoted to Anne-Marie, placing her interest first on every occasion.

At Netherfield, they were met by an anxious Mrs Perrot, who bustled ahead as Charles carried his sister up the stairs to her room, which had been prepared for her, and placed her in a warm bed with fresh linen and comfortable pillows, which made an immediate improvement to her demeanour.

She thanked him with great affection.

"Thank you, dear Charles, you have made me so happy just by being here with us again. We have all missed you, especially Papa," and, when he tried to hush her, urging her not to tire herself, she shook her head and said, "No indeed, I am not tired. It has actually helped me get well, seeing you back again. You will be good to dear Anna, won't you? She is an angel."

He nodded and smiled.

"Of course, I shall be on my best behaviour, I give you my word. I can see that Miss Faulkner has done a wonderful job caring for you."

He left and went downstairs and found Anna with Teresa and Cathy in the sitting room, where tea had been served. His younger sisters greeted him effusively, not having seen him in many months, and there were tears a-plenty.

After tea, they took him upstairs to show him their rooms, and when he returned, he was full of praise for Anna's excellent taste.

"Miss Faulkner, I must congratulate you. The girls' rooms are exquisite. When I get my rooms in town and set up my practice, I should apply to you for advice on their refurbishment," and, noting her look of disbelief, he protested, "No, I beg you to believe me, I am not teasing you. You have superb taste and I could not do better, I am sure of it."

Jonathan, meanwhile, had been around the park with his steward and came indoors to find a happy family gathering in the sitting room. Seeing the look of pleasure that suffused his countenance, Anna and Charles exchanged glances and smiled. They both appeared to understand how he must feel, though neither had discussed it before.

That night, Anna slept in Anne-Marie's room, and to her great relief, there appeared to be no adverse reaction to her journey from London. On the morrow, it was intended to send for Dr Faulkner to ensure that Anne-Marie's recovery was proceeding satisfactorily.

The Faulkners, who had only recently returned from Ramsgate, had had no news of Anne-Marie's illness, and when called, Dr Faulkner rushed over to Netherfield, fearing the worst. He had met a colleague at Ramsgate, who had warned him of the virulent strains of fever that were common in London, some of which had caused deaths among the elderly.

Having read Dr Morton's notes, Dr Faulkner was most impressed with Anne-Marie's recovery. Assured by both the patient and her father that it was more than the medication, it was Anna's excellent nursing that was responsible, Dr Faulkner felt very proud of his daughter.

Some days later, Charles was preparing to leave for Edinburgh. It had become plain to him that his father and Miss Faulkner were in love, and although he had no knowledge of their secret engagement, he was certain they must have an understanding.

As they parted, Jonathan expressed the hope that they would see him again at Netherfield soon, to which Charles replied, "Sir, if I have read your feelings correctly, I think I will soon be returning on a much happier occasion. Congratulations, she is without doubt one of the finest, most charming women it has been my pleasure to meet. I think you are very fortunate and I am sure you will be exceedingly happy."

His father was so moved he could hardly speak and struggled for words to thank his son. Little had been said of their estrangement or its cause.

But, by his concern and support during the last few difficult weeks, as well as his genuine desire to be as amiable as possible to everyone, Charles had indicated clearly that the feud between them was over.

Anna was sorry to see him go and said so.

"I have enjoyed our talks," she said, and Charles, replying that he had too, promised he would be back, quite soon.

She had known him not at all, yet now she felt she knew and understood him. As they had tended his sister in her illness and talked together during the long afternoons or, after dinner, when at Jonathan's request she had sung or played for them, Anna had discovered more about this rather angry young man. Occasionally, he had revealed a gentler side of his nature that, for her, was special, because it linked him to the man she loved, his father, whose gentle kindness was the very heart of his nature.

Before leaving, he sought her out in the sitting room upstairs, where she often went to work or read on her own. Apologising for intruding upon her, he spoke warmly and sincerely, thanking her for her devoted care of his sister as well as the friendship she had shown him.

"I very much appreciated our conversations and your beautiful music, Miss Faulkner; that was a most unexpected pleasure. I look forward to returning soon, when I am sure we shall have much more to celebrate."

Anna thanked him and noted as he kissed her hand that his eyes were very like his father's.

※

As the weather improved, Anne-Marie grew stronger.

When her grandparents, the Bingleys, arrived together with Emma and James Wilson, her spirits lifted considerably, and she was almost her former self again. She, like Anna, had deep affection and admiration for Emma Wilson, whose singular qualities of strength and generosity of spirit, coupled with an elegance of taste, had set her apart as an example to the younger women in the family.

"I confess, I do not know how Emma manages to deal so well with all the busybodies and troublesome constituents that James must cope with," she said to her father as they sat together listening to Emma tell some of her many amusing anecdotes. "It must be her kind heart and great charm."

Jonathan laughed. "I think, my dear, you will find that in most cases, she finds a sense of humour even more useful than her kind heart," he said.

When James was called upon to declare which of his wife's qualities were the most useful in coping with his constituents, he replied without a moment's hesitation.

"I have no difficulty there; it has to be her courage. Indeed, if you had seen her calm the nerves of an irate farmer who would have had me hanged when he discovered I had supported the Repeal of the Corn Laws, you would agree with me. I cannot believe that I would have survived in the Parliament without her considerable courage and honesty."

As he spoke, he looked across at Emma, and none of those present who saw the warmth of their affection, could have doubted his word.

Anna, who loved her prospective sister dearly, wondered if she and Jonathan ever would discover the kind of love that sustained Emma and James.

The sad news about Mr Gardiner's illness had taken some of the gaiety out of their party and cast a pall upon their Easter festivities. His daughters Emily and Caroline were helping their mother care for their father, while Colonel Fitzwilliam and Mr Darcy were both on hand in case of an emergency.

Anna, sensing some of the family's sadness, decided it was time for her to return to her own parents at Haye Park. Despite her inner feelings of happiness and her tender feelings towards Jonathan, which she knew to be returned in full measure, she felt no sense of elation.

Now that her parents were acquainted with her decision to accept Jonathan Bingley's proposal, she knew her mother would press her for a wedding date, and she asked that they keep news of the engagement secret for a while longer.

At first, her mother, who had been delighted with the news, was disappointed that she could not tell her friends.

"May I not tell my sister Charlotte?" she pleaded, but when Anna explained to her mother that it would seem a little insensitive to be celebrating engagements and fixing wedding dates while poor Mr Gardiner's health was still uncertain, Maria Faulkner agreed.

She did, however, caution her daughter that secret engagements could be troublesome, what with "pesky neighbours and relations always asking when was the happy day?"

But any reservations she may have had were overwhelmed by contemplation of her daughter's future as the wife of Jonathan Bingley and Mistress of Netherfield Park. It was a prospect she could not have dreamed of a few years ago.

"Indeed," she remarked to her husband, as they went to bed, "he is a man whose character and fortune are of such quality as to make her the envy of women all over the county. Do you not agree, my dear?"

Dr Faulkner did agree, though he may have expressed it rather differently.

He had received from Mr Bingley a very gracious letter, in which he had informed Dr Faulkner of his gratitude and joy at having been accepted by Miss Faulkner and pledged himself to make her happy. Jonathan had also mentioned Anna's wish that their engagement remain a matter of confidence for a while longer.

Anna herself had not stopped to think about it, but when her mother spoke of pesky neighbours asking questions, she laughed.

"It is very unlikely that they will be sufficiently curious about me to ask such questions, Mama. Many of them have probably consigned me to spinsterhood, by now. I am almost twenty-seven and certain to be an old maid, in their eyes. I think you will not be bothered by too many questions from curious neighbours," she had said.

It was an indication of her lack of vanity and also of a certain naïveté, which she was only later to realise and perhaps to regret.

Discouraged by her father and her own sound common sense from indulging in pointless gossip herself, Anna did not believe that she could ever be the subject of such activity. She was genuinely convinced that at her age, when most women were either already married or else confirmed spinsters, being in no way a threat to any of the eligible young ladies of the district, she was an unlikely target.

Moreover, she reasoned, the long-standing connections between their two families would surely protect Jonathan and herself from such mischief.

She was to discover, too late, that in this she was, unhappily, mistaken.

Jane Bingley, who by now had decided that her granddaughter Anne-Marie was sufficiently recovered to enjoy a picnic in the park, felt also that it allowed her to indulge her feelings of satisfaction at the happiness of her son. She could not wait to write to her sister and tell her all about it and in fact began her letter while the preparations for the picnic were afoot.

My dearest Lizzie, she wrote:

Imagine my joy, when we arrived to find that not only was Anne-Marie very much recovered from her distressing illness, but here was my dear Jonathan walking around as if an angel had just brought him a gift!

One did not have to look far for the cause of this amazing condition, for it was soon clear that Anna Faulkner had a similar if less obvious version of the same.

They are quite clearly in love and secretly engaged, I said to Bingley, who would not go so far, but later that evening, they came to my room and told me themselves. Oh Lizzie, I cannot tell you how happy I was; they seem so right for one another.

Now, as if there was not enough joy for one woman's heart to hold, young Charles had arrived from Edinburgh on hearing his sister was ill and stayed with them for three weeks! During which time, it seems, his feud with Jonathan has ended. I feel Anna has had some part to play in this as well. Lizzie, she is a wonderful young woman; Anne-Marie swears she saved her life, but even if that may be regarded as an exaggeration, no one denies that Anna's devoted care helped make her well again.

Jonathan is very fortunate, as indeed are we, for as I said to Bingley, being so accomplished, she could quite easily have married some eligible young man about town in London or even in Paris (there are so many Americans in Europe now) and she would have been lost to us.

As it turns out, she will make Jonathan, who loves her dearly, an excellent wife and be an exemplary companion to his daughters. They are already good friends. I can see they will all be very happy at Netherfield, dear Netherfield, which holds so many happy memories for us ...

Completing her letter later that day, Jane sent her love to her sister and brother-in-law, her dear aunt and uncle, and all her cousins. Clearly, she was content and happy at Netherfield.

Before closing her letter, she stopped to write a final line.

Oh Lizzie, if only we could all be as happy as I am at this moment, would life not be perfect?

Reading her sister's letter, a few days later, Elizabeth sighed.

"Oh Jane, will you never realise that life just isn't like that?" she smiled as she passed the closely written pages across to her husband, who was just finishing his breakfast.

Darcy read it through quickly while Elizabeth poured out more tea; then, with a somewhat indulgent smile, he said, "Jane would not be Jane if she did not believe in perfect happiness and the innate goodness of human beings. She is an idealist and refuses to think ill of anyone, until their guilt is conclusively proven."

Elizabeth laughed.

"Indeed, you are right, she will give the most malevolent villain the benefit of the doubt," she said, recalling how reluctant Jane had been to condemn Wickham totally, even after his iniquity was exposed. Similarly, with Lydia, she had always hoped for some amendment in her behaviour.

"She would be the one to ask, hopefully, 'Could it be that he really loves her? Can there have been some dreadful mistake?' My dear sister has never been the one to point the finger at anyone. Yet of us all, Jane, with her goodness and kindness, has the best credentials to judge any conduct."

Mr Darcy was more philosophical.

"Lizzie, we need people like Jane in the world. They provide the antidote to all the cynical and suspicious minds that tell us that society is full of malice and corruption. Your sister believes in people, and that is important; she is not naïve or foolish, she simply hopes to find goodness where most of us expect to find evil. She aspires to be happy and share her felicity with others. It is a genuinely blessed intention."

He was warm in his praise of her sister, and Elizabeth was happy to hear it. He continued, "Bingley has confessed to me that, on occasions when he returns home after a difficult business deal or one in which he has found it hard to trust the men he was dealing with, it is Jane who restores his faith in human nature."

Elizabeth had no wish to argue with him.

"Jane is a darling and I would not have her any different. She is very fortunate that her husband and all her children are so amenable she has had little or no strife to contend with. Our children were never so willing to accept my ideas and opinions," Elizabeth said, and Darcy relented.

Understanding the source of his wife's sadness, he sought to comfort her, but would not indulge her.

"Come now, Lizzie, I will not have you feeling sorry for yourself. I know Cassy and Julian are strong willed and have their own opinions about everything, but I have always supported you, have I not?' he asked, and she smiled.

"Yes indeed, you have, and I am truly grateful, Darcy. I would like to be more like Jane and think well of all my fellow men, at least until I am proved wrong or their pretence is clear. As you well know, I did just that on at least one infamous occasion, only to be badly deceived and have my entire family imposed upon most shamefully; quite apart from the pain and mortification to yourself and the continuing aggravation we all suffer, as a consequence," she said. "So, there is now a cautious streak in me, which will not let me believe everything people say or claim to be, unless I know them well enough to be confident of their character."

Seeing his grave countenance, she apologised.

"I am sorry, dearest, you do not deserve to be subjected to this complaint. I have never needed so much as a second thought before accepting your word, and for that alone I am more grateful than I can say."

He was pleased and honoured by her words, understanding in every particular what they implied. That there had never been any mistrust or suspicion between them was, for both of them, the crowning achievement of their marriage.

He knew her earlier remarks referred to the iniquity of Wickham, whose elopement with her sister Lydia had caused them so much distress. Yet, gratified though he was by her confidence in him, Darcy was quite determined that this fine Spring day deserved to be remembered for something more.

"Well, my dear, Jane's letter has confirmed the best news we have had in many months—Jonathan's engagement to Anna Faulkner will, I confidently predict, be the start of a truly felicitous marriage. I have rarely met two people, apart from our own Cassy and Richard, who seemed so well suited in every way. We must celebrate it."

Happy to lift herself out of a mood of gloomy introspection, Elizabeth readily agreed.

"Indeed, we must. I shall write to Jonathan and suggest we have a dinner party for them at Pemberley, as soon as their engagement is announced. How would you like that?"

Darcy said he would like it very well, and preparations were set in train for one of those great occasions at which Pemberley and its staff excelled.

Within a day or two, Jane received, as well as a happy reply from her sister, a note from her cousin Caroline, which brought good news.

Caroline wrote that her father Mr Gardiner had survived his illness in much better condition than had been expected.

Though weakened, he had been declared out of danger, she wrote:

Indeed, dear Jane, my brother Richard's friend from Harley Street has seen Papa and has declared that he may well live for years if he is very careful and does not overwork or become agitated. He must vary his activities and be mindful of his condition in everything he does.

Dear Jane, I cannot tell you what a difference it has made to us all, especially to Mama, who had almost accepted that we were going to lose him, this time.

Changing the subject and simultaneously her mood to one of light-hearted banter, Caroline concluded her letter with a message of congratulation.

I know it's a secret, but I am sure Jonathan will not mind my saying how very happy we are about his engagement to Anna Faulkner. Do tell him, dearest Jane, that Fitzy and I wish them every happiness and look forward to seeing them soon.

Your loving cousin,

Caroline Fitzwilliam.

A few days after Easter Sunday, the party at Netherfield, taking advantage of some fine Spring weather, were considering if they should drive to St Albans or simply enjoy the pleasure of a picnic in the woods, where a profusion of blossoms made a carpet under the trees. As they talked of the relative merits of each prospect, a letter arrived for Anne-Marie. It came from Harwood House, and Mr Harwood wrote to inform her that Eliza had been safely delivered of a son, to whom they hoped she would consent to be a godparent.

Anne-Marie was delighted; her only sorrow stemmed from her inability to be at her friend's side. Dr Faulkner had ruled it out already.

"Quite out of the question, my dear Miss Bingley," he had said. "You will need to become a good deal stronger, and the weather will need to get much warmer, before I would even consider letting you travel to London."

She was deeply disappointed, but Anna added her voice to persuade her.

"You can see how happy it has made your papa to have you here. Stay a few more weeks, especially since the baptism is not for some time yet; it will do you good," she had said.

Young Anne-Marie, however, turned the tables on her, saying archly, "It is very kind of you to say so, Anna, but Papa's happiness is more dependent on your presence than mine, I think! Now, I understand that you could make him a good deal happier, ecstatic in fact, if you would only name the day!"

She was only teasing, but Anna was completely taken aback and struggled to maintain her composure.

Anne-Marie apologised, not wishing to embarrass her.

"I am sorry, Anna, I did not intend to discompose you so, but I did ask Papa when it was to be and he said it was your privilege to name the wedding day. Well? You do love him?"

Anna reddened, unused to being quizzed with such frankness but, recovering her composure said, "Yes, Anne-Marie, I do. I should never have accepted him if I did not. But, as your papa knows, I have been reluctant to name an early date or even to announce our engagement, because I have felt it would not be seemly to do so. I thought it best to wait at least a year... ." Her voice trailed off, and Anne-Marie felt deep sympathy for her. Clearly, she was uncomfortable talking about it.

"Yes, I know and I love and respect you for your delicate sensibility, but Papa has suffered badly and he needs you, Anna. He loves you, I know he loves you desperately, but will do nothing to compel you. He believes it is a matter on which you must feel at ease, else you will not be happy. For my part, I know how much he suffered during the weeks and months before my mother's death and how deeply grieved he was by her conduct. It is my dearest wish that he should find some happiness again. It is in your power, Anna, to grant that wish."

They were interrupted by the maid, who brought Anne-Marie her medication. Anna was grateful for the opportunity to change the subject. Much as she loved Anne-Marie, she was ill at ease with her questions.

Convinced that it was wrong to announce their engagement with what might be seen as unseemly haste, she had chosen to defer the fulfilment of her own happiness for a few more months. Anne-Marie's words had stirred the first doubts in her mind, regarding the correctitude of her decision. She needed more time to think.

Jane and Charles Bingley returned to Ashford Park after their stay at Netherfield, and Jane's only disappointment was that no date had been fixed for Jonathan's wedding. Indeed, she was not supposed to speak of it openly, she complained to Elizabeth when the sisters met at Pemberley.

While she respected Anna's scrupulous sense of propriety, Jane abhorred deception or guile, believing it was more important that Anna and Jonathan be open about the nature of their friendship. She was uncomfortable with being a party to concealment, however well intentioned.

Jane had met their cousin Jessie Phillips while visiting her sister Mary and Charlotte Collins at Longbourn, and Miss Phillips, a noted gossip and busybody, had been very curious about Jonathan and Anna Faulkner.

"Jessie as good as told me the story was all over Meryton," she said. "Everyone knows they are lovers and it is generally expected that they will soon be naming the day."

Jane reported Jessie's words and added, "Lizzie, if I were Anna, I would rather have it known that I was engaged to be married to Jonathan, than have women like Jessie Phillips gossip about me. I may be wrong, but I do not think she means well."

It was obvious that Jane had been disconcerted by the remarks, however little regard she had for their author.

Elizabeth agreed, "No, Jane, you are not wrong. Neither Jessie Phillips nor our Lydia has a brain or a scruple between them. They will, by their loose talk and insinuation, besmirch Anna's reputation and ruin her chances of happiness. Anna is probably unaware of the harm they can do to her good name. I think, my dear sister, the time has come to write a note to my friend Charlotte. If I suggest tactfully that she speak to her sister Maria, and they advise Anna on the dangers of becoming the subject of gossip in the village, it may work."

Jane agreed that it was indeed an excellent idea and urged her sister to write at once to Charlotte Collins who, as Anna Faulkner's aunt, might well have some influence upon her.

Later that day, Elizabeth did just that.

In a carefully composed letter, she detailed Jane's concerns and her own, suggesting that Charlotte may wish to speak with her niece and draw her attention to them.

I know you will not mind me writing to you on this matter, my dear Charlotte, because I am sure you are as concerned about your niece Anna as Jane is about Jonathan.

It seems clear enough that they are both very much in love and should under normal circumstances be already engaged. However, Jane believes that Anna's reluctance to announce their engagement is due chiefly to her sense of propriety, which dictates that Jonathan should wait at least a year before remarrying.

My dear Charlotte, while neither Jane nor I have any quarrel with Anna for the delicacy of her feelings in this matter, we are both agreed that were she and Jonathan to become engaged openly, it would not only promote their own happiness, but it would certainly put a firm stop to the kind of idle gossip of women like Jessie Phillips and our own sister Lydia Wickham.

*We feel, and Mr Darcy agrees with me on this, that you are best
placed, being Jonathan's mother-in-law and Anna's aunt, to advise her.*

*I hope you will agree with me, Charlotte, and forgive what may seem
like interference on my part. Please believe me, it is with reluctance and
only because of our great affection for both our nephew Jonathan and Anna
that I have taken the liberty of writing to you on this subject.*

Elizabeth concluded her letter to Charlotte with an invitation to her to join
them at Pemberley, at a dinner party to celebrate the engagement of their niece
and nephew, "whenever that happy event is finally announced," and expressing
a hope that it would be soon.

Having despatched her letter, she went in search of her husband, who was
indulging his love of Art, supervising the hanging of two new paintings in the
long gallery.

When Elizabeth joined him, Darcy was in an excellent mood, having
received a letter from London which authenticated the antiquity of a favourite
piece in his collection. She let him tell her all about it before detailing for him
the purpose of her letter to Charlotte Collins.

He listened attentively and, to her delight, agreed absolutely with her.

"There is no question that more damage may be done to both Jonathan's
good name and Anna's reputation, should their secret engagement become a
topic for malicious gossip and innuendo, than would occur if they were married
before the twelve month anniversary of his wife's death.

"The latter may cause some uncharitable comment, perhaps, but that would
soon be overwhelmed by the congratulations and good wishes that must surely
follow. The former, on the other hand, would introduce the taint of corruption
which may well defile a perfectly good marriage," he said.

"Then you think I was correct to write as I did to Charlotte?" she asked,
and he agreed without question.

"I certainly do, my dear. I have too much affection for our nephew and far
too much respect for Miss Faulkner to wish to see their reputations sullied by
malicious gossip. I hope Charlotte follows your advice, Lizzie. Better still, I
sincerely wish that Jonathan and Anna will do so, too."

The arrival of their daughter Cassandra with two of her children,
bearing the good news that Richard had pronounced Mr Gardiner to be

much recovered, cheered them all up. But, as things turned out, the feeling did not last long.

Elizabeth, sworn to secrecy by Jane, had said not a word to her daughter about Jonathan and Anna. Which is why she was astonished when Cassy revealed that her mother-in-law, Mrs Gardiner, had received a letter from an acquaintance in Meryton, detailing the prevailing rumours about Mr Bingley, the handsome widower, who had recently purchased Netherfield Park.

Probably unaware of the close link between their families, she wrote of him having a secret liaison with a young woman in the neighbourhood, whom she had described as "an artist, who has spent some years in Paris and was probably freer in her ways than the other young ladies of the area."

Cassandra confessed to being diverted by the description of the young woman. "Can you imagine anyone describing Anna Faulkner in those terms?" she cried, and Elizabeth almost leapt upon her to demand how she had come to fix upon Miss Faulkner as the lady in question.

Cassy looked bemused. "Mama, because everyone knows they are secretly engaged! Caroline told me a week or more ago. I thought you knew, already," she said. "Surely Aunt Jane must know and I assumed she would have told you."

Elizabeth explained the complex and confusing circumstances that obtained in the case of Jonathan and Anna.

A thoroughly practical young woman, Cassandra could not believe that two people who loved each other would waste any time at all pandering to the small minds of local gossips.

"Oh Mama, it's absurd! If I were Anna, I would surely have married him already, or at least become engaged. I cannot imagine why they would put their happiness in jeopardy, simply because they fear the censure of people who are in no way connected to them and have no right to lay down rules for their behaviour."

Elizabeth agreed, pointing out that while it was customary to observe a year's mourning, Jonathan's situation with three young daughters would surely serve to soften any possible criticism. She was glad she had written to Charlotte. She hoped very much that her letter would have the desired effect.

❧

It was almost the end of April.

In Hertfordshire, the afternoons were becoming warmer and more soporific. In the village, with the promise of fine weather, preparations were afoot for the May festival.

Charlotte Collins and Mary Bennet had spent a very pleasant hour with Jonathan Bingley and Anne-Marie, who had come to tea. Anne-Marie had recovered from her illness and was making plans to return to London and her work at the hospital. She was looking forward also to seeing her friend Eliza and her new baby and insisted upon giving her grandmother all the news from Harwood House.

After tea, Mary Bennet invited Anne-Marie to play for them, but unfortunately, she claimed she was very out of practice, having been ill.

"I know you are accustomed to have Anna play for you, she plays so beautifully, I should be ashamed to let you hear me play, until I have practiced some more," she said.

Mary was most censorious.

"You must never let yourself get so out of practice that you cannot play at all, Anne-Marie. I hope, when you next come to visit, you will have improved your performance sufficiently to let us hear you play. Anna Faulkner is a perfectionist; we cannot all be as good; but she is an example to us, and we can be inspired by her to try harder," she declared, laying down her own philosophy in a single sentence.

Chastened, Anne-Marie promised faithfully to do better next time.

They left soon afterwards, undertaking to call again before Anne-Marie returned to London.

They had hardly been gone ten minutes when a pony trap drew up in front of the house, and without any warning, Lydia Wickham and Jessie Phillips burst into the room.

While Jessie, who was several years younger than her cousin, was as fast a talker as Lydia, she had at least a trimmer figure and a quieter manner.

Lydia Wickham, on the other hand, had started out as a plump young girl with a boisterous manner and remained a buxom, loud-mouthed woman right into middle age.

Her predominantly silly and empty-headed comments, spiced occasionally with an unpleasant coarseness of phrase, were rarely appreciated by either her sister Mary or Mrs Collins, but this did not seem to deter her in any way. She had very little to do, now her large family had grown up, and could be counted upon to arrive, usually without warning, and impose herself upon her relations and friends and proceed to regale them with the latest gossip in the county.

Unencumbered by any sense of fairness, she was totally unconcerned about those of whom she spoke, casting aspersions with abandon, her only aim the pursuit of a vindictive form of entertainment.

On this pleasant afternoon, it appeared that that was exactly what she had in mind. Even before they had been invited to sit down, Lydia had collapsed into a large armchair, one that used to accommodate her mother many years ago, and reached for the food.

"Oooh! Fresh scones with cream and fruit cake! Jessie, we have certainly arrived at the right time for tea. Are you expecting anyone?" she asked, and when Mary informed them that Jonathan and his daughter had just left, having had tea with them, Lydia and Jessie exchanged conspiratorial glances and giggled like schoolgirls.

"Lord! I am so hungry, I could eat up all that cake! We walked all over Meryton trying on hats. Jessie needs one to attend a wedding, and I must have a new hat for the May Parade. But, you will not believe, there was not a single one that would suit. I cannot think what has got to the milliners in these parts, Charlotte, they make boring, old-fashioned bonnets, yet the ladies of fashion are wearing very chic *chapeaux*," she complained, as she ate more cake and urged Jessie to do likewise.

When a fresh pot of tea was brought in, she barely waited to ask if Charlotte or Mary wanted any, before helping herself and, talking all the time, she proceeded to attack the cake.

Watching her, Charlotte was reminded of Mrs Bennet, whom she resembled so closely in looks and manner that it was quite uncanny seeing her sitting where her mother had often sat in years gone by.

The irony of the situation had not escaped Charlotte, who had known how deeply Mrs Bennet had resented her since her marriage to Mr Collins, who, had he lived, would have inherited Longbourn, under the entail.

As Lydia groaned and complained again of being exhausted, Mary, growing ever more irritated, said, "I wonder at your bothering to come at all, Lydia, if you were so tired," to which Lydia replied, "Ah, but we had to come, because we had to bring you the latest news."

"And what news is that?" asked Mary, not really interested at all.

Lydia and Jessie Phillips giggled and exchanged glances again, and then

Lydia, leaning forward, spoke in an exaggerated whisper, "Did you know, Charlotte, that your precious Mr Jonathan Bingley and your niece Miss Anna Faulkner are engaged? Indeed, their secret liaison has been going on for quite a while and nobody, not even Maria Faulkner, knew of it."

Charlotte's retort was sharp. "Don't talk nonsense, Lydia. Shame on you! You should not repeat gossip and rumour. It is quite wrong."

"Oh, you may choose not to believe it, if you wish, but I know it to be true. Indeed, if they are not engaged, then they must have some explaining to do, because I happen to know that Anna Faulkner and Jonathan Bingley both stayed at the Bingleys' house in Grosvenor Street, not too long ago."

Seeing Charlotte's expression of disbelief, she said, "Now, Charlotte, don't you scold me, this is not gossip or rumour, it is true. I have it from my sons Henry and Phillip, who saw them when they were visiting a friend in the same street. They saw Jonathan and a lady, whom they did not recognise at the time, arrive in a hansom cab and go into the Bingleys' house together.

"Some time later, they saw Jonathan Bingley leave and return alone, but the woman remained in the house throughout. Now, when Henry was here over Easter, he saw Anna Faulkner twice in Meryton with her mother and knew at once that she was the woman they'd seen with Jonathan in Grosvenor Street.

"Henry says he has no doubts at all; indeed, on one occasion, she was wearing the same gown and hat as the woman in London. So, how do you explain that?" she asked defiantly, and when poor Charlotte, stunned, made no immediate reply, she went on, "Henry says it was quite clear that they were not mere acquaintances, he could tell by their manner. La, Jessie, would it not be fun if little Miss Goody Two-Shoes turns out to be not quite so innocent after all, eh?"

Charlotte's patience was at an end. She exclaimed that she would hear no more and ordered Lydia to hold her tongue.

"For shame, Lydia, you of all people have no right to defame other young women in this way. I am sure there must be some perfectly reasonable explanation; I do know that Anna helped nurse Mr Bingley's daughter, Anne-Marie, who was very ill, and it is quite likely she stayed with her at the Bingleys' house in London."

But Lydia was not so easily silenced.

Her outrage was expressed in a tirade against members of her family, many of whom had continued to help her and her feckless husband for years.

That neither Anna nor Jonathan had ever played any part in what she saw as her own humiliation was of no significance.

"Well, I hope there is an explanation, because if there is not, and they are not engaged, then everyone will want to know what is going on."

"It is none of their business, Lydia, and you should tell them so," snapped Charlotte, but undeterred, Lydia raved on.

"Well, it will serve them right, Jane and Lizzie and all those people who have been preaching at me for years. There's Aunt Gardiner, too, she would go on and on at me as though I were some criminal."

Her face red and angry, she was determined to have her say.

"Lizzie and Jane have been no better. Ever since Wickham and I were married, they have been looking down their noses at us whenever we meet, usually at weddings and funerals. Why, you'd think we had done something that no young couple had ever done before or since. Mr Darcy will not receive Wickham or my boys at Pemberley, indeed, he is so high and mighty, he pretends he has no connection with us at all. Mr Bingley is barely polite and Cassy Darcy and her precious husband sat next to me at Amelia-Jane's funeral and said not a word!

"I am heartily sick and tired of them all. It would do them good to have a bit of scandal of their own, and I for one do not apologise for mentioning it," she declared, and with that, she rose to her feet, marched out into the hall, twirled her parasol, and was gone in a flurry of flounces and frills, with Jessie Phillips following meekly in her wake.

Mary looked up and remarked that Lydia had always fancied herself in fussy gowns, but she thought they only made her look foolish.

"She is much too old for frills and flounces, anyway," she said.

Charlotte was too upset to listen and said not a word for fully five minutes, and then she sighed and declared that she did not know why Lydia had become so vicious. Charlotte was well aware of the innumerable occasions on which both Jane and Elizabeth had helped Lydia pay her bills. She had received Elizabeth's letter that very morning and, until the arrival of Lydia with her "news," Charlotte had not been too perturbed by its contents. She had intended to approach Anna, in private, but only to ask her to beware of the local rumour mill. But now, the possibility of Lydia Wickham defaming her niece's good name, and with it her chance of happiness, threw her into confusion.

Charlotte Collins had never had to face such a situation in her own life. A sensible woman before she married Canon Collins and a good wife and mother afterwards, she was at a loss to know what to do. But, forewarned, she was determined to do something to prevent a possible disaster.

～❦～

As May Day dawned, preparations for the festival were going on apace in the village. Groups of dancers, buskers, fortune tellers, and itinerant performers jostled for space on the green, while the usual fairground attractions had been set up around the square.

Anna, who was on her way to Longbourn, decided to visit the fair to buy some preserves, which she knew her Aunt Collins favoured. She had almost completed her purchases and was about to get back in her little pony trap, when she caught sight of her aunt, who appeared to be in a state of some agitation.

Anna, moving quickly through the crowd, reached her aunt's side, and was careful not to alarm her, taking her arm gently as she spoke.

"My dear Aunt, I did not know you wanted to come into Meryton today, else I would have called at the house for you," she said, but Charlotte, all but ignoring her words, said in an urgent voice, "Anna, oh Anna, I am so glad to see you. I have already been to Haye Park and spoken with your mother, but it is you I wanted to see."

Anna was astonished.

"To Haye Park?" she exclaimed. "My goodness, how did you get there?"

"My brother sent the carriage round for me," Charlotte replied, "but it was required to return to Lucas Lodge, so when your mother told me you were coming down to the fair, I walked here hoping to find you."

"Walked? My dear Aunt, you must be exhausted! Pray, tell me, why were you in such a hurry to find me? Has something happened? Is it Miss Bennet? Has she been taken ill?" she asked, concerned and surprised at her aunt's actions.

Anna knew something was wrong. Her Aunt Collins was a sensible woman, who would not lightly leave her home to wander around the village in search of her niece unless she was seriously troubled. She pressed her for a reason and Charlotte replied that Mary Bennet was perfectly well.

"It has nothing to do with Mary, but there is a matter that concerns me very deeply, about which I wish to speak privately with you."

Even more bewildered, Anna offered to drive her home either to Longbourn or to Haye Park, where they could talk.

"Not Haye Park, no, it would upset your mother. She must already be wondering at my arriving on her doorstep this morning. However, I did at least succeed in confirming one thing; I know that you and Jonathan Bingley are secretly engaged to be married. Anna, my dear, why did you not tell me?" she asked sadly, adding considerably to Anna's confusion.

She realised that whatever her aunt's concerns, they must have something to do with her and Jonathan; it was not possible to have a discussion about them standing in the roadway in the midst of the bustle of the May Day festivities. The parade would be getting ready to move off very soon, and she did not intend to be caught up in it. She could already see the groups of young people in their bright costumes gathering in the square, and the Meryton band was tuning up rather noisily. Many people had come in to Meryton for the festival, attracted by the fine weather and the promise of fireworks at nightfall.

Eager to be gone, Anna urged her aunt into her vehicle and started off, taking the road that led in the direction of Oakham Mount, which was a fair distance away if one were walking, but a far less arduous undertaking when driving. Charlotte was so agitated she hardly noticed where they were going.

As they had no intention of attempting a walk to the summit of the mount, whose celebrated view of the surrounding country they had both seen on many occasions, they stopped in the meadows below and tethered the pony in the shade of an old spreading oak.

The day was already warm, and Anna was glad of the shade. She was keen to discover what had disturbed her usually imperturbable aunt.

"Now, Aunt Charlotte, tell me please, what is it that has been troubling you? Have you had some bad news?" she asked.

Charlotte, who loved her niece and wished only to protect her from the cruel gossip that Lydia was spreading around the district, could not hold back her tears as she blurted it out. Anna listened as her aunt told of the visit of Lydia Wickham and Jessie Phillips, her outrage at their insinuations increasing every moment.

Charlotte Collins was reluctant to speak of them.

"Anna, ordinarily, I would pay no attention at all to gossip of this sort. But these women are quite without scruple and will destroy your reputation and that of your family. They are neither respectable nor honest, but have sharp tongues that will spread their lies throughout the district. Jonathan will suffer, too," she said. "Lydia, especially, has a particular grudge against Jonathan Bingley. She believes that Mr Bennet used her ill and treated her son unfairly when he left Longbourn to Jonathan. She has said as much to me, and I am ready to believe she, urged on by her husband, will do or say anything to damage him. In his position in public life, such a story may be used against him."

Seeing Anna's shocked expression, she added, "Please tell me, what plans have you and Mr Bingley made?"

Anna told her aunt the complete truth, apologising first for having caused her so much distress by keeping her in ignorance.

"My dear Aunt, I never dreamed we could become the target of wicked gossip. Jonathan has no enemies here, the Bingley family is well liked and respected, and I live quietly with my parents. I have simply been reluctant to let it appear that I was trying to secure an early engagement, even before a year had passed since Amelia-Jane's death. I truly believed it was right to wait. If we had anticipated anything like this, we might have acted differently," she explained.

Somewhat reassured, Charlotte then begged Anna to let her parents announce their engagement, immediately.

"Let it be done at once, Anna, make it known publicly, and if you plan to marry within the year, set a date for your wedding. Please do not let them destroy the happiness I know you both deserve."

Anna embraced her aunt. She was grateful indeed for her concern and counsel. She resolved to take Mrs Collins home to Longbourn first, before deciding what she would do. On reaching Longbourn, she waited only a very short time, even refusing refreshment, before setting out again.

Anna had thought deeply about her aunt's words and it had resulted in growing feelings of guilt about her own conduct. However unintended, if the consequences were to damage not only herself but her parents and Jonathan as well, she knew she would never forgive herself.

Even as she considered her own behaviour, she grew ashamed.

"How arrogant have I been, considering only my own wishes, never thinking how my decision might rebound on him or others in my family?" she thought, wretchedly blaming herself and hoping desperately that it was not already too late to reclaim the situation.

She had set out in the morning expecting to travel only as far as Longbourn, for which her little pony carriage had been quite adequate. However, it was, she decided, essential that she go on to see Jonathan, and there was no larger carriage available to her at Longbourn.

It was a little over three miles to Netherfield Park.

Meanwhile, at Netherfield, Jonathan had been contemplating the long Summer ahead. Anne-Marie would soon be returning to Harwood House and her work at the hospital, while young Cathy and Tess had been invited to join their grandparents at the Darcys' farm, Woodlands.

He had no doubt that the invitation would have been extended to him too, except that it would have been assumed that he would prefer to remain in Hertfordshire with Anna.

He would, but the situation was far from simple. With all his daughters away, it would not be seemly for Anna to be visiting Netherfield alone. He was already aware of the quizzical glances of some of their neighbours at church and in the town. People who had known him for years appeared curious.

As for calling on Anna at Haye Park, it would present no problems, since Mrs Faulkner was hospitable and friendly and Dr Faulkner always made him welcome, but they would have very little time together on their own.

He yearned for the days they had spent in Kent, at Standish Park; walks in the woods, tea on the terrace, picnics by the river, it had been idyllic. And, it had helped them explore and express their feelings for each other.

But, being a practical and sensible man, as well as being in love, Jonathan knew that, idylls apart, if he wanted to avoid a long and unhappy Summer, he must persuade Anna to let her parents announce their engagement.

He understood and respected her reservations, but hoped to convince her that it was in their own interest to make it known that they planned to marry. They could then be seen together without causing undue comment and would no longer need to conceal their feelings from their families. It was a charade he was finding increasingly difficult to maintain, feigning indifference to a woman he passionately loved.

It was afternoon; the May festival would be in full swing. Everyone, including most of the servants at Netherfield, had gone into Meryton for the parade and fireworks. Cathy and Tess had gone too with their governess and Jonathan's manager, Mr Bowles.

Except for Anne-Marie, who had shown no interest in the festival, Mrs Perrot, and a couple of her maids, who claimed they had too much to do, there was no one in the house.

Growing impatient, Jonathan went down to the stables, saddled up his horse, and set off for Haye Park.

It was a sultry afternoon, and by the time he reached his destination, he was tired. To his dismay, a servant informed him that Miss Faulkner had left some hours earlier, intending to visit the May fair before proceeding to Longbourn. He learned also that she had taken the pony trap and was alone. She was expected to return by dinner time, the maid said.

Disappointed, Jonathan rode back to Netherfield, stopping at Longbourn on his way, only to discover that neither Anna nor her aunt had returned from Meryton. None of the household knew where they were.

As he rode home, Jonathan noticed the darkening sky and clouds gathering on the horizon beyond Netherfield. The prospect of a Summer storm looked very real indeed.

He was anxious about both Anna and Charlotte. He had no idea where they might be. Since they were neither at Longbourn nor at Netherfield, he assumed they were still out on the road in a pony cart!

When Mrs Perrot brought him tea in the sitting room, he inquired if any of the servants had returned from Meryton.

"Tom's back," she said. "He said he didn't want to catch his death getting soaked by the storm that's coming."

The gardener was sent for and asked if he had seen either Miss Faulkner or Mrs Collins at the fair. He recalled seeing Mrs Collins, he said, but that was quite early in the day, and no, he had seen nothing of Miss Faulkner.

The sound of a carriage in the drive took them to the door, but it turned out to be Tess and Cathy with their governess and Mr Bowles, arriving just minutes before the storm broke, with great claps of thunder and streaks of lightning, around the house. Rain fell in sheets, drenching everything, sending everyone scurrying to close the windows and draw the curtains.

Upstairs, Jonathan found Anne-Marie looking out of her window, complaining that she could see nothing beyond a few yards of the house.

"Papa, where could they be? Tess and Cathy saw neither of them in Meryton. What has become of them?"

She was fearful, and he comforted her.

"At least there is still light in the sky and Summer storms in this part of the country are, mercifully, short lived. When it abates, we can send out a search party. They may just be sheltering somewhere, out of the rain."

Anne-Marie looked up at her father and seeing the anxious expression on his face, she was not convinced by his words.

Anna had left Longbourn noting the gathering storm in the distance.

The unusual build-up of heat through the day had become quite oppressive. It was the kind of weather in which a short, sharp shower of rain would be welcome, if one were not out in it, she thought, as she set out, taking a route she knew well, avoiding the main road between Meryton and Netherfield, which she judged might be busy with traffic from the fair.

Overhead, the clouds had begun to swirl around and gather in great greyish lumps, and very soon, much of the blue sky had been blotted out. So gloomy were her surroundings, it seemed much later than it was, but Anna had forgotten her watch and could not check the hour.

She was still a mile or so shy of Netherfield Park when the first drops of rain began to fall. At first, she drove on untroubled, pulling her cape around her and tying the ribbons of her bonnet more tightly.

The pony seemed not to be disturbed by the rain, but Anna was afraid the thunder and lightning might scare him into bolting. She kept him on a fairly tight rein and talked soothingly to him; as the storm broke, she became anxious and looked for some shelter, but there was none, for they had left the farm houses and cottages behind as they entered the woods around the Netherfield estate.

There was nothing to do but plod on, wet, cold, and miserable as the wind drove the rain in and swamped the pony carriage. To make matters worse, broken boughs from trees snagged the roof and cluttered the path of the vehicle, and Anna was terrified lest the poor animal should stumble and throw her or overturn the light vehicle. By the time the rain eased, Anna, her pony and the carriage were all soaked through.

As they emerged from the copse below the park and made their way slowly up the lane leading to the gate, Anne-Marie saw them first from her bedroom window, and calling out to her father, she ran downstairs and raced to the front door. Jonathan was beside her immediately and as he flung open the door and went to help her, Anna alighted and almost collapsed into his arms.

Anne-Marie and Mrs Perrot together took her drenched body from him; with the weight of her sodden garments, she almost needed to be carried up the stairs. The maids had already run upstairs to prepare a hot bath and Jonathan worried about her catching a severe cold or a chill.

He remembered that the Faulkners had lost a daughter, Kitty, from pneumonia in similar circumstances, and was very afraid for Anna. He took comfort from the fact that she was older and stronger than her sister had been at the time.

Mrs Perrot and her helpers removed her wet and muddied clothes, bathed and dried her, washed her hair, rubbed her down with warm herbal oils, and finally wrapped her in a thick blue dressing gown, several sizes too large for her, and tucked her into a comfortable chair in the upstairs sitting room, where a lively fire burned in the grate.

After what seemed like an interminable wait, but was in fact not much more than an hour, Anne-Marie came downstairs to tell her father that Anna could see him.

Jonathan Bingley must have reached the top of the stairs in seconds and the sitting room in not much more. Seeing her there, pale, anxious, and quite unlike her usual confident self, Jonathan, appalled by the fearful prospect of what might have been, went directly to her and before she knew it, had gathered her into his arms.

It seemed all his pent-up feelings had rushed to the surface and would be denied no more. Smiling, Anne-Marie left them alone and even Mrs Perrot was persuaded to wait a while before returning with a hot toddy, guaranteed to keep the chills away.

Having been assured that Anna was surprisingly well, though still a little shaken by her experience, Jonathan declared with a passion that surprised her that this charade must end. They must announce their engagement at once, he said, so he could assert his right to look after her properly.

"I cannot have you wandering around the country in a fragile little pony trap. Just think, Anna, what might have happened if the poor creature had stumbled or bolted. I was sick with worry. For two dread-filled hours, my darling, I thought we had lost both you and Mrs Collins."

Anna was deeply touched and confessed she had been very frightened indeed. It was an experience she would not want to repeat.

"I realised soon enough that I had done something very silly, driving into the storm, but I did so want to reach you. I did not stop to consider the danger. I am very sorry to have caused everyone and especially you, my dear Jonathan, all this worry."

He held her close, reassuring her and while there were some tears, mostly there were loving, comforting words.

Not surprisingly, they found they agreed completely on what their future should be. It was settled that their engagement would be announced at once.

Indeed, moments later, Mrs Perrot, arrived and was greeted with the news.

"You are the first to be told," said Anna happily, and she was very honoured and wished them every happiness.

Together with many of the staff at Netherfield, Mrs Perrot had been hoping for just such an announcement. There had been far too much talk about the master and his lady, below stairs and in the neighbourhood, for her comfort. She was glad it was out in the open and very happy for both of them.

Anne-Marie was the next to know. She hugged and kissed them both, and more tears were shed, but this time they were unashamedly tears of joy. Teresa and Cathy joined them, and the news was told and retold until everyone in the household had been informed and had expressed their pleasure. Jonathan and Anna basked happily in their general approval; the knowledge that their love could bring so much satisfaction to others added considerably to their own happiness.

Jonathan's countenance had undergone such a remarkable change since afternoon as to be barely recognisable, so content did he seem in the fulfilment of his dearest wish.

As for Anna, it seemed that no amount of repetition would suffice to confirm her happiness. Now, they were impatient to tell their friends and family of their mutual felicity, all the more for having kept it from them for several months.

When, after an hour or so, Mrs Perrot suggested that perhaps Anna might need some rest, there was outrage.

"Oh no, not yet," said the girls, who wanted more time, and Anna, insisting she was well enough, remembered that messages had to be sent to her aunt and her parents to reassure them that she was safe and well.

"My aunt Collins will be most anxious," she said and asked for pen and paper.

These were soon fetched, and two notes were immediately written and despatched. Both stated in the clearest way that she had been stranded at Netherfield by the storm, but was quite safe. To her aunt, she sent many thanks and told her of her engagement, urging her to announce it to anyone who cared to enquire.

"Indeed, dear Aunt, I must be the happiest woman in the world, at least for today. I am totally indifferent to anything anyone might say and give you authority to proclaim my happiness to the county, if need be!" she wrote, to Anne-Marie's great amusement.

Her parents were informed that her engagement to Jonathan Bingley could be announced without delay. Turning to more mundane though equally essential matters, a postscript was added requesting that some suitable clothes and shoes be sent for her, as her own had been so muddied in the storm, they were beyond repair.

The responses of Charlotte Collins and Dr and Mrs Faulkner were quite predictable; they were delighted.

Anne-Marie, meanwhile, had begged for a wedding date to be set.

"I must know before I return to Harwood House," she pleaded. "Everyone will ask me and I shall feel foolish to admit that I did not know."

Her father assured her that it would be soon.

"Probably before the end of Summer," said Jonathan, urging patience and promising she would be the first to know.

The storm blew itself out overnight and the dawn brought a fine day, washed clean by the rain. Everything seemed clearer and brighter, like the joy that had suddenly enveloped the household at Netherfield.

"It's the kind of day a painter dreams of," said Anna, as she stood in the saloon with Jonathan and Anne-Marie, looking out at the park.

It was, certainly, a day that had materially changed their lives.

For Anna and Jonathan, it had brought freedom to express their love and enjoy each other's company without concealment.

For Anne-Marie and her sisters, it had ended a year or more of enduring their father's sorrow. Now they could share his hopes for happiness.

Anna had not realised how much had depended upon her decision. The night before, after her compliant acceptance of his determination that it was time to declare their intentions to friends and family, she had apologised for what she saw as her selfishness.

"I am sorry, Jonathan," she had said. "I know now I should not have acted as I did. I insisted on having my way in this matter, never stopping to think of you or my family. I thought only of my own inclinations, it was unforgivable self indulgence on my part. I never realised that you may well have been damaged by gossip and rumour."

She was deeply contrite. But, as is often the case with newly acknowledged lovers, he sought to absolve her of any blame, declaring that he was culpable, because he had not been more persuasive, nor had he tried to explain more cogently the reasons for announcing their engagement and setting a wedding date.

In any event, he pointed out firmly, it was her privilege to name the date for their wedding and it was no one else's business.

When they had confessed their love once more, recounted with regret their transgressions—imagined or real—and granted each other remission of their sins, they were able to return to the more ordinary task of making plans for their wedding.

Once again, Anne-Marie was consulted, as she would be often in the future. Though not yet twenty-one, she was an intelligent young woman, with a strong affection for her father and the woman he was going to marry. Such a happy circumstance came but rarely and was not to be squandered.

Anna, who had no younger sisters or cousins, asked Anne-Marie if she would be her bridesmaid, an honour she accepted with pleasure.

The day chosen by the couple was the last Saturday of Summer, when the leaves of the oak would be turning to gold, while the birches in the park still shimmered silver and Netherfield would look its best for its new Mistress.

"I think that would be just the most perfect time," said Anne-Marie, before she went away to write to her friend Eliza and give her the happy news.

Jonathan and Anna drove first to Haye Park to receive the blessing of her parents and then to Longbourn, where they found Charlotte Collins and Mary Bennet so excited, they completely forgot to order tea.

Only when their guests rose to leave did Charlotte remember, to her chagrin, that they had been offered no refreshment! Neither of the ladies had forgotten, however, to tell the pair how pleased they were about their engagement and wish them every happiness.

Anna was deeply touched.

"If I had known that one little decision of mine could bring so much pleasure to so many people, I would not have dreamed of putting it off," she said as they returned to Netherfield. "I expected to face censure and severe criticism."

Jonathan assured her that he had known all along that she would not be condemned.

"If any one was to face censure for not waiting long enough, it was I, not you, Anna. I am pleased that you have seen it for yourself. No one has so much as hinted that we were wrong to have sought happiness together. Why would they? We have injured no one and indeed we may claim to have greatly increased the joy of many among our family and friends who wish us well. Anna, my dear, everyone who matters to us is happy for us," he said.

It was a statement that she had no reason to doubt.

All that day and for most of the next, plans were made and letters written by both Jonathan and Anna.

For Jonathan, his first thought was to inform his parents and the Darcys, all of whom were by now at Woodlands. A letter was written and promptly despatched, assuring them that all was now settled between himself and Anna, with Dr and Mrs Faulkner giving them their blessing and announcing their engagement in the *Times*.

"Dear Mama," he wrote, "you can rest assured that my heart, for which you have expressed so much concern recently, is now in very good hands."

There were other letters to write, including to his dear aunt Elizabeth and Mr Darcy, reminding them that he owed a good deal of his present happiness to them, for it was at Pemberley that he had met Anna Faulkner again—grown up, handsome, and recently returned from Europe. He promised they would soon see them all at Woodlands.

Anna, too, had letters to write before she could turn her mind to anything else. Her letter to Emma Wilson was as loving and intimate as a sister's could be.

If only I could tell you, my dear Emma, how much happiness this decision has brought, not just to both of us, who have longed for it, but to all our friends and family. Jonathan and I are both deeply indebted to you for the time we spent with you at Standish Park, in Spring, for it was there, in your gracious home and amidst your beautiful grounds, that we first understood, and indeed acknowledged to one another, the depth of our love.

It had been growing slowly over several months, and we might never have recognised it for what it was, except for those lovely days together in Kent. Since then, it seems to have come on so fast that, speaking for myself, it has virtually taken over my life to the extent that it is almost an ache in me, unbearable, yet sublime.

I know you, above all, will understand how I feel.

Thank you, Emma, and to James too, please convey our heartfelt thanks.

We hope to see you when Anne-Marie returns to Harwood House, next week.

Your loving sister
Anna Faulkner.

To her dear friends, the Armandes, she wrote somewhat differently, but with no less affection, of the joy this love had brought her. She thanked them for their kindness to her.

I know in my heart, dearest Marie and Emile, that much of the pleasure Jonathan and I share, the appreciation of Music, the love of Fine Art, I owe to you. What talent and skills I possess, and which he delights in, were nurtured by you.

They would have been poor indeed, without your enlightened guidance.

You have meant as much to me as my dear parents, and it is indeed possible that you have done more to make me who I am than they have.

The years I spent with you so enriched my life that I was able to contemplate the future with calmness, even before I knew I loved Jonathan. Now I look forward to it with excitement and serenity. We have often spoken of the days we spent with you in London and then again, when you were at Netherfield last Winter. They were such happy times, and though we were not even aware of it at the time, I have no doubt that we grew to love each other then. There is no other explanation for the happy way things have turned out.

Jonathan sends his best regards and please let me thank you with all my heart for your kindness. We both owe you so much.

We look forward to seeing you at our wedding, at Netherfield.
Your loving friend,
Anna.

The delight that both letters provoked in their respective recipients was quite remarkable, for though both Emma Wilson and Madame Armande had known in their hearts that Anna and Jonathan should marry, they had both been afraid that what was obvious to all the world, may not necessarily be as clear to the people most intimately concerned. As Mary Bennet, with her great love of aphorisms, was wont to say, "There's many a slip ..." But this time, everything had worked out right.

James Wilson had been far more optimistic than his wife.

When she told him the news and read Anna's letter to him, he had smiled and said with the merest trace of smugness, "I did tell you, did I not my love, that Jonathan Bingley was far too sensible a fellow to let such an excellent young woman get away?"

"Indeed you did," said his wife, "but it seemed to take so long that I had become fearful it might all come to naught, as happens often when these matters are delayed."

"Your brother made a mistake once, when he was young and impressionable, and it cost him dearly. He is a very different man today, and I was confident he would make the right decision," said James, adding, "I am happy for them and indeed for you, Emma, for I know how dearly you have wanted this for your brother."

Emma smiled. She neither could nor wished to hide her satisfaction, both in her dear brother's happiness and in the fact that Anna, whom she loved and admired, would soon be her sister.

There had developed such a warm and affectionate friendship between the two women as is given to very few. For her brother, Emma prayed this marriage would bring the kind of satisfying, passionate contentment that she had found within her own.

They had both made hasty and unsuitable marriages in their youth, which was why Emma was not critical of the time Anna had taken to reach a decision. Clearly, she had wanted to be certain of her feelings and his.

As for Jonathan, Emma, who had never understood how a man of his education and intelligence had become so bewitched by Amelia-Jane, was sure that this time, his judgment was right.

The intelligence and sensitivity of Miss Faulkner had attracted her attention well before she had become aware of her brother's interest in the lady. Since then, every meeting between them had served only to confirm her approval. They were undoubtedly right for each other.

It was a sentiment with which their general acquaintance clearly agreed.

At a grand dinner party given by the Darcys at Pemberley, in honour of the couple, friends and family and several of Jonathan's political colleagues gathered to celebrate. Apart from all the sound reasons that presaged a successful union, he looked so delighted with her and she was so obviously proud of him, that their happiness appeared to be guaranteed.

Indeed, a young wag from Westminster was heard to remark that the couple seemed to be "almost indecently happy," to which Colonel Fitzwilliam retorted that the only indecent thing about their happiness was that "it was so damned public."

"They are in love and don't give a damn who knows it," he declared in mock indignation, recalling, no doubt, the enforced concealment of his own love for Caroline Gardiner, for several months before he could apply to her parents for permission to court her.

With less than three months to the wedding, Anna's parents were keen to make preparations for their daughter's big day. But both Anna and Jonathan pleaded to be allowed to have a quiet, private ceremony, with only their dearest friends and family present. It was a request the Faulkners found hard to refuse, being themselves uneasy with much pomp and circumstance.

⚜

Seldom had Jane Bingley been happier than on the morning when her son married Anna Faulkner.

For both Jane and her husband, whose union had been unvaryingly happy, the grief of seeing their son's marriage crumble and end in tragedy had despoiled their chief source of joy—the happiness of their children.

While she had not deemed Amelia-Jane to be unsuitable, as Lizzie had, her extreme youth and lack of learning had caused Jane to wonder at her son's choice. Youth and beauty appeared to have won the day.

Many years later, after the early glow was gone and the marriage had turned dull and passionless, Jonathan had suffered terribly for his youthful mistake, and Jane had suffered with him. His wife's recalcitrance and her tragic death had dealt him a terrible blow, and Jane had feared he might never find the happiness she knew he deserved. The apparent injustice of it had left her bewildered.

On this fine, late Summer's day, all that was put to right, and she looked forward to seeing him share his life with a truly remarkable young woman, whose heart and mind were no less worthy of admiration than her looks.

Indeed, Mr Darcy, whose judgment in these matters both Jane and her husband regarded as impeccable, had declared that Anna and Jonathan were ideally suited and would make a very good marriage.

There were certainly no dissenting voices to be heard. Surrounded by friends and family, the couple accepted the good wishes and accolades of their guests, confident that the well-springs of their own felicity were deep and enduring.

Afterwards, when they were alone, Jonathan expressed his love and gratitude to his wife in the sincerest terms. He owed her, he said, his very sanity, for being there to support him at a time when his spirits had been at their lowest ebb.

"For surely, dearest Anna, you showed great charity by favouring me. You, who were so contented and self-contained, who wanted for nothing, filled as your life was with Art and Music, friendship, and the satisfaction of artistic achievement. Yet, you chose to come to Netherfield and share my life, rather than return to Paris."

Deeply moved, Anna took his hand in hers and said very simply, "You must not exaggerate my contentment, Jonathan. Yes, I was certainly happy with my Art and Music, and perhaps I had become self-contained, but how long can such satisfaction last, if there is no one with whom to share the joy? How long would I have remained happy and fulfilled, alone? I know I had my dear friends, the Armandes, but I know also that without the love we share, I should have been only half alive," adding with a smile, "I have not only accepted your love, indeed, I have given you all of mine in return."

The delight which this endearing recital produced was more than Jonathan had ever known, and he assured her of his affection in the most ardent words he could summon.

As he had proposed the toast to the bride and groom, Jonathan's long-time friend and political mentor Colonel Fitzwilliam had wished them every happiness and then, in a typical gesture, with his wife Caroline at his side, he dared them to do as he had done.

"I speak now, only as I know. The advice I give you, my dear friends, is to love each another as truly and as passionately as you know how, much, much more than you could ever love yourself. Then, look within your hearts and find some love to spare for your fellow man, for it is from love and service that lasting pleasure comes. I know you both too well to believe that anything less would bring you genuine happiness. You are neither of you selfish beings."

While their guests were still celebrating in the elegant surroundings of Netherfield, Jonathan and his wife said their goodbyes and slipped quietly away.

They were off, not to Paris, as some of their friends had speculated, but to a place they loved more than any other: Standish Park, which the Wilsons had obligingly vacated for a fortnight. Anna and Jonathan could think of no more appropriate place to spend the first weeks of their life together.

Later, they travelled to Europe to spend some time with the Armandes, with whom they would always remain on the happiest terms. Their joy was immeasurable, combined as it was with the satisfaction of knowing that they had played a significant part in bringing their friends together.

End of Part Two

An Epilogue

1861

Prince Albert is dead. Britain and its Queen are in deep mourning.

For the family at Netherfield Park, it is the second funeral in a month.

The unexpected death of Miss Mary Bennet had shocked the family, for though she had been troubled by a respiratory complaint for many years, she had shown few signs of deterioration and indeed had appeared especially happy during this last year.

Mrs Collins had found her, having passed away as she dozed in her chair after tea, and summoned Dr Faulkner. She had also sent a man to Netherfield, with a note for Jonathan.

He had found Jonathan and Anna engaged in their favourite pastime—playing with Nicholas, their son, who was only a few months old.

Jonathan read the note and was immediately on his feet, explaining to his wife that he had to leave at once for Longbourn. Anna wanted to accompany him, but was dissuaded from doing so; her husband suggested that she had better wait until later.

Saddened, she accompanied him into the house, where she surrendered her son to his nurse.

"I cannot believe it," she said. "I was with her on Sunday and she seemed cheerful and perfectly well. She was particularly pleased that one of her pupils had been chosen to play for the function at Hatfield House."

"We shall have to see what your father says. He has been her doctor for many years; he would know if there was some condition of which we were unaware."

Jonathan comforted her and promised he would be back before nightfall.

Alone, except for the servants, Anna remained upstairs, and asked for Nicholas to be brought to her after his bath. At least with him, she could try to overcome the shock of Miss Bennet's sudden death.

She recalled the many stories that were current amongst members of the family about Mary Bennet. Though she had not been the most popular or the best favoured of the bevy of Bennet girls who had lived at Longbourn, she had probably worked harder than all of them.

While her two elder sisters, Jane and Elizabeth, blessed with both beauty and brains, had married fine, prosperous young men and moved away, and her younger sister, Lydia, continued to flaunt her foolishness, Mary had worked very hard to achieve modest success. Lacking the attributes that her sisters possessed, she had been compensated with a degree of earnest persistence which served her well in her study of both Literature and Music.

While it may not have been possible to say she had excelled at any of her studies, she had reached a level of competence through dedication and practice that enabled her to teach successfully a number of young children in the area who had attended her classes at Longbourn.

More recently, after a bout of illness had forced her to reduce her work, Anna had been helping with some of the older pupils, adding the extra excitement of instruction in drawing and painting, which had attracted quite a few young ladies to Longbourn. Their youthful enthusiasm and bright conversation seemed to cheer the old place up, and Anna recalled that both Miss Bennet and Mrs Collins had enjoyed the musical evening she had organised for their pupils and their proud parents.

So clear were her memories, Anna could not believe Miss Bennet was dead and with so little warning.

Jonathan had returned, rather later than expected, to find his wife tearful and depressed from too much reminiscing and spent some time comforting her.

The news he had from her father Dr Faulkner was that Miss Mary Bennet had died peacefully in her sleep, probably as a consequence of heart failure.

While this gave her some comfort, greater consolation flowed from the story told to Jonathan by her Aunt Charlotte. One of Mary's students had stayed on after her lesson to practice a favourite piece of music. Mary, having completed her lesson, had taken a cup of tea and decided to remain downstairs to hear her play.

Sometime later, the girl had finished playing and gone over to the chair in which Mary sat to bid her goodnight. Supposing her to be asleep, she had left quietly, leaving the instrument open, lest the sound of its closing disturb her sleeping teacher.

"I cannot think of a happier way for Miss Bennet to have died than while listening to one of her own pupils playing," said Jonathan, and Anna had to agree. It seemed fitting, somehow.

The entire family came to Longbourn for Mary Bennet's funeral, which was well attended by her pupils and their families. Even Lydia and her daughter arrived, though neither Wickham nor any of their sons attended. Mary had been quite severe in her condemnation of their behaviour and was, consequently, not popular with them.

Afterwards, the family returned to Netherfield and many of them stayed to dinner. The question of what to do about Longbourn and Charlotte Collins weighed heavily on their minds. According to the terms of his grandfather's will, Jonathan was now the sole owner of the Longbourn estate.

After Mrs Collins had returned to Longbourn, various views were expressed.

Elizabeth and Darcy declared that it was a matter for Jonathan alone. They had no wish to interfere, believing that Jonathan and Anna were best placed to do what was right for Mrs Collins.

Jane agreed. She knew their friend would not want to move to Lucas Lodge, where she had been made to feel unwelcome before.

Lydia Wickham simply wished Mrs Collins would go—anywhere.

"She has no right to be at Longbourn," she declared, fiercely, no doubt hoping she could persuade Jonathan to let her family move in.

Mr Bingley thought Charlotte may be persuaded to move to Derbyshire to live with her daughter, Rebecca, who was very well established there. Her husband Anthony Tate owned a number of provincial newspapers and their daughter Josie was recently married to Julian Darcy.

Jonathan was not comfortable with this idea, believing it would make Mrs Collins feel awkward. She was an independent woman and would not want to feel as though she were imposing on her relations.

Jonathan knew how much she had valued being invited to stay at Longbourn, of which, if her husband had lived, she would have been Mistress. His untimely death and Mr Bennet's generosity had placed Jonathan in his present position, and he felt responsible for her.

"I told Mrs Collins she was welcome to stay at Longbourn with Miss Bennet. They were good companions, and I had hoped they would help each other for many years to come. Mrs Collins has taken an interest in the place and done a great deal to improve the park and garden," he said to his wife, as they went upstairs that night after the others had left.

It was then that Anna, who had stayed out of the discussion about her aunt, wondered almost as an afterthought, whether Mrs Collins could not simply continue at Longbourn, in much the same way as she did now?

After all, there were Mary's students to be taught and her own Art classes, she pointed out, asking Jonathan whether he would have any objection if her aunt continued to live there, while she took over the teaching.

Jonathan was surprised; it was an idea they had never discussed before.

"Do you mean to do it all yourself? Would it not be too much of a task?" he asked, not being sceptical, just concerned for her. He wondered if she would be taking on too much.

Anna spoke quietly.

"Well, Miss Bennet asked me some time ago if I would look after her pupils, should she become too ill to teach, and I promised I would. So, if you've told my Aunt Charlotte Collins that she may stay at Longbourn, and I've given my word to your aunt that I would take over her pupils, that fits together rather well, don't you think, my dear?"

Jonathan put his arms around her. Her capacity for warmth and kindness never failed to delight him.

"What a good idea. I do believe, my dearest, you have solved the question of Mrs Collins' stay at Longbourn. I shall continue to manage the property and send a man over regularly to help with the garden. Mrs Collins has her own maid, and if we provide her with a servant who will attend to her household duties, Mrs Collins could then assist you with the school.

"Do you suppose she would like that? We could go over and talk to your aunt about it tomorrow," he said and then added, "Anna, are you quite sure about taking on all Miss Bennet's pupils?"

Anna nodded.

"The older ones, certainly, but I am sure we could find another teacher from Meryton or even further afield, perhaps a former student, who will help with the younger ones," she said, and Jonathan, pleased with her enthusiasm, added his own.

"I am happy to let you try it, if that is what you want, so long as you promise me you will not take on too much and overtire yourself."

Anna smiled. It was the easiest promise to give and she looked forward to the challenge.

A school of her own, teaching Art and Music; it was almost a dream come true!

～※～

The funeral of Prince Albert was a very solemn, grand affair, attended by several princes and dignitaries from Europe. It was quite spectacular, Jonathan said.

The Queen was said to be distraught.

James and Jonathan both agreed that the death of the Prince Consort was a blow to the cause of public education.

"More has been lost by his untimely death than a consort for the Queen," Jonathan had remarked when he and James returned to Standish Park.

"It was well known that Prince Albert was interested in the idea of public education and, in time, would probably have convinced his Queen that all her subjects, not just the children of the rich and famous, were entitled to a national system of education."

Though Jonathan had decided not to stand for re-election to the House of Commons, he had continued, with Anna's encouragement, to maintain his interest in his Party and, in particular, the Reform Group.

There were several areas in which his wife's ideas coincided completely with his own, and she had insisted that he continue his work outside the Parliament.

James Wilson was particularly grateful and had remarked to his wife that Anna was proving to be the perfect wife for Jonathan, just as Caroline was an absolute asset to Fitzwilliam when he was in Parliament.

"It is plain to see how much happier Jonathan is," he said. "My only regret is that he is no longer in the Commons himself. We miss his eloquent support in all our debates. I am sure Anna would have been quite happy for him to continue; she appears to have an active social conscience and some strong views herself, as do many intelligent women today."

Emma teased her husband.

"Have a care dearest, or they will soon be counting you among the supporters of Votes for Women."

James laughed and confessed that it was a cause for which he had much sympathy. However, Parliamentary Reform was his first priority, he said. Now that Italian unity was out of the way, with Lord Palmerston's friend Mr Garibaldi victorious, it was generally hoped that the reform agenda could be taken up again. James Wilson was quite confident that Lord Russell would keep his word.

"I have spoken with him on several occasions, and he has never prevaricated or evaded the issue. He is sincerely committed to reforming the electoral laws," he said.

Unlike Fitzwilliam, Jonathan did not miss the cut and thrust of Parliament; indeed, after the birth of Nicholas, he had taken to spending more time at Netherfield, conferring with his steward and attending to the concerns of his tenants and his estate.

He enjoyed far more now than he had in his first marriage the domestic joys of home and family, but he did miss the intellectual stimulation of the Reform Group's discussions, and James often invited him to join them. He involved his brother-in-law in much of the preparation for the next Reform Bill that Lord Russell had promised he would bring into the house, just as soon as he could get Palmerston's attention.

There were other matters too which he pursued, in which his wife shared his concerns. She had begun to take an active interest in the work Emma Wilson had been doing for many years, in the poorer districts of London and in the villages around Standish Park. Helping with the schooling and health of children, pressing for better conditions for women, Anna seemed to derive great satisfaction from the hard work involved, and it gave her a chance to spend time with her dearest friend and now her sister Emma Wilson.

Whether working with the children of the slums or in their own gracious homes, two more contented women would have been difficult to find. Whenever they met, their conversations were eager and warm, often extending late into the evening.

Anna was experiencing a new intensity of living, like she had not known since childhood when, as a bright and earnest little girl, she had enjoyed life to the full.

Her marriage had opened her life up to new and deeper experiences. Anna had found herself Mistress of a fine estate and an affectionate family. In her husband, she had a man so close to her ideal that she asked little more than the joy of being his wife.

Yet life seemed always to be offering her more and she grasped it eagerly.

When Nicholas was born, she had thought she would never again know such happiness, but each week seemed to bring keener pleasures.

She confessed to Emma that she had expected to become domesticated like many women she knew, married and with children who gave them no time for anything or anyone else. Instead, she had found that marriage to Jonathan had brought her more, not less freedom, with opportunities for involvement in areas into which she had never ventured before.

"I understand, far better than I did, what it is that drives men like James and Jonathan to strive for the improvement of laws to help the poor and protect women and children. I have learnt so much, Emma, thanks mainly to you and your wonderful work. Thank you for letting me share it."

Emma was pleased and asked if Jonathan approved of her new interests.

Anna nodded. "Indeed, he does. He shares my concerns and encourages me in the work we do. For himself, he says he has never been happier," she said, her eyes shining. Emma had to agree.

"Anna, it is plain to see. Anyone who knew Jonathan would tell you the same thing, but as his sister, I can assure you, both James and I have spoken of it often. He is more content now than we have ever seen him. My parents feel the same and we are all indebted to you, my dear Anna. My brother was deeply unhappy, you have transformed his life."

Anna blushed at her words of praise.

She had not spoken of her own happiness, because it had seemed self serving, yet nothing in her life at any previous time had matched its present intensity nor brought such contentment.

Postscript

1862

Two letters from the collection of family documents in the library at Netherfield Park will suffice to conclude this narrative.

Charlotte Collins writes to Mrs Jonathan Bingley, about the program for the School of Fine Arts for Ladies, at Longbourn.

August 4th, 1862.
My dear Anna,

Since we have settled on the manner in which the classes for the new students will be organised, would you let me suggest that we have a regular woman who will come in and do the cleaning downstairs, so my maid Harriet Greene may be free to help with the school's paperwork?

She reads and writes a fair hand and keeps accounts, in addition to being very honest. We should therefore try to use her gifts to benefit both her and the school. I should wish, also, to pay her at least one additional pound per month for this work, if that meets with your approval.

On another matter, I have had two very encouraging letters. The first from Mrs Georgiana Grantley, who would be happy to endow a scholarship for a Music student and looks forward to visiting the school in the

Autumn. I thought we might try for a little presentation and a musical item on that occasion. I am sure Mrs Grantley will appreciate the girls' efforts on her behalf.

The second is from a woman who used to teach Music in London, and has recently moved to Meryton. She is a widow, I think, a Mrs Lucy Sutton, who wishes to enrol her two girls, seven and nine, for Art and Music classes.

As well, she has offered her services as a teacher, if we require one.

The accounts for the past three months are ready. Harriet has checked them and you shall have them at our next meeting, at which we could perhaps also decide on the entertainment for Mrs Grantley. Something short and sweet, I think.

Thank you both for the generous basket of fruit from Netherfield Orchards. The plums are especially fine, so sweet and fresh. We do very well here with our vegetables and herbs, but I am disappointed that, apart from the apples, we do not do so well with fruit.

Thank you again for your kindness.

God bless you both,

Your loving aunt,

Charlotte Collins.

Anne-Marie, who was now permanently settled near her friend Eliza Harwood, having married Mr John Bradshaw, the chaplain at the Harwood military hospital, wrote to her father and Anna in October 1862.

My dear Papa and Anna,

This brings good news. We are not being moved to the country after all, because Mr Harwood, who hopes to enter Parliament, has donated the hospital and its grounds to the church and appointed my husband to the living at Harwood Park.

That means the work of the hospital can go on without interruption, even if the army moves its patients out. Mr Harwood believes that there are hundreds of people in the community who need care and Mr Bradshaw agrees.

He has urged me to complete the next level of my training too.

Last Sunday, we dined with Mr Darcy and Aunt Lizzie at their town house in Portman Square, which has been recently refurbished. It is truly beautiful. The new lighting is splendid. Colonel Fitzwilliam and Cousin Caroline were there too, having come to London to attend a reception for a colleague.

We spent a very interesting evening hearing so many stories of times past, of which one of the best has to be the tale aunt Lizzie told of the week my grandfather, Mr Bingley, first arrived in Hertsfordshire, having taken out a lease on Netherfield Park, and the excitement it aroused at Longbourn.

As Aunt Lizzie tells it, the news was all over the town in a flash; there was so much excitement, with all the young ladies setting their caps at him and all their mothers, including Mrs Bennet, urging them on! You see they had discovered that Grandfather had just inherited a fortune and was looking for a house in the country.

As she put it so amusingly, "and of course, a single man in possession of a good fortune, must be in want of a wife."

So it seems every mother and daughter in the district had their eyes on Mr Bingley ... he was forever being invited to dine or dance with the young ladies of the area ... but all to no avail, for he, Mr Darcy tells us, had eyes only for Miss Jane Bennet. Once he had met her and danced with her at Netherfield, he was quite smitten, and no other woman, no matter how rich or famous would do.

Everyone enjoyed the droll tale of Grandfather's arrival at Netherfield. Some of them had heard different versions of the story before, but only Aunt Lizzie could tell it as she always does. It was very funny indeed!

I was quite amazed and said how things have changed, because when Papa moved to Netherfield a few years ago, no one paid any attention to him at all. I wondered why, when he was, after all, quite eligible himself, being a handsome widower with a very good income.

At that, both Mr Darcy and Aunt Lizzie laughed heartily and Colonel Fitzwilliam said, "Ah, Anne-Marie, that was because your papa was already spoken for."

Aunt Lizzie and Mr Darcy hushed him up and said they must not tell on you, Papa, but then they all laughed and seemed very amused indeed.

Cousin Caroline said she thought everyone in the family knew and yet they all pretended it was a secret, because they wanted to protect both of you from gossip.

Dear Anna, forgive me, I do not mean to be nosey, but had you already decided to accept Papa ? I would love to know ...

Yours very affectionately,

Anne-Marie

It is not known if Anne-Marie received an answer to her question, but it would not be difficult to imagine the mirth with which this innocent piece of speculation would have been received by Jonathan Bingley and his wife, whose lives had by now settled into an enviable state of contentment at Netherfield, setting all previous vexations at nought.

Appendix

Netherfield Park Revisited – A list of the main characters:

Jonathan Bingley – son of Jane Bennet and Charles Bingley

Amelia-Jane Bingley, neé Collins – wife of Jonathan, daughter of Charlotte Collins and Reverend Collins (deceased)

Charles, Anne-Marie, Teresa, and Cathy Bingley, (Francis and Thomas, deceased) – children of Jonathan and Amelia-Jane Bingley

Emma Wilson – sister of Jonathan Bingley, married James Wilson (previously married David Wilson, deceased, brother of James)

Catherine Harrison – sister of Amelia-Jane, eldest daughter of Charlotte Collins, married Reverend Harrison of Hunsford

Cassandra Gardiner – neé Cassandra Darcy, daughter of Mr and Mrs Darcy of Pemberley, married Dr Richard Gardiner, son of Mr and Mrs Gardiner

Julian Darcy – son of Mr and Mrs Darcy, brother of Cassandra, married Josie Tate, granddaughter of Charlotte Collins

Anna Faulkner – daughter of Maria Lucas and Dr John Faulkner of Hertfordshire, niece of Charlotte Collins, neé Lucas

Eliza Harwood, neé Courtney – daughter of Emily Gardiner and Reverend James Courtney of Kympton, close friend of Anne-Marie Bingley

Monsieur and Madame Armande – of Brussels, friends and confidantes of
   Anna Faulkner

And from the annals of *Pride and Prejudice*:

Charles and Jane Bingley – parents of Jonathan and Emma

Fitzwilliam and Elizabeth Darcy – uncle and aunt to Jonathan Bingley

Colonel Fitzwilliam and his wife Caroline (neé Gardiner) – cousins of the
   Darcys and close friends of Jonathan Bingley

Mr and Mrs Edward Gardiner – uncle and aunt of Elizabeth and Jane, parents
   of Richard Gardiner, Emily Courtney, Caroline Fitzwilliam, and Robert
   Gardiner

Acknowledgements

The author wishes to acknowledge her debt to Jane Austen, who has been her inspiration, and to the BBC for their magnificent dramatisation of *Pride and Prejudice*, which started it all.

Thanks are also due to Ms Claudia Taylor, Librarian, for the historical research, to Robert and Ben for work on the computer, and to Ms Beverley Farrow for her invaluable work in organising the preparation and printing of the text.

May 1999.

About the Author

A lifelong fan of Jane Austen, Rebecca Ann Collins first read *Pride and Prejudice* at the tender age of twelve. She fell in love with the characters and since then has devoted years of research and study to the life and works of her favourite author. As a teacher of literature and a librarian, she has gathered a wealth of information about Miss Austen and the period in which she lived and wrote, which has become the basis of her books about the Pemberley families. The popularity of the Pemberley novels with Jane Austen fans has been her reward.

With a love of reading, music, art, and gardening, Ms. Collins claims she is very comfortable in the period about which she writes, and feels great empathy with the characters she portrays. While she enjoys the convenience of modern life, she finds much to admire in the values and world view of Jane Austen.

PROLOGUE TO

Ladies of Longbourn

October 1862

When Jane Bingley heard the news, delivered by express post from Harwood House, she was at first so numb with shock that she could not move for several minutes from the chair in which she was seated.

Afterwards, she rose and went to find Mr Bingley and tell him that John Bradshaw, the husband of their granddaughter Anne-Marie, was dead of a sudden seizure, the result of a completely unforeseen heart condition, which had caused him to collapse unconscious in the vestry after Evensong on Sunday.

It appeared from the letter, written hastily and despatched by Anne-Marie's friend Eliza Harwood, that only the verger, Mr Thatcher, had been with him at the time and despite his best efforts to render what assistance he could, poor Mr Bradshaw had passed away before the doctor could even be summoned. Mr Bingley, when he had recovered from the shock, had ordered that the carriage be brought round immediately and they had set off for Pemberley to take the news to Darcy and Elizabeth.

On arriving at Pemberley, they were spared the need to break the bad news, by virtue of the fact that a message sent by Anne-Marie's father, Jonathan Bingley, via the electric telegraph, had reached Pemberley barely half an hour earlier. Elizabeth was at the entrance to greet her sister as she alighted. It was clear from Elizabeth's countenance that she knew already.

Now, there was need only to speak of the terrible sadness of it all. Mr Bradshaw was still a young man, being not yet thirty, and though not a particularly inspiring preacher, he got on well enough with everyone, and of course, here was Anne-Marie, married no more than fifteen months, a young widow.

Then, there was the need to prepare for the funeral. Mr Darcy had said his manager would attend to all the arrangements and they could travel down together. Jane was particularly happy about that. She liked having Lizzie beside her on these difficult occasions.

The letter had said the funeral would be at the parish church in Harwood Park; both the Bingleys and Darcys had houses in town, and preparations were soon in train to leave for London on the morrow.

When the Bingleys were leaving Pemberley, Elizabeth said softly, "It is difficult to believe that Mr Bradshaw is dead; they were dining with us at Portman Square only last month, together with Caroline and Fitzwilliam. We were such a merry party, too, were we not, Darcy?"

Her husband agreed, "Yes, indeed, and Bradshaw looked perfectly well."

They were all a little uncomfortable in the face of the sudden departure of someone they'd had little time to get to know and so could not mourn with any real conviction, except as the husband of Anne-Marie, for whom they all had great affection and sympathy.

At Harwood Park, where, in a small churchyard amidst many old graves, an assorted collection of relatives, acquaintances, and parishioners had gathered to bid farewell to the Reverend John Bradshaw, many could only sigh and wonder at the suddenness of his death. Jane still seemed stunned by it all. Her granddaughter Anne-Marie, veiled and clothed in deepest mourning, her small, pale face moist with tears, clung to her grandmother, accepting her comforting embrace even though Jane had no words of consolation for her.

Afterwards, there had been a very simple gathering at Harwood House, where Mr and Mrs Harwood mingled with the mourners, but Anne-Marie retired upstairs until it was time to leave. Then she said her farewells and kissed, embraced, and thanked them all before leaving with her father, his wife, and their family in a closed carriage, bound for Netherfield Park in Hertfordshire, some twenty-five miles away.

❦

Returning to Derbyshire, other members of the family were staying overnight in Oxford, at a favourite hostelry not far from St John's College.

When the ladies withdrew after dinner, Jane, who had remained silent for most of the meal, approached her sister.

"Lizzie, this has been a time for funerals, has it not? There was our sister Mary, then the Prince Consort, and now poor Mr Bradshaw."

Elizabeth nodded; she knew Jane was feeling very depressed.

"Yes indeed, Jane, though I am quite confident that if our sister Mary could speak at this moment, she would surely point out that 'these things are sent to try us' and they usually come in threes."

Elizabeth was not being flippant or facetious, merely noting their late sister Mary Bennet's propensity to produce an aphorism for every occasion, whether happy or catastrophic, thereby reducing everything to a level of banality above which it was virtually impossible to rise. Jane, however, was not amused.

"Oh, Lizzie, how could you say such a thing! Do be serious; I was thinking of our poor young Anne-Marie and how this wretched business has blighted her life," she cried.

"So was I," said Elizabeth. "It must be a dreadful blow, but as for blighting her life, look at it this way, Jane. She is still young, not yet twenty three, still very beautiful, and well provided for by her father. No doubt she will inherit something from her husband as well. With no young children, she will have very little to trouble her, and when she has recovered from this terrible shock, I am quite certain she will not remain a widow for very long."

Jane was aghast. "Lizzie, how can you say that, with poor Mr Bradshaw barely cold in his grave? Anne-Marie will be very cross with you."

"I am sure she would, so I shall not be saying any such thing to her," replied Elizabeth, adding, "of course she must mourn her husband. I mean only to reassure you, dear Jane, that life has certainly not ended for young Anne-Marie. I am confident there will be a better future for her."

Entering the room at that moment, Elizabeth's daughter, Cassandra Gardiner, heard her mother's words and, on being applied to for an opinion, agreed with alacrity.

"If you really want my opinion, Mama, Anne-Marie was wasted on Mr Bradshaw. Neither Richard nor I could ever understand why she married him and in such haste, too," and seeing her Aunt Jane's outraged expression,

Cassandra added, "Oh I know he was good and kind and all that sort of thing, but dear me, Aunt Jane, he was quite the dullest person I have ever encountered. When they came to visit after their wedding last year, he had nothing at all to say unless it was about church reform. Poor Anne-Marie did all the talking. Mr Bradshaw insisted on walking miles to visit all the village churches in the district and wanted to attend everything from matins to Evensong, and he would drag poor Anne-Marie along, even when you could see she was longing to stay and chat with the rest of us."

"And he made some boring sermons," said Elizabeth with a sigh. "When they came to Pemberley after they had become engaged, Darcy and I could not believe they were really going to be married. Darcy still believes that Anne-Marie would never have accepted him if she'd had the opportunity to meet more people, especially more eligible and intelligent young men. He would agree with Cassy that Anne-Marie was much too good for Mr Bradshaw and so, I am sure, would Colonel Fitzwilliam. He was at Pemberley at the time, and I remember his astonishment as Mr Bradshaw got up from the table after breakfast and hurried poor Annie, as he used to call her, off to church. She went quite cheerfully, I will admit, but Fitzwilliam was amazed and said as much.

"'Upon my word,'" began Lizzie, who was a good mimic and could do Colonel Fitzwilliam very well. "'Upon my word, Darcy, I cannot imagine he is in love with her if he just keeps dragging her off to church so often.' Whereupon Darcy said, 'It appears to be his only interest. Church reform is his pet topic; I have heard him speak of little else.'"

"And did Mr Darcy not regard Mr Bradshaw as a fit and proper husband for Anne-Marie?" Jane asked, anxiously.

"Oh he was certainly fit and very proper, too, Jane," replied her sister, smiling, "but I do not believe he was interesting or energetic enough for her. She is so full of vitality and energy, feels everything so deeply, while he . . . I cannot honestly say I could pick a single subject upon which I have heard him speak with anything approaching passion."

"What, not even church reform?" asked Cassy, with a wicked smile, to which her mother replied with a doleful look.

"No, not even church reform. It was a subject he addressed at length and with some conviction, but in such measured tones that it was difficult to listen to him for more than a few minutes, which, if he meant to enthuse us, must surely have defeated his purpose altogether."

Jane, still shocked, did recall on being prompted by Lizzie that Mr Bingley had fallen asleep during one of Mr Bradshaw's sermons, much to her embarrassment. "Poor Bingley," she said. "He was mortified."

She was promptly assured that no one would have blamed her dear husband for the completely understandable lapse.

Cassy said she had frequently wondered what had prompted the marriage, and Richard had been of the opinion that after her mother's death, Anne-Marie must have been so deeply hurt and troubled by what she clearly regarded as her mother's betrayal of their family that she had sought the safety of a marriage with a good, dull man, who would never dream of doing anything similar.

Jane agreed that in all her letters as well as in conversations, Anne-Marie would only refer to Mr Bradshaw as "dear Mr Bradshaw" and would always tell them how very good and kind he was.

"I do not doubt, Aunt Jane, that he was a good man, but one cannot live out one's life with a person whose only claim to fame is 'goodness.' Doubtless he will have saved her soul, but surely one needs some warmth, some rapport, some shared love of music or reading to nourish the soul, which must learn to enjoy and delight in God's gifts, before it comes to be saved." Cassy, in full flight, had not noticed her father and Bingley as they entered the room until Darcy said, "That was a fair sermon in itself, Cassy."

She smiled, knowing he was teasing her, but Jane applied to Mr Darcy for a judgment upon his daughter's opinion.

"Let us ask your father if he agrees," she said, whereupon Darcy smiled a wry, crooked little smile and declared,

"If Cassy was speaking of the late Mr Bradshaw, I have to admit that I am in complete agreement with her. Neither Lizzie nor I could ever get much more than exhortations to virtuous living from the man. I am in no doubt at all of his worthy intentions, but for a young man—he was not yet thirty—he was an amazingly dull fellow." Turning to his wife, he added with a smile, "Not quite as tedious as your late cousin Mr Collins, Lizzie, but close, very close."

Jane pressed him further, "And do you believe, Mr Darcy, that Anne-Marie was mistaken when she married him? Was she deceived, do you think?"

"Mistaken? Probably. Deceived? No indeed, Anne-Marie is an intelligent young woman. She may have been mistaken when she decided that Mr Bradshaw was the right man for her, but I would not accept that she was deceived by him. Bradshaw seemed incapable of deception. He was honest—

transparently so—and dull; he had few remarkable qualities, but honesty was, I am sure, one of them. No, Jane, my belief coincides to a very great extent with Cassy's. I think, though I cannot know this for certain, that Anne-Marie was so disturbed by her mother's irrational behaviour and by the terrible events that led to her death that she accepted Bradshaw, believing that marriage to him offered a safe, secure life without risk of betrayal or hurt," he said, and his sombre voice reflected his sadness.

It had been only a year or two ago that Darcy had, in conversation with his wife, expressed the hope that Anne-Marie would widen her horizons beyond her nursing career, hoping her friendship with Anna Faulkner would engage her mind and encourage an appreciation of the arts.

"Do you believe she never loved him then?" asked Jane, sadly.

Darcy found it hard to answer her.

"I am not privy to her thoughts, but I do know that she always spoke of him with respect and affection. But whether her feelings were deeply engaged, I cannot judge," he replied.

"I saw no sign of it," said Cassy, firmly.

"No indeed," Elizabeth agreed, "yet, they always seemed content. I cannot believe she was unhappy."

As her husband Richard Gardiner came in to join them, Cassy spoke.

"Not unless you believe that the absence of deeply felt love in a marriage constitutes an absence of happiness," said Cassy, of whose happiness there was never any doubt. "For my part, such a situation would have been intolerable."

Cassy had once declared she would never marry except for the very deepest love, and no one who knew them doubted that she had kept her word. Recalling her own determination that she would rather remain unwed than marry without an assurance of deep and sincere affection, Elizabeth could only express the hope that Anne-Marie would find that life had more to offer her in the future.

The return of Mr and Mrs Bingley to Netherfield with their widowed daughter was certain to cause comment in the village and on the estate, but knowing the esteem in which the family was held, Mrs Perrot, the housekeeper, was quite confident it would be uniformly sympathetic.

Ever since the news had arrived by electric telegraph late on Sunday night, the house had been in turmoil, with the master plainly shocked and Mrs Bingley, who was usually so calm, in floods of tears.

"Poor Anne-Marie, poor dear Anne-Marie," she had said over and over again. "Oh, Mrs Perrot, it is just not fair!"

Mrs Perrot, who had lost a husband in the war and a son killed in an accident on the railways, agreed that life sometimes just wasn't fair.

Mrs Perrot and the manager, Mr Bowles, had had a little discussion and decided that no special fuss would be made when Mrs Bradshaw arrived at Netherfield House. "It's best we let the young lady rest a while," Bowles had suggested and she had agreed. He would convey the sympathies of the entire staff and, if Mrs Perrot wished, she could add her own, he had said. So it was resolved and the maids and footman were urged to restrain themselves, lest they cause Mrs Bradshaw even more distress.

LOOK FOR Ladies of Longbourn IN OCTOBER 2008